THE ~~MOST~~ BEAUTIFUL GIRL IN THE WORLD

THE ASKENES TRILOGY: BOOK 2

KEITH POLLARD

Published by Keith Pollard

ISBN 9781685830403

First published in 2021

Design and typesetting by Hawk Editorial Ltd, Hull

To my wife, Jacky – thanks for putting up with being a wannabe writer's widow.

I would like to thank Sam Hawcroft at Hawk Editorial for all her help and patience with me while proofreading and editing my trilogy, for without her help this would never have happened.

Many thanks too to Mackinley McNab for the use of her brilliant photo on the cover.

DEDICATED TO THE
HULL 4 HEROES CHARITY

Winners of the Viking FM Local Hero Award 2016
Finalist: Heart of East Yorkshire Awards 2016
Finalist: Hull Health and Care Awards 2017 and 2018

CHAPTER 1

LEIF

Back Home Again

It was November 6, the day after Bonfire Night, and the plane landed at ten-thirty in the morning. I lifted the window blind, and it was pissing down. I had come from a humid 32C to a damp, cold November day that felt like a winter's day. What had I done?

I got through passport control, customs and was out of the arrivals hall in about three-quarters of an hour. I had decided to hire a car and drive up to Hull the next day, having booked a hotel near the airport rather than do it all in one go. I was shattered. I'd been cramped up in baggage class with my six-foot four frame stretched to the limit; it was a good job I'd had a seat with plenty of legroom. I had struck lucky there; I think when I checked in early the girl on the desk took pity on me and allocated me that seat.

I took the shuttle bus to my hotel, went for a meal and a few beers, hit the sack and woke up eight hours later. I hadn't even rung home yet to tell them I was back safely; they did not realise I was coming home that particular day; all they knew was I was coming back sometime that month. I rang Mum, and luckily she was in.

'Hi, Mum, it's me, Leif.' It was a bit stupid saying who I was, as the word 'Mum' would have given her a clue. After all, I was her only son... but, there again, I wasn't.

'Oh, Leif! It's great to hear your voice. Where are you? It's a clear line.'

'Mum, it should be – I'm in London. I will be home this afternoon.'

She asked me all the usual questions, and I told her I would tell her everything when I saw her later. Just as I was about to say goodbye, she said she had had a phone call from a bloke; his name was Freddie something and he was calling from Bangkok, but he said he would call back.

I got my bags and looked around the car hire company desks for the cheapest one-way deal to Hull, for these places knew how to rip you off. One of them had an older woman on the desk; 'try her' passed through my head – flirting usually worked.

'Hello, and how are you today, Julie?' I asked, reading her name on the lapel badge.

She fluttered her eyelashes; 'Got her,' I thought.

'Hello, sir, how can we help you today?'

'I'm after a one-way hire up to Hull; what's the best deal you can offer?'

'Well, do you have a company account with us? They get the best rates.'

I had noticed two invoices for McClelland Civil Contractors on the desk.

'Yes, I work for McClelland. I'm moving up to a new job in Hull, just flown in from the far east, and left my card at my old address; it won't be here for a few weeks until I get the rest of my stuff. I know their reference number if that will do? Please, Julie, I would really appreciate it.'

'I shouldn't really, er, but OK, seeing you have a friendly smile, I will.' She started to fill out the relevant forms. 'What's your name and address? Have you your driving licences, please?'

I handed her my licence; she never asked me for the company number, just copied it from the other invoice.

'There you go – with company discount that's £25, and it includes their insurance. All done, then; I have upgraded you to a mid-range as you are so tall.'

'Thank you, Julie, you are a star. Can I ask you something? You ever been on TV? I know that beautiful face from somewhere.'

Those eyelashes fluttered again. 'Away with you; flattery will get you everywhere.'

'Wish I was stopping the night now, I could have booked a hotel as well; maybe next time we could have a drink, what you reckon, Julie?'

'Well, you know where I am, Leif.' She handed me the keys and the documentation. I touched her hands, looking into the lashes.

'Yes, I certainly do. Bye,' I said, and winked at her.

The journey took me about four hours once I had found my way out of London and on to the M1. I stopped for a coffee a couple of times, arriving in Hull about three. I went for a ride down Hessle Road first to see how it had changed, if indeed it had, then back up to Gipsyville and Mum's new house, the one with the bath.

As I drove into Pickering View, I looked at the numbers, and I had to turn right to Mum's house; it was the one on the end of the block with a lovely garden to the front. It was in a good position with a back garden overlooking Pickering Park and the boat hire building. You could even see the motorboats for hire; I had been on them lots of times when I was a kid along with the rowing boats; it was ironic that, having been all over the world, being here brought back such great memories.

I knocked on the front door, which was painted council green; no answer. Maybe I should have rung up first to say I was back. I hadn't seen a telephone box, but then I realised that I was looking for the wrong thing. I forgot they were white in Hull, not red, like the rest of the UK.

I went around the back; there was a shed at the bottom of the garden. Mum was in there, messing with some plants or something.

'Anyone home?' I called out. Mum dropped the trowel she had in her hand, screamed, and jumped on me. I held her in my arms; it felt so good to be home.

'Oh, Leif, Leif! Oh, it's so good to have you home… oh baby, oh my…' She started crying, tears rolling down her cheeks.

'Hey, stop it; you're supposed to be happy to see me; no need to cry, Mum.'

We hugged for a few minutes, then we went inside. Mum had done an excellent job of decorating the place. It was not that big, but larger than the two up, two down in Rosamond Street. She took me upstairs and yes, of course, first of all was the bathroom, then the bedrooms, all three of them.

'This one is yours,' she said proudly, 'and that one there is your office if you need it.' She had got a desk, swivel chair and filing cabinet all set up; even a map of the world on the wall. I so loved this woman.

I choked a little with emotion at what she had done, and wondered how long it had been like this, but never asked.

'Come on, I will make a cuppa; you must be gagging?'

We went back into the kitchen and she put the kettle on, still asking lots of questions about the past six years – what had I done, who had I met… I had to calm her down; it was doing my head in, trying to get an answer in.

'Mum, I must ask something; what did Freddie say? The last time I saw him, I told him I was looking for Intera, a girl I met in Bangkok. You should see her, Mum – she is the most beautiful person you could ever meet. He said I was mad what with the number of girls; spoilt for choice were his words.'

'God, you sure are smitten, son – funny name, Intera, for an English girl?'

'No, Mum, she is a Thai girl; they are kind and gentle; it's unreal how they treat their men.'

'He said he would ring you back; he had some information or something. He was a bit vague, to be honest, but never mind, it will have to wait.'

'Where is Billy? Is he at work, then?' I asked, before realising it would be too late for him to be still at work.

'No, he is at his allotment just across the road; why don't you go and surprise him? He would love it. It's plot number fifteen as you go through the gate. And don't forget to put the bolt on when you have gone through; it's the first path you come to, then it's the eighth plot on the right. You can't miss it – it has a green shed and greenhouse. He will be sitting in his deckchair having a cuppa; always does this time of day, regular as clockwork.'

I went for a walk; it wasn't far, as Mum had said – I crossed Hessle High Road, went through the gate, remembering to put the bolt on, then down the path, as instructed. Sure enough, there was Billy sitting in a deckchair, flat cap down over his eyes. I walked up to where his shed was; he never heard a thing, just snorted.

I decided not to disturb him and had a look around. At first glance, you could tell he was very orderly in the way the plot was laid out. All the rows of plants straight as a die, with string you could hardly see with the naked eye stretched out as a deterrent to keep the birds off. But the one thing that stood out was his greenhouse; no doubt this was his showpiece, his place of tranquillity away from the turmoil of his usual place of work, the fish dock.

When you stepped inside, the heat was thirty degrees hotter than the exterior. The smell of the sea hit your nostrils. It was as if you were out sailing with the wind blowing into your face. It was the seaweed; Mum had told me he put that on his tomato plants. He had been told that if he put that down as compost, they would come up ready salted. I took one off the vine, a plump red one, and they were right, whoever they were.

Each plant stood in line like soldiers on parade. Some of the younger ones were only just flowering; their best time had yet to come. The mature plants bore both green and red fruits hanging on the point of being picked, ready for the table.

There was one corner that had been allocated to his unique plant, the one Mum told me he didn't think would take – his black grapes, his pride and joy. Once again, looking to see if he had stirred, I pinched one from the back, hidden out of his view. It was something to relish; the sweetness, the succulent taste was superb.

At the front of the greenhouse was a workbench, above it a rack with all his tools – a fork, a small trowel, a medium one and a large one, and a dibber that looked like he had created it from a spade handle. The various pots were all stacked neatly in the corner, all cleaned, ready for their next implant. The miniature cucumbers hung from the plant like baubles on a Christmas tree. They must have tasted beautiful when used in a salad with his lettuce and celery fresh from his garden.

All this from a man who had worked with fish for more than fifty years. You just never know how well you know a person.

I went back outside. Billy was still fast asleep; I could have stolen anything I wanted. I tapped his foot and said, 'Hey, it's the police.' He opened his eyes with a start.

'What the fuck? What? What you want?' He then saw it was me.

'You fucking bastard! You twat!' He jumped up and hugged me. I was worried for a minute that he would stick the lips on me, but he didn't. 'Oh, mate, it's so good to have you home; your mam will be over the moon.'

Another inquiry started. I went through the same scenario as with Mum, answering what I could without going into too much detail. He put the kettle on the paraffin heater he had in the shed and we had a cuppa; I was busting for a piss.

'I need a leak, Bill; where is the bog?'

'Oh, just go behind the greenhouse in the bushes; it's what we all do.'

We talked for an hour at least; time just flew by. I looked at my watch; it was gone six. Billy screamed, 'Oh, quick! Come on, tea is at half-past six prompt, so we better go; she will fucking kill us if we are late.'

'Bloody hell, mate, are you always as keen to get home?'

'No, but we have a routine – tea at this time of day every day, saves any messing about. Christine is a stickler for time; she likes to know what time I will get home no matter where I have been. I have to be back for tea, so come on, move your arse.'

As we walked back, Billy pushing his bike, it seemed like time had stood still; me and Billy just yarning about all the things we had done over the years. He told me he had been made redundant on the dock; the fishing industry was almost gone. 'All I've got now would be this allotment; if I did not have this, I would have gone crazy.'

We laughed about him liking a bet, and Mum hated betting and didn't really know why; she just did.

'You know, many years ago, my old man loved a bet; I think that is why I got into it. I can remember when betting shops first opened, must have been around 1961. They never had machines then; the settler, or the man who worked out the bets, all he had was a book – that is why they call them bookmakers. Anyway, I got well in with this lad who worked for the guy who owned the new betting shop down our street. We had a thing going on; he had to write the bets in the book, who had placed what, you know the general information. He used to leave a gap in the list of bets, and after the race was over, he would put my name in with a winning bet. I would go in later and not even know I had won, for I did not realise I had backed a certain horse. He would say as I walked through the door, 'You lucky bastard, Billy, you did it again – how you pick them I will never know!' He handed me our winnings, and we would then meet up later and share our ill-gotten gains. Then they put machines in that timed your bet, which fucked us right up, that did, but before that, we did OK. Then in fucking 1966 they brought betting tax in, and that shagged it good and proper.'

'You never got caught, then? The bookie never found out you were robbing him?'

'Nah, but once he put in those machines, we knew we were fucked, so just gave it away.'

*

I had been home a couple of weeks, and it was time I looked for a job. I'd been away too long and lost contact with guys in the know. I went to my previous employer, Paratec, but all the guys I knew had gone; my old supervisor and mentor Mike Peterson had retired. Johnny Cappelen, the former workshop foreman, had retired and moved away. Even Jack and Len, the two site supervisors I had worked with, had moved on.

A week later, I was sitting looking through the job advertisements when the phone rang. 'Hello, Askenes residence,' I said in a posh voice.

'Oh, hiya, is Leif there, please? It's Freddie; can I speak to him?'

'It's me, Leif; how are you? Mum told me you rang a couple of weeks ago; what's up?'

'Yes, I did. I have some news for you about Intera. I managed to get hold of Pino; he had gone missing. He was distraught when I collared him. I don't know how to tell you, mate, but I am so sorry, mate.'

I knew it must be really bad news from his tone of voice.

'Leif, I'm so sorry – she died… Intera was killed; her scooter was hit by a truck. She was going home after meeting you. I am so sorry, mate.'

I was fucking gutted. Dead? How could she be dead? I was only with her a few days ago, sharing our lives. I would come back and live with her; I had made my mind up to come out and stay with her forever. I just broke down and cried; I was devastated.

I could not believe I had lost her. Was I some sort of Jonah, first losing Donna in a car accident, and now Intera was dead after being with me – oh, how I'd loved them both, for different reasons, I suppose, but still – two fantastic women were no longer with us.

'Hello, you there, Leif. Talk to me, mate. I am so sorry, I didn't know how to tell you; I can't say much more, pal. I am so fucking sorry, she was a beautiful girl.'

'Yes, Freddie, she was; thank you so much for letting me know. I appreciate it; we will have to get together next time you are in Hull. I owe you one, pal, Thanks again; bye.'

*

I signed on the old 'King Cole' or unemployment benefit for the first time in my life, and went round to one or two employment agencies, not that there were that many, after updating my CV. I had purchased a word processor while I was in Bangkok; such modern times.

I started buying the *Yorkshire Post* and *Times* newspapers looking for work; I was not concerned whether it was in the UK or abroad; I just needed a job. I could not bludge on Mum and Billy and did not want to spend too much of my savings that'd I brought back from Australia.

I kept being pulled up for using Australian slang words, and often my accent suddenly sounded Aussie. 'G'day' was the most used and then 'fair dinkum for you telling the truth'. I could not help it; it just came out. I had gone swimming one day and mentioned budgie smugglers for swimming trunks and crikey when I sounded surprised. I remember calling Billy a galah, and when I told him it was an Australian cockatoo that was not very smart, he was not impressed. Manchester was another word; it meant bed sheets or linen. If I was talking about something easy to do, it was a piece of piss. Rack off was a less cruel way to tell someone to fuck off. Tucker meant food. One no one understood was 'sickie', when you could ring up work and tell them you were having a day off and still get paid.

CHAPTER 2

LEIF

Advertisement in the Times – Two Years Later

After almost two years of jumping from contract to contract on numerous dead-end jobs, often with three or four months in between, times were getting desperate; my bank accounts were getting lower. Christmas 1980 had come and gone, and in January 1981 I had almost given up on getting work when I saw an advertisement in the *Times* for construction personnel in Aberdeen for the North Sea industry, working on oil platforms in the Netherlands.

It was a box number, so I had no idea who it was; I knew agencies did not usually use box numbers, it was nearly always the companies direct.

'Now then, how you doing? Any luck on the job front, son?' said Billy.

'Maybe… I have sent my CV off more in hope than really thinking I would get a start, but had to put feelers out.'

I did a bit of investigation into the new North Sea industry; one headline read, 'Production tops one million barrels of oil per day for the first time.' Things were starting to look up, and I wanted to get into it.

I was sitting at home wondering what my next move would be, and then the phone rang.

'Hello, Leif Askenes, can I help you?'

'Hello, my name is Andrew Green from Don Offshore. We are an agency. I have got your CV in front of me and wondered what your situation is. Are you currently working, Leif?

'No, as they say, I am in between jobs; why, are you looking for people?' It seemed a stupid question, in hindsight; why would they be ringing me if they weren't?

'Yes, I am in Aberdeen, and we are interested in your details. Would you be willing to fly up here? It will be at our expense.'

'Er, yes, of course, I will.'

'OK, great – listen, I will get back to you as soon as I have arranged the details at this end; thanks for your time, Leif – I will be in touch.'

A week passed with no news, and I was starting to get worried when they eventually contacted me a few days later, asking me to fly up the following Tuesday.

I was booked on the flight from Humberside; I was picking up the Norwich and Humberside Teesside Shuttle to Aberdeen; it was around an hour and a half's flight, arriving in Aberdeen around nine in the morning. It was thick snow; I hadn't seen snow in years, and had never been so bloody cold for a long time.

I got into a taxi pre-arranged by the company and was driven to a hotel in Aberdeen where I met the company representative. As the meeting was scheduled for ten o'clock, I had time for some breakfast.

I was sitting in reception when this guy approached me. 'Good morning; you must be Leif. I am Terry Baxter, HR manager for Vangleeson Offshore – how are you? And thank you for coming.'

I was pretty impressed by his friendly attitude towards me. I thanked him for asking me to come for an interview. He asked me to follow him as we were going up to meet the others; that did not alarm me but made me wonder what third-degree interrogation was waiting for me.

I was sitting in front of four people – Terry; Richard de Freis, head of planning; Hans Backer, head of quality assurance; and Faye de Jong, head of mechanical engineering. They introduced themselves in turn, saying their name and position in the company; it all seemed so informal and helped me to relax, and they all asked me to call them by their first names.

Terry was a tall – six foot, at least – good-looking guy; I suppose you would call him distinguished; one of those guys who had always been a leader. I guess he was head boy at school, most likely private. Very well-spoken, the educated type, that women would fall all over for.

Richard was quite the opposite; not very tall and of medium build, he was a mysterious, studious-looking guy with rimless glasses and a huge moustache. He was married to a doctor who was also university-educated; the typical company man.

I got to know Hans quite well; he was a bit of a jack the lad, but a European version, of stocky build, around five foot eight; he loved the ladies and had a few good nights out together.

Then came Faye. She was elegant, and looked like a film star, with all the right things in the right places: high cheekbones, pert nose and beautiful skin to match – and she knew it. When Faye walked, she floated across the ground, untouchable – she should have had a tattoo on her forehead with 'Keep Off' on it.

We had an excellent meeting, and I was asked what I had done in my career so far. Without a doubt, they had my CV in front of them, so I needed to remember not to tell any untruths. We did not discuss money, which surprised me as it was the company I was being interviewed by, not an agency; we had finished talking, they then asked why I wanted to join their company. I could not say that much about the company as I did not know anything about them, for no names had been given to me, but I spoke about how I felt that the North Sea was a booming economy and that it would be an excellent opportunity to further my career. I spoke for five or ten minutes, and they listened intently, each one making notes; the good thing was that they were all smiling and nodding, and at the end they asked me to leave the room.

There were several chairs in the corridor outside the interview room, but no one else there, which was good; if they had no one else lined up to interview, that was a favourable sign.

It must have been fifteen minutes, but it seemed longer, then the door opened, and Faye asked me to return to meet the group.

Terry thanked me for being patient and started to talk about the company and what its aims were. 'Now we must come to the important thing – salary,' he said, smiling. 'We are looking for the best young engineers in the world.'

This seemed a bit over the top to me, but he was an HR man. 'We are willing to pay over the top to get those people on board, and we feel that you are one of those guys.'

This was unusual because you usually discussed terms with the agent, not the client. The only problem I could see with this was I did not know the going rate, nor did I know what they had me lined up for – piping engineer, project management, estimating/cost control? No one had mentioned which discipline.

It made it difficult to put a salary to any position they hopefully were going to offer me. I was led to believe that there were different variations of payment terms for working offshore.

Most engineers, management and supervision rolls were paid a daily rate; I was aware of that, for I had read it somewhere, with trades on an hourly rate and nothing when they were on leave, primarily working a two on, two off rota.

The going rate for tradesmen was around £5 per hour, which was very good for they worked twelve-hour days on fourteen-day trips, giving them £840 per trip, but nothing when on leave, giving them £210 a week. Some guys signed on the dole when they were off, considering the rate for pipefitters and welders working 'on the tools' in Hull was about £1.50 per hour, or £60 less stoppages. I was aware of this because a couple of lads I knew were in the game working locally on petrochemical plants, and they told me what they were on. The offshore game was the thing to be in. Nevertheless, this did not help me in any way. The question was, what would I be willing to accept if an offer was to be made?

'Having said all that,' continued Terry, 'we are hoping you will join the company as a piping design engineer working in our design office based here in Aberdeen. You will be on a staff payroll for work in the home office. Any questions, Leif?'

'No, fine, thanks; all sounds good to me.'

'When the projects go from design into fabrication, you will be based in whatever country the jacket and modules are constructed, as we are going to start modular construction as against the systems being used now. Where most of the construction takes place offshore, it has been found that this proves to be very costly as against modular. Hans will explain more on this subject.' Terry nodded to Hans.

After Hans and Richard had talked more on the design and QA element, Faye said her bit. Wow, she must be wise as well as good-looking to be in that position, I thought. She liked my history and believed I would fit in nicely with their vision of the future. Faye handed the baton back to Terry.

'Right,' he said, 'so I know you will be wondering after all this talk – what is the, as you say, dosh? Well, the package we would like to offer is as follows – while you are based in the home office, it will be £200 a day for eight hours a day, five days per week, plus a living allowance of £20 a day. All hotel bills will be paid by the company, including B&B and evening meals. No alcoholic drinks included, all taxi bills to be paid by the company and air fare back to your local airport once a month. You will be paid a full long weekend once a month; by that we mean four full days at home, travel to and from the office base, on the works day rate.' While on the construction phase of the project the day rate would increase to £300 a day for ten hours per day, five days per week, any other hours to be paid extra, pro-rata, with all other benefits staying the same. I must add that, dependent on accommodation costs, we have the option of providing an apartment rather than a hotel, but all costs would be to the company account, and the daily allowance of £20 would become £50 a day. During the offshore hook-up, the day rate would increase to £400 a day for twelve hours on a fourteen-day trip on a two on, two off rota, and you would fall back on to your staff rate for all leave days. On fulfilment of the contract, there will be a 10% bonus on all hours worked payments. We envisage the agreement's total time to be four years, from start to first oil; once the four-year term reaches its time, the bonus would be paid up. No other dividend would be paid for any extension of time, as that would be on a week-by-week basis. There is one other thing I must add – all payments will be subject to British tax laws. The rates will be increased every April as per British tax year ending April 5, and an increase will be paid at 3% per annum; all expenses will be paid tax-free. What do you think, Leif? I realise you would like to think it over and let us know.'

He handed me a folder with my name on it and title of lead piping engineer.

'Please take this with you; could you give us your answer by the end of the week?'

I was stunned. Trying to work that lot out in my head had burst a few brain cells but even at the minimum, £200 a day or £1,000 for 46 weeks, it came to £46,000 a year, and four years was £184,000. I just could not believe it.

'Well, thank you for your offer, and yes, please, I would like time to go through it in more detail, although I must add it seems very attractive,' I replied, without trying to sound too keen.

I had a night in Aberdeen and went over the contract with a fine-tooth comb, but could not find any glitches in it. Was it all too good to be true?

I checked out the company as best I could by ringing one or two guys I knew in the game. They all seemed to think they were an up-and-coming company, although as it was Dutch, they did not know that much about it. It was time to make my mind up – I was out of work anyway, and this looked like an excellent opportunity. What was there to lose? I decided I would accept the offer.

I slept better than I had for a while and was up early for breakfast, sitting in the reception again waiting to be picked up.

Back at the offices, Faye came down this time; as I said, she was a good-looking woman, very tall; mind, many Dutch women were, as I was going to find out.

I had been involved with Dutch companies before, admittedly not offshore but in the oil industry; this was what they had taken into consideration when offering me the job.

I joined Terry, Hans and Richard; they went over one or two items that they had not mentioned the previous day. We chatted for a while, then Terry asked me if I had made a decision. I said I had, and agreed to join them. They all stood up and came round the table to shake my hand; it was decided that I would start with them on the first Monday of the next month, February 5.

CHAPTER 3

LARS

Back on the Trail – Eight Years Later

It was now 1983, and my life had changed drastically over the past eight years. I had not looked into the Leif trail either for a very long while; I had been too busy setting up our new crane hire fleet. Along with other ventures, all our businesses were going great, and, while not quite sitting back, we were not doing so much on the job work. We had set some great staff on and, seeing as I had time on my hands, I started to look at him again.

I had saved all my findings, so I pulled out the file and started going through it. I still wanted to find this brother.

I was back in touch with Mum and Dad; he was seventy-five now and not too well. Mum was sixty-three; they were both failing and, to be honest, Dad had lasted longer than we thought he would. Outstanding doctors in the private hospital had kept him alive, but I often wondered how much longer he had left. I had asked him a couple of times if he wanted to go back to the 'Old Dart' for a visit. They both said no as the travelling would be too much for them. I even offered to pay for a world cruise for them, but they weren't interested.

I intended to go before I got old to see if my brother was still alive. I knew he had gone back; I had traced him during his time in Australia; he was last in the Byron Bay area around 1976.

I had hired a private detective; he had found some more information about Leif and the person he contacted (he would not divulge names) had told him he had gone back to the UK. The problem I had was that he was adamant he would not disclose 'her' name; that was a clue. He then added she had worked with Leif in Sarawak and that they had both got very close, having worked together previously up in Queensland at Mount Isa.

Surely she shouldn't be hard to find? Whoever it was had made the guy promise not to divulge her name for reasons she wasn't willing to say, but she had seemed worried that a private investigator was trying to find Leif. It seemed odd to me, but having said that the PD would not tell her, whoever she was, why he was trying to find him.

Two weeks had passed before I set off to Byron Bay; it couldn't be that big a place, surely? I did have not a clue how I was going to get on, but I just had to try. I booked into a hotel in the centre of town; I had taken my board with me, thinking I might as well catch a few waves while I was up there.

I was hoping that someone might recognise me and think I was Leif; I thought we must be identical twins, or just look very alike, or why would people going into Dad's old bank have believed I was him?

It was late afternoon when I arrived up at the bay, and a great day. I went down to the beach, took the board off the roof bars, and went down to the water; the surf was up, looking good. The old board could have done with a bit of waxing; I could not remember the last time I had serviced it, but it was good enough. I went in, swam out a few yards, and sat waiting for a wave. I didn't have to wait long – I was off. Oh, boy, I loved it – I did not realise how I had missed it.

There were quite a few guys down at the same time and I soon got chatting to one or two of them. I spent a couple of hours until my shoulders were beginning to ache a bit; not used to this much exercise, I decided to call it a day. I waited for one more wave, and I was off.

I was having a shower back on the esplanade when a guy came up and said, 'G'day, mate – not seen you for a bloody long while; when did you start to surf? You couldn't get up on a bloody board last time I saw you.'

Bloody hell, he thinks he recognises me; I must play this a bit crafty, I thought. 'Nah, mate – went down to Sydney and took it up. Can't keep away now. Sorry, I remember your face, but the name has gone.'

'Jamie, mate, Jamie Flanagan. Bloody hell, you have picked up the Aussie accent as well. You wouldn't think you were a bloody Pom; you still seeing that Mel? Couldn't keep away, eh? Mind, I don't blame you, mate – she was a good-looking sheila.'

Mel, so that was her name. I'd only been there a day and got her name.

'I am hoping to catch up with her, but I've been looking for her house. I went round to where she used to live but no one was home. I'm not even sure if she still lives there or not… suppose she could have moved, as it was now about four years ago. Don't suppose you have seen anything of her, have you?'

'Yes, was a while ago, I suppose,' he said. 'Must be at least seven or eight years, I reckon, since I saw you last. Bloody strewth, mate, don't time fly by?'

He told me he had not seen her but would make some enquiries about her if I wanted him to. I thanked him, saying any help would be appreciated; he asked where I was staying, and then he said, 'I will either see you on the beach or, if not, in the Great Northern Pub. I drink there with the other surf guys.'

Just as he was leaving, he remembered something. 'That mate of Mel's, er, what's her bloody name? It will come to me… you know, the sheila whose mother was in a home.

Then you and Mel put her mum in with her, then buggered off overseas. She never forgave you bastards, you know, or so my mum told me. She knew her well, even went to her funeral. Oh, yes, Stella – that's her name, and her mother's name was Mary; bloody memory, eh… she is a barmaid in there.'

I did not know what he was talking about, obviously, but Leif mustn't have been bothered about who he hurt along the way, not on the information this guy Jamie had told me.

I had another few days surfing, hoping Jamie would have found out more information for me. I didn't see him; maybe he was working. I went into the pub he had mentioned, and was a bit disappointed no one said 'G'day' or seemed to recognise me. I was wondering whether I had wasted my time coming up here.

I went back down to the beach; at least the surfing was good, if nothing else. I was sitting having a burger and a coke – my staple diet when I was younger – when this girl, or, rather, woman, stopped to say hello.

'Well, I'll be buggered, Leif, you bastard; when did you get back? Must be ten bloody years at least. You remember me, don't you? Karen – Karen Stephens, Mel's mate from the surf club.'

I acted like I could not recall her, which did not take much of a performance as obviously I didn't know her. She went on, giving me more clues about who she was and why I should remember her. It's funny whenever you say you do not recognise anyone; they always tell you why you should make it ever so easy to say, 'Why, of course, I remember now,' even if you don't. It seems she was a big buddy of Mel and Leif when they were together. She told me the whole story; I made mental notes and could not wait to get back to the hotel to write them down for future reference.

Did this Karen know where Mel was now? She had not mentioned her whereabouts, but just kept going on about what a great time we had. She told me everything about how we had worked together in Mount Isa and went overseas to Sarawak, and then put Mel's mother in a home. She was another one who considered it wrong, but added, 'None of my business, though.'

I had heard enough from Karen – what a talker. She did not stop to breathe, just kept going on and on. I had to stop her.

'OK, Karen – the big thing I need to know – have you seen Mel lately? I went round to her house, but no one was home?'

'Oh, right, which house did you go to? She doesn't live in the same place, she moved out to Suffolk Park when they got married. You know Mel got married, don't you? Such a great guy, was such a pity, but that's life…' Once again, she was rambling on.

'What was a pity? Why, what happened?' I had to keep interrupting her, or she would never have told me.

'Oh, you mean you did not know Brad died?'

I told her I did not know she had got married, never mind him dying;

she then gave me the full story, not that I expected anything else.

Karen went on, in full flow. 'Well, they met about a year after you shot through and left her. She never got over you – you know that, you bastard, don't you? Anyway, Brad came to town. He was a footballer from Newcastle, I think; he came up to play for the Bears, good-looking guy, similar build to you, tall, blond, great surfer. He played for one season, and had got himself a decent job as well, then he stopped playing after a bad injury; his knee was buggered. I think it was his knee… anyway, he had to give footy away.'

I interrupted her again. 'Karen, just get to the point, will you?'

'Oh, right, yes – well, as I said, he had a good job, he worked for the bank – that's why they came here; he had been transferred with his bank, the Bank of NSW. They had moved in together; he had a house in Suffolk Park just south of here, about ten minutes' drive; Alcorn Street was where it was. I don't know the number, but it's that street, without a doubt. They were such a lovely couple. He was a wonderful guy; they got married around twelve months after they moved in.'

It was a great story, but all I needed was where Mel was now.

Karen continued, 'Then they had their first baby within the first year; people say she was pregnant before they got married, you know how people go on, don't you?'

'Oh, yes, I do, Karen.' She had a bloody degree in it.

'Anyway, child number two came along a year later, then the accident happened. He was driving home from work one afternoon, and hit a semi-trailer head-on as he went round the bend near Old Bangalow Road. He never had a chance – the semi driver was pissed as a newt; stupid bastard was killed as well, they reckon. Brad's car was welded to the front of the Big Mac, no bloody chance. The police found a flagon of wine in the cab of the truck, and when they were getting his body out, he was half hanging out of the windscreen; the ambulance men said he stunk of booze. Brad's car was a write-off; he had no chance. I said that, didn't I? Oh, yes, of course, I did.'

I was stunned. I did not know Mel yet, but I felt for her, I truly did – to be left with two young children, so bloody sad. I had to meet her now. I was even more intent on getting to know her. I wondered if my brother knew of the tragedy. I asked Karen if she had kept in touch with Mel.

'Is she still in the area? Do you know, is she still in Suffolk Park? What's her married name?'

'Her name is Ledgard; she's in the telephone book under that name.'

'Karen, you have been a great help. I don't know how to thank you.'

I left her still rabbiting on about how tragic it all was; she hoped I would find Mel and asked if I wanted her to ring her, but I told her no; I wanted it to be a surprise.

I got back to the hotel, knowing they always had a local telephone book in the rooms; I was right – they had; I just hoped she was still at the same address.

CHAPTER 4

LEIF

Aberdeen

February arrived, and I was asked to go to Aberdeen on the Friday before starting work, to give me time to settle in and get my bearings, so to speak. I once again picked up the Air Anglia Norwich to Aberdeen shuttle as the company had a block booking on this flight to save any messing about trying to book at short notice. It gave me three full days to get to know Aberdeen.

They had booked me at the Station Hotel, one of the city's oldest hotels, yet still one of the best, right in the city centre. The room was more of a suite with a separate bedroom and living area, not just a square box. I was booked in for a month; after unpacking and settling in, I went down to the bar.

There were quite a few people in; mind, it was a Friday and, being lunchtime, a few of the companies used to finish around that time of day to enable the travellers working for them to get home for the weekend. I got a yarn on with a guy sitting at the bar; he was called Ken and from North Wales. He only went back once a month; he was an expeditor for Shell, and it was his job to ensure all the materials required for offshore construction projects in the North Sea were available when needed.

I told him who I was working for, and he had heard of them; he also gave them a kind word, which pleased me as I was still apprehensive about them; if it sounded too good to be true, it most likely was too good, that syndrome.

'What are you doing tonight?' he said.

I told him I had no plans as I did not know the script about Aberdeen and its nightlife.

'Gabriel's is the in-place to go, especially on a Friday – best disco in the place, but Monday is grab a granny night; full of fanny, you will love it.'

Sounded good to me – I hadn't had my leg over for quite a few weeks. I'd had a couple of old flames I knew from my younger days – not girl-friends, just one-nighters, good fucks, but most of the lads on the road also learned that; one of them had had more pricks than a second-hand dartboard.

Ken and I arranged to meet later that day; we did not want to get there too early, so we had a few beers in different pubs on the way to the club, then paid our couple of quid, and entered the crowd. Ken was right. It was heaving with fanny, all shapes, sizes and colours – best range I had seen for many a day.

I had a walk around looking at what was on offer; quite a few of the girls were obviously wives of guys working offshore – while the cat's away – some only young kids and others must have been grandparents, all out looking for a bit of fresh meat, I hoped.

I didn't know this until Ken had told me on the way to the place, that the city was full of them, as Aberdeen was the Houston of the UK, the capital of the UK oil industry. It had brought a lot of jobs and money to the city, but as the value of the houses, etc., had shot up, so had the cost of living and supposedly the divorce rate. That was only rumoured; how true it was I don't know. Anyway, I was a single man in a strange city and with a bevvy of women to choose from, but the only problem I had was understanding the language and vice versa.

I finished up the night with Helen, a not too bad-looking lass of Scot-tish descent, reasonably tall, with long dark hair and a beautiful body. She finished up in my hotel bed for the night; no wedding ring to be seen, but very good between the sheets. After a hearty breakfast and a sweet kiss, she said, 'I hope I see you again,' put her business card in my hand, and left the hotel. She was a reservoir engineer for one of the oil companies and also worked offshore, as I was later to find out.

I started work on the Monday at 8am and was introduced to all staff members at a 'Monday meeting' by Peter Andrews, project manager. He had all the design team heads along with each discipline engineer – eleven in total, including Peter.

They were Neil Brooksbank, head of design; Mitch Goodway, a Yank process engineer; Jim Watson, cost control manager; and all the discipline engineers. Doug Petty (materials), Nick Wood (E&I), Mark Jones (structural), Billy Cook (mechanical/rotating), Jess Richards (procurement), and I made up the head team.

They had already been working on the project for quite a while. I just sat in the meeting listening and learning. It was evident from the start that Peter was the 'gaffer' for when he spoke, they heard. I won't go into all the detail, but this was going to be some task, one much greater than I had imagined. I was not daunted at the undertaking in front of me, though – I was looking forward to it.

Two Years Later – December 1981

I had been in Aberdeen for two years and enjoyed every minute of it. I had moved into a flat in a new apartment block built out near Dyce Airport, so the only commuting I had to do was on social occasions. However, there were quite a few of those. As such, I had no regular girlfriends; I did not want to fall into that trap, as previous experiences had taught me lessons in more ways than one about the so-called fairer sex.

The design packages had been completed, and we were ready to go into the project's construction phase. Enquiries had gone out to the big module manufacturers, and the jacket was almost certain to be built in Scotland up in Nigg Bay.

They were specialists at making the 'jacket', or legs – the part of the rig that went into the water; this yard was established in 1972 and custom-built to service Scotland's emerging oil and gas industry. About seventy hectares of land were reclaimed from the eastern edge of Nigg Bay to create the yard; they turned out some great work from an outstanding local workforce. We had a meeting to discuss who was going where. It was disclosed that I was going to be sent to the module yards to look after the piping scope. Deep down, I was hoping to be sent to Holland. I had visited a few times but never lived there for any length of time, and it was only a short flight home or even an overnight ferry trip. The choice of location was between a yard on the Tyne in Newcastle, one in Holland, and one in Hartlepool. After much deliberation, the company chose DeGuyr in Holland at its Zwijndrecht yard, not far from Rotterdam. I was rubbing my hands when Terry informed me.

CHAPTER 5

LEIF
Zwijndrecht

I worked in Zwijndrecht on a ten days on, four off, basis and travelling in the ten on. I decided to use the ferry, travelling overnight, getting home early the following day, which saved waiting in airport lounges, and also gave me a night on the piss, going both ways.

My boss appreciated me even using the ferry as I did not lose that much time on the job. I had a week off at home before starting, catching the Sunday night ferry from Hull, which left around 9pm, arriving in Rotterdam at around 7am.

It was just a day out for me, but I did not argue; it got me out of the office for a day every other week.

I was picked up by a taxi which took me straight to the yard; the actual work of fabricating the modules had not yet started; the pipe-spool fabrication was well on its way. One of the reasons that DeGuyr was chosen was that the pipework had been left to another Dutch company whose fabrication facility was not far away. I was to float between the pipe fabrication yard and the module yard as we already had a piping engineer set up in the piping fabricators. He was looking after the QC side of things using Dutch NDT contractors and British inspectors. All of the crew from the Aberdeen office had joined us in the management team in Holland, and a new member of the group joined us.

Asta Jacobs was a Norwegian girl from Bergen who spoke four other languages, Dutch, English, French and German. She was to act as the construction coordinator, liaising between all companies involved in the project – a hell of a task considering the enormous costs involved. Apart from being very good at her job, she was a stunning-looking woman. She was tall, well over 6ft, with an athletic build – broad shoulders, but beautiful and long blonde hair, down to her shoulder blades, mostly kept up in a ponytail; on social occasions, she let it fall.

We got pretty close over the next few weeks, going out for the odd drinking session; she sure liked a beer. We went for meals sometimes, even to the cinema; just friends, as they say, although the chemical reaction was there for sure. One of her finer points was her voice; it made your balls crawl up your belly when she spoke. She had the sexiest voice I'd ever heard; I think husky is how you would describe it. I was at Dewsbury before I left the station, just listening to her.

Six Months Later

Things had changed quite a bit. Asta had moved in with me to save the company money. That, of course, was the main reason; the other being she was a fantastic cook and even better in bed.

I was still working ten and four but not always going home every other weekend; I stayed in Holland, and the company didn't mind as I was saving them the ferry costs.

Asta had managed to get on the same rota as me, so we had four days off every fortnight to see more of Holland and Europe. What made things easier was that Asta could speak all those different languages. I did try to pick up some of them, but could not get past yes and no, please and thank you, or feeling horny, which were good ones to learn.

There were a lot of Hull guys working in the module yards at the time. I got friendly with a couple of them, and we became drinking partners. It seems a few of the riggers who had previously worked at sea were off Hessle Road. Some had moved up to the council estates such as Longhill and Greatfield in the east of the city. Also, one or two had moved to Hessle and the Anlaby Park area. What made life a bit easier – there was nothing better when you were getting homesick and fed up with working away, for I had been travelling for quite a few years now – was to be among your own kind, hearing the same accent. The Hull accent is one of its own, and their sense of humour is also something different; they take the piss out of each other something terrible. What might offend others is often found to be hilarious among 'Hully gullies', for that was our nickname.

Being the main contractor, we were invited to lots of team bonding sessions. Most of the time, these get-togethers were mixed parties, meals at five-star restaurants or hotels in Amsterdam or Rotterdam, at exclusive clubs or bars.

One of them was at the Kristof Meester Club in Rotterdam. This was a fantastic men-only club with the most wonderful 'girls' in the city. It was costly, but you got your money's worth. We all met in the Three Musketeers pub on the Oude Binnenweg, one of the city's prewar streets lined with shops, bars, cafés and the odd gentleman's club, although it was not as well known as Amsterdam's red light district. Still, like many cities around the world, there was always somewhere you would find the more seedy side of life, but a high-class type of seediness was what was on offer here.

No actual money changed hands; it was all on the bill to be paid for by the company hosting the get-together. Attendees were supposed to be senior management only from the two companies: us, DeGuyr, and the hosts, one of the leading materials suppliers.

We went to the club and were welcomed with champagne as we walked through the door. We were then asked to go to the dressing room and get naked and take a shower, before putting on swimming trunks and bathrobes. Swimmers were compulsory, to start with anyway, and we all went in, ten of us in total.

After changing, we went into what could be described as a lounge area, with six sofas and chairs around a large coffee table arrangement. There was also a bar about thirty feet long along one side of the lounge. I suggested we sit at the bar and have a drink or two, and it wasn't long when two girls, both scantily clad – some would say naked – appeared and started dancing on top of the bar. As they passed each person, they squatted down to expose their better bits.

We had been given some twenty-five guilder notes and told to lay our head on the bar looking up, and to put a note on our forehead or just hold it between our lips; the girls would squat down and pick the notes up with their vagina. It was unreal just watching them lower down on to your face and it more or less sucking it up off your lips or forehead; it was so erotic.

Now, this was only the beginning of the evening. As the night went on, the drinks were flowing and things got hornier. There were enough girls to go round; in fact, there were more than enough – two each if you were so inclined, possibly three. Evil was at its highest; I'd never been to a party like it in my life – obviously I hadn't lived.

They even had boys working behind the bar who batted for the other side if you were so of a mind; it wasn't my cup of tea, but I must say they were outstanding-looking boys, if you liked that sort of thing.

We all finished up naked, and in one mass orgy. It was like something out of a Roman bathhouse – there was a swimming pool, but not that big, more of a plunge pool. Along with a sauna and steam room and three bubble baths, plus private cubicles complete with mini-fridge and double beds, the place was much bigger than I had visualised; no one would have ever guessed the size of it from the outside.

As we left, very satisfied, to say the least, we were promised another couple of visits as the contract went on. They certainly knew how to entertain; no wonder oil and petrol were so expensive. There were quite a few parties as the job went on, but this one had been what I might say the most rewarding; not all companies offered so much return for obtaining services rendered, but it was quite often the case; the stakes were so high it just went in with the cost of the job. I remember later on in life working on a project. The client wanted a golf driving range built at their site offices, complete with one bunker and artificial grass forty yards long, fully enclosed with floodlights. It was supplied and constructed by a scaffolding company and paid for out of purchasing the fire blanket for offshore use; this was the norm for many projects.

Life was excellent once again; living with Asta was great. She had even been over to Hull with me. She used to love coming out with me and some of the lads. They had their regular pub crawl in Dordrecht, where most of them lived; the Frick De Witt was one pub, and Dick & René's was another most frequented waterhole. An excellent Indonesian restaurant just up from the De Witt served a fantastic 'rijsttafel', a mixture of Indonesian dishes, washed down with plenty of Amstel beer.

Then it would be back to my apartment for some 'happy time'. Now, I found out that Asta was a bit of a nympho and trick cyclist when it came to sex; very diverse in her wants was one way to describe her. We were sitting having a glass of wine when suddenly she said: 'You ever had a threesome, Leif? I fancy one of the lads off the job, Mike, you know him; he is an E&I engineer for one of the subcontractors. Would you like to share me with him one night?'

'What… why? What brought that up?'

'There is nothing wrong; I just fancied him, that's all, and it would be fun, especially if you have never done it. Just a thought… up to you.'

I was a bit dubious, to be honest. I didn't fancy losing her but was quite intrigued as to how it might turn out. I knew the guy; he was a bit younger than me. We had talked about rugby, as he played rugby union for a local club in Manchester – big back-rower, tall guy, a bit too tall for league but perfect in line-outs.

'OK, then, yes, I will go along with it but not until we set it up. We can bring him back here one Saturday night after being out on the town.'

'Yes, it will be fun, him not knowing he is going to be used, if that is the right word.'

The night came, and we were out doing the usual haunts finishing up at the City Bar, another one of the regular bars we used.

Sure enough, Mike, our target, was in there; as I said, he was a big fit-looking guy and could understand why Asta wanted to fuck him. We were standing at the bar; she was flirting with him – you know, laughing at his jokes, touching his arm whenever she could, looking deep into his eyes, passing on the message that she was on heat. He was getting the message OK but kept looking at me to see if I showed disapproval, which I didn't, of course.

It was getting late, and they were looking at closing the bar a little early for them; we suggested we go back to ours for a nightcap, just the three of us. We told Mike we didn't want a crowd but seeing we had been chatting to him most of the night, did he fancy coming back for a drink?

We grabbed a cab, and I got in the front, leaving the other two to get in the back seat. Asta was wearing a short skirt and low-cut blouse, no bra or panties. To be honest; she looked stunning. She sat next to him; her dress was now right up, her legs showing her thighs. She was making sure her leg was touching Mike's, rubbing against him so he could feel the heat of her body. She had her hand on the top of his thigh as they talked, faces almost touching, not yet kissing, but not far off it. I could see it all happening through the rearview mirror, as it was just at the right angle. The driver was looking too and nearly hit a couple of cars en route. It was apparent he was getting nervous about what was going on, by the look on his face; he watched me to see if I could see what was going on in the back.

We arrived at our place, they got out, and I hung back to pay for the cab; by the time I got in, they were embraced in a long snog.

'Hey, what the fuck's going on here, then?' I said as I walked through the door.

'Oh, Leif, don't be so mean, it's only fun; come on, let's sit down and relax,' whispered Asta.

'OK,' I said. 'I will get the beers. Amstel, Mike, or something stronger?'
'Beer, please.'

We had a big three-seater settee in the apartment; it was well over seven feet long, and we all sat on that, with Asta in the middle. I got up to put some music on the record player; nothing too noisy or fast, more easy listening.

We were sitting there, just laid-back, and the plan was that I was to nod off, and she would go for the kill, then I would wake up and agree to both of us making love to her.

I had closed my eyes, and she started to seduce the victim. I could hear Mike saying, 'No, please, what if Leif wakes up? He will kill us…

don't, please… oh fuck…' Then they kissed; it went silent. I was getting quite aroused by what I was listening to.

She was stroking him. I heard the zip come down on his jeans; it was then I woke up.

The look on his face was priceless; he was trying to stand up but was struggling. I said, 'What you doing, Mike, with my girlfriend? What the hell is going on?' Then I smiled. 'You want to fuck her, Mike, is that it, you want to shag my girl? There is only one way you can make love to her, and that is if we do it together. Not me and you as in homosexual stuff, but a threesome, with Asta. If we do, you do not tell a soul about what happens here tonight, for you can stay all night; you will sleep in the other room when we have finished, the three of us. If Asta wants you again alone, then it's OK by me, but in the separate room, OK?'

He just stood there, speechless. I was pretty taken aback myself at what I had suggested, for this was a surprise to Asta and me, but she did not argue.

We made love, the three of us taking turns in all positions, swapping over whenever one of the guys had reached the station. I'd never done anything like this before and found it quite erotic, this swinging thing. I managed three times and Mike twice before we all laid back and relaxed. We had put some porn on the video player to help us through the session.

Asta and I often made love watching porn; it was good fun. I never lasted as long as those porn stars, and they must have found the women with the most petite hands in the world to act in them, for the cocks were always gigantic.

We went to bed in our separate rooms. I crashed out, and I don't know if Asta went for more or not, and the following day, I never asked.

We had breakfast, and Mike left to go to his digs agreeing never to say a word, for I promised him more of the same, and if the story did get out, I would make sure he lost his job on the project, without a doubt.

We did play again on a couple of occasions, but the next time, Mike brought his girlfriend over, a Dutch girl called Greta, and it turned out she was as randy as Asta; they never got into a lesbian situation, although it was pretty close. I think they were both tempted, but she was a great lay all the same.

The fabrication work was coming to an end; Asta had left the project to go back to Norway on another assignment, promising to keep in touch and hopefully get me a start when my job had finished, for I had no real intentions of going offshore with it.

CHAPTER 6

LARS

Alcorn Street

I grabbed the book as soon as I got in my room. Yes, there it was – M Ledgard, 177 Alcorn Street. I wrote the address and number down, had a quick shower and was off; I wanted to look the place over before I rang her, and didn't want it to be too much of a shock for her, me just turning up out of the blue.

Karen was right – only ten minutes and I was there. Bloody hell, it was a long street, especially when you were looking for a specific house number. Would you believe it – it was right at the southern end on the corner. I drove past slowly, seeing if anyone was around. It was a typical fibro-board house, a decent block, well-landscaped; a lovely home. There was a car on the drive, a Holden Premier station wagon, a couple of years old, yet a smart set of wheels.

I drove along, turned around and went past the house, and pulled up about 100 yards from Mel's place. I noticed a small café nearby and decided I would hang around here for a few minutes to see if Mel came out.

The garbage bin was on the kerb. I wasn't sure if the truck had been past yet, but just as I was thinking that, it came round the corner, the guys, as usual, running behind it, picking up bins and emptying them on the move. I hoped Mel might come out once they had passed, rather than leave the bin out.

The truck had been gone about ten minutes when I looked in my mirror and saw Mel come out of her drive to collect the bin. Wow, she was a good-looking girl; still had a good body after two kids – she must work out or swim a lot, I thought. Lovely old Leif had good taste in sheilas, that was for sure. She was in shorts and a vest and wasn't wearing any shoes – very sexy. It was make your mind up time, Lars. I was sitting there arguing with myself what to do. Should I just go and knock on the door say, 'Hello, I am Lars, Leif's brother!' Or should I ring her first, so it won't be so much of a surprise. I knew there was some reason she did not want to be found as the PD had told me she did not want to be named. But if I ring up, I thought, Mel might panic. I gave it another twenty minutes of deliberation, before reversing nearer the house, and I sat there for a while trying to get up the courage to make a move.

OK, fuck it, I said to myself; here goes. I walked over to the house and went down the drive, and knocked on the door. I heard someone shout, 'Hang on a sec, Rhonda, please, I will be there. I'm in the shower; you are early.'

Oh, fuck, she was expecting someone. Damn – that might be a bit messy. A couple of minutes later, the door opened, and Mel was still wrapping a towel around her hair; she could not see me.

'Come in – shut the door behind you, go into the kitchen. I will be there in a second,' she said, still not realising I was not Rhonda.

I went into the kitchen, and I still hadn't said a word; I sat down at the breakfast bar waiting for Mel to appear. She walked in, still barefoot and wrapped in a bathrobe, and I assumed she had nothing on under the robe. She was still rubbing her hair as she looked up at me; the look of surprise was unreal. She just stared, not believing it was me, for she didn't know yet it was not Leif.

'Oh my God! Why didn't you ring me? Why have you not been in touch? When did you get back?' Question after question. She started to cry, I did not know if they were tears of joy or what. She moved towards me – I had not said a word yet – and she came close and put her arms around my neck and kissed me, full on the lips. Then she stood back and looked at me.

'Why are you kissing different, Leif? That was not the same, you did not respond like you used to. I know it's been a while, but that was different.'

'I am different, Mel,' I said, and she took another step backwards. She did not say anything, and I could tell her mind was working overtime.

'I don't understand this; what is happening? You have an Australian accent now. I thought you went back to the UK, went home – have you not been home? If not, why has it taken you eight fucking years to get back in touch? Eight years, Leif, why? I thought you loved me? Why did you lie to me and leave me just like that? I honestly believed you were dead, that something had happened to you. I hoped you would have written at least one letter, but nothing – fuck all, and you were in Australia all this time. Why? Did you hate me that much?'

I stood up and moved towards her; she backed away, 'No, don't touch me. I don't want you to touch me – get out of my house! Don't think you can just walk back into my life, just like that, after all this time.'

'Mel, please listen; it's not Leif. I am not Leif. I am his brother, Lars Mellows; we were separated at birth in 1946. My adopted parents emigrated from the UK just after I was born; I only found out the truth a few years ago. I do not even know if Leif knows he has a brother; did he ever mention it to you?'

She did not speak; she was in shock. She just kept repeating, 'What? What are you talking about? I don't believe you, Leif; why are you lying to me like this? You can't just come back telling me you have changed your name and all this bullshit.'

'I am telling you the truth, Mel; you noticed a difference straight away in the way we kissed; you said it was different. In what way was it different? The taste? My lips feel different? What was it?'

'Well, your lips just did not feel the same; when our tongues touched, yours did not roll around mine. You did not nibble my bottom lip or suck on my top lip as Leif did. You had always done this, especially when you wanted sex. It was a sign I had learnt because he was always horny. I was surprised when I got close it was not hard, for he was always hard; one kiss and he became erect. That's what I meant about it being different.'

39

She was thinking that, after all this time, Leif or I would react the same when their bodies touched. Apart from that, her husband had died and it had been a long time since she had been with a man. She was ready; she clearly could not believe what went through her mind when setting eyes on me, and she just wanted me there and then.

'Listen – it has been nearly four years since I have been with another man, and I am only a young woman. Yes, I have been tempted on a few occasions lately. Do you realise I never saw anyone, not even close friends, for nearly two years? I was in mourning for Brad, but if the truth was to be told, I had never gotten over Leif leaving me. Brad was more or less on the rebound; he was so much like Leif – looks, body, mannerisms, not as good in bed, but Pommie men had the reputation of being better lovers. They indeed are, not that I can compare anyone, but Leif has always been the best I have ever had. I was winding him up one day. I once said to him in a joking kind of way, "You are not that good-looking, Pom, but you sure can root!"' She giggled when she spoke; it was the first time Mel had laughed since we had met, she was starting to relax.

'Just listen to me, talking to a stranger like this; you must think I am a right weirdo!'

'No, it's OK. I don't think you are weird at all; I understand you must be in shock, me surprising you like I have. I am sorry, but I didn't know how to approach you. I had found it easy when you had thought I was Rhonda.'

She gasped when I said her name. 'Oh, fuck, she will be here soon. What am I going to tell her? What will she say?'

'Just tell her the truth – I am Leif's twin brother, and I had tracked you down. No need to hide anything. Anyway, I will be going soon; where are the children?'

'They are at the childminder's, as I work full time; I am just having a day off to go into the town with Rhonda for a girly day.'

We arranged to meet up at the weekend; the kids would be home. Mel wanted me to meet them. We were going to have a barbie, and said we could talk more about Leif and when he went back to the UK. I was just about to leave, and Rhonda turned up; she knew nothing about Leif as she had never met him. She hadn't lived in Byron Bay area for long but worked with Mel at the surf club.

She was younger than Mel, about twenty-four or so, and a good-looking girl; one would call her a typical surfer, with long, blonde hair, and a trim body, but muscular with it. All that swimming gave surfers broad shoulders. She was a lifeguard, so she had a great tan. My past life was coming back to me – when I did nothing but play footy, work on the building sites and surf. Wow, I was getting old.

I rang home and told Maya what was happening; I said I had made progress, but it would take a bit longer than I estimated and I'd be home by the middle of next week.

I was told not to worry, that everything was OK. 'You enjoy your break, honey; you have earned it,' was the last thing Maya had said to me.

When I was making inquiries about Mel, I was told that her mother had died about six months after Mel got home from Sarawak. It seems Mel had split up with Leif because she had insisted that she brought her mother home, and he could not cope with playing second fiddle. He did not want to be an assistant to a carer. Mel had changed; the feelings were not there any more. Leif knew there was no coming back when the final goodbyes were said, and she turned and went into the house without looking back.

'How do you know all this intimate, private stuff, Karen?' I had asked.

'Because Mel told me – we were big buddies in those days, you remember; it was you who shot through. Don't tell me you can't remember the last time you left her? Gee, you men.'

I arrived back at Mel's in the middle of the afternoon, rang the doorbell, and heard kids running down the hall.

Mel opened the door with two children hanging off her legs; she looked gorgeous. She had a bikini on, and a sarong-type wrap around her. They had a swimming pool in the backyard. Brad had it built along with a small gymnasium with a weights machine in it; he had always been a bit of a keep-fit fanatic even after his footy injury. Mel had used it as well; she said that having a workout took her mind off things, and that was how she kept her trim figure.

I had not seen the backyard on my previous visit the day before. It was great; it had a high fence all around, and was not overlooked as it backed on to the scrubland that led down to the beach; a little bit of paradise, as Mel called it.

CHAPTER 7

LARS

Jo Jo

'Hey, Mel, how long you had that?' I said, pointing at a giant dog – the biggest one I had ever seen. 'He is huge; what is it?'

'Oh, Jo Jo – he is a bull mastiff. We have had him a while now; about three years, I suppose. Some friends bought him, but he grew too big. They were talking about having him put down as no one wanted him, so I adopted him. I love him to bits, even though he has his bad points.'

'Why, what's wrong with him? He looks friendly enough. Come here, boy, come on.' Jo Jo waddled over, drooling like he was rabid, but his stubby tail was going off like the clappers.

'Oh, he is – he's a great dog but he has one fault: his love of milk. Have you seen the new plastic bags they now deliver milk in instead of bottles? Well, he used to collect them; he is not stupid. He used to sit on the front porch waiting until the milkman went past, then he used to steal them and bring them back here. There was no denying it was him, as there were trails of milk from the houses down the street to here. I tried everything I could to stop him, but he just loved milk and some guy every day delivered as much as he could drink.'

We were sitting on the back porch having a few glasses of wine. Jay and Leif – guess who he was named after? – had been put to bed.

'Do you want to stay the night?' said Mel. 'You will be way over the limit, and they're pretty keen on DUI in this area due to the number of young surfers they get in the neighbourhood.'

'If you don't mind, yes – I'd love to,' I said. Deep down, I hoped I could have more than just a few bottles of wine to finish the night. Mel had gone to check on the kids, and to refresh the drinks. After the second bottle had gone down she was getting even more relaxed.

'That's them both crashed – too much sun and fresh air, mate. You won't hear anything from them now until morning.' Jo Jo had also fallen asleep, and he was snoring like an old warthog.

I could not believe my feelings towards Mel; I had only just met her, yet I felt like I'd known her all my life. Was it unusual that twin brothers could fall for the same woman?

Mel came back with another bottle; the sun was just going down, and it was still a warm evening. 'Fancy a swim, Lars, to cool down a bit?' She stood up and slipped the sarong off. Fuck, she looked hot.

'I have no swimmers with me.'

'No worries,' she said. 'No one can see you – just strip off and jump in. I don't mind.' She gave me a big smile, and I didn't need telling twice.

It was not a big pool; it was not in-ground but was built into the decking, as the plot was on a bit of a slope along with the house, which was built in typical Australian style, up on stilts to allow airflow underneath. There was a deck leading out from the back of the veranda; the pool was about twelve feet wide by about twenty long and five feet deep, all one depth.

I jumped in and joined Mel. 'Fuck! It's not that warm, babe?'

She laughed and said, 'You will get used to it in a second once your balls have dropped back down.'

I swam up and back a few lengths, if you could call them that. Mel had gone down to the end away from the house. The deck dropped down into the pool to form a seat.

She was sitting on there as I came back; I got out of the pool, and as I sat beside her, she handed me my wine. We were as close as we had been, bodies touching. She put her hand down and stroked my thigh. 'Mmm,' she said. 'You just look like Leif. Can I kiss you, please? Do you mind? I know I have had a drink, but I want to taste your lips again.'

I put my glass down on the deck and took Mel's and put it alongside it. I took her in my arms, as she came to me I undid the top strings of her bikini. Her breasts were still firm, even after two children. Our lips met, and I tried to do a Leif, nibbling and sucking her lip, and taking her tongue in my mouth and rolling it around. 'Mmm, oh yes,' she sighed.

I was erect now; we both dropped back into the water, standing there in each other's arms, holding each other close. Mel took hold of me and stroked it. I was getting close; I undid the strings on her bikini bottoms, and they dropped down. The buoyancy floated her up, and she docked on to me; it didn't take me long.

'That was wonderful; it's been too long since I had such fantastic sex. Thank you, baby. God, I feel so hot,' whispered Mel as she got out of the pool. She walked over to the chair to pick up her towel and dry herself off as she stood there naked, smiling down at me.

Was I as good as my brother, I thought? She seemed satisfied. I wondered what else he did that I didn't do; should I have taken my time, maybe gone down on her? My mind was running away with me. I got out of the pool and joined her on the deck.

'Mel, I really enjoyed it, too – if enjoyed is the right word. Can I ask you something? Please don't get upset, but are you comparing me with Leif?'

Mel looked at me, and then, closing her eyes, looked away. I took her by the shoulders and turned her face towards me. She was crying; tears were rolling down her cheeks.

'Yes, sorry, I was. It all came back to me when I first saw you; everything you do I have compared to him. I'm sorry, I just can't help it. I had never experienced anything like it, meeting two men who look the same. I thought I had lost the man I was so in love with, and I suppose I still am. Even when I married Brad, I still had Leif in my mind; when we made love, I was making love to Leif. I know it sounds so bad, but that is the truth. I'm not a slut, Lars; I was besotted with him; he meant everything to me. I turned him away when we came back from overseas; it was my fault I had a guilt thing about Mum, but I was wrong – again, I was wrong. I got with Brad on the rebound; he just happened to come to town at the right time; it's been so hard for so long then you turn up – the same body, same looks, everything the same… I'm so sorry.'

'Hey, baby, don't be sorry, I understand; he is one lucky guy to have had you. I know how it must have been with your mother; it must have been terrible, the shock when you saw how she was when you returned. I just hope one day I can find Leif and tell him how you felt so much remorse after he had gone. Don't worry, baby, he would understand. You are a beautiful and caring person, and I am so glad I found you.'

We both dressed and sat down at the table.

'You want a coffee or something stronger?' Mel asked.

'Coffee, please,' I replied as she walked into the house.

I wondered what to do next. Should I suggest I slept in the other bedroom, or call a cab and go back to the hotel, and pick the car up tomorrow? Then Mel appeared with the drinks. She had stopped crying, but still looked sad.

'Hey, come on, cheer up; it's OK. I don't mind you comparing me; I just hope I lived up to my brother's standards. Well, did I?'

Mel smiled and took my hand, squeezing it. 'I will keep that secret to myself, babe,' she said, 'but I need you again – in bed the next time, for we had never rooted in the pool.'

We drank our coffee, not saying another word, just holding hands. Mel stood up and, taking my hand again, she started to walk into the house, turning off the lights as she went in.

She led me up to her room, and we stood by the bed, looking at each other. We kissed slowly, our eyes devouring each other's body. After lying down together, the passion was hotter, more intense. We made love again and again until we fell asleep in each other's arms.

We both woke up about 2am; a thunderstorm had come over the coast, the rain was pouring down, and at one point, you could hear hailstones rattling on the metal roof. We cuddled up.

Mel whispered, 'You know I have been comparing you with Leif all the time; well, there is one difference. I know it's nothing; it does not bother me. Some people say it makes a difference, but I know now there is none.'

'Why, what's wrong with me?

'Well…'

Just before she got it out, there was a cry of, 'Mummy, Mummy, wake up, Mummy!' The bedroom door burst open, and the two kids were standing at the end of the bed.

'Why is he in bed with you, Mummy? Couldn't he sleep because of the storm? He's a big suck, Mum,' said Jay.

'Can we come in with you as well, Mummy? Please, please, can we?' said Leif Jnr.

'OK, jump in, both of you.'

I moved over and let the two kids get in; Leif Jnr snuggled up to me, while Jay snuggled up with his mum. We all fell asleep again, and the only one not in the bed was Jo Jo.

*

The sun was beaming through the Venetian blinds as I woke up. I looked around; the others were still all sound asleep. I slowly got out of bed; I had woken up with a boner on and didn't want the kids to see me as I tiptoed out of the bedroom, picking up my shorts and shirt on the way.

I went into the kitchen and made myself a coffee; I decided that I would leave before they all woke up. I found some paper cups to take my drink away with me, then left a note on the worktop, telling Mel that I would ring later on, and I left the house.

I decided it was better to ring Mel to arrange another meeting, for we had not discussed Leif in depth, or nothing that could help find him anyway, as we had been somewhat waylaid. I got back to the hotel, had a shower, then went down for breakfast before ringing Mel.

It rang three times before she answered. 'Lars, that you why did you go like that? The kids were looking forward to spending the day with you; why did you sneak away? Is there something wrong?'

'Whoa – no, there is nothing wrong. I needed a change of clothes, so I thought I would nip back to the hotel and get some, and I had a shower while I was here. Do you want me to come back straight away?'

'Yes, please come back. I was hoping to spend the day on the beach with you and the kids. They are taken with you; they miss their father something awful. I have never seen them take to a stranger as they have with you. Please come back – you will, won't you?'

We arranged to meet at the surf club; she could take the kids' boards on her car, and I would take mine.

I arrived early at the beach; it was a gorgeous day. The sun was shining; it was going to be a hot one. I was sitting in my car at the meeting point as Mel drove up. The kids ran over, shouting, 'Lars, Lars! We are here,' jumping up and down as young kids do, like spring lambs. Mel was unloading the two bodyboards for the kids, so I jumped out and ran over to give her a hand; she hugged me and kissed me on the cheek.

'Thanks, hun; here you are, take them. I'll get the Esky. I have made a picnic for us; can you manage the umbrella as well, please? I have to bring so much bloody stuff with the kids.' With that, she shouted at them, 'Get your hats on, you two – what did I tell you?'

The boys had taken their T-shirts off and were heading for the water; no fear, these kids, I supposed they were both in the Little Nippers club.

We got the gear out of the cars and took it down to the spot I had found in between the flags, not too far from the club and the car park. I helped Mel set up camp and sat down on my towel; she took off her shorts and T-shirt, revealing that body again; wow, she was so beautiful, I could not get over how fit she was.

'Come on, Lars – come for a swim!' The kids were back, pulling me to get up and go in the water.

'Get your boards, then I'll be there in a second, OK?'

Mel just laughed; she looked so happy. I just smiled and took off after the kids.

It must have been at least an hour with the boys, and I could not believe how much I enjoyed it. I had never been a kiddie person, but this seemed so natural.

Jay called me Uncle Lars – and that little comment it hit me hard. He was right; I could have been his real uncle. I know circumstances meant I was not related, but this woman had been the lover and partner of my brother – my long-lost brother. I had never believed I would ever be an uncle, and I loved it.

I got back to Mel, leaving the kids still playing in the water; they had endless energy, and they had worn me out.

'Mel, what have you told the kids? Jay just called me Uncle Lars.' Mel just looked; her eyes got bigger, and she smiled.

'Nothing – it was funny, but he had asked me, "When is Uncle Lars coming back, Mum? I like him." Why? Do you mind? I did not want to say you were not his uncle as I didn't want to upset him.'

'No, it is fine. I quite like the idea. While we are on the subject – can I ask you more about Leif and what you know about him? Where he might have gone when he left you?'

I could see it hurt her; her expression told me there was a pain in her heart when discussing him. In the end, though, she did not know much more than I already knew – that Leif had gone back to the UK and as far as she knew he was never coming back.

'I have moved on; it took me a long time. Then I met Brad, and there was the tragedy of all that. I had had it rough, no doubt about that – then you show up and open a can of worms. I was getting used to the idea of being a single mum, a widow with two boys to bring up on her own. What you have done is took me back to the best time in my life, being with the man I loved – not just loved, but adored.'

I felt kind of guilty; I had more or less taken advantage of her kindness. Why had I made love to her? Had I used her? She had come to me freely, but only because I was the double of the man she had thought she would never see again, never mind make love to.

We sat there, not saying much more to each other; I was thinking about Maya back in Sydney – my partner, the woman I had lived with like husband and wife for the past few years, with whom I'd had set up in business. I was now cheating on her. Fucking hell; what was I going to do? I had never felt the same at any period of my life. I was now in love with two women simultaneously. Yes, in love – I had said it to myself. I had not realised it, but I was.

The day ended, and we had had a great time – family time, as some people call it. I had often heard guys talk about 'family time', how every Saturday was the man's day, and he would go to the pub on an 'arvo' and have a few beers with his mates, maybe go to the footy or spend a few quid having a bet on the TAB. Still, Sundays were always 'family time' when the whole family would get together and do what they wanted to do – go to the beach, or into the bush for a picnic, whatever, but it was their day of the week. It was the first time it had happened to me, and I loved it. I wanted more of it; the only problem was the family I was with at the moment was not my family. I did not have a family; I'd never really had one – no grandparents, no siblings. I had never been involved like I had been today.

I stayed another night with Mel, and it was beautiful, but it had to end. I told her I had got to get back to Sydney as some problems had come up at work. I did not know how I was going to feel when I got back to Maya. Was this just a fling, a one-off? No, I didn't think so. I honestly had feelings for Mel and the two boys; I don't know why. I still had this thing in my mind about how much Leif and I were alike. How could two men be in love with the same woman? Just because they were twin brothers, the same flesh and blood, from the same mother and father – the real blood mother and father – and made up of the same genes; was this just a figment of my imagination, or was there more to it?

I got my stuff in the car; I had checked out of my hotel that morning, knowing full well I was going to spend the night at Mel's place, whether I wanted to or not. The kids had gone to bed, and we were sitting by the pool, just holding hands like two teenagers on their first date. It felt so good, too good; I had a pang of guilt inside me. I knew I was doing wrong, but I just could not help myself.

'Babe, what are we going to do? How can we go from here?'

I stood up and walked towards the door. My mind was in turmoil. I turned to put out my hand and said, 'I don't know, Mel, but what I do know is I am in love with you. Forgive me if you think I am bad – a cheat on my girl in Sydney – but my feelings for you are deep. I had no idea it would come to this, but you have got into my heart.'

Mel stood up and put her arms around my neck. 'Oh, baby, I want you to make love to me – fuck me like you never have done before.'

We were saying our goodbyes when Leif Jnr said, 'When are you coming back, Uncle Lars? You will come back, won't you? Please come back and visit us. It's been great.'

I was filling up. I could feel that lump in your throat when you want to cry, but you try to hold back the tears. Mel gave me a hug, and whispered, 'I love you; please come visit us soon, you hear.'

As I walked out, Jo Jo passed me, going the other way with a bag of milk dripping from his jaws. I heard Mel shout, 'Oh no, not again! Jo Jo, come here with that, you bad boy.'

With that memory in my head, I was gone. I turned out of Alcorn Street, heading for the highway and south to Sydney.

CHAPTER 8

LEIF

Tragedy – A Year Later

It was now August 1983, and the offshore hook-up and commissioning were expected to last eight months as all the testing of the modules had been completed in the yards.

We only had the final connections of modules and the wells' eventual opening up, which had been pre-drilled and then capped off by the drilling rig months earlier.

I landed on the platform and was informed I would be on the night shift that night, covering all disciplines. Any problems were to be noted and handed over to the day shift team, who would sort them out with the beach office.

I was told I would be doing alternate trips – days one trip, then nights the next, which sounded good to me. We were living on an accommodation barge as the platform accommodation was not complete as yet. There were no catering staff on board anyway to man the kitchens; it'd be a while before that happened.

I looked at getting about six months more out of the project before the job was handed over to the commissioning team and the OCE (offshore construction engineer). Whoever he might be, he would more or less be a jack of all trades; it was a job I did not fancy anyway as I knew nothing about E&I engineering, so six months would do me.

Unfortunately, it did not last that long – well, not for me anyway.

It was my fifth trip, and this time I was on the day shift. It was a freezing night. The wind was gusting to forty knots with waves up to twelve metres high. I had had my shower and had gone into the mess room for my evening meal.

I was sitting talking with Stephan, one of my colleagues, when we heard a loud bang. The guys in the room cheered, for they hoped we were about to be pulled away from the platform as it often happened due to bad weather. It was done as a safety measure to ensure the barge did not collide with the structure's jacket, or legs.

The accommodation barge was the Musk, a semi-submersible, meaning it was built on legs with pontoons attached to the bottom of them. When the barge was being towed, as it did not have self-propulsion, they would fill the pontoon with air, then when it reached its station, they would pump water into the floats to make it sink. It had anchors operated by winches; this enabled it to be pulled away as and when required.

Another loud bang – this time the barge shuddered. Someone came in and said one of the standby vessels had crashed into the barge and was on fire. These vessels were old sidewinder-type trawlers; since the cod wars, instead of being scrapped, they were turned into safety vessels that sailed around offshore platforms during construction phases to provide emergency assistance.

On this occasion, the safety vessel was the problem. How and, more importantly, why it had collided with the barge was yet to be found out. All I knew was I had to get to a lifeboat. But first of all, I needed my survival suit, which was hanging in my cabin.

As I got up, there was another bang and the barge tilted. Panic erupted; guys fought to get up the gangway to get out on to the main deck. I decided to take another route, running to the back of the mess hall and through the galley. The catering crew had already gone. I went out of the back door and started to climb the ladder up to the top deck.

I stood mesmerised for a second or two when I saw what had happened. The standby vessel was impaled into the main deck, right at the connection points of one of the main legs, which had broken off. This was why the barge was tilting; it was sinking, and the only thing keeping it up was the anchor lines, and the air in the other pontoon. We later found out that the safety boat had lost all its power and steering and the gale, along with the strong current, had smashed it into the barge.

The barge was now heaving over at more of an angle. The mangle of steel and cables, with the old trawler's weight, was pulling the barge with it. We were sinking fast.

I still did not have my survival suit; mayhem was the name of the game. To get to my cabin meant an uphill climb along the deck – which, by now, seemed impossible.

I was going for a swim; there was no doubt about that. Thirty-foot containers had slid across the deck, and I could hear men crying for help as they had been trapped between them. 'Sorry, guys,' went through my head – I could not take a chance in trying to help; it was every man for himself. I still feel guilty for not going to their assistance.

I was just going to turn, and then there was a mighty twang. I heard a crack, and when I looked up, one of the anchor lines had snapped and was flying through the air above my head; then the barge heaved and went over, throwing me into the water.

There was no chance of getting to my cabin for my survival suit; I started swimming as hard as I could away from the platform. I turned and saw one of the deck cranes' jibs coming towards me; it was like watching a slow-motion movie, but I was in the film.

I rolled in the water and swam as hard as I could. I was trying to get away as fast as possible in the raging sea. My thoughts were for my family. It is said your life flashes past you when you are drowning. Well, I was sure I was going to die, but the fact that I was a good strong swimmer held me in good stead. Surely this must help, I was saying to myself; swim, you bloody fool, swim – go for it.

I turned again and then there was another loud twang. Another anchor line had snapped, and the whole barge was turning over. I saw the legs up in the air as it rolled like a giant sea monster diving under the swell. The jib had missed me, and I was now watching the barge sink. Men were swimming about, but they had no chance.

There was oil on top of the water. It was lucky that it had not caught fire; it had broken up into small clumps due to the waves and wind.

I tried not to take any in my mouth; it was hard enough to keep the seawater out, never mind oil. Then, all of a sudden, I could not believe it – a life raft capsule bobbed up in front of me. It opened automatically, upside down, but here my survival course training came into play. The wind had died down a bit, and I still had enough strength to climb on top and find the end where the compressed air bottle was. Luckily it was the right way for the wind to blow it over me. I stood up, both feet on the bottle, pulling the rope attached to the bottom. I leaned back, trying to get the life raft on its edge. Amazingly, it worked. That course in Vlissingen, which I had always believed was a load of shite and would never need, had now become reality.

My main worry now was trying not to freeze to death. I knew you would be dead if you were in the North Sea for any length of time with no survival suit, for all I had on was a T-shirt and tracksuit bottoms, and bare feet, my flip-flops long gone. I appreciated I did not have that long left to live if I did not get rescued soon, and the standby boat had gone. I was in deep shit.

I finally had it the right way up, and clambered inside. I was being blown away from the barge and platform. I heard the sound of a supply boat, but it was going away from me. I shouted, but there was no chance of anyone seeing or hearing me; it was pitch black. I must have been a hundred yards away by now.

I could not believe my eyes; a man was swimming backstroke. He had a life jacket on and he was waving. I was heading straight for him.

I managed to pull him in; he was blue with the cold. We wrapped our arms around each other, and I tried to transfer my body heat to him.

'What's your name, mate? Come on, we must keep warm.'

'Oh, thank fuck for that. Jimmy; what's yours?'

'Leif – now come on, just do as I ask, please.'

I tried to look through the raft entrance and keep the bit of warmth in the capsule when a lifeless body bobbed up next to the raft. We both pulled it in.

'Pull him in and strip his clothes off him – we must share them,' I said. The other guy looked at me as if I was demented. 'Just fucking do it, or we both will die with him.' Then another body bobbed up. This guy had even more clothes on him, so we stripped him too.

I know it sounds harsh now, but if we had not done this, we would have perished. Those extra layers, and huddling together, kept us alive.

Then another guy floated alongside. We had turned direction; now we were going back to the platform. Don't ask me how – I will never know. Currents, wind – who knows? We pulled this guy on board; he was shivering, only a young boy about twenty, I supposed. I recognised him – he was one of the stewards on the barge. He joined our huddle; it hadn't been long when I suddenly became hot. The boy had thrown up on my shoulder; his warm vomit felt so good. The boy was staring at the two bodies on the other side of the raft; I don't think he had ever seen a body before. 'Forget them, son; we can't help them,' I said. 'We only pulled them in so that their relations will have some closure if and when we get picked up.'

Then I had an idea. I said to the other two, 'Can you piss? Come on – piss on each other if you can.' I started to strain to piss, and some came out. Then the first guy I had pulled on began to do so too. Time and time again we did it, until we were dry; nothing left inside us. The boy threw up again. He was crying like a baby. 'I want me Mam,' he said, spewing and pissing himself, and we hugged him tightly. We were getting warmer, I could tell; it was working – we were keeping ourselves warm by being on the piss together.

I looked at the boy; he had gone quiet. His grip was not as firm as it had been. I asked him if he was OK; no answer. 'Hey, son, come on – you will be OK, keep awake,' I said, but there was no response; his eyes were open, but they were dead.

I was looking into the eyes of a dead boy. I'll never forget those eyes, looking back at me. I started to pull his clothes off him. 'What are you doing?' Jimmy said. 'The boy is fucking dead – what are you doing?'

'He won't need his clothes, then – we have got to get as much cloth-ing on our bodies as we can, for we don't have a clue how long we are going to be in this raft. Now just do it – if they don't fit, wrap them around your feet or use a scarf – just use them.'

They did not fit me. I wrapped the boy's T-shirt around my neck. I put his socks on, which were also too small, but I needed to convince the other guy to use as many layers as we could get.

I heard a chopper above us. I left Jimmy and opened the flap on the door; looking up, I was waving, but the helicopter's downdraught was blowing us back away from the platform.

Then I saw the winchman, through the mist and rain, coming down on the wire. Within seconds he was hovering above the door. He dropped in, unfastened his harness, and smiled, 'How you all doing?' as if he had just called in for a cup of tea.

I told him there were only the two of us alive, me and Jimmy; the chopper was still hovering above.

'OK, you're going for a ride, guys; one at a time – can't take the two of you. Who's first?'

'Take him, mate.' I pointed at Jimmy. They buckled up and were gone. Within minutes the winchman returned and put me in the harness.

'What about the bodies in the raft?' I asked, and he just shrugged his shoulders.

'Sorry, there are more important things to do. They are beyond help. It seems harsh, but you are told that in a survival situation, only worry about those who can be helped.'

With that, we were gone.

We were flown on to the platform, for that was not in any danger. The barge had now disappeared beneath the waves, with no sign of it ever having been there.

We were tended to by the medics onboard the platform. A fleet of choppers was mustered up from Norway and Aberdeen to ferry the injured and dead to the shore.

That was the end of my offshore career for a while. I was out of action for a few months before I recovered both physically and mentally.

CHAPTER 9

LARS

Back Home to Maya

I had been back home in Sydney for six weeks; everything was OK with Maya and me. We discussed what had happened in Byron Bay, how I had found Leif's ex-girlfriend, how we had talked and discussed Leif, my feelings towards him, and how I wanted to see him somehow.

We were sitting in the lounge one night, having a glass of wine, talking about my favourite subject, finding Leif. I was getting obsessed with it, and I think Maya was getting a bit sick of it too. We had also discussed having children; Maya was not that keen.

'What would you say if I said I don't want children?' she said. 'I like my life as it is. I like the way we live, being partners in everything, work, our lives – how we have now reached the point where we can do what we want when we want, not having kids to tie us down. I'm sorry, babe, I'm not the mothering type. It does not get to me when I see mothers with babes in arms. I do not get clucky when I see them, or whenever our friends bring their kids around – it's just not me. Do you truly want to change all this? Our sex life is good, isn't it? Am I not satisfying you in bed? Or do you just want more? You want to play away, is that it? If you do, that's OK with me as long as it works both ways. I can go and root whoever I want, is that it? Is that what you need? It seems we have we grown out of love. Do you not love me any more?'

She stormed out and went to the bedroom, slamming the door behind her. I could hear her crying. It was not like Maya to get emotional. She was a hard woman; she had had a hard life, taking over her father's business all those years – no doubt, she was a career woman.

I went to the bedroom; she had locked the door. 'Maya, please open the door; come on, don't be stupid.' Silence. I shouted again. 'Maya, please come on, we need to talk; I don't want to go separate ways. Come on now, please, Maya?'

The door opened. Tears were rolling down her cheeks. 'Why now? What's got into you? Why now? You never mentioned it before; why bring it up now?'

I told her about Mel and her two boys, and all about the tragedy she had had – the whole story, and how that had started me thinking about my past life; how I did not want us to be too old to enjoy kids. I was now thirty-six and not getting any younger.

Maya looked at me funnily and said, 'Fuck me, mate, she got to you, didn't she, this Mel? She has done something to you – did you root her while you were up in Byron Bay? Or would you like to have done it? I have noticed you're a changed man since you got back.'

I told her not to be so stupid, and that it had got me thinking, that was all – that there was more to life than just work.

'I don't believe you,' she said, and turned and went back upstairs into the bedroom, slamming the door.

I left her to herself for a couple of hours before going up. I opened the door, and saw she was asleep. I did not disturb her, and went and slept in the guest room.

The following morning I got the silent treatment again. Maya never said a word, just went about her daily routine. It was a Saturday, so we were stuck together for the day. I broke the silence. 'What are we doing today?' No answer, so I asked again. 'What are we doing today? How long is this going to go on, Maya? We need to talk – we can't go on like this.' I was starting to lose my temper now. 'Maya, for fuck's sake, answer me. I'm not putting up with this shit; what's wrong?'

Maya looked at me with disdain; she had never acted like this before. She must have believed that while I was away, I had been unfaithful to her. She was right, but I did not want her to know that. I did not want to break up with her. I loved her so much.

She went upstairs again, so I followed her back up. She was sitting on the bed, sobbing. I went over to her, grabbing her shoulders, but she shook me off.

'Go away. I don't want you to touch me. Fuck off! You had Mel, didn't you? I know it. Don't lie to me – be honest, you rooted her, didn't you? Come on, be honest – tell me you had her. I can tell – you are a different guy since you came back. You haven't touched me. Usually, if you had been away, even for a weekend, you couldn't wait to get into my knickers, but this time all you talked about was this fucking Leif and Mel. Well? Tell me the truth.'

I was dumbstruck, which made my guilt seem even more obvious. I did not deny it, and never spoke a word.

'That's it – you don't have to say it, Lars. I know now. I want you out of the house. We are through. I will go and see a solicitor about breaking the businesses up, and we will put the house up for sale. We will share everything down the middle.'

She walked out of the room. She had stopped crying and was stable now; she had her business head on. There would be no turning back, for I knew that once she had made up her mind, that was it, but I had to try to resolve the situation.

'Maya, please listen to me. Nothing happened. I don't want us to split up, please, Maya. I love you so much. How can I get you to understand it's the last thing I want? We have too much to throw away, just like that – for god's sake, please, believe me. It's you I want.'

Maya was looking out of the window. She turned back and said, 'All you are worried about is losing half of the businesses. That's all that concerns you; you don't give two fucks about me. Just be honest for once in your life. I don't care if that is what you want. Go back to her in Byron Bay, go fuck your precious brother's ex-whore, keep it in the family! Go on, fuck off! I don't want you, do you understand? I do not fucking want you.'

For the first time in my life, I felt like hitting a woman. No man had ever spoken to me like this and got away with it, never mind a woman. Did she truly hate me that much?

I grabbed her; she started hitting me. She was crying again, beating my chest with her fists, and was hysterical by now. I got a grip of her, pulling her towards me; she stopped and rested her head on my chest. I wrapped my arms around her as she calmed down. The sobbing had stopped.

CHAPTER 10

LEIF
South Africa

I returned to work after about a month at home. I just could not face offshore again. The company sent me back to Holland to work in the office on future projects that were in the pipeline, excuse the pun; they had a revamp job coming up off the east coast that would suit me. It was a long project and did not require a lot of travel to Aberdeen.

I was very interested in this. But this was only a job that they were negotiating for; it would be a while before it started, so I had to make my mind up whether to stick around in Holland or look elsewhere.

I continued with Vangleeson in the Holland office, mainly because I could not find another job that had a better deal. I was not assigned to any particular project, just helped on anything needed – a general dogsbody that could cover any discipline. This was OK; I enjoyed the freedom.

An enquiry came into the office; I was asked to look at it and do a feed estimate on the information supplied. The project was for Saprole in South Africa, near Durban, on the east coast. I was called into the office by the cost control manager, Richard.

'Leif, have you taken a look at the SA job yet? It's a big project, one we would like to win. We're hoping it will give us a foot in South Africa as we have not worked there, and feel there could be a lot in it for us if we can just get a presence in the country.'

'I have only just got the package, Richard, I've not got to grips with it. It could take me a week or so to create some sort of discipline breakdown – you do realise we don't have any rates to work to as yet, don't you? Or plant and materials costs for that area of the world?'

'Don't worry about that; we can just come up with the hours, for now. The other reason I brought you in on it is I know you don't mind travelling. We want you to go out to Durban for about a month or so to get a feel for the place and gather information from suppliers and local contractors while you do the Level 1 estimate – is that OK with you?'

Great – another trip away, I thought. South Africa – I'd always fancied working out there but until now had never been offered the chance.

'Yes, for sure, when do you want me to go? Give me a week to prepare what I need after I have broken the job down?'

'You can do all that out there. What about next week? Is that OK? As I say, you will be away for about a month, maybe longer. We will pay all expenses, just send in receipts, as usual; we will give a per diem payment, say 500 rands a week for your incidentals – all other expenses, just claim them, OK?'

'Yes, no problem. Next week it is, then? Just let me know the details when personnel have got it organised.'

I carried on doing what I had been doing on the project – getting to know more about it, trying to envisage what information I needed before I left for Durban. I created some work packs from the information we had, which made it a bit easier to price up.

I arrived at the Louis Botha Airport, named after the South African statesman, late on a Wednesday afternoon. As I stepped out of the plane, it was like stepping into an oven. The heat was unreal, just as it was in Australia; why do I get all these gigs, I wondered.

They were having a bit of unusual weather for April; the annual temperature was around 75 degrees, but this was nearer 90. I was not dressed for this; in long trousers and a shirt and tie, I had begun to melt.

I got to my hotel, The Royal, and was ready for a beer and a shower, in that order. I checked in without any problems; the company had organised everything.

They gave me a free upgrade to a suite rather than the standard box, which was a bit of a bonus. There was a minibar in the room, so I grabbed a nice cold Lion beer and stripped off. I downed the beer in one and went straight under the shower; god, that felt great.

I was lying on the bed, with another couple of Lions down me. I was reading the local information the hotel had given me when the phone rang. 'Hello, yes – that's me; how can I help you? I did not realise we had anyone working for us here; no, no problem. See you in the morning. Yes, thank you.'

Well, that was a surprise – Vangleeson's local agent, Hansie Botha, had just rung me; he had arranged a meeting for the morning. Funny – why I had not been informed of this before I left? I needed to ring Richard later to find out the script. Luckily, Durban was only one hour ahead of Amsterdam; I would ring him first thing.

I went down and had a decent meal; at least I would not starve here. The menu was quite extensive, so it all looked good. I had an early night, as I was buggered. It wasn't long before I must have nodded off.

The alarm went off at 6.30am; the sun was streaming through the Venetian blinds. When I looked out of the window, I saw it must have rained during the night; the steam was rising off the road. It was going to be a humid day; fuck the tie. Good job I had brought some short-sleeved cotton shirts with me just in case.

Bang on 7.30am I was sitting in reception when this tall, lean-looking guy around thirty-five, I suppose, approached me. 'Mr Askenes, my name is Botha – Hansie Botha. We spoke last night. Welcome to South Africa.'

'Hello, Hansie. Yes, I'm Leif. Call me Leif – no need for formalities. How are you? It looks like another stinker of a day.'

'Ya, we have some unusual weather for this time of the year. It is generally a bit cooler in April, but you never can tell.'

Hansie was a tall, dark-skinned lad, well over 6ft; he was not a black African as he had European features and more of a German or Dutch overconfidence about him. You could see he considered himself superior to the blacks; mind, this was South Africa in the 1980s, after all. I had read that within the country at the time there were three creeds – the whites, the coloureds, and, at the lower end of the scale, the blacks.

The white ideology saw whites mixing with blacks as an offence. At one point, a white man could go to prison if he were caught with a black woman. They had split the country up. The white South Africans also used the term 'coloureds' to cover any Asian, especially Indians who came to the country to work. There had been quite a few in the Durban area in their thousands, as they thought themselves far superior to the blacks. What a fucking country; no wonder no one liked them.

I did not like the bloke from the off, but there again, it was his country and how he had been raised; I suppose he could not help himself. I had noticed his arrogance even more so when he was anywhere near a black person; he looked at them like he had brought them in on the bottom of his shoe.

We left for the office, and during the trip, Hansie explained the situation with him and Vangleeson, and why Richard had not told me about the link, for it had only happened the day before I left Amsterdam. He had spoken with Richard, but he had told him to explain what was going on. He would guide and drive me around to the area, taking me to different companies and suppliers in and around Durban.

Just to be sure, I rang Richard once I had settled in the office they had given me in their facility. He confirmed that they were a consultant engineering company that Vangleeson had been in touch with but had not established before I left. Once again, there was a lack of communication with our setup; it was sorted to organise the link out here at the eleventh hour.

There was a knock on the door, and Hansie appeared with a couple of A4 files for me with numerous lists and brochures from companies and agents in Durban and surrounding areas.

'Hansie – no need to knock, mate, you can leave the door open. There's not much air in here, and I noticed the windows don't open that much – only a couple of inches. Why's that?'

'Vandalism, sir – we tend to have a lot of break-ins. It's the blacks; they are terrible for it. If it's not screwed down, they will take it; you must be very careful when you are out alone, sir. Do not go anywhere without me and on an evening do not walk anywhere – always take a taxi.'

'That is another thing – don't call me fucking sir. I am not a knight of the realm. Not yet, anyway.' He did not see the joke. 'Leif is the name, OK – you understand?'

'Yes, sir, oh – I mean, yes, Leif. Thank you, sir – I will try my best to get used to it.' He handed me a list and a copy of a map of Durban. 'These are the places we will visit today. I have set up meetings with the four steel suppliers, one that I know give the better prices, and will come back with a more detailed quotation.'

I was wondering what he was getting out of this; he have must been on a bung from these companies. I thought I'd look up a few others and visit them myself. The first rule was never to trust anyone when it came to purchasing; they were all as bent as corkscrews.

We visited the four he had listed, and all were very helpful and came back with a detailed list as an example of what they could supply. I told them I had made out a sample BOM, or bill of materials, to quote on to give me an idea of what their prices would look like in my model. I insisted that they complete my document as it was written. Also, I wanted it in electronic form in Excel on a floppy disc to use when I got back to Amsterdam.

The next day we visited a couple of fabricators and site installation companies to look through their facilities and quality control systems. I would reduce the bidders to four from the ones I would visit during my month in SA.

Most of the first week, I was taken around by Hansie, but I wanted to explore the area myself and visit some companies that he had not put forward, to make sure he was not just looking at his interests or company. We had visited all of the companies that Hansie had put forward for all disciplines, including electrical and instrumentation.

The civil's scope of work was being taken care of by the client, something we always made sure was the case. If there were any delays in the programme you could hit them for extras, same with the scaffolding and crane hire – anything that was not able to be controlled by us, we made sure they gave it as a free issue, as and when we needed it on the plan. This was known as free and unfettered access.

The second week of my visit, I hired a car and made appointments with some other contractors I had picked out of the local directory. The reason we were trying to get into South Africa was that it was the largest oil refiner in Africa, with four complex refineries scattered around the country. Not many leading engineering companies had managed to break the stranglehold that Goodway Engineering had gained, and we wanted some of it. The refinery had been upgraded in 1972 and again in 1980, with the main contractor being Goodway. We were trying to break into a very lucrative market and get our feet under the table at the largest refinery in South Africa – Saprole, in Durban. There was quite a lot of money to be earned, but we needed street credit in this country.

If I could win the contract here, it would be a real feather in my cap. I was reading some literature I had picked up from the library on my search for local information when Hansie walked in. 'Hi, Leif – what's that you got there? Oh, I see; why didn't you ask? I could have filled you in with all that info.'

'I got it from the library yesterday when I was out and about. By the way, I went to a couple of other fabricators that you had not listed. Can I ask why?'

He went red and looked sheepish.

'OK, just tell me what you know about the refinery business. We can discuss others after.'

'South Africa is the largest oil refiner on the African continent,' Hansie began, 'with four complex refineries scattered around the country. Saprole, which is jointly owned by two of the big players in the oil and gas industry, has a capacity of 155,000 tons a year, which is possibly the largest base oils refinery in Africa, contributing substantially to the South African lubricants industry.'

'OK. You sure know your stuff, very impressive – go on, tell me more, smart-arse.'

'There are five refineries in total in South Africa. One is Sapref, owned by Shell SA and BP SA. Another in Durban, Natref, in Sasolburg, is owned by Sasol Oil and Total. Then there is Enref Durban Engen, opened in 1954 by Mobil. Then a joint venture – Engen, Caltex and

Total – owns the Safor lubricating oil refinery. The fifth, the Calref refinery in Cape Town, is owned by Caltex. All South African refineries were built on grass-roots sites well away from urban areas. However, over time suburbia has spread to the point where the refineries are now being surrounded by habitation.'

'Hansie, how come you know so much history? Did you study this as a subject as school or something?'

'I was told that you wanted as much information as I could give you, as you are trying to break into the oil business here in South Africa. I am trying to provide you with that information; the more knowledge you have, the better chance you will have of obtaining work. With regards to how I know, I will come to that later, Leif, if you don't mind. Please, let me tell you more about the oil business in SA; all will be revealed. Where was I? Oh yes, It was originally opened in 1963, with an integrated unit and associated storage facilities. In the years following, it has had a bitumen high-vacuum unit, blowing unit and blending facilities, first crude distillation unit and lube oil plant added.'

'Has there been much more added to the plant since it was first brought on stream?'

'Yes. It had other expansions in 1970 and 1975; it is one of the most up-to-date in the world, or so the story goes. The first crude oil was processed in 1971, and there have since been several revamps and upgrades. The owners are looking to increase their capacity further. In addition to increased refinery throughputs as a result of one modification, they are hoping to complete a further upgrade in 1993, and then refinery will able to process heavier crudes more efficiently. I can tell you more about the others if you so wish, Leif; it would be my pleasure to discuss this with you. As you can see, the work is my passion. I love being involved, and I have done quite a lot of research over the years.'

'Hansie, I bow down to your knowledge, son; it seems that what you do not know is not worth knowing. While I think on, what does nameplate mean? I remember reading about it, but I don't seem to recollect where and when. Just remind me, will you please – when you talk about refineries; I have never heard it mentioned in any conversation.'

'That is an easy one, Leif. Nameplate capacity is also known as the rated capacity, nominal capacity, installed capacity, or maximum effect. It is the intended full-load sustained output of a facility such as a power plant, electric generator, chemical plant, fuel plant, metal refinery, mine, and many others; you understand now – you remember?'

'Yes, thanks, mate. I recall it now.' I didn't have a clue what he was talking about, but I did not want him to know that.

'One thing I think I must tell you before I go any further,' said Hansie, 'I don't know if you realise that all young men in South Africa are initially called up for two years of national service, with ongoing short-term service requirements. Troops are generally fully trained for operational duty within the space of four to seven months; they are part of the South African Defence Force or SADF for short – a bit like your Territorial Army, I believe, only these are conscripted. I think you should know this, for it will have an impact on your quotations. I think you should put a contingency cover for this, either as a clarification that you have not included it and should there be a requirement, it will be charged as an extra to contract, OK?'

'Never heard of that before – cheers Hansie; a good one.'

'Anyway, will you be coming to the party? You are also invited to stay the night – we have lots of room in the Big House, as they call it; it's an old colonial building my father bought years ago. It has eight bedrooms so no problem about a bed for the night.'

'Yes, thank your father so much – I will look forward to meeting him.'

'There is no need to drive up. Father will send the driver for you; shall we say 4pm, which will give you time to settle in and shower before dinner?'

'OK, great – looking forward to it. Hansie, do you mind, but can you tell me a bit more about your family? I hate to be sitting around people I know nothing about – unless you don't want to tell me.'

'No, I don't mind one bit. Well, where do I start? It is a long story, but here goes. My father has always been what you might call rich, always had good jobs, and has always been frugal with his money. He has built up quite a private empire of companies, mostly involved in the oil industry; he just happened to fall into it back in the early 1950s. I call him my father, and he is, but I was the bastard son of a black woman; it was immoral back in those days for a white man to have any sort of sexual contact with a black woman. Still, father loved what he calls "black meat"; he finds them very erotic, sensual, and is quite open about it now. You will most likely think him racist, and maybe he is, but he just can't help himself. Anyway, my mother died in childbirth. We lived in Swaziland; it was not against the law for whites to have black girlfriends there. When she passed away, he took me from the family and brought me here to Durban, and both he and my now stepmother adopted me and gave me their surname of Botha. My stepmother is Indian by birth. Her family came out as immigrants; there was a massive labour shortage, and lots of Indian people took the chance of a new life, which is how the "coloured" part came about.'

'Yes, I know all that – I've read about it. You don't need to go into all that. Sorry to interrupt you – go on.' I was beginning to warm to the lad now he had told me his background and how his father was. I could see where he got the arrogance from; what a strange culture.

'Do you realise that the Indian nation is one of the most racist on earth, for there is a social structure based upon the caste system? The society is divided into four significant castes – the Brahmans, Kshatriyas, Vaishyas and the Sudras. A lot of difference in what you might call tribes, but it is boring to the Europeans. I won't go into great detail. This scenario still goes on today; my mother came from the Kshatriya sect. They came to South Africa quite a few years before the mass influx. She was also classed as an Anglo-Indian because one of her ancestors was part of the English army that took Indian wives back in the early 1800s; I am not boring you, Leif, am I?'

'No, not at all. I find it fascinating learning about other cultures; it's amazing. Please, go on.'

'I think not – I have said enough. Please, when you meet Father, do not think too badly of him. It has been his upbringing during the apartheid days; he has built an empire on more or less slavery.'

CHAPTER 11

LEIF
The Big Man

The car picked me up bang on 4pm as arranged; an old Mercedes was my mode of transport. The driver, Meshach, did not say a lot on the journey, but seemed quite happy with his lot; he did say his wife was part of the house staff and worked in the kitchen as a maid. They were all black Africans, as I was to find out when I arrived.

I kid you not, it was the butler, James, who showed me to my room, which was more like an apartment. Some of the furnishings must have been antique. Very posh, as Mum would say. I was informed that Mr Botha was waiting for me in the Orchard Room, when I had made myself comfortable; it seemed there was a bit of old colonialism coming out.

I went down to find said room, not knowing where it was. This house was huge, like Buckingham Palace on a smaller scale. I was wandering around, obviously lost, when one of the servants asked me if she could help. I told her the problem, and she took me to meet Mr Botha; still, no one had mentioned his first name or even Mrs Botha for that matter.

'Hello, you must be Leif – so nice to meet you at last. I hear you are enjoying your trip to Durban; I hope you are finding all you need. Looking to get into the construction field, I believe?'

'Yes, I am. Hello, Mr Botha, and the same to you – been looking forward to meeting you; I've heard quite a lot about you.'

'Nothing bad, I hope – and call me Fricke, less of the "Mr", please. My wife, Aarushi, will be with us shortly and my daughter Bhrithi also should not be long; she has been out on her horse most of the afternoon. I got her a new Arab stallion for her birthday; she is over the moon with him. Mind, she should be, cost me a bloody fortune.'

'Wow, they are beautiful names, if I may say so, Mr Botha – I mean, Fricke. Do they have English meanings?'

'Yes, my wife's translates as "first ray of the sun", and Bhrithi is "cherished". Beautiful, aren't they? Been handed down from ancient times, I believe. I find some of the old cultures are intriguing, don't you agree, Leif?'

I was lost for words. Coming off Hessle Road where Fred, Harry, John or Pat had all been handed down… it just did not have the same ring to it.

'Ah, here they are – Aarushi, Bhrithi, come and meet our guest, Leif. Er, sorry, Leif, I did not catch your surname. Oh, how stupid – of course I did. Hansie did tell me. Forgive me, please – Leif Askenes.'

I moved forward and shook both of their hands; they were both exceedingly beautiful women, with that aura about them. They could both have come out of an old English movie about the Raj.

'Hello, ladies, so pleased to meet you; thank you for inviting me to your home, and also may I wish you a very happy birthday, Bhrithi. I hope I pronounced it correctly.'

'Yes, thank you, Leif; just call me Biri – everyone else does apart from Father, and just call Mum, Mum.' Her mother nodded in agreement. 'And thank you for coming; it appears you are my partner tonight as my husband Ajit is away on his war games this week. He has no option when they get the call – they just have to go. My married name is Devi; it is a bit like your Smith, the most common surname in India, or so I am told. He was born here in South Africa, so he got conscripted.'

I liked this girl – she was stunning. It was her thirty-third birthday and she did not look her age. Mind, I had noticed that South African women all looked younger; it must have been the fact they didn't work for a living, as even the lowest white families had servants and house boys.

'Leif, do you like horses? Come and see my new stallion, Lancet. I did not pick a name; he was already called that, but I like it anyway. Dad, can I take Leif to see Lancet? We won't be too long.'

'OK, if he wants to go to the bother.'

'I don't mind; I would love to see him.'

'Come on, then.' She grabbed my hand and off we went to the stables.

'Here, he looks wonderful – isn't he magnificent? A great specimen, isn't he – a bit like yourself, Leif.'

I was silent for once in my life; I did not know what to say.

'What's wrong? Don't you like compliments, Leif? You are a very handsome man, and your body looks amazing; you don't mind me being so forward, do you?'

'No, not at all; it's just that we have only just met, and you being married… it just seems odd that you are coming on to a stranger – someone who is a guest under your father's roof.'

'Who said anything about coming on? I am a healthy sexual woman who loves sex. We Indians wrote the Kama Sutra, you realise that? My husband is a skinny Indian boy who is useless in bed; the chances of me getting an heir to my father's fortune are just about nil. You know the story about Hansie and how he came into the family, the illegitimate child of my father's black whore, and how she died?'

'Yes, I know – Hansie told me all about it. So sad; his birth mother died during labour.'

'What a load of bullshit. Is he still telling that story? Unreal. She did not die; she was paid off. My mother could not conceive, and my father was desperate for a son. She was Cape Coloured, and dad knew if he made her pregnant, the child had a great chance of being the same colour as us, more of a milk chocolate, not black like the Kaffirs. And he was the perfect match. He could be my brother; well, I suppose he is a half brother, but that's about all. He will never get his hands on my father's millions. I need a child, a boy, and then Hansie will go back down the pecking order of the Botha family.'

'If your mother could not conceive, how come you arrived on the scene?'

'Before you ask,' she butted in, 'no, I am not another manufactured child; she did get pregnant not long after Hansie arrived. It was about two years – in fact, yes, it was two years; he is thirty-five. But I was a girl, as you no doubt noticed, and after that, she had a problem down below, with her womb; not sure what it was, but no chance of any more children. Dad reckons it's my job now, and I don't think he minds where it comes from. Hansie has been talking about you and described what you looked like – big, blond, almost Afrikaans-looking. It was father's idea to get you here, for he knew Ajit would be away. He also knows I like fresh meat, and it doesn't have to be a horse, just hung like one.' She laughed. 'The second bit is just wishful thinking on my part. Anyway, come on – we have talked enough. Better get back, or father will be thinking you are having your wicked way with me. It's a bit early for that.'

Well, I thought, looks like you have struck lucky here; she sure was a great-looking woman and horny as fuck. Tonight was going to be interesting.

I got back to my room, still enjoying the idea that Biri wanted me, not for lust or sexual enjoyment, just for breeding purposes, similar to old Lancet, for one day he would go to stud. If she wanted my sperm, she could have it, for I was sure I would enjoy the ritual of insemination.

I had a shower and was lying on my bed contemplating the coming evening's events when I must have nodded off. A noise awakened me, then I saw Mildred, one of the maids, standing at the end of the bed. She was not saying a word, just staring at me, for I was naked, sprawled out like the proverbial starfish, with an enormous erection; I must have been dreaming of the night to come.

She realised what she was doing and suddenly said, 'Oh, sorry, sir, I did not mean to stare at you. I just came in to bring you some clean towels. I did knock, but no one answered. I thought you must still be out with Miss Bhrithi; I am so sorry.'

'It's OK, don't worry – you never saw a white man naked before, is that it? Do I look OK to you – will I pass the test?' I said, laughing.

'Oh, yes, sir, very nice; I only ever seen black boys, never seen a white one before. It looks OK to me if you don't mind me saying, sir.'

'Don't mind at all; you want to try it out for anything? Want to hold me, see how it feels?'

'Can I, sir? I will get into lots of trouble if they find out I have been in the guest's room. Can I touch a white dick? They would put us in jail if anyone found out and throw away the key – especially in your case; they would flog me.'

'Come here – come on over here.' I took her hand and placed it on my penis, 'Well – does it feel different to a black guy?'

'It is bigger than white men are supposed to be. I have seen bigger, but in a different colour, that's all – but bigger than most Asian men, those I have seen anyway. I must be going, sir, sorry. I must not be caught in here. I hope you won't say anything. I would hate my husband to find out.'

'Who is your husband? How will he find out?'

'Meshach, the driver – he is my husband. Have you met him? Did he bring you to the house? He did, didn't he – oh my god, you won't say anything, will you? They will fire us both. Please, sir, do not say anything – please.'

'No, it's OK. I won't tell a soul; go on, you better get going.'

I was pondering after she left my room. It was a shame she had to go; she had an adorable body and I never got to see her naked, but it was very nice all the same.

I went down to dinner. There were only ten people there, including Fricke, Aarushi, Biri, Hansie and his girlfriend, Ahyoka, which I believe means 'she brought happiness'. I hoped she did – she was another cute-looking girl. Also there were another two couples who worked at the plant, an Afrikaans bloke called Guy and his wife, Belinda. Lastly, an English guy called Mike Watson and his wife Lesedi, who told me her name originated from a tribe that dwelled in southern Africa called the Sesotho; it meant 'light' in Sesotho.

Anyway, the food was terrific. I had a monkey gland steak. I had never tasted such an incredible sauce. I asked Mike what it was. Had he any idea?

'Yes, I love cooking myself and use this sauce quite often. It's made with onions, garlic, ginger, fruity chutney, tomato puree, soy sauce, mustard, Worcester sauce, and port red wine mixed with chicken broth; it's a fantastic taste, isn't it?'

'Yes, unreal – cheers for the cookery lesson.'

It was great meal, all finished off with cheese and biscuits.

Biri was sitting next to me, and all through the meal she was rubbing her foot up my shin, and on my foot. I had kicked off my sandal; fuck, it was horny.

'How long you staying in Durban?' asked Mike.

'Another week or so, my company is considering opening an office here. We are in the construction industry working on refineries, off-shore petrochemical plants, that sort of thing.'

'We are always looking for more companies to locate to SA; one of them is getting too much work monopolising the industry, in my opinion. They seem to charge what they like,with no competitors to make them sharpen their pencils.'

'What do you do, Mike? What is your role at the plant?'

'Contracts manager and cost engineering, that's why I say we need more; let's hope you can come in with a decent proposal. I am sure it will be considered and given the utmost attention.'

Now, what did Mike mean by that? An Englishman in South Africa – maybe I was reading too much into him. He seemed OK, if a bit boring, to be honest; all he talked about was work. Was that because he was at his boss's house and did not want to let himself go? It was our first meeting; I made a mental note to see him again on his own turf.

It wasn't the only thing that was getting the utmost attention. Biri's foot had just about rubbed the skin off my shin, and her hand was stroking my inner thigh. It was hard as hell; I hoped I did not have to stand up quickly, as that could have been a bit embarrassing.

We finished dinner and went out on to the terrace for coffee; Fricke came over to me and his daughter.

'Hope you are enjoying your stay, Leif; thank you for coming. I don't want to discuss business tonight, but I see you had a bit of a conversation with Mike. A good man, Mike – he will keep you right. We need more contractors. By the way, nothing goes past my desk without my nod, if you know what I mean,' he said with a wink. 'I will leave it at that.'

'Fricke, what about Guy? Can I ask how does he fit into all this?'

'Well, Guy is my number two in the organisation, my majordomo, as you Brits like to call them; he takes care of the day-to-day running of my companies, but mainly the head office. If you want to know anything, just ask Guy; if he can't get you an answer, no one can'

'Right, thank you. I will keep that in mind.' He's his fucking spy, more like, I thought.

I knew what he meant. OK, he wanted a bung for us to get work; I needed some advice on numbers here before I could commit to anything.

'Hi, Biri, I think I will go to my room. I'm feeling a bit, well, you know – tired.'

'Don't be too long,' she whispered as she held my hand and kissed my cheek.

'Goodnight, Biri; see you in the morning,' I said as she walked away.

Hansie came over. 'You like my sister, don't you, Leif?'

'Yes, she is a beautiful young lady, Hansie; her husband is a fortunate man, no doubt about that.'

'Would you like to make love to her? I know she would.'

'What? Why ask me that? I am a guest in your father's house, and you suggest that I sleep with his daughter and your sister? Now, come on, Hansie, you can't catch me out like that. What are you trying to do? Trick me into letting my company down? We are honourable, and that is the last thing I would want. Now if you will excuse me I will also get to bed. Goodnight – I will see you in the morning; there is something I need to discuss with you – I believe you know what it is.'

I got back to my room, which just happened to be across the hall from Biri's.

I undressed and put on the robe that was laid out on the bed for me; I was now pondering how I could get across the hallway. No way was I going to miss out on giving the gorgeous Biri an excellent seeing to. She was gagging for it, and Leify baby was going to provide it. I heard voices as the others eventually went to bed, then there was silence for about half an hour. Now was the time to make a move. I opened my door and peeked out – no one around. I silently closed the door and went across to Biri's. I tried the handle – it was unlocked, so, gently turning the knob, I opened it and went in.

'Where have you been, baby? Come on, I need you; what took you so long?'

'I could not get away. First your father, then Hansie came to chat. Now, come here.'

Our lips met; mmm, she tasted nice. We were standing at the end of the bed. She had on a similar robe to me; it was just held with a slim belt of the same material. We undid each other's, and they fell open. Biri shrugged her shoulders, and hers fell to the floor, exposing an incredibly slim, well-proportioned body, with firm breasts that were not too big, and just perfect dark nipples, to go with her golden skin. Yes, she was a sight to behold, no doubt, and a small tuft of pubic hair that had been trimmed and waxed was waiting for my attention.

She took the robe from my shoulders and let it drop alongside hers. Her arms reached up and pulled my head down to meet her lips, and we kissed again, this time with more passion; she was ready for the taking. I picked her up and carried her to the bed, and she lay there like a sacrifice on the altar ready to be used. I lay alongside her and took her in my arms; Wigan was not far away, but I was not going on the express tonight.

We made love all night; she was like a rabid dog that could not get enough. I was well and truly fucked by the time the sun came up.

We got up, and I ached in places I didn't know I had. I went back to my room, had a shower, got changed and went down to breakfast, and when I arrived Biri was already there. I sat next to her, and her father was at the head of the table, as usual – the master of the house.

'Leif, could I have a minute? I would like to have a word with you before you go, is that OK? Come into my office where we can talk privately.'

'Yes, sure, Fricke, no problem; what can I do for you? I must, first of all, like to thank you for your hospitality. I have enjoyed my time here; it's been wonderful.'

'No problem; hope you got some pleasure spending time with us. It is not often we get white people to stay with us, and I do not mean that with any disrespect, but it is South Africa after all.'

'What do you want to know? Is it about my company? Is there anything more you need from us? Please forgive me, I am not trying anything underhand by that comment. I was not offering any sort of inducement for favours – you understand that, don't you?'

'Leif, I will not beat about the bush; I will be open and frank with you. That is why I asked you into my house – for your company to stand any chance of getting on the bid list, you must ensure that I personally get my palm crossed.'

'With silver?'

'No, not silver – gold.'

CHAPTER 12

LARS

Good and Bad – Two Months Later

Two months had passed since the near-breakup; things had settled down. I talked with Maya after dinner one evening. 'I fancy going to Europe for a trip,' I said. 'Do you fancy coming? We have not had a decent holiday in years. Not since we got together back in 1970, which was nearly 14 years ago; I think it's about time we had something out of this partnership. In fact, how about us getting married?'

Maya just looked at me; she started to cry, 'Oh baby, you mean it? Get married? Oh, fuck, yes, please!' She put her arms around my neck and gave me the sloppiest kiss ever.

What the fuck had I said? I had not even been thinking about getting wed, but hey, yes, why not? We were not getting any younger. 'I am 37, you are 42,' I said. 'It is about time we tied the knot.'

We had talked about having kids, but Maya was not that bothered; she wasn't the maternal type. 'Too tying,' was her remark when I had brought up the subject before, and she had said we were too old and set in our ways to have lots of kids in our feet. She liked the luxuries of life as they were.

For me, I still had the same feelings about kids. Again, I had realised she was right; I was too tied up with our businesses to worry about children; it's not that I did not like them, but seeing other couples I knew whose children had fucked up their social lives, I went along with Maya, even though it might sound selfish.

I contacted my parents in Maitland and told them the news – we said we were going to Europe, looking at getting married in either Venice or London, but nothing fancy. Then when we got home we'd have a get-together with all our friends' families.

Mum was not a happy bunny. 'Why get married without us there? It's not on. We should be there on your happy day. Why can't we be there?' She shouted at Dad. 'Jon, come here, just talk to your son, will you; he is going to get married without us being there. Just tell him he can't do that – tell him, will you?'

Dad came on the phone. 'Maya's parents aren't going either,' I said. 'They will not travel overseas. I have told you before, Dad, she does not have a mother; she passed away a long time ago, and her father has been ill ever since I have known her. He has kept hanging on in there, but no one expects him to last much longer. Regarding her new stepmother, that is not so true because they have never got married. The least said about her, the better, as she is mental. It seems she had been playing around for years. Maya hates her, so there was no chance of her being invited to the wedding anyway.'

'Bloody hell, Lars – what on earth do you think you are doing getting married on your own with none of your parents there, neither of you? Who else is not going?'

'No one, Dad, it only leaves Maya's other sister; she is a school teacher living in Melbourne, and she only gets a Christmas card from her, that is about it.'

'Just because Maya hasn't got any real family, you are punishing your mother. What has become of you, Lars? You have changed over the years. Is this because we did not tell you the truth about how we adopted you? Is this the reason you are you going to England? To find your birth mother and get her to your wedding, is that it?'

We argued for a bit longer until Dad put the phone down on me. His last words were, 'Oh, do as you like.'

I started to think about them – I supposed they were right, especially as they were getting older. Dad had had that bad scare a few years when we thought we had lost him, but he came back from the dead. We just did not think before telling anyone; we wanted to do it our way – we had not done it out of spite or anything. OK, Maya's parents, or parent, did not come into the equation; we knew mine would not travel, or could not, so we wanted to do it our way. Why do you always have to do things to please everyone else when all that matters is you?

Our plans of travelling to Europe and getting married were put on the back burner for a while. In 1985, the first thing that went wrong was when one of our cranes was involved in a tragic road accident.

I was sitting in the office alone on the early morning of June 18 when the phone went.

'Hello, yes – speaking; how can I help you?'

'My name is Constable Jefferson. I am afraid we have some bad news; one of your mobile cranes has been involved in an RTA on the Princes Highway just outside Wyong; I am afraid your driver was injured in the crash and is on his way to the hospital as we speak.'

'How did you know how to contact me?'

'Your company name and number are on the crane?'

I felt dumb; what a stupid fucking question. I hadn't asked how he was, or who he was, as I did not know all the crane movements that particular day.

'OK, I am sorry, officer, can you give me his name? Or if you can't do that, give me the reg number of the crane in question, please.'

'I have his name, sir; it's Mike Thomas. He is not too bad, but we have sent him to the hospital just for a check-up.'

'How… what… how… I am sorry – I'm just shocked about what happened; who was involved, can you tell me, please?'

'Unfortunately, it was a car; there were four other people in the ve-hicle. I am sorry to say they did not make it. Looking at the wreck, it was not your man's fault, but I am not at liberty to say. I was first on the scene, and it was not pleasant, to say the least. We have interviewed your man, and what he has told us ties in with the scene of the accident. I can't say much more, you understand. I just needed to get in touch with you; your man has been taken to Wyong Hospital. If you want to contact them for an update, that would be good. Also, if you're going to get someone out to recover your crane, it is drivable; there is not a lot of damage, only to one side, the nearside rear. The other car ran into the side/back of your vehicle, how I do not know – it was at a junction at the top, Windy Creek Road, do you know it?'

'I am just trying to find it on my map, officer. Oh, yes, I know it; that is a bit of a lousy bend if I am right – just over the brow of the hill where it goes down to turn off for Wyong?'

'Yes, sir, there was a bit of a hold-up, and it looks like your crane was stationary in traffic, and the other vehicle ploughed into the back of it. Anyway, I can't say much more; thank you for your time, sir, we will be in touch.'

'No, thank you, officer. I will get someone there as soon as we can to recover the truck. Do we have to take it to a compound or anything for inspection, or can we bring it back to our yard?'

'Er, we should inspect it, if you can take it to our station in North Sydney, you know it? Would help us no end. I can see by the look of the crane it looks brand new and should not be a problem. We should by law tow it in ourselves, but it would mean a load of hassle; if you can help us out it would be appreciated, OK?'

We got the crane taken round to their compound, and as expected, there was no problem with it, and Mike was OK. At the inquest, it came out that the car had been speeding as it came round the bend at the top of the hill and ran straight into the back of the crane head-on. They never stood a chance – a complete family wiped out in one go; terrible.

After the accident, things improved notably for the other side of our company, the mechanical/steel fabrication arm. With the help of Bruce's contacts in Queensland, we had opened a second fabrication shop in Ipswich and one in Gladstone, about 350 miles north of Brisbane. We'd had a new Boyne aluminium smelter built in 1982, and the coal mining industry was on the way up and we wanted to be in on the upsurge. Alongside this was the fact that housing for the new workforce and other civil projects were becoming available.

Bruce was interested in a steel fabrication company whose owner was an old schoolmate of his and, like Bruce, was looking to sell up, yet still take part in the business. I met Bruce up in Brisbane to discuss the deal we were putting together to take over Crownsteel.

'Here are the figures Mike gave me for the past five years; it has been a gradual growth, nothing spectacular, mainly because he did not want to take on more staff. He was quite happy to look after the guys already employed, as he had a great working relationship with them.'

'In what way, Bruce, can we learn anything from him? What does he do that we don't do? I think we do all right by our people.'

'Yes, we do, but one thing he does, that we don't, is, if they don't take any sickies during the year, he gives it to them as a cash tax-free lump sum at Christmas, losing the money somehow away from the taxman. Also, along with the basic state sickies, five a year, he doubles them by giving them a full week of extra holidays – both these things are accrued every week, starting on January 1 until the end of December.'

'What happens if they leave during the twelve months?'

'They forfeit all benefits, simple. Don't forget, sickies can only be claimed for one day at a time, and once they have taken the five statutory, then the five extra are automatically lost. If guys are generally sick, they can claim off the federal department. That is why no one ever leaves. He never has any union problems, and he won't employ Poms, for he believes they are trouble. No disrespect to those who turn out OK when they settle here, but it has been found that the majority suffer from Pommie disease – the love of bad industrial relations.'

'I have never realised that – most of the Poms I know are decent blokes; we have a couple working for us and never had any problems. One of them is the shop steward at the shop in Maitland – one of your boys, Bruce, he is spot on.'

'Eddie, you mean? Yes, I interviewed him when he first came to Maitland. He had been in Sydney for a few months when just off the ship; he didn't like big city life. Do you know how he picked the Hunter region? By sticking a pin in a map with his eyes closed, and it landed on Maitland. Well, near enough anyway. He did leave us once; he went to the Dockyard in Newcastle, and lasted six weeks. Then he came back. I remember him telling me he'd left because of the days off on strike, bloody Pommie stewards and rednecks. He said it was being ruined, same as they had ruined the shipyards back home, as he put it. That is when he took the shop steward's duties here when old Bobby retired, and they wanted someone to take his place; we never lost another day. Any problems that arose, we sorted then out as best we could between either the foreman, the manager, or, if required, me. One time I gave them a bonus for going twelve months without a lost day. Mind, I did have a problem with him once, but that was through the manager I had at the time; he tried to con him, but Eddie was too smart for him.'

'How come, what happened? I don't think you have ever mentioned it. Come on, I'd love to hear it.'

'It was a few years ago – we had won a contract to supply new twenty-ton gantry cranes for a job in Wollongong. In point of fact, the Pom, as the lads called him, was given the job of fabricating the main beams – bloody good boilermaker, the guy was too. Anyway, we had always said whatever the going rate was in Newcastle, we would match to ensure we did not lose anyone. The local union organiser had been to the shop about six weeks previously and said they were, as they put it, going for the ton – a $100 basic rate. He had approached the manager with his request for the increase. My manager had told him he had to run it by me, but he never did.'

'Why not? He was asking for trouble, surely?'

'Yes, you are right. He tried to take the piss, mate, but he was too smart for him. The boys had asked for a meeting to discuss what results their steward had got for them, and he told them he would give him another a week – the manager, that is – and if they had not come good, he suggested that they should start lightning stoppages. The fool was using me as an excuse, saying he could not contact me, which was a damn lie, for I spoke to him every week, and he had never mentioned it to me. He knew that he was going to plan a stoppage that would hurt us and cost me a lot of money – a lot more than the extra wage bill for the past six weeks would have cost us.'

'Why wasn't he foreman for you if he was that clever?'

'I asked him after the event if he would, but let me finish.'

'OK, sorry, go on – this is a great story, Bruce.'

'Where was I… oh, yes – one of the beams that he had fabricated was due to go out for delivery on the Friday of the sixth week. They were fifty feet long, five feet high, by three feet wide – some piece of kit. We needed to get them out of the shop through the front doors; you have seen the shop – you know the layout, don't you?'

I nodded. 'Yes.'

'We were using a rig where the beam became part of the truck. One set had a separate steering system where the wheels could be turned from inside the tractor's cab. It seems there was not enough room for the rig to turn. I don't know the full technicalities, but anyway, the back-end wheels had been set into position. The driver had reversed the tractor into position, and his offsider had made that safe. They had moved the beam out ready, which was still hung on the gantry crane in the shop ready for the iron fairy to take it out, allowing more manoeuvrability in the yard; they were prepared to lower it on the back set of wheels when the Pom called a stoppage.'

'Well, you can imagine the chaos it caused. The Pom went into the office and informed my man. I was told these were his words: "Considering your lack of cooperation in our negotiations for the increase, we have no alternative than to withdraw our labour." My man went berserk, calling him a Pommie bastard; you can imagine the frustration this had caused twelve o'clock on a Friday lunchtime. Eddie was crafty; they were only losing two hours, for they worked six until two on a Friday to enable them to get to the pub early. It meant the truckie could not go anywhere; his convoy ute was also stuck. They all walked out straight to the Rutherford Pub; the manager was running around like a headless chicken trying to contact me. What the fuck did he think I could do? I was up here in Brisbane; he was going home to Sydney as it was his long weekend, so he had to be off. The Pom also knew this; I reckon he had inside information on the manager's movements. After he had gone about half an hour later, Billy, our crane driver, returned to complete the loading operation to let the truckie get away. Billy told one of the girls in the office that this was all planned. No one knew this;

the Pom had planned it all. It was a show of strength; don't fuck with the Pommie.'

'How did you find out about it? When did you get involved?'

'I got a phone call from the office manager; I had heard nothing from my so-called manager. I went back down on the following Monday morning and called the Pom and all relevant parties into a meeting, individually of course, and heard both sides of the story.'

'What did you do? What was the outcome?'

'After listening to both of them, I sacked the manager on the spot. I gave the lads the rise they were asking for, backdated it the six weeks they had been waiting. I also paid them for the two hours they had lost, gave the shop foreman the manager's job, and offered the Pom the foreman's position, which he declined – and that, Lars, is what you call good industrial relations.'

'Bloody good story that, mate, like it.'

We had also purchased two construction companies on the Gold Coast, which needed the personal touch. It also got me out of Maya's hair for a while and meant I had to spend quite a lot of time on the road again. Still, it just had to be done; there was nothing like face-to-face commitment when dealing with not only your new clients but also the staff of the companies you had taken over. I understood their trepidation about new management and owners coming in – would there be any retrenchment? Would they miss out on any benefits they were getting? All that had to be sorted and my having one-to-one consultations with them was the best way to do it – but this would mean travelling up the coast to meet them, and I wasn't sure how well that would go down.

CHAPTER 13

LEIF

Down to Real Business

'Now, this conversation never happened. If anyone asks if you offered any bribes, I will tell them no, because you did not offer me any. Is that understood? How do you think a coloured man gets by in this country? Yes, I am coloured. I may look Afrikaans, but no, I am coloured. My father was a Boer, but my mother was black as coal; I just came out white. As I was saying, how do you think I can live as I do in this shithole of a country? Why? Because I am, as you English say, fucking bent. Oh, I do love those old English quotes.'

I was shell-shocked; at least I knew where we stood. Now, what could I say to that? I couldn't commit to anything. 'OK, how do you determine how or what should the amount be,' I said. 'Does it depend on the size of the contract or a nominal lump sum? In what currency would you require it to be paid and where?'

'Usually, on the scale of agreement, and it is negotiable. I realise it is a tight margin you work to, dependent on how much you need the work at that moment in time. I am not stupid, and I know you want to get into the marketplace in South Africa. Your main competitor is getting greedy and is reducing his, shall we say, bonuses being paid out. He needs a lesson in manners, so I will help you. For the first contract that you shall win, I will not only tell you his price, but I will take a minimum amount of, say, $1 million. I know that the cost will be about $12 million; our company estimating team has worked on this project for more than twelve months and they have it down to a tee; we do that on every project – we can't rely on just contractors' prices or how would we know we weren't getting ripped off? We know how much we have to pay; we include inducements, or I will tell him he has to pay me $2 million, so his price should come in at $14 million. It is not a science; it is easy numbers. We know you have allowances for contingency and what you might call unallocated provision and escalation. Therefore, our – or should I say my – pittance can be lost in those items without anyone ever noticing them. I realise you will not be able to commit today; you will need to speak to your people. You may think that a million dollars is a lot for me, but I have to "look after" – to use another one of your sayings – other people within the system, you understand?'

'Yes, I understand. You could not have made it any more precise. Let me talk to my people back in Amsterdam.'

'Now, as I said, this conversation never happened, but I will look forward to your first quotation, and may our arrangement bear fruit throughout the coming years. I know you would like to say goodbye to my beautiful daughter Bhrithi before you leave, and once again, I hope you have had a nice time. I am sorry, but I must leave you. I have another commitment this morning.'

In other words, fuck off. OK, I could take a hint; I went to see Biri to say goodbye.

I got back to my hotel just after tea on the Sunday and decided to go out for a meal, so asked the concierge if he could recommend a decent seafood restaurant nearby. He told me that Die Vangs – or The Catch, in English – was a decent one and not too expensive, so off I went.

He was right; the food was fantastic. I had the seafood platter and I'd never seen anything like it – you name it, it was on it, OK, the fish was not what I was used to – no cod, haddock, halibut or any flatfish I could name, but the southern ocean specimens were wonderful. I had never heard of carpenter or angel. The dusky cob was very much like cod, and kingklip, monkfish, cape dory and gurnard were all on the platter too, and in decent-sized portions. I was glad I'd only asked for the serving for one; I was going to ask for a double but was advised not to by the waitress. It was served with chips and salad and all for twenty rands – about five quid; unreal. I washed it all down with a beautiful bottle of South African De May chardonnay.

I walked back to my hotel full as the proverbial boot – the end to a perfect night… or was it?

I had just got into bed when the phone rang.

Who the fuck's this at this time of night, I said to myself. 'Hello? Who… what? OK, put her through. Hi, Biri, what's up?'

'Nothing – I can't sleep. I want to come to you.'

'What – now?'

'Yes. I loved it last night, and I want more, please, Leif.'

'But I am fucked – just had a big meal; honestly, babe, I'm shagged.'

'You will be if you let me come now. Please, you won't regret it.'

'Oh, OK… how long will you be? Where are you now?'

'At the reception phone booth; they would not let me come up because of the time unless I got permission from you. Can you call them to let me come up, please, Leif – please?'

Five minutes passed, and there was a knock on my door.

'Come in.'

She closed the door behind her after putting the do not disturb sign on the handle.

'Does your father know you have come here?'

'Yes, of course he does; I told you he wants you to make me pregnant, and so do I.'

She unbuttoned her coat and dropped it to the floor. She wasn't wearing a dress, just a bra, panties and suspender belt along with black stockings and high heels; oh my god, she looked ravishing.

She put her arms around me, and we kissed. She was a fantastic kisser; our tongues met, and I just melted. It proved to be another night without sleep. She must have woken me three times after I'd nodded off, licking me where the sun don't shine.

Her husband had never come into my mind until the morning when I asked her.

'Oh, he is still away, not back until Wednesday, so we can do this again – if you want to, that is?'

'But Biri, I have work to do. I am not here much longer; I am away back to Holland end of next week. I realise that's almost two weeks away, but I have a lot to get done, and it will be tight.'

'That's not the only thing that's tight,' she smiled. 'You don't work at night, so no problem. I can come here every night until Thursday when he gets home. Do you want me or not?'

There was no doubt I was a sucker for a sweet vagina. Biri had won me for the next four nights. She arrived at nine-thirty prompt and we made love all night on and off until we left the hotel, me to go to my job and she back home.

Apart from being shagged, the work I had done on the enquiry we had received before I'd come to Durban was a complete waste of time; it was a whole different ball game. Fricke told me that it was a hoax to get someone down to go through the company to make sure we were not a fly-by-night outfit and talk face-to-face with a company representative to ensure that they could do his line of business. I managed to gather all the relevant information needed, and wrote my report and basic FEED estimate for a job that had already been done. With the kind help of Hansie, who had provided the relevant facts, all I needed to do was enter details into our estimating model. According to Hansie, we were under the winning bid; without the bung required with a million added, it would still be under their estimated cost for a FEED, which was great news. What we were not aware of was that all alongside the civils, scaffolding, and craneage, all structural and piping materials – vessels, pumps, etc. – were a free issue. We had to cost labour and management above the foreman; the rest was supplied by the client using local labour and done on a day work rate. The scope covered the 'black trades' – welders, platers, pipefitters – plus electrical, instrumentation, erection, riggers and banksmen, including all local labour plus Filipino labour.

I called Fricke after he had asked Hansie to request a call. Lo and behold, his spy had been keeping him informed of what we had been doing. He told me that the courier would send an invitation to tender for the next big job coming up in two weeks. He also told me it was worth around 15 million US dollars, plus the million he wanted and that we would win it, assuming we could do it for that sum of money. His last word was, 'Do not forget it is day work rates, and you know what that means.' With that, he put the phone down.

I did not see Biri again before I left. Was she pregnant? I did not know. In a way, I hoped I had sowed my seeds in her, and she'd got what she hoped for. It wasn't for want of trying, for I had worked hard on her. Would I ever find out?

I left Durban at the end of the week, arriving back in Amsterdam on a Thursday evening. I had been informed by Richard back in Amsterdam I was not needed until Monday; everything could wait until then.

I had not been home for a while and did not fancy getting the ferry across, so I had a relaxing weekend in Holland, soaking in its specialities – say no more.

On the Monday morning, I got in to work at seven-thirty and made a few copies of my report and estimate for the job I had used as a model, as it was nothing like the information I had worked on before leaving. Richard, nor anyone else, was aware of what was wanted. I went into the meeting with Richard and the head of engineering, where they went through my report with a fine-tooth comb. The one pleasing fact was everything was free to issue. We did not have to import anything but a management team and European supervision, mainly superintendents and general foreman. The rest was to be South African labour with a mix of Filipinos.

I had not mentioned the bung to anyone as yet; I was leaving that for Richard's ears, as loose lips sink ships and all that.

'What? How fucking much? You must be joking – a million dollars, he is taking the piss?'

'Richard, it is the only way we will win any work in South Africa. It will not cost us anything – they are paying the "favour". At the end of the day it's coming out of the price of the job. We add it on, and they pay it; what I would suggest is we put two million on the price, one for them and one for us, just to try them out. It's worth a try. Fricke was quite open about it, and I think he will come back to us if it is too expensive.'

'OK, I suppose you are right. Let's see when the inquiry gets here and take it from there.'

It was nearly a month before the inquiry came through. The rest was quite simple. We had already sent off for quality control systems, and all the other paraphernalia required. I had a phone call from Hansie a week later.

'Hi, Leif, it's Hansie; how are you, OK? I was just wondering how you were getting on? Everything there that you need? Any more information required?'

'No, it's spot on. Just one thing – could you ask Fricke to get in touch, please? He said he would ring me on some finer points but he has not been in touch. I know he is a busy man and all that; just a couple of clarifications, that's all.'

'Oh, OK – you sure? It's nothing I can't handle; after all, I am your contact with Saprole, and all correspondence should come through me – you must remember that.'

Now, this was the first time he had ever pulled rank on me, and I smelt a rat. Was he fishing for something, or was he just trying to do his job?

'Hansie, it is something personal about… well, I would rather your father dealt with it, if you don't mind.'

'If it is about Biri, I understand – she is my sister, and I believe you and her got, shall I say, rather close on your visit here. It is OK, Leif – I know all about it. I must say I was quite surprised when she told me she was in love with you and was leaving her husband for you, and was coming over to the UK to find and be with you. It did surprise us all; Mum was shocked; nearly hysterical when she found out. Father said he was going to hunt you down like the dog you are – fucking his daughter under his roof; he called you a dirty, low-down… sorry to use the C-word… no, I won't say it – but you know, don't you?'

What the fuck was he talking about? Fricke knew I was fucking her; he wanted another son or grandson to be in the family line, someone to leave all his wealth to… or had I been set up by Biri? Oh, fuck – had she used me as an excuse to get away from her husband? This was a fucking nightmare, and it wasn't on Elm Street either. I had been led right up the fucking garden path, hook, line and sinker. I needed to speak with her father on the subject to see what he had to say, or was Hansie not aware of all the facts? This I had to find out – and soon.

'Hi, OK, Jaclyn, yes – please put Mr Botha through, and put any calls on hold. Tell whoever they are, no matter, I will ring them back – OK, thank you.'

'Hello, Leif. I believe you have been trying to get hold of me. I am sorry, but I have been rather busy at home – family crisis, I hope you understand?'

'Oh, I hope there is nothing wrong – are your wife and Biri both OK? No problems there, I hope?'

He seemed relatively calm and collected – no mention of Biri leaving her old man and coming to find me. What the fuck was going on?

'No, son, nothing; well, yes, there is, but nothing I can't handle. It will be fine, don't you worry, it will be OK. I will sort Biri out, silly little fool.'

I had to act as if I did not know anything; I did not want to drop Hansie in the shit for telling tales, and I did not know if he knew about our little arrangement.

'Why, what is the problem with Biri? What has she done? I hope it's nothing serious.'

'Well, Leif, she has only gone and got herself pregnant. She has admitted it's not her husband's, but she won't tell us who the father is. He is talking about wanting his revenge; she has brought disgrace to his family. His father is talking about her having an abortion to get rid of the "bastard child" – that is the only thing that will save their marriage, and it is a right mess.'

I'll say it was a mess. The cunning little bitch had well and truly conned me; she wanted out of her marriage. The only way she could get rid of her husband was to get herself up the stick to any poor bastard who was willing to shag her. There must have been hundreds that would volunteer; the back of the queue would have been in Johannesburg – why pick on me? How the hell would I get out of this one? I was worried that this could destroy all the work we had put in trying to get a foothold in SA. If – and it was a big if – Fricke had not put her up to it, no way would he let me and my company in. I was well and truly up shit creek without a paddle. Could Hansie keep his mouth shut? He was the only one who had any idea I was the father. But why was she blaming me? How many other guys had been hanging out of her? She had said she wouldn't name the father; maybe, just maybe, she did not know who the father was – it could have been anyone. I needed to contact Hansie again and have a good heart-to-heart conversation with him on what he knew about his sister's sex life – before it was too late.

'Hello, Hansie, good morning; how are you this fine day?'

'I do not want to discuss my sister; sorry, I do not want to discuss her with you.'

'Hang on there, mate, what are you going on about? Why should I ring you about your sister?' Was this guy psychic? How did he know I was going to ring him?

'Leif, you made love to my sister. I know that you know that the chances are the baby could be yours – you agree?'

'OK, I hold my hands up, but you said "could be". Now, how many other guys have been fucking your lovely sister? Come on, tell me the truth – she dropped her knickers quicker than a lump of hot coal. Who else has been poking the fire? Come on, I need to know.'

'Leif, OK, you are right. I know of five other men who have been seeing her; she does not know I know, but Father had told me to keep an eye on her.'

'Why have you been told to watch her? Is she that bad?'

'Yes, she does like it; she just can't do without it. She's been like this since she was a teenager. One of her schoolteachers was the first man to have her; I caught her in the changing rooms with him. Biri told me if I told anyone about her, she would tell them the truth about me – the fact I prefer men to women.'

'What – you are batting for the other side, Hansie? How long you have known you are homosexual? When did that start? You never said anything to me, not that I am that way inclined, you understand?'

'No, I understand, it is OK. I know you did not give any indications that you would be interested in me. I have been more attracted to boys and men all my life, but anyway, this is about Biri – she is still seeing men outside of her marriage. I suppose it could be any one of them, but you were the last one I know of who has been with her.'

'Hansie, how close an eye do you keep on Biri? Do you know she came over to my hotel in the middle of the night to be with me?'

'No, I didn't. What night was that?'

'It was on Sunday before I left to come home.'

'No, I did not know; she has always been secretive, though.'

'Fucking secretive – sounds liked she has fucked half of the men in Durban, and you are trying to put the finger on me as the father of the unborn child. No way, Hansie, am I taking the blame for this one, son. You better tell your father that, or I will, for I am not jeopardising all the work I have put in to win this contract if I get the blame. What would your father do if he knew you were gay? How would he take that news?'

'Are you blackmailing me, Leif? Would you really tell my father my secret? No one knows but you and Biri. Please, Leif, I beg of you – he would disown me and throw me out; please, Leif.'

I had him by the short and curlies; he was in tears on the phone. I had played my ace and come up with the money.

'OK, Hansie, do not worry; as long as you steer the spotlight off me, tell Biri to do what she has to do to put it right. Or you will tell your father everything about who she has been seeing, and how many men are involved in the full script. Tell her you have spoken to me, and if she put the finger on me I will tell her father, as you have told me everything – this way we are both covered, OK?'

'OK, I will, and thank you, Leif. I will let you know how it goes. If you do not hear from me again on the subject within the next three weeks, it will be sorted, OK?'

I heard nothing more from Hansie, and we won the contract with no problem; everything was sorted. I decided to leave and handed in my notice. Richard was not too pleased, but I told him I wanted to look for work back home; I was sick of travelling and needed a rest. He said to me that if any time I wanted to return, there would always be a job for me – and, on that note, I left.

CHAPTER 14

LEIF

Back in Hull Again – Three Months Later

I was now back in Hull was renting a flat in Hessle, just up the road from Mum and Billy but not too far.

I was drinking in the local pubs, the Marquis of Granby and Admiral Hawke, both next door to each other in the square. I also used the Ferry Boat Inn; this was my favourite pub when I was a youngster, and they always had rock groups on back in the 1960s.

It was good to be back home; the feet had stopped itching, for the time being anyway. I had been transferred from Aberdeen to the Middlesbrough office that covered the southern North Sea. I was to become part of the team running a three-year project just off Hornsea on Yorkshire's east coast.

We landed on the West Sole B platform for our first trip; I was the OCE (offshore construction engineer) for this platform, looking after the black trades. On the other two platforms, A and C, the OCEs were for E&I and mechanical pumps. The project had been set up this way to ensure that, if any problems arose with any discipline, someone was available to be transferred while still offshore as the three platforms, although not identical, were the same gas platform. It was a good job, with primarily local labour, including the supervision; all the guys knew each other, and it was a happy ship.

The only problem I had was with the OIM, or offshore installation manager – Patrick Donaldson; for want of a better description, he was a fucking idiot. I won't go on about him, but he was unreal. He was a legend in his own lifetime. The stories told about him are beyond belief, such as one Christmas day when the general manager of the owners, the oil company, decided it might be a good idea if some senior management paid the guys offshore a visit. When their chopper landed on the platform, Donaldson acted as the HLO (helicopter landing officer). Just as the manager was about to get out, Donaldson told him to stay where he was and took the bag of goodies from him, then told him to fuck off, saying it was bad enough having to work over Christmas and new year without some sanctimonious bastard coming out to rub it in.

I had my moments with him, but he knew where he stood with me. One day I was having a discussion with him about some scaffolding that had been put up in the tank area, by my back-to-back – that was the supervisor who came on when I went off on leave. He had been told it would only be up for a few days.

'Listen, I want this lot down,' he said. 'It has been up too long. I want it down – now.' He started poking me in the chest as he talked down to me.

'Don't do that, Pat; there is no need for that.'

'I am telling you now, I want this lot down.' His finger hit me in the middle of the chest.

'Sorry, it stays where it is. We are still working on it. The pipework we are installing – the deluge system is all screwed fittings, and they are, for want of a better word, shit. Your mob have bought a load of crap foreign fittings and on half of the screwed sockets and elbows, the threads are rubbish. We are having to take our time in putting a thread on each piece of pipe and trying it one at a time. Sorry, but the scaffold stays.'

He was not satisfied with my explanation, and the finger-poking started again.

I asked him to stop doing it on four occasions. Still, he kept on poking me. In the end, I said to him, 'Stop poking me, Pat, or I will break your finger off and shove it right up your fucking arse. And this conversation never happened. Because if you get me sacked, I will come round to your house. I know where you live and I'll give you the biggest hiding you have ever had. Your own fucking mother would not recognise you.'

I must point out we were alone at the time, so there were no witnesses. I had no bother with him after this incident.

Another time, the scaffolders were working over the side in a basket slung off the crane, doing some preparation work to erect a working platform the entire width of the main deck; they only had a couple of hours of work left to complete the task.

It started to rain heavily, and they radioed for the crane driver to bring them up. Donaldson heard the call and told the crane driver to keep them where they were as he wanted that particular work completed that day; he would not let them up.

They eventually were brought back up after an hour or so, absolutely drenched like drowned rats. He did allow them to take a hot shower and change of clothing but told them to be back on deck after lunch.

The onshore representative of my company used to visit the platform once a month to see how things were progressing. He was terrified of Donaldson, and Donaldson knew it.

One particular day when he came on to our platform, he was in the office and asked Donaldson how he was getting on with me.

'Quite well, to be honest,' he replied. 'When I tell him something, he just tells me to fuck off. No one has ever spoken to me on my platform like that in my life, so I admire him for it. He is his own man, and I like that – not like some of the wimps I have had to deal with over the years. He is very good at his job, the crew work well for him, and the job is being run safely and productively; I could not ask for more.'

When the rep came to see me after this and told me what Donaldson had said, he could not believe the relationship I had with him. He was sure he would have asked for me to be replaced, and with him being the OIM, the company would have had to do it.

My future at the company was only short-term, so I handed in my notice and started looking for another job. I would leave when I wanted to, not on Patrick Donaldson's whim.

It was not long afterwards that an agency called me about a position they believed I might be interested in. It was on a new plant construction that was going through some teething problems, and they needed extra staff to bring it online.

CHAPTER 15

LARS

Not Again

I had booked in a hotel in Surfers and had called in a local burger joint on my way back after spending a hectic day in the office.

I had pulled up at the first screen in the drive-in to order my meal, and a girl answered when I pressed the button.

'G'day, how can I help you this evening?'

'Er, I will have a double burger with fries, er... extra onion rings – actually, make it double fries – and a Diet Coke, thanks.'

'Anything else, sir, or will that be all?'

'No, that's it, thank you.'

I drove around to the pickup window. There was a beautiful young woman with headphones and a microphone; I assumed she was the one who took my order. She was not looking at me, just putting the ketchup and tissues in the bag. As she turned, she greeted me with the biggest, most beautiful smile.

'Jesus Christ! Bloody hell, Leif, it's you; when did you get back? I wondered what happened to you. Oh, jeez, it's so good to see you again.'

Not again – not another sheila that my brother had serviced on his journey around Australia? I played innocent, and pretended I had not a clue who she was referring to.

'I'm sorry, do I know you? You must have got the wrong person; I have never seen you before in my life, sorry.'

She looked again at me, and put her head and shoulders through the hatch.

'No, it's you. I will never forget you. Come on, you are taking the piss. It's me, Steph – Stephanie Longbottom. You must remember that name; you even made a joke about my bottom looking OK – on the beach that day. God, you must remember me? We spent the night together in your hotel.' Then it dawned on her. 'Hey, have you been here all this time? You got a bloody Aussie accent now. How come? Have you never been back? You told me you were going back home; did you not go?'

There was now a queue of cars behind me, all with their windows down getting ready to place their orders; a couple of them blew their horns, getting impatient.

'Please, I am sorry – I will repeat it; I do not know you. Fair dinkum, I have never met you before. I must go – sorry… bye.'

I drove my car around the side of the building, and she was standing in the road. Horns were now blowing louder from the growing number of vehicles in the drive-through. She came and stood in front of my car, both hands on the bonnet. God, she was beautiful. I had to come clean with her, or she was going to be in bother with her boss, who was standing in the doorway. I assumed it was her boss – he did not look too happy. I waved for her to get out of the way and started to pull into a parking space.

'What are you doing to me, Leif? Do you think I am stupid? You can't just ignore me. I had got the idea in my head that we had something special, I know it was only one night, but I thought it meant something to you, the way you talked to me as you made love to me.'

'Stephanie, I must tell you something. I have never met you before. I did not have a clue who you were.'

She was getting agitated. 'But –'

'No, hang on a second, let me speak. I am not Leif. He is my twin brother from England. Believe me, we have never met, not me and you – not even me and him, for we were separated at birth. My name is Lars Morrison, and I was brought up by foster parents who adopted me.' I did not tell her the truth – not yet; I let what I had told her sink in.

'Let me take a break; I have one due. Let me speak to the boss, please?'

I was about to speak when the manager of the restaurant came up.

'What the hell is going on, Steph? Do you want this job or not? People are waiting to be served, girl. Now move your arse and get them served, or go; I don't need this hassle.'

'OK, Tommy, just a second – can I take a break now? Please, Tommy... please?'

'I have put Melanie on taking orders. Just get that lot over there served,' he said, pointing at the serving hatch. 'We have a business to run here. Chris is due on in fifteen minutes; you can take your break then, OK?'

I was weak as piss and agreed to talk with her; she deserved an explanation, I suppose.

As she disappeared into the building, I grabbed my burger and fries, which had not entirely gone cold but were not that hot now, and went into the restaurant area, picking a seat at the back out of the way and waiting for Steph to join me.

'Sorry about that, but I'm free now; want another drink, or you OK?'

'No, I'm fine, thank you. How long you got?'

'Half an hour. Now, please tell me all about how come you are not Leif. That sounds stupid, but you know what I mean. I am confused, you are so much alike. Fair dinkum, it's incredible.'

'Well, where do I start? In the beginning, I suppose. As I said, at birth, we were separated, but my adopted mother told me they had actually bought me. I only found out I had a brother a few months ago. It was just the same as you had. You mistook me for Leif because of our likeness. Well, Leif was mistaken for me in the Hunter region. He had been through there and was spotted in Maitland or Kurri Kurri. Someone had seen my photo on the wall in a bank – no, it wasn't a wanted notice for a robbery, my father was the manager, and he had my picture on the wall, as I was playing for St George at the time; someone told my father that they had seen me.'

'You played for the Dragons? Wow, jeez, good on ya, mate.'

'Yes, mostly lower grades but I did make quite a few first-grade appearances. Anyway, it is not about me – well, yes, I suppose it is. As I say, Leif had been seen in the area, and as I had not spoken to my mum and dad for a while, I gave them a ring. When they eventually answered the phone, I could feel there was something wrong; just the tone of their voice seemed odd. It turned out they had not contacted me because they believed I had visited the area without going to see them, and they had the shits.'

'Fuck me dead; I don't believe it. Have you never met him then, or does he even know you exist?'

'Not as far as I know. He doesn't know yet, but we are planning to go back to Hull – that is where my mother, my natural mother, lives – and get married over there.'

'Oh, you are married.' She sounded disappointed

'Yes, well, I might as well be – I have a partner, Maya; we have been together for a long time, and we live in Sydney.'

'What do you do? Got any kids? Oh, sorry for being nosy.'

'No, we have no children, and we run a group of companies in the construction industry. We have done quite well; it has been a lot of hard work, but we have done OK, without getting up myself.'

'That's sick, mate.'

'Anyway, enough about us – what about you? How long ago was it you met Leif, and how did that come about? He certainly left an impression on you, that's for sure?'

'Yes, he did. It was, oh, I don't know, about, what… I am twenty-eight now, must be eleven years, I suppose. I was a bit of a wild child at the time. He was around thirty, I suppose – well, you will know if you are his twin,' she giggled. 'How old are you?'

'Thirty-nine.'

'Well, there you go, it was about 1974, then. I had written Leif a note as I was at work early that morning, but I forgot to leave my phone number. He wouldn't have found me in the phone book, as it was under Mum's name; she had gone back to that after Dad had passed away. You talk about making an impression – yes, as I was saying, I was a bit of a root rat – couldn't get enough; I thought I had bloody invented it. Leif showed me how to do it properly; I'd never done it until that night, and if I am honest, never had it the same since.'

'You not married now, then?'

'Nah, had a couple of boyfriends that lasted a while but never got married. One of them turned out to be a right mongrel – a real dickhead; he stayed two years. The other lasted three, but he finished up a right bogan and started acting really weird. I think he started batting for the other side, mate. Since then I've been on my own – I prefer it that way, doing my own thing. I have my little place, which is no palace but it's good enough for me. I still go down the beach – I love surfing and hanging out with my mates, and I can still live on a burger and a coke, which I get from here as freebies. Old Tommy there thinks the world of me, as long as I give his dick a twitch now and again' she said, smiling. 'That is why I work the back shift here; this place is open until one in the morning, seven days a week. I work five till one, five days a week, and my weekend is Wednesday and Thursday, which suits me down to the ground, mate.'

'What about your mother? Is she still around? She still lives up here?'

'Oh, yes, she met another guy; he seemed a decent sort of a bloke, had a servo down near Burleigh Beach. He was OK at first – that was until he took a fancy to my knickers… not wearing them; he tried to get inside them. I did not dob him into Mum but decided to move out; it cost him a few quid, mind. It had to, or I would have told Mum about him – that's how I got my place.'

I looked at my watch; it was just gone ten, and our half-hour was nearly up. I didn't want it to end. I liked this girl; she was different – odd, in fact – but honest, dead straight, no edges. You got what you saw. But she had to get back to work.

'How long are you up here for? I am off tomorrow; would you like to meet me for a coffee or something? I will be down the beach – the surf club does a great cappuccino. Fancy meeting up, or are you at work?'

I was at work, but hey, I was the boss – I could take an afternoon off. It would be nice to spend some time with someone who was not up themselves. I wished I'd brought my board with me; it'd been a while since I caught a few waves.

'Listen, OK, I will meet up with you. I just wish I had brought my swimmers and board with me; it would have been nice to have spent some time on the surf.'

'No shit! Aw, that's great, mate. Hey, you can borrow a board from the club; I know plenty of guys who would loan you one. What you got at home?'

'Oh, I have always used Hobie boards ever since I was a kid; never owned anything else – can't beat them. I suppose I could go and buy some shorts on my way to meet you at the club.'

'You can buy some at the club; I can get you a decent discount, mate, no worries. I have a McTavish Bluebird – best board ever, mate. Bought it when I was a kid just before they phased them out in '79; mind, it was a lot older than that.'

'Good choice – a few of my mates have the same board, and swear by them.'

'Fuck me dead – I can't believe I am going to spend the day with you, mate. It will be awesome. See ya tomorrow arvo, about one-ish, OK? You know where I mean.'

'What club?'

'Nobby's Beach – can't miss it, mate, just on Albatross Ave. Just follow the signs. I must go – bye!'

She hugged me and kissed me on the cheek as she left; I liked her – liked her a lot.

I was sitting outside the surf club at one o'clock, and she turned up; I wouldn't have guessed it was her. She was in a Ford panel van with a board on the rack, and surf scene painted on both sides of the van. Bloody hell – I'd not seen one as old as this for years.

'G'day, mate – jeez, I am really pleased you turned up; thanks for your time, mate.'

'Did you think I would not come? Would not have missed it for the world, babe.'

Behave yourself, Lars, I told myself; just think about Maya back in Sydney.

'Come in, let's get you sorted with some bathers and board; we will go to the shop first.'

We went into the club's retail store. 'G'day, Ken, this is Lars, an old

110

mate of mine from Sydney. He's up here for a few days and wants a pair of bathers – can you sort him out? What's the best deal you can give him? We don't want any shit, OK. I will be back – just going to organise you a board.'

'She is something else, Lars, ain't she? Like a facking whirlwind, never stops yapping. Great girl all the same. So, how can I help? I reckon about a 34 should fit you; what size do you take?'

'Yes, mate, a 34 should be OK. I remember the day I was a 30, but that's going back a few schooners ago.'

'Here you go – try these. Changing rooms are just over there. These are on special – they're a good make, O'Neil; last season's stock. To be honest, mate, I found them in the stockroom only yesterday, hidden under some boxes. Brand-new, not that they have been used or anything; they would set you back fifty bucks. Go on, see if they fit – and you can have them for twenty. Got to be cash, mind', he added with a wink.

'Yes, they are fine, thanks, Ken. I appreciate your help; I will keep them on.'

'Take the bloody label off, then – give it here.'

I turned around, and Ken came at me with a pair of scissors. 'There you go, blue, you have a good day now, you hear – nice meeting you.'

'And you mate – see ya later.'

Steph was waiting outside with the board. 'Come on, mate, where've you been? I have been waiting for ages. I am ready, are you?'

I was stunned. I could not believe what I was seeing. At twenty-seven, Steph had the body of someone ten years younger. I kid you not – what a figure; talk about toned.

'Er, wow, yes, OK… you look… good.' I had to be careful what I was saying here, but she was dead-set beautiful. I'd never imagined that was hidden under the Rooburger uniform from last night.

'What you looking at? Something wrong, is there?' she said, looking down at her legs and arse.

'No, not at all – just a very nice pleasant surprise. I think Leif was right when he said there was nothing wrong with your Longbottom.'

She just smiled and said, 'Come on; let's catch some waves.'

We had a great afternoon – one of the best times I have had for a very long time. I need to do more of this when I get back to Sydney, I thought. I did not realise how much I had missed being in the water, just sitting there on my board waiting for that wave, the one wave that would test me to the full.

Steph was still out there. I had gone and sat on the beach; my body was aching in places I had forgotten I had. I could see her riding a wave, disappearing in a spray of water time after time, then jumping on her board, and swimming back out to catch the next one. What a bundle of energy.

About half an hour had passed, and she came running up the beach carrying her beloved Bluebird.

'Facking beaut, mate. What a great day! I enjoyed that; the surf was spot on. What d'you reckon mate, you rooted or what?'

'You could say that – I ache all over; I need a bloody massage. I am as stiff as a board.'

'Don't look stiff to me, mate,' she smiled. 'Come on, let's get rid of this sand. Take my board to my van, will you, please? I will take yours back to the store. We can take a shower over there and then get changed. What you reckon? I am bloody starving, mate, could eat the proverbial horse.'

I took her board and fastened it on the van, then went back into the men's side of the changing rooms and had another shower in there. Those on the beachside were OK but always bloody cold water. I needed a hot torrent on my body, which took a bit longer than Steph, as she was waiting for me as I reappeared.

'You always late in everything you do or just taking the piss, mate?'

'No, sorry – needed a hot shower. God, I am aching. Been a long time between drinks, Steph – have not spent so long on a board for a while. I need more of it, though. Thanks so much for a wonderful day.'

I put my arm around her waist and hugged her. Bingo, something clicked – she felt so good pressed against my body. She looked up at me; that smile again.

'No, thank you, babe. I have enjoyed your company. I really mean that.'

Then it happened – our lips touched, ever so gently, not sensual; it just felt right.

'You want to come back to mine, Lars, for a coffee and a sarnie? Won't be a lot – we can grab some bread and salad from the deli on the way. I have wine in, or beer in the fridge – finish off a lovely day, what do you reckon?'

Without a doubt, this was the best offer I had had for a very, very long time.

'Sounds good to me – love to.'

She took my hand in hers, and then we got in our cars, and I followed her back to Mermaid Waters.

*

I looked at my watch; it was seven-thirty. We had slept in – not that we'd had much sleep. Leif had taught her well; she was undoubtedly a great lover.

I was just about to get out of bed, and she rolled over. 'Mmm, morning, darl… sleep OK?'

I just looked at her again; without saying a word, I bent over and kissed those lips.

'Yes, thank you, Steph; that was wonderful, that massage you gave me. Well, what can I say? I've never had anything like it; where did you learn to do that? Was that another Leif special?'

'No – I had a friend, a girl I went to school with, she was Thai. Her mother was a masseuse who came from Bangkok. She showed me how to do it. It is based on muscle stretching; mind, I developed the body bit myself. It was good, wasn't it? Feeling our bodies rubbing together, all oily and that sandalwood aroma… mmm… it always turns me on. Fancy another?'

'I have a better idea. I will give you one, OK?' I wanted to explore that body – I wanted to touch her all over without having sex. I had read a long time ago about giving a girl a sensual massage. I had tried it with Maya, but she wanted a root straight away and I never got to finish it.

'You game, then, Steph? Can I do you ?'

She rolled over on to her belly. Oh my god, what an arse.

I started on her shoulders and her arms, working on her neck and upper back, and down to her lower back, massaging that bum. It felt so good in my hands. Then I worked down her legs – her calves were like two small loaves of bread.

After about twenty minutes, I said, 'OK, Steph – turn over slowly; keep your eyes closed – do not open them.'

I began massaging her breasts; oh my, they were beautiful, just to feel them in my hands. Her nipples soon stood to attention. Then I did her stomach, arms again, and then back to her legs. I spent quite some time on each foot, rubbing under the arch, relaxing them, and then each toe. They were so straight – it seemed like had never worn real shoes, always thongs or sandals. All I could hear was her sighing; she still had her eyes closed. I spent about five minutes on each part of her body.

Now that she was fully relaxed, I could start on her select areas and the surrounding places, slowly stroking the oils into her. Once again, I could hear her moaning with pleasure; she was gone. Gently, I moved on to the finger-stroking technique, which led to a G-spot orgasm. We both finished up with a happy ending.

'Oh my God, where did you learn to do that, Lars? That was fantastic. It's a long time since I felt like that. Must be the Pommie blood in you, although Leif never did that. He was a specialist in other departments. Sorry, I should stop comparing you.'

'No, that's OK; naturally, you will. Considering you have tried both models, are we that alike? Is there any difference in looks, stature, mannerisms?'

'Lars, do you mind if I tell you something and please do not get annoyed? It is not an attack on you personally, but one difference that I have found, and it has only been one night, is he took longer to climax.'

'Climax – you mean, shoot?'

'Yes, we had about four fucks, and he lasted longer, but when he was rooting, he always had his eyes closed and was mumbling to himself. Just before it finished, when Leif was really at his best – the last one of the night – he just opened his eyes wide, took a deep breath, and shouted "Wigan".'

'Wigan? Why Wigan? That's a place in the UK. Great footy team play at Central Park, but why Wigan? He was from Hull.'

'Yes, he said that word as well, Central Park; it was as if he was trying to keep his mind off fucking. Whatever – it worked, mate. But I was not complaining – the sex last night was great; believe me, it was good.'

'But not as good as Leif, is that what you are saying?'

'No, I am not saying that – you are both great lovers but different, if you know what I mean. Both two of the best roots I have ever had. There is one other different thing, and that's –'

She stopped as the phone rang. 'Oh, fuck, just a sec, babe. Hello? Oh, it's you. No, I haven't forgotten. Yes, I will bring it when I can. OK, goodbye – yes, I have to go. I'm busy. Bye. Bloody nuisance mate of mine wants to borrow my electric frypan.' With that, she gave me the biggest kiss and jumped up. 'Must get a shower again.'

I left Steph's place around nine that night. I needed a good night's sleep, as I was back at work the following day and had to ring Maya and let her know how things were going.

'G'day, Maya – hi, babe, how are you?'

'Hi, Lars, why did you not ring me? It's been two days now?'

'I have been up to my bollocks in it, babe.' Well, I was not lying there. 'Been non-stop, but we are getting there.'

'OK, when will you be home? I have something special for you. Will you be home before Monday?'

Monday – I wasn't thinking about staying over the weekend, but it sounded an excellent idea to me.

'Yes, should be. I will try and make sure I am; why Monday?'

'You have forgotten, haven't you?'

What was she talking about? What was so special about Monday… oh fuck, yes – it was her birthday.

'No, of course not, course I know it's your birthday.'

'You lying bastard, you never remember it.'

'OK, you're right. I never know what to buy you anyway – what do you buy a woman who has got everything? I will give you some money or, better still, you get what you want, and I will you for it, OK?'

'I already have. I will show you when you get home, OK? See ya babe, love you.'

It was easy to get to see Steph again. Not having to be home until Monday gave me Thursday until Sunday afternoon; I booked a flight back on the Sunday evening and then called Steph.

'G'day, Steph, how's you, OK? Listen, I don't need to be home until Sunday night. You wanna get together for some fun?'

'My fucking oath, mate – but what about work? Don't you have to be in?'

'Same goes for you. Can you get a couple of days off? Tomorrow's no problem, you are off anyway; what about Friday and Saturday? Can you throw a couple of sickies?'

My dick was ruling my brain again; if one of my employees was to pull this stunt, I would have sacked them – now here I was doing the same.

'Yes, no worries, it will be sweet. I will just tell Tommy I'm crook – the old red flag's flying. He will understand; I have done it before – you start talking about women's problems, he goes the colour of bad shit.' She was giggling away to herself.

'OK, when are you going to call him to let him know you are not going in to work? I was thinking about going up the coast, maybe Mooloolaba.'

'Nah, too far, mate – two to three-hour drive. Why waste six hours sitting in a car?'

'OK, why not Brisbane, then? Nice hotel with a swimming pool – bit of luxury for a change, fancy that?'

'Too right I do, but don't go too fancy, not got clothes for that. I never wear much more than a T-shirt and jeans.'

'OK, I will take a look for somewhere.'

I put the phone down; it suddenly hit me. I needed to look at myself. As it happened, I was standing in front of a mirror. What are you doing? I asked myself. Wake up to yourself. I was feeling guilty; I had cheated on Maya. We were looking at getting married – why throw it all away, and for what? A root? Don't be so bloody stupid.

The following morning, I rang Steph. I needed to knock her back. Deep down, I did not want to, but I had to do the right thing, I know, it was a bit late for that.

'Steph, hi – sorry, change of plan. I need to get home. Something has come up.'

'Oh, OK. Good job I didn't ring Tommy at work, then.'

'Yes, I know, sorry – it's business.'

'Can't you get out of it? I need to see you again; I did enjoy our meet, babe.'

'My partner just rang me – one of our biggest clients has called a meeting, and we both need to be there. Really sorry.'

I was lying to her, but it had to be done. I did not want to get in any deeper. I was better to get out now than break her heart further down the track. And I was kidding myself; she was still in love with Leif, not me. I just happened to look like him. I would always be compared to him. No, get out now, I told myself.

'I am sorry, Lars – you will keep in touch when you are back up here again? You do want to see me again; please say you do.' Her voice was breaking; she was upset.

Then there was a silence. I did not want to hurt her; it had been good, no doubt about it – but no, I had to back away.

'I will contact you next time I am in Surfers. OK, bye, babe, I have to go – someone wants me… bye.'

CHAPTER 16

LEIF

South Africa Again

I could not believe it. I was interviewed by the company and was offered a job in South Africa, near Johannesburg in the Northern Transvaal. I was going back for the second time. I never dreamed I would be heading back there so soon. I was offered a piping superintendent's position, something I had never actually done.

Johannesburg was a ten-hour drive from Durban, the last city I had visited in South Africa. It was so different; you could feel the tension in the air as you walked about the streets or even drove a car around. I had read articles about apartheid, and the first sign of it I witnessed was the segregated railway station in Johannesburg. I could not believe my eyes – there were big signs saying 'Whites Only'. It was more multi-racial than Durban. There were lots more Asians and Indians there, or coloured, as they were classified.

The project I was going on was near a new town about three hours' drive from Joburg. It was like a wild west town, the ones you saw in the old American cowboy movies. Life seemed to be cheap; there was an accident at Satoil when a structure collapsed, burying ten men. I was told they dug the bodies out with a front-end loader, and if a body fell out, so be it. Another accident occurred when a man fell off the site's highest building, the 200-metre chimney. They never even stopped the process of building, as it was a continuous pour and would have cost thousands to stop the plant and machinery.

The project was at that time reputedly the biggest construction site in the world. It was made up of five separate companies running different sections of the job. It took half an hour to drive from one side to the other, it was that big.

The town was built due to the proximity of the coal mines, as it was on top of 6,000 feet of a mountain of coal. It seemed like the scum of the earth had moved there, for the town was the only place I had ever been where the Holiday Inn bar had bullet holes in the ceiling.

We were sitting in a bar in another part of town, having a beer one night, when this pissed-up guy from the site – I wasn't sure of his nationality – was slagging off the South African people. This big Afrikaans guy sitting near us, who also had had one or two too many, was chuntering, 'Not taking this crap from that bastard' – then he put his hand inside his jacket.

I heard the click of a safety clip, and it wasn't his trouser braces he was undoing. 'Come on, we are going,' I said to my mate, grabbing his arm and pulling him up before he could argue.

That night, some guys were walking back to the site in single file; there was a decent gap in between them, and the middle one of the three was killed in a hit and run accident. I don't know it was the same guy from the bar, but wouldn't have been surprised if it was. I never found out; it was never mentioned by anyone.

We did not frequent the bars in Springs; we often travelled to Johannesburg as we worked an eleven-day fortnight, having a long weekend off every two weeks.

Everything was so cheap compared with the UK. We used to stay in Johannesburg, in an area of the city called Hillbrow. It had plenty of bars and pubs, but the only one with live music on a Saturday was the Alexandra Hotel. It was a great afternoon spent with the guys off the site, just relaxing and letting your hair down after the job pressures.

I had been for a haircut one day and I was having a wander around. I heard an argument over the road, and two guys were shouting at each other in Afrikaans. All of a sudden there was a crack like a car backfiring, and one of the guys just dropped to the floor. He was a black guy; no one around seemed to take any notice. The other man just walked away, leaving him lying in the gutter in a pool of blood. I could not believe my eyes. No one stopped to help him; someone passing by had to step over him but they never stopped to help. No wonder they hated the whites in this country.

The next eleven-day cycle over, and I had once again gone to Joburg for the weekend.

I was having a coffee in a cafe in Pretoria Street; it was packed. I was alone reading the local paper when I heard this voice, a woman's voice, asking if she could join me. She was English, with a bit of a Yorkshire twang as well. I looked up, and this rather elegant-looking woman was standing over me with a cup in her hand and book under her arm.

'I'm sorry, but there are no other seats available,' she said. 'May I sit here?'

'No problem,' I said, and she sat down, smiling as people do, if even they don't know one another.

I had to make conversation; I would never miss a chance. I asked her where she was from in England, assuming she was, and she told me, 'Yorkshire.'

The accent was so familiar. 'Are you from Featherstone?' I said.

'How did you guess that?' she laughed. 'My parents live in Featherstone. I am Debra Middleton, by the way – and you are?'

'Leif Askenes. Pleased to meet you, Debra. The thees and thys gave it away.'

'I have been here in South Africa for three years,' said Debra. 'I am a doctor at Charlotte Maxeke Johannesburg Academic Hospital; it is the biggest hospital in the city – we have a staff of well over 4,000 people.'

'Bloody hell – that's a big place. Is it just a hospital for sick people?'

'No, it is also the main teaching hospital for the University of the Witwatersrand. I work at the faculty of health sciences, teaching medical students.'

I had not got a word in; she was clearly very proud of what she was doing.

She was quite a good-looking woman, with her blonde hair up in a ponytail; I didn't know if it was natural or not. I would have said a size ten, maybe twelve, but she looked fit under her tight-fitting low-neck jumper and jeans. She was very confident – perhaps that was the doctor and teacher in her; they always seemed to give off the air of being in charge.

We'd been talking for quite a while when I looked at my watch.

'I am sorry, Leif; am I boring you? I am talking too much, sorry. I don't mean to – it's one of my faults, sorry.'

'No, on the contrary – it is great meeting and talking to someone about other things than pipes and work; believe me, it is a refreshing change.'

'What are you doing in South Africa and particularly Joburg?'

'I am up in the Northern Transvaal at Springs.'

She pulled a face; she'd obviously heard reports about the place.

'It isn't that bad,' I said, with tongue in cheek. 'We only work eleven days, then get away for a long weekend, and I come to Joburg most times.'

I was very taken by this woman – I'd not met someone so intelligent for years, and with the looks to go with it – impressive. She had said she was single; I'd gleaned as much from some of the things she mentioned in the conversation.

'Debra, it's been wonderful to talk to you. Can I ask you if you would like to meet again on my next weekend off? I would love your company again; it is refreshing to meet a girl who can string sentences together.'

'Yes,' she laughed. 'I would love to. Here's my phone number – it's the works number, but it has an answering machine on it.'

'Are you busy this evening? We could maybe have a meal and a drink?'

'No, I am sorry – I have something arranged. I've already agreed to go to some friends' house to a braai, and I can't get out of it. Sorry, I really am.' She looked at her watch. 'I need to get going – I hope we will meet again in two weeks. Don't forget; please ring me.'

As she rose to leave, I took her hand; she leaned forward and gave me a peck on the cheek. She smelled gorgeous; yep, I was hooked again.

I rang Debra on the following Saturday afternoon and then on the next Wednesday to arrange our date. We were to meet in the same cafe on the Friday evening. I had not booked my usual hotel to ensure none of the lads from the site was lurking around. One or two did lack a little in the decorum stakes.

I had booked in at the Carlton Hotel next to the Carlton Centre, which was a bit more expensive, but it was nearer to where she lived, and its restaurant, the Three Ships, was renowned as one of the best in Johannesburg. She was there on time, just as she promised and looked even better than the first time we had met.

I was sitting at a small table by the window; we passed the usual pleasantries, and she kissed my cheek. I ordered another two more coffees and we started to discuss the last two weeks, our history, where we had been and what we'd done in our lives – all deep, meaningful stuff, that sort of thing. She was thirty-eight and single. She had been in a close relationship and almost got married, but her fiancé had passed away tragically at a young age, with pancreatic cancer, five years ago.

'I was devastated when Peter passed away, thinking my world had ended, but, as he always said, "Shit happens, babe." I got over it, and I told myself to live my new life to the utmost. That is when I decided to come out here.'

'What do you think of it? Is it as good as you hoped?'

'It is OK, but one thing I am not that happy about is the social life. It is almost non-existent; you are the only guy I have been out with on an actual date for over eighteen months. I find that I just can't seem to click with any of the people at work – doctors and hospital workers are so wound up in their own little world. A social life is not on their agenda. Some of the younger nurses have great sex lives. Then, realising what she had said, she blushed slightly. I was a bit taken aback by the comment, but it sounded good to me. She was quiet for a few minutes, then said, 'I hope that did not put you off me. I sounded a bit like I was jealous of them. Well maybe I am, I suppose,' she added, laughing.

After a couple of drinks in a nearby bar, she opened up a bit, telling me how she had had a great sex life with her fiancé and missed him terribly. We talked and talked. I suggested we go for a meal in the Three Ships to cheer ourselves up a little, as it was so sad listening to her tales of frustration.

After the meal and a couple of bottles of wine, I was starting to take a different view of Debra; I suppose it was the drink. Was it time to go in for the kill, so to speak? We left our table and adjourned to the bar, taking a booth out of all the other revellers' general view.

We sat next to each other, close enough for me to feel the heat from her leg. I moved my leg to put a little pressure on her thigh; she did not pull away, but I believe she pushed back against me as she smiled. I took her hand in mine and looked at her eyes; she was ready for the taking. The mixture of the fillet steak and wine had relaxed her to the point of no return.

'Can I ask you a personal question, Debra?' Now, I had used this line a few times before in my boudoir techniques, and it had worked quite well.

She nodded. 'What is it?'

I took her hand in both of mine. 'Can I make love to you?'

There's always a moment where a question like that risks getting you a slap on the face, but I believed Debra had missed the lovemaking part of her last relationship. She squeezed my hand and nodded again.

'Would you like to stay the night with me?'

'I would love to, but I have no change of underwear.'

'It won't matter; we can go into the mall tomorrow and buy some more. I know there are bathrobes in the room if needed, plus a king-size bed.'

'That sounds wonderful, Leif; it has been so long since I had a man hold me close and make love to me.'

We sat there looking at each other, holding hands; she could see I was aroused. She looked down, smiled and licked her lips – always a good sign.

We finished the bottle, and I suggested another, but to be sent up to the room this time – champagne. I ordered a couple of Irish coffees too. We finished our drinks, signed the cheque, and took the lift to the eighth floor. Once inside and alone, we kissed for the first time. Debra felt so good in my arms. It was a long, slow kiss – not too much pressure from either of us, and our tongues just touched at one point. God, she tasted so good. There was that nervous moment when you both either go quiet and just have that pause before seduction begins, not knowing who will take the lead, or you both try to undress each other in record time. We took the first option – or Debra did. She suggested that she powder her nose; I opened the champagne, poured two glasses, and awaited her return.

She had undressed to only her bra and panties. God, she looked good. She still had her heels on, which made her legs look even better – long, slender, yet muscular. I wondered whether she worked out or played tennis. She walked towards me, with that slow, sensual walk that cat-walk models do – arms by her side, head held high, looking so proud; one foot directly in front of the other.

I was still fully dressed in a polo shirt and trousers. I kicked off my shoes as Debra stood close, just enjoying the moment. I took her glass from her and put it on the table. We were standing in front of a full-length mirror. I had gone behind her, kissing her long, slender neck, cupping her breast in my hands. She threw her head back and sighed. It was like watching an erotic film. I undid her bra; it fell to the floor. She turned to face me and put her arms around my neck; a long, sensual kiss followed before she removed her arms from my shoulders to loosen the belt on my strides. She then lifted my shirt above my head, throwing it on the chair; we were joined at the lips, my hands were holding the cheeks of her firm bottom.

I was already at Bradford; my penis was thinking more Wigan, but it could even have been Workington. We more or less fell on the bed, with our mouths still stuck together; she slipped my briefs down, then pushed me backwards as I sat on the end of the bed, and dropped on to her knees. Oh my God – I wasn't expecting this; she was taking control. She was making love to me, not me to her, but who was I to complain.

I woke up about 6.30am and Debra was still asleep next to me in the foetal position. I watched her body rise and fall as she breathed, her smooth skin glistening with tiny beads of sweat from our lovemaking last night. God knows what time we had our final copulation. I was so good I had been to St Helen's twice and Wigan once before I fell asleep. Too much wine and champagne had taken its toll in the end.

I was getting in the mood again but needed to powder my nose before she woke. I returned from the bathroom as she opened her eyes. She rolled over on her back, smiled and spread her arms and legs into the starfish position.

'Now? You want me now?' I asked. I touched her foot, stroking her toes gently. I saw her breathe in deeply – she liked her feet being touched. I bent over and kissed the arch of her foot, then, working my way up to her toes, I kissed each one in turn. I heard her moan. I looked up at her, and her eyes were closed; she loved it. I started running my tongue around her toes, kissing, licking each one in turn while holding her foot in both hands; she reached Wigan within seconds. Her body trembled as she arched her back, and a massive orgasm followed. 'Oh, fuck!' she shouted. 'Mmmmm, oh yessssss.' She then turned a switch off in her head, got quickly off the bed, and said, 'I need a piss bad!' and ran to the bathroom.

Within minutes she was back, and grabbed my hand. 'Right, where were we, babe?' We stayed in the room all day, sending for breakfast, then lunch. What a session – she certainly made up for not having sex for a while. We were lying on the bed watching TV after our last engagement, and I suggested we go out for a meal.

'Do we have to?' she frowned.

'I am hungry,' I told her.

'Eat this; you don't need food,' she said, pointing downwards.

'Later – I will have that for afters, if that's OK? Come on; I need something more substantial.'

I got up and went for a shower. My hair was full of shampoo, and I felt this body touch mine – she had joined me. Her hands took hold of my lower regions and she started to massage me – was there no satisfying this woman? I went under the water to clear the soap out of my eyes.

'Please, babe, later – not now, please.' Mind, I was erect again, and she was stroking me now. Then she squatted down. With the water cascading down my body and on to her back, Workington arrived within seconds – it must have been an express, the last train.

We left the hotel looking for a restaurant. I fancied Italian; this had become my favourite food ever since my time in Perth – was I getting old? We found a small side street with a choice of nationalities, but Italian it was. We both had panzanella, a Tuscan bread salad, and then had my favourite Florentine steak, and Debra had lasagne – all washed down with white wine for the starter and a bottle of the house red for the main meal.

I was full as a boot as we walked back to the hotel hand in hand. We stopped next to an alley, and Debra pushed me down it.

'I want it here and now,' she said. This woman was crazy – not in public, not here on the street, surely?

'No chance – not here, no way. Just wait till we get back, for God's sake; are you mad?'

I pulled her out of the alley and started walking briskly back to the hotel. She was sulking; what had I let myself into? She was sex-mad; more than anyone I had ever known.

She never spoke until we got back to the room, when she set about me, not sexually – but punching me.

'You bastard, you want it all your way; when I want to fuck, I want to fuck, no matter where or when. If you wish to carry on seeing me, you do it my way – understand?'

With that, a mug flew past my head. Good job it was a hotel, and most of the stuff was screwed down.

I grabbed her hands as she was flailing into me. 'For fuck's sake, calm down; what's gotten into you?'

Then she bit me. Fuck this, I thought. I slapped her to break her out of her frenzy, but her eyes were glazed; she had gone. She collapsed on the bed. 'I fucking hate you!' she screamed, and began crying; anyone in the next room must have thought I was murdering her.

After a while, she calmed down. I sat next to her on the bed; she was still sobbing.

'I'm not staying another minute with you. I'm going – fuck you.'

She started gathering her stuff together, which wasn't much. Her soiled knickers were about all she had to put in her bag; we had used the complimentary toothbrushes and stuff that was in the room, so that was it.

I tried to talk to her. 'Come on, let's not end it like this; what's gotten into you? We were getting along great.'

'No, you have had your chance. I told you, when I want sex, I want it there – no foreplay, just raw cock. Goodbye.'

She left, slamming the door behind her.

I just stood there. I could not believe what had just happened. She'd gone from one of the most sensitive, sensual women I had ever met to a raving lunatic in twenty-four hours. That was the last thing I ever heard or saw her – one to put down to experience. God help anyone who got together with her.

*

I had been thinking about going home as I had been on the job for four months and had enough. I was ready for off. I called home, and Billy answered the phone.

'Hi, Billy, will you do me a big favour?'

'Oh, hi, Leif, yes – what's up? Don't you want to speak to your mother?'

'Yes, OK, go on.'

'Well, you can't; she is out,' he said, and he started laughing. 'Got you, didn't I?'

'Bastard, stop fucking about. Will you do me a favour?'

'OK, what is it?'

'Call the works office here tomorrow.'

'What, in South Africa? It will cost a fortune – your Mum won't like that.'

'Fuck the money, do it; there is a pack in the sideboard I gave Mum. It has the emergency number on it. Just tell them that she is gravely ill, on death's doorstep, with not much longer to live. Really lay it on – they will fly me home first-class, no expense spared. Fuck 'em – I have had enough. Will you do that? Do not let me down now, Billy, OK?'

'OK, no worries, I won't let you down, but I will not say a word to your mother; you know how she worries – she will say it is a bad omen telling lies about someone being ill. You know how superstitious she is. Just leave it with me, OK?'

'Thanks, Billy, you are a star.'

*

I was out on site and got a message to go into the office. I looked at my watch, thinking they should have got the news by now.

I got a call on my radio at 11.55am. 'Leif, come back – Leif! Leif, come back.'

'Hello, Leif here.'

'Hi, Leif, this is control – can you come round to the office, please.'

I punched the air; Billy had done the right thing.

The company flew me home on the next available flight, all first-class; I waited at home until the end of the month, and they had kept ringing me asking when I was going back, but I intended to resign my post when the money was in the bank on the first of the month, for if you did not finish the contract the company was entitled to take the airfare out or your salary. And fuck that for a game of soldiers.

*

It was now May 1985, and I decided to take a bit of a holiday to Portugal for a couple of months. I rented an apartment in Praia da Rocha on the Algarve; I'd never been there so, I thought, why not? Give it a go.

I finished up staying four months before I decided I had better get back to work. Billy and Mum had been over for a month; she was now fifty-four and never been on a holiday abroad. It was my treat to them. Billy was now finished on the fish docks and picked up the odd job as a pipefitter's mate with a local company. I got him a start through a lad I knew, and he loved it, working a regular job outdoors. However, he did not like working 8am until 4.30pm every day and quite a few weekends, but it was a job.

On my return I decided that I needed to settle down and get myself a house or apartment. The only problem was I loved travelling and seeing other parts of the world, and other women, if available; if God made anything better than sex, he kept it for himself, that was a certainty.

Being with the same woman did nothing for me. My marriage would not last. It would not be fair to marry someone and then play away and hurt her.

I stayed with Mum and Billy for a week or so and could not stand it; I had to get a flat or something – it was doing my head in, Mum fussing over me. I loved her to bits, but she could be overpowering at times.

I found a flat in Hessle – 2a, The Birches, South Boulevard, not far from Mum's house but far enough for my independence. The flat was on a short rental system, which was a bit more expensive, but there was no deposit and I only needed a week's notice to get out of the lease, which suited me down to the ground.

I met one or two local girls over the weeks I was in Hull; nothing regular, but good fun all the same. One married girl whose hubby worked away on the oil platforms was incredibly tasty in more ways than one. Him being away for two weeks at a time worked out well – she was just greedy. She couldn't have children; I felt sorry for her, as she was a really nice girl. To meet her you would have thought that the proverbial butter would not melt, but in private… wow.

Another girl I met was a physical education teacher at a local girls' high school. She knew every position in the book and some that even I had not tried. She was a former gymnast, with the most flexible body I had ever seen – or been inside. She was so lithe, yet muscular, and along with her job she still trained and went to the gym. She had her own gym at home, too, in a spare bedroom. She used to love working out on the equipment, working herself into a lather while I lay on the floor watching her. Then she would strip off her leotard and come and fuck me, and we would shower together afterwards – oh, sweet memories. I didn't often get past Castleford; I was so worked up. But I had plenty of train journeys with her over the months.

CHAPTER 17

LEIF

Across the River – Four Months Later

I had been on holiday for four months and then found a local job, right out of the blue, across the river in Immingham.

The annual shutdown was always in August. The position was for piping engineer, for a contractor working at Conoco Phillips Humber Refinery. I was to be covering the night shift. I had started two months before the actual shutdown and begun to create the work packs from the estimated hours produced by our planners and estimator along with Conoco engineering staff.

We had compared our estimate and plan with theirs; it was found to be nearly the same. I believe this is why we won the contract; there was maybe a bit of insider trading as the company I had joined was one of the listed contractors on site and had been for quite a long while – ten years, I believe. It seemed to me that the Conoco staff wanted as much relaxed time as they could get; who and what you knew served itself well in that situation. If the client could trust his contractors and knew they would not rip them off, as quite a few did in those days, hitting them with extras the day they walked on site was one of the favourite money earners. Go in cheap, then tickle them under the chin while you are fucking them, was one way of describing it. I know of one company who employed four quantity surveyors from day one to follow every stoppage or waiting time, like vultures ready to pounce.

The plan and work packs had to be spot on, with all the materials being purchased by the client. It was then issued from the client's stores as and when required according to the programme, otherwise the contractor could hit them for standing men down, for you could not just find more work for a squad of riggers, pipefitters and welders, or a crane standing waiting, just like that, as all other jobs would be already covered.

When I think back, some of the tricks the contractors pulled were nothing more than extortion. I sometimes blamed the client, for they agreed to manning levels suggested by the contractor to cover all eventualities, most of the time way over the top. Take scaffolders, for instance – when a shutdown is on, the last thing you need is men standing around because they are waiting for a scaffolding modification, something as simple as a tube needing moving. Under safety regulations, no one is allowed to undo a scaffolding clip to move a tube in case of the scaffold collapsing or the possibility of a board coming loose. There were always too many scaffs on the job – another way of plundering the client.

All plant and equipment had to be on site, the correct crane age had to be available, and lifting zones checked for lifting over any live plant. However, this was not that critical, as the plant was shut down. Any locations the cranes were to be placed had to be checked to ensure there was no underground pipework or ducting. Once the shutdown commenced, it was flat-out, twenty-four hours a day for twelve weeks, and when the programme showed that the twelve weeks were complete, if the plant did not start when they hit the button, all hell would let loose, for you were talking millions of pounds a day that would be lost.

Under the permit to work system, run by the Conoco health and safety department, every man had to be inducted to the site safety rules, was issued with a site booklet, and was expected to adhere to the standards, or it was instant dismissal.

My role was more of a construction manager than a piping engineer; it was my responsibility to ensure the smooth running of all mechanical work; the E&I was by another specialist contractor. We had to coordinate with them for any scaffolding requirements. I must admit it was bloody hard work. After twelve weeks, Conoco would push the button, and bingo – the plant started up. Certain areas such as the boiler house had to be completed before any other to provide steam.

Shutdowns are driven to a stringent plan; on the one I had, the initials 'MHH' were written next to the date that the plant was to be brought on stream. When I started in the oil and gas industry in the UK, it was overrun with US nationals coming through, as they had the most experience in this industry. They used abbreviations all the time, such as LNG (liquefied natural gas) or OIM (offshore installation manager), that sort of thing. So I asked the planner, Geoff, what MHH stood for. Being the joker he was, it meant 'Magic Happens Here'.

I was invited to a start-up party by Conoco at a local hotel in Grimsby, where everything was on the company – as much food and refreshment as you could consume. We were also booked in the hotel for the night, all on Conoco. I often wondered why the guys on the job, who did the manual work, never got invited to these sorts of parties – but how silly of me; of course, it was them and us, and always would be: the rank and file against the management. It was a class thing; there were times when I hated it, coming from a working-class environment. When they get a bit of power and a few quid in the bank, why do human beings want to treat the lower earners like shit?

Anyway, at the party there were one or two tasty young ladies who worked for the contractors, but I was so pissed I did not bother. That was not like me – I must have been getting old, and at thirty-eight I suppose I was. Would I ever settle down with pipe and slippers? I doubted it, although I was looking for a regular partner – someone I could live with, as I was fed up with going home to an empty flat, cooking my own meals, although I was a good cook, even if I say it myself. It was either that or living on fish and chips or going to the local Chinese.

I received my £1,200 bonus, which was not a lot, but not bad as I was already on a reasonable rate in those days of £350 a day. The contract finished a month later, after we had tidied up all the relevant documentation, and there was nothing for me in the pipeline (excuse the pun), so I was let go.

It was now getting towards Christmas, and I fancied spending it at home in my own flat – a few parties, maybe I'd get myself a steady girl-friend after the festivities; it was no good tying yourself to one girl over Christmas as they were open season that time of year.

I did the usual boring things on Christmas day with Mum and Billy – a pint in Tavern, the nearest pub to Mum's house; walked back, had dinner, watched the Queen's speech, then had a few more beers and fell asleep; it was a toss-up who started snoring first, Billy or me. Why did we do it? Spend a fortune that we couldn't afford, all for the sake of two hours?

'Wake up, you two; what do you want for tea? There is cold turkey or beef – do you want sandwiches or on a plate?'

'What? We have only just had dinner, Mum. I don't want anything, thanks.'

'Me neither, Christine. I'm shagged, think I will go have a nap,' said Billy after being woken from his slumber.

'You've only just had your dinner? It's nearly seven o'clock – now, come on, what do you want? Or you can get it yourself later, but you won't sleep if you go to bed on a full stomach.'

'Oh, OK, I will have a bit of both,' said Billy, 'with pickled onions and that red cabbage, please.'

'Fucking pickled red cabbage; why do we only ever eat that at Christmas? Go on, then, I will have the same, thanks Mum; put the kettle on while you are there, will you, please? I'm gagging for a cuppa.'

I didn't do much between Christmas and the following week; I went to a couple of piss-ups in King Edward, then on New Year's Eve I went to a party in Hessle. I had been in the Ferry Boat Inn all night and I had met a girl who was thirty-two and worked for a solicitor in the old town of Hull. She was OK. Her father was a bank manager who lived in a big house in Hessle, but she was a bit soppy and wanted to settle down. You could hear fucking church bells when she opened her legs.

I saw her for a month or so, then met this other stunner in King Edward's upstairs bar. It was always full of fanny, all ages. I was now thirty-nine and I couldn't drink and fuck as I used to; I was feeling my age, but I intended to beat it. I stood at the bar talking to two guys I had known since I was at school. We were chatting away, and these two girls walked in and were trying to get served. I used my influence and called Dennis, the barman, over.

'Hi, Leif, same again?'

'Yes, please, mate.' I turned to the girls. 'What's yours, while I'm at it?'

'Oh, er, two lagers and limes, please.' One of the girls had some money in her hand.

'No,' I said. 'Have these on me – no worries; if I can't buy two beautiful young ladies a drink, there is something wrong.'

I was then at it again in full flow; the chat-up lines were coming thick and fast. One of the two girls was not interested, but I had the smaller one eating out of my hand. She stayed with me, while the other one went off to talk to some other guy.

'I am Leif, and you are?'

'Penny.' She gave a slight smile.

'Hi, Penny, so pleased to meet you.'

'Do you come in here all the time, Leif? Oh, I do so love that name.'

'Before you ask – Norway. And, yes, I do, when I am at home. I work away quite a bit. I am an engineer in the oil and gas industry.' Always impressed them, that line.

'Wow, how long have you been doing that for, then?'

'Most of my life, since I came out of my apprenticeship.' I never told them the year as it gave away my age – I didn't want to put the younger ones off. 'Where do you work, Penny? What do you do?'

'Oh, not a lot, not as exciting as you; I work at HRI. I am a nurse, been there ten years now. Don't suppose I will ever leave.'

'Great job, Penny – do you like it? Do you specialise in anything in particular?'

'Yes, I am in the theatre. I work with the surgeons, which is a bit more interesting than being in a ward all the time. I assist in doing operations, mostly on cancer patients, and it is fascinating.'

We went and found a seat and finished up being together the rest of the night; I'd totally lost track of time. This girl had me mesmerised with her knowledge of just about everything. The barman rang the bell for last orders. 'Another one for the road, Penny?'

'No, thanks, Leif. I need to be going. I have to catch the last bus.'

'That's OK. I will take you home – if you want me to, that is? I have a car.'

She did not say anything at first, thinking about my offer. Then she smiled and said, 'OK, thank you, that would be nice.'

We finished our drinks and went to get my car. I opened the door for her, as any gentleman would. 'Thank you,' she said, ever so polite. I had never met any girl like Penny before; it must have been the nursing job, having to be with people who were poorly and possibly suffering from terminal illnesses. She told me she had a flat on Beverley Road just up from the hospital.

We arrived, and once again, there was that agonising moment where you do not know what to do for the best.

'Would you like to come in for a coffee, Leif?'

Now, did she really mean 'come in and make love to me', or was it just for coffee? There had been no sign from this girl of her intentions; I'd never dreamt she would be a willing party to any sexual matters, 'Yes, love a coffee, thank you.'

'Take your jacket off, make yourself comfortable – I will just put the kettle on.' She disappeared into the kitchen. I was having a nosy around; it was a nice place, neat and tidy, obviously a single person living there.

'Beautiful place,' I called to her. 'You live alone, Penny?' I looked through her record collection; she liked Elvis, the Beatles, and some older artists – including one of my favourites, Tony Bennett; now, he was a crooner. 'Can I put a record on, Penny?'

'Yes, you choose one; I won't be a second.'

I put *Tony Bennett at Carnegie Hall* on; I had the same album. I was singing along with one of the tracks when Penny came into the room. I took the drinks from her and put them on the table. I took her in my arms, and we began to dance; it was just the right tempo and mood. Our bodies were touching for the first time, and there was a feeling of this being just right.

The song finished, and we standing there holding that moment. I bent down and kissed her. I was not sure she wanted it, but it just seemed the right thing to do. 'Mmm, nice… it feels just right, Penny.'

'Yes, me too.' She rested her head on my chest. There were four more tracks to go, and we continued to dance. Yes, this was going to be another marvellous ending to a beautiful evening.

*

It was seven o'clock when Penny's alarm went off. I looked over at her; she was still sound asleep, cuddling the pillow; her naked back and beautiful arse were laid bare in front of me – so smooth, so slim, but with curves in just the right places. I moved across the bed and kissed her shoulder, snuggling up to her. She whimpered as my penis rubbed against her cheeks. 'Penny, you awake, babe?' I cupped her small breast in my right hand, she pushed her arse against me; she was awake, OK.

'Mmm, that feels nice, Leif, what time is it?'

I turned back to look at the clock. 'Er, 7.25am; lots of time.' I pulled her closer; my penis slipped between the cheeks of her arse.

'What? 7.25am? Oh, fuck – I will be late. I am at work for nine, Jesus! Sorry, babe – must dash.'

With that she was up, and as she ran to the bathroom she shouted, 'Leif, put the kettle on, please, and do me some toast on the cooker – slices of bread are in the tin on the bottom shelf of the pantry. Two rounds will be enough for me; jam's in the pantry as well. I will be two ticks, OK? Thanks. A quick shower and I will be with you.'

'OK, will do.' I was trying to get dressed as fast as I could as well as trying to get the grill to light on the cooker. Bastard things never worked when you wanted them to.

Penny came out of the shower; she looked so sexy wet through, but there was no chance.

'So sorry, Leif – I need to dash to get the bus, or there will be hell to pay. We are in the theatre at 10am. It totally went out of my mind. I was enjoying myself so much last night; it was wonderful.'

Then I remembered I had my car; I could run her to work. 'Penny, slow down. I will drop you off; we have no need to rush. Now, sit

137

down, have your breakfast, drink your tea –no panic.'

'Will you? Oh, that will be great; yes, I forgot you had a car. Thank god for that.'

I dropped her off at 9am on the dot; she kissed me and said, 'Ring me, please,' as she was getting out of the car, and then ran off.

I set off for home, and then realised I did not have her number or her address, or even her second name. I would have to go round again tonight, but what time? When did she finish work? I knew which street it was, so I went round after tea, found her flat and rang the bell. No answer. Then she walked up behind me.

'Hi, Leif, what you doing here? I did not know we'd arranged to meet again tonight?'

'We didn't. I just thought I would come round as I loved our evening, and –'

'You thought you would come back for another fuck. Think I am some sort of whore, do you?'

'Hey, hang on a minute, Penny. It was you who invited me in for coffee; yes, I wanted to get you in bed, but it was you who made the first move, not me. You did not knock me back when we made the initial move. Forgive me if I am wrong; have I got the wrong end of the stick here? Can we go into the flat? I do not want to discuss the situation out here.'

'There is no situation; you seem to have got it all wrong, Leif. I am happily engaged to Michael. He is away at the moment, and he would not be happy to think I had been unfaithful to him. I think you should go before I call the police.'

That was enough for me; it was time I went before I said something I shouldn't.

'I'm sorry, Penny, I will say goodbye, and good luck with Michael. He will need it.'

Thank fuck for that; she was a headbanger. I was just a one-night stand. It had happened to me before, and I did not like it. That would never happen again; lesson learned.

CHAPTER 18

LARS

Nice Surprise

'Lars, do you want rice with this curry, or fries? Rice is easier – I can throw that in the microwave?'

'Yes, rice is fine, no worries – rice will do.'

Six months had passed since my last trip to Surfers. I had not been in touch with Steph; it had been very close – too close – and I decided it was better to forget her altogether.

Maya had surprised me when I told her to buy herself something she wanted. I was sitting on my new boat – well, our new boat. Maya had purchased a twenty-five foot, twin-onboard, four-berth motor-cruiser. I'd always promised myself one when I could afford it. She had only gone and bought it as a joint present for her birthday – how good was that? She did this while I was cheating on her. I was so glad I had done the right thing in coming home when I did. It was now 1986, and there had been a few changes in our lives. No more womanising, no more close calls – I had seen the light, stopped travelling and settled down.

'Lars, I am just nipping out to the mall. Do you need anything bringing back? Are you OK for beers, or do you want some more Crown Lager? No? OK, won't be too long, bye.'

We'd also moved house, for the third time, and we were now living in North Harbour, not far from Welling's Reserve in Balgowlah. We had splashed out on a block of land that cost us just short of a million bucks. We designed our new home, a unique split-level Spanish-style house complete with a four-car garage and an in-ground swimming pool. I must admit, when it was finished it was worth all the heartache and hassle. I told Maya we were never moving again.

'Hi, babe – got two cartons; they were on special. Twenty-five dollars a case or two for forty. Can you go get them out of the car? I could not carry everything. Are we still going out on the boat today? Aren't the Jacksons coming round for a trip on the water? If we are, I will leave the beers in the car and take them with us.'

'Yes, I am expecting a call from them.'

'In that case, go put them in the fridge in the garage; they will need to be kept cold – you know you don't like warm beer. You might be a Pommie, but that is one thing you don't like.'

As I got up, the phone rang. 'Hello? Hi, Greg, yes, that's no problem. See you down at the jetty around eleven. No, we have plenty of grog. Yes, bring some of that piss your wife likes – yes, that's the one. I refuse to buy it. OK, mate, see ya later, cheers, No, we have everything… if you got some more snags, bring them, OK?'

'Maya, did you hear that? Greg and Rhonda are coming to meet us at the jetty.'

'We had better get a move on, then; it's nine now. We need to get out to the boat and back to the jetty if we are to be there for eleven.'

'They are always late. Don't panic. Are we sleeping onboard tonight or coming home? I think we should just crash out when we are pissed, no need to worry about driving; it is not as if it's cramped, there's loads of room.'

'See what they want to do – and keep your bloody hands off Rhonda's tits. You know what you are like when you have had a drink.'

'OK, but they are a wonderful set; best thirty grand Greg ever spent, that boob job he bought for her birthday – a lot cheaper than the bloody boat cost me.'

'Yes, but she can't lie on her tits and sunbathe in the nuddy, although I bet you would like her to fucking try, wouldn't you?'

We got down to the jetty just before Greg and Rhonda arrived.

'G'day, Lars, how are ya, OK?' said Rhonda. 'Great morning for a day on the piss. The ship is looking OK, mate.'

'It is a boat, Rhonda, not a bloody ship,' said Maya, shaking her head. 'What's the difference? I can never tell, Maya. Still, it looks nice; what make is it?'

Maya shook her head again; she had already told her. 'A 1982 Johnson – they call them an enclosed fly-bridge, I don't know why; we looked at a new one, but we could not afford it. This is just under four years old. Anyway, it suits us – it has two double beds in it, that's all that matters.'

'OK, girls, get that stuff on board, and we can get off. I'm gagging for a beer; what about you, Greg?'

'Good thinking, mate – long while between drinks, and it's five o'clock somewhere.'

We set off out into the channel heading for Hornby Lighthouse and then out to sea. We weren't planning to go far offshore, just south for a bit and dropping anchor just off Bondi Beach.

'This the life, mate,' said Greg. 'Wonder what the poor people are doing. Beautiful day, sun shining, plenty of grog in the Esky. Two decent-looking sheilas; pity they are our wives – whoops… well, one is – and nothing to do but enjoy ourselves. Cheers, mate.'

'Lars, did you look at the forecast before we left? It's getting a bit dark – just look over there; it's pissing down towards the eastern suburbs.'

'Bloody hell, Maya, stop worrying. It said sunshine with possible squalls, winds southerly moderate, so don't worry. We are OK where we are. If it blows up any more, we can head back into Watson's bay and anchor there; it will be fine. Another beer, Greg?'

'Might as well.'

'Take it easy, you two – don't want you pissed if we have to move.'

'No dramas, Maya; it's not as if we are legless,' said Greg. 'We've only had five – you can't get done for being pissed in charge of a flaming boat.'

We had decided to up anchor as the wind was starting to increase; it had changed direction. It was now an easterly blowing us straight in towards Bondi; we didn't want to rely on the sea anchor, and had too much draft to drop a standard anchor. We needed to get around to the leeward side of Watson's Bay.

'You OK there, Rhonda? Don't want any technicolour yawns on here, thank you.'

'Yes, I will be fine – just had too much of the old cab sav; mind if I go below and lie down on the bed? I don't feel seasick when I am lying flat.'

'No worries, mate, off you go. Maya, take Rhonda below. Give her a couple of bags just in case, but once we get around Hornby, you will be fine; won't be too long.'

Maya took her below, and returned ten minutes later. Greg had nodded off.

'How is she, OK?'

Maya nodded and whispered, 'Yes, but she said the only thing that makes her feel sick is that fat bastard up here.'

'Wow – that's a bit strong.'

'Yes, it surprised me as well. She fucking hates him; she wishes she'd never had her tits done. It was his fucking idea, give him something to skite about, to tell all his mates how he spent thirty fucking grand on a pair of booboos – fucking bastard.'

We managed to get back into Watson's Bay and dropped anchor opposite Robertson's Park.

'There you go – wanna beer, mate, while I put the barbie on? I need a bloody feed now; all that drama has made me bloody hungry. How's Rhonda now? No more chunders?'

'She sure sounded crook coming round the heads there; mind, it was a bit choppy, even my old guts gave a bit of a wobble. Don't know who the fuck Hughie is, but she kept calling his bloody name.'

'You are a rotten bastard, Greg. I don't know why the fuck she puts up with you.'

'Cos I bought her new tits and kept her in the finest clothes and bloody high standard of living, that's why, mate.'

Maya looked up at me from the hatch and gave me the 'tosser' sign, mouthing 'fucking wanker'. I nodded in agreement.

Greg was getting on his high horse again; he always did when he had a few beers. Still, he was OK; he wasn't a bad bloke. I was waiting for a mouthful from Maya, for she was not that keen on him anyway; she only put up with him because he was a good customer. As a housing developer, he put a hell of a lot of work our way.

It had calmed down a bit, and we managed to get a decent night's sleep. I was first up and got the breakfast on – steak and eggs; you couldn't beat it after a night on the piss. Greg was up before the women; he looked like shit.

'G'day, mate,' I said. 'Gee, you look fucking awful, blue – feel OK?'

'Yes, have been better, but will be OK when I get some of that down me; I'm bloody starving, mate.'

With that, the two girls came up. 'You two OK with steak and eggs, or want something lighter?'

'No thanks, babe, I will just have cereal and some fruit; thanks, here – I will get it. What about you, Rhonda?'

'Just coffee for a start, please. The old guts feel like hell. Too much bloody wine – I keep telling myself never again but no, like a bloody galah, I do it every time. Maybe some cereal and toast when the coffee has settled me down.'

We had breakfast and then set off back home. It didn't take long when we dropped the anchor. I took Greg and Rhonda across first; we had a load of stuff to bring back. They said their goodbyes to Maya. I could see the joy in her eyes as we pulled away; she hated Greg with a vengeance. I went back to pick Maya up while Greg went to get his car, arriving back at the jetty ten minutes or so later.

'Thanks for a great weekend; you must come out to Shoal Haven some time; it's been wonderful.'

'No worries, it has been good seeing you must do it again soon, safe drive home now. Bye.' As their car drove away, Maya came up to me and said. 'Thank fuck for that; why do we put up with him; he is a fucking Galah?'

'Why, because he gives us thousands of dollars of business that's why as long he keeps doing that we will put up, with him, sounds a bit two-faced, but it doesn't bother me, Maya, while he keeps crossing our palms with silver we will continue accepting it. Come on, I need a beer and a nice hot shower. Wanna join me, babe?'

'Is that all you think of? It won't last long if we do, you know what you are like, what's the record again, ten minutes?

She was right. I wish I could be like Leif wonder how he managed it. I could still hear Steph's words; when she said he was always mumbling something, she even got the idea he was thinking of other girls when he was rooting, Donna, Cass, Kayla, Leigh. Steph swore blind that she heard those names mentioned, but why Wigan just as he climaxed could not understand it.

CHAPTER 19

LARS

Embarrassing

I went to a sex therapist. Maya had talked me into it. She came with me; it was kind of uncomfortable talking about our sex lives in front of a stranger, and a woman at that, but it went OK.

We sat in the waiting room; all I was thinking was, what was this going to cost – must have been the Pommie in me coming out. The number of times I had heard the comment 'How fucking much?' when in negotiations a price or cost was given to a client, who just happened to be a Pom. Especially those from Yorkshire; it sounded too funny with the dialect. That was another thing I could not get my head around – how many different ways there were to say something, and it was all supposed to be English. It was beyond me.

We had not been waiting long, and the lady we were booked in to see joined us. I was relieved to see she was relatively young. I expected some frumpy older schoolteacher-type woman with horn-rimmed glasses and grey hair up in a bun. But not Terry Anderson – she was a gorgeous-looking woman, about my age, I suppose, very well dressed, which prompted my 'how much?' question again; she clearly wasn't on the sort of money I paid my staff.

'Hello, good morning, how are you? Sorry to keep you waiting; I had to finish a report for my last clients while I had it in my mind. Right, come in, Lars, Maya – can I call you by your first names? Far less formal; this is not an examination. It's getting you to talk about your problem, if there is one, out in the open?'

We entered her office, which was all glass and modern furniture – no sign of the settee I expected where the psychiatrist sits behind you asking questions and making notes: instead there were three leather lounge chairs, green in colour. I'd read somewhere that green was supposed to be a soothing colour. I guess I was nervous.

'Now, who wants to start, or do you want me to give you what we know first?'

'Rather you go first, please, Terry,' said Maya, 'it's all new to us, this, and we're not sure how to attack the problem. Well, we think it's a problem – it is something that has been happening all the time we have been together, and it's so frustrating, that right, Lars, isn't it?'

'You seem to think it is. Well, yes, suppose you are right; it is frustrating, for sure.'

'It is premature ejaculation, isn't it? That was what you put on the form. I already knew, but needed you to admit to it. It is a common problem; there are approximately twenty to thirty per cent of men in Australia who suffer from one sort of problem, but there are no actual records kept. First of all, I must say there is no clear definition of "too early"; it depends on the individual. I must point out that quite a lot of men ejaculate prematurely, or come too early, at some time in their lives. It is more common in younger men. Also, it has been found there is no fixed time that a man should ejaculate. It is a fact that premature ejaculation is customarily considered when you ejaculate within one minute of your penis entering your partner.'

'One minute? Is that all? Even I can beat that. Bloody hell… one minute?'

'Shh, Lars, let Terry finish.'

'Should it happen only occasionally, then do not worry. If you have found it a regular thing that you come earlier than you or Maya wants, she is right; it is an issue, and you are right to see me. You must remember it is important that ejaculation problems are nothing to be embarrassed or shy about. It is good that you can discuss this with Maya, and now you have come to see me with your concerns, and in most cases, we can often help to reassure you. This is important. Most men with premature ejaculation can be helped, which can help with developing and maintaining intimate relationships. Before we go any further, I must advise you that you may wish to try several ways before seeking medical help – such as prescribed medicines, or you could try a local anaesthetic spray that you spray on your penis ten minutes before the sex act. It has been found that this could the last resort as it can cause the opposite effect, as often the best sex happens on the spur of the moment, when you do not plan to make love. Other ways include: one, masturbating an hour or two before you have sex. Two, using a thick condom to help decrease sensation. Three, taking a deep breath to briefly shut down the ejaculatory reflex, which is an automatic reflex of the body during which ejaculation occurs. Four, having sex with your partner on top, as you may find this position less arousing, and five, you could try taking a break and thinking of something other than sex.'

Lars then realised that Leif must have had the same problem, for option five was how he was doing it.

'Have you any questions? Do you think I have helped in any way? I would suggest you take the pamphlets here, read through them, discuss your options and try a few, see if that helps – and don't forget your problem is not just you; lots of men after a while come good, excuse the pun.'

'No, Terry,' said Maya, 'you certainly gave us a good explanation of our problem, and ours is not as bad as others, or so it seems, as ten minutes is our record, but like some, it has been the norm.'

'What do you think, Lars? Want to add anything?'

'No, nothing… only that looking at what you have said and at the five options you think we should try – number one, I have tried, but that did not work.'

Maya looked at him, surprised.

'Number two – I do not fancy that at all; I'm not using an inner tube. Number three – OK, it could be a possibility. Number four – we already do that; it is Maya's favourite position.'

Maya nodded in agreement.

'Number five sounds like it could be another one we should give a go, for when we are having sex. I do agree with the idea that what we are doing helps me come. Have you any suggestions about how I can get sex off my mind while still keeping an erection? It sounds a hard thing to do, and like you, sorry about the pun.'

Terry smiled at his last comment.

'One thing you could try is saying the alphabet to yourself – A, B, C, D… I am sure I do not have to say them all – or even try saying it backwards from Z; that is also supposed to help. My partner also used to have the same problem as you – that is how I got into this job. I had a personal interest, for he was terrible; I only had to take my knickers off in front of him, and he came.' She laughed out loud. 'He loves footy – he's a Rabbitohs supporter from being a boy. He knew every team, all the great players, and was an encyclopedia on the game in Sydney, he knew every club every ground they played at. He decided he would use the original Australian rugby league clubs in Sydney (before the Knights, Canberra Raiders and Brisbane Broncos were invented after the Super League war and the NRL was started up). It was one thing he loved but not in a sexual way. He used to think about them in alphabetical order – Balmain Tigers, Canterbury-Bankstown Bull-dogs, Cronulla-Sutherland Sharks, Eastern Suburbs Roosters, Manly Warringah Sea Eagles, Newtown Jets, North Sydney Bears, Parramatta Eels, Penrith Panthers, St George Dragons, South Sydney Rabbitohs, Western Suburbs Magpies. Do you know them all as I do? I heard it so many times, I know them off by heart, too.'

That was it; that was what Leif was doing when he was having sex. He was naming all the Pommie clubs and their grounds. 'Cas' wasn't a girl's name; it was Castleford. Kayleigh was Keighley, Lea was Leigh. It was too obvious – the last club was Wigan Central Park. Still, it wasn't actually the last club – Workington Town was; he never finished the list. That was one thing I could do better than him if I tried, I thought. I needed to get to Western Suburbs Leichardt Oval.

CHAPTER 20

LEIF

The Isle of Wight, Here I Come – A Few Months Later

I was thinking to myself, Leif, it is now getting towards the end of April, and you have been out of work now for quite a few months over the wrong part of the winter; there's never much work around at that time of the year. I just did not want to go back.

Not having any significant debts, I had no one to tell me what to do. I had been sending my CV to numerous clients and agencies without a lot of success. I had done a couple of quick front-end engineering design, or FEED estimates as they are known in the trade, for cash in hand, which was welcome. I had a few quid in the bank. It was time to have a few days away again, but I decided to go to the south of England for a change. I looked at the map and read a few advertisements in the Sunday national newspapers for different areas of the country, as I'd never really holidayed in the UK.

I decided on the Isle of Wight; why, I don't know. I'd never been there, but I loved the sea and ships. It was the Mecca for the yachting fraternity. I thought I would try it out.

At the time, I owned a car, a Ford Cortina GTI, the model before the 'jelly mould' Sierra came out. I loved it – it was black with loads of chrome and a vinyl roof; classy. I drove down to Portsmouth, intending to catch the ferry across to Ryde, but stayed a couple of nights in Portsmouth.

I did the tourist bit and went to look around the new Mary Rose Museum to see the 16th-century Tudor naval warship and read about the historical context in which she was active.

I also went around Lord Nelson's HMS Victory, and kept banging my head on the bloody beams between decks; they must have been small people in those days, but it must have been a hell of a hard life being a sailor during the wars then.

I was pleasantly surprised by what a lovely city Portsmouth and the surrounding area were; it was nice, but I was looking forward to getting to Cowes, where I had decided to visit.

It started a beautiful sunny morning as I boarded the 10am Wightlink ferry from Portsmouth to Ryde, which is on the north coast of the island.

I had a twelve-mile drive to my hotel in Cowes, where I had booked a room at the Duke of York, an old pub not far from the centre of town and near to everything. I had chosen this after researching hotels; it got useful reports. It had a private car park, rooms were a bit basic but good enough, and the food was spot on with complimentary breakfast. I was, after all, only sleeping there.

I loved Cowes. Walking around the Yacht Haven (they don't call it a marina; that is reserved for the Shepards Marina a bit further away), it was great looking at the boats on show; they were beautiful, along with some of the women lying out on the decks sunbathing and posing.

I could walk everywhere. I wanted to be in the town. I was in a pub one lunchtime and was sitting next to an older couple; they were Yanks. I got talking to them, as you do, and it seemed they were of Norwegian extract. Their forefathers had even travelled the same journey as mine, during the great famine, through Hull. They hadn't settled in Hull, like mine; they had taken the train and moved on to Liverpool, then New York.

They continued to tell me about their family history after a while. The families who had initially made the long journey to the States had intermarried and eventually moved to Texas, where one of the grandparents got a job in the oil game. Most of the family had followed him as pioneers in what was then a new industry.

'We are not boring you, young man, are we?' said the lady.

'Not, not at all. Oh, by the way, my name is Leif Askenes; I am also of Norwegian blood. My ancestors came over in the 1800s – please carry on.'

'Well, that is a coincidence,' said the man. 'My name is Einar Hegdahl, and this is my wife, Borghild. As I was saying, my family got into the oil industry in the early days, and yes, they had all made fortunes, and luckily for me, I followed them.'

'Where does your surname come from? I know from the history lesson I have had from Mum that they were old-fashioned names handed down through generations?'

'Yes, you are correct; Einar comes from Ein, meaning one or loan, and arr meaning warrior. Also Borghild, in Norse mythology, was Sigmund's wife. Hegdahl was derived from the name bird or cherry (Hegg) and valley (Dahl); it's a little confusing to non-Norwegians, but that is how it is.'

I just loved hearing about Norwegian history, for we did not learn it at school. I had read as many books as I could on the subject, but not enough.

They were an amiable couple, who were touring Europe, having come over from Florida where they owned another home, and were nearing the end of their vacation, having been away for three months.

They had hired a motor cruiser in Holland and sailed over to Cowes. Their plan was to cruise around the island to Yarmouth via Ryde, over to Lymington and back to Cowes. They estimated it'd take no more than a couple of weeks, if that; maybe even less. Then perhaps they would go up to Southampton before heading off home back to Texas, via Amsterdam.

They invited me to see their cruiser. I jumped at the chance, having not had the opportunity to go aboard one, only look at them and drool.

'Well, here we are; what do you think to her?'

'God, what a boat! How long is it?'

'She is 40ft long, with twin onboard engines. She rides quite well – bit heavy on fuel economy, but hey, it's only money.'

God knows what it cost. I had been thinking that these two must have had a few quid, but when I saw their boat, I knew they had. Mind, they were both around their mid-fifties, possibly older, I reckon, and both looked fit for their years.

We went on board, and they started to show me around. It had two cabins separate from the lounge. There was also a lounge area on the top deck with a flying bridge where you could steer the boat in good weather, with the same controls undercover below for lousy weather.

Above the accommodation was an area where you could sunbathe or just relax. I was taken aback by it all; it was beautiful.

'What you think then, Leif?' said Einar. 'It's a bit small in comparison to ours at home. But it is the largest we could get without a crew; I have a licence from the States which allows me to skipper a boat; I got it in the military. Now, to obtain one privately in this day and age, so to speak, costs the earth.' He continued, smiling, 'I let Borg take the helm when we are at sea. I take over when coming in and going out of the marinas, just to be on the safe side. How would you like to stay for lunch? We've loved your company today. Thank you for being so friendly towards us.'

'Yes, thanks very much – I would love to, It's nice to meet other people from abroad, with different ideas. I also love to travel.'

I would not have missed it for the world – few beers and a barbecue (gas-fired, of course), T-bone steaks… they knew how to eat, those Yanks, that was for sure; they were monster portions.

We had a beautiful afternoon loving how the other half lived. I was thinking about it when Borg asked if I would like to stay the night; there was plenty of room, with the two cabins both having double bunks in them. I said there was no need. It's not as if I was miles from home. It was within walking distance back to the pub.

'Don't tell me you would rather stay in the old pub than remain on board with us? Anyway, we aren't leaving for a couple of days – just stay on board until we go, no worries.'

He was right; it was a no-brainer, really. 'Yes, thanks,' I said, 'but I need my toothbrush and change of clothes; I've got no toiletries or anything with me – wasn't imagining I would be staying out all night.'

'No worries, we have everything here. You tend to carry spares of everything on a boat,' said Ein.

So it was settled. I stayed the night, and what fantastic hosts they were, too.

Borg had got changed into a bikini and top and had been lying out on the deck. I was sitting in the top lounge with Ein when she came up after getting changed, and, me being me, I had to comment when she passed, 'What a great body for your age, if I may say so, Borg.'

She just smiled and said, 'Why, thank you, kind sir,' and wiggled her arse. Mmm, even at her age, I would give her one, maybe two if she asked nicely, I thought.

The wine flowed – only the best, primarily Californian, but still, I was no wine buff, so wouldn't know. It was another great meal; this time it was a buffet with lobster, crabs, every sort of seafood, with salad. I was being spoiled here, and didn't want it to end. Fuck the bar meals or restaurant; this was far superior.

Ein had loaned me a pair of shorts; admittedly they were a bit tight they but covered my modesty and gave me a chance to get some sun on my body.

I went up and lay down next to Borg; as the sun was going down, the heat had gone out of it, but was still a pleasant English spring evening. As I lay down, she touched my hand and smiled, 'It's nice to have your company, Leif. Oh, how I do just love that name – really glad you decided to stay the night.'

I nodded off – what with the food and wine, it had knocked me out; I don't know how long I was asleep, but the sun had nearly gone down when I opened my eyes.

Borg was on her side, leaning on one elbow and looking at my body; she did not see me open my eyes, so I closed them again quickly. I left it a couple of minutes, then slowly opened them a bit; Borg was still looking down at my shorts area, not just looking, but staring. I realised why – I had a semi on; the bulge was more pronounced because the shorts were that tight on me. Fuck, what should I do?

I was pleased and excited that she was watching my dick, but I needed to go slack. However, the more I thought of her watching me, the hornier I got and the more erect it was trying to get. It was no good. I opened my eyes and shuffled a bit to show her I was awake.

She moved her eyes on to mine, and I apologised to her for what she had seen. 'Don't be silly,' she said. 'I was enjoying seeing a younger man enjoying a dream. Was it about me, Leif? I do hope it was.'

I think I blushed because she touched my hand again, this time holding hers on mine longer than just a touch, and kissed me on the cheek.

'Come on – I need another drink after watching you. It's been a long while between drinks,' she said, laughing as she got up – and what a dirty laugh.

I was now thinking, would she? Was it that Ein could not perform? Was I being set up? Nah, no chance… but maybe. Nah, you are kidding yourself, Leif, old son, not a cat in hell's chance.

I had a great night's sleep. The bunk was that comfy; it was about four feet wide and seven feet long. There were two beds with a gap of about two feet between them, and a cushion at the back that you could drop down to make a full-width double king-size bed by pushing the two mattresses together. This was the same in the master cabin, as I found out later.

I woke early; it must have been about five o'clock. It was too hot, so I went up on deck. You could smell the sea, and there was a soft breeze blowing. It was a perfect morning – but I was not the first up, it seemed. Borg was already sitting in the captain's chair with her legs wide apart on the handrail, tanning her nether regions – in fact, tanning all of her body, as she was naked. She had not heard me come up the stairs, as she lay back in the chair with her sunglasses on.

I was right – she had a great body for her age; no doubt she had been to the uplift shop as her breasts were substantial, and her tummy had been tucked in; her legs I was not sure about. It was a beautiful view to start the day, without any question.

I closed the two doors softly as they were already open, then opened them again, making sure I made a noise to ensure Borg heard me, giving her time to make herself decent – if she wanted to, that is.

She did – so, not the brazen hussy I'd hoped she would be. I got to the top of the stairs as she pulled her wrap around her. 'Oh, hello, good morning, Leif; how did you sleep? OK, babe?'

'Yes, OK, thanks, and thank you once again for letting me stay aboard. I have enjoyed myself.'

'Listen, Leif – me and Ein were talking last night; we decided – if you want to, that is – seeing as you were telling us you were going to tour the island, why not come with us for a few days? We would love your company.'

Once again, I was lost for words; this was what I was going to do, tour the island – and what better way of doing it than on a million-pound boat?

I came up with the polite response, 'Are you sure? Won't I be in the way? It's your vacation, not mine.' I hoped like hell that she would say, 'Yes, of course, we are sure.' Which she did.

She then added, 'There is only one stipulation on the trip – that is, as we are both naturists, it means the whole trip you will have to be naked. We just love the freedom of not wearing clothes. Letting the sun get to our bodies is so invigorating – is that OK with you?'

I was a bit nervous, to be honest. 'What happens if we see another boat, or, say, a ferry passes by?'

'It's OK. When we are in any port, we dress, but we are naked out in the ocean. If we do pass a boat while under way, we slip on a top. Well, I do – Einar can't be seen. Not that he has that much to show anyway!' There was that laugh again.

With that, Einar came up on deck wearing just a pair of shorts.

'He has agreed to come with us. Isn't that excellent news, darling?'

Einar looked at me and nodded, but something told me he was not that over-keen.

I had to go back and get some clothes, not that I would need much. I had to check out of the pub and pay my bill, anyway.

As I was leaving, Einar said, 'Bring your car back to the marina and park it here; there's a slot allowed for each boat, and we do not have a car, so it will be empty. We are coming back here in a week or so, dependent on the tides and weather; it's better doing that than paying for parking.'

'Great – I have an open ferry ticket, so it does not matter to me when I get back. I have plenty of time.'

'Very well; try to get back to the marina before lunch as we want to get away as soon as possible – is that OK?'

I was back at 11am and parked; I locked the car and had to give the keys to the marina office in case of any emergency. I left most of my gear in the boot of the car, just taking one pair of shorts and a change of T-shirt, one polo shirt, a couple of pairs of dress shorts in case we went ashore somewhere, to a restaurant or something, and clean briefs, along with toiletries, etc. Right, I was set – it was off back to the Blue Moon and my naked companions for the next week or so.

We left the harbour at bang on 11.30am and turned left – sorry, to port – as we came out of the marina heading towards Yarmouth. It was a fantastic day; the Channel was like the proverbial millpond. We had not been travelling twenty minutes when Borg said, 'OK, all off now – that's an order from the captain!' That laugh again.

They both stripped off, and I went along with the order, standing there naked with the breeze blowing between my legs; I felt great, to be honest. I did feel a bit embarrassed, but it soon wore off. Einar looked me up and down, more down than up, and said: 'Very nice indeed. I just knew Borg was right in asking you along for the trip.'

My mind was starting to ask questions; why had they asked me? I had the feeling there was more to it than just being friendly.

It is fifty nautical miles around the coast of the island – not that far in actual time, but they intended to stop off at one or two coves for the night or two, to make the trip a bit longer, as sailing ships do it in around four hours, once again dependent on winds and tides.

'Where are we intending on going, Einar? Have you got a plan or just playing it by ear?'

'We intend just to take our time, no rush – not go too far from shore; a steady cruise and see how we feel when we get there.'

'How many places are there where you anchor up and stop the night?'

'Quite a few – Totland Bay, Alum Bay, Steephill Cove, Ventnor Bay, Bembridge Marina – if we can't get to the beach we can always lay anchor for the night, once again dependent on the weather.'

I knew I had got the terminology wrong; it was lay anchor, not anchor up; you could tell who the nautical man was on board.

Talking to the two of them sitting naked seemed so natural – they had no inhibitions, and weren't trying to look anywhere you wouldn't generally if fully dressed. It was great; I must admit I liked it. I thought I could get used to being a nudist.

'What made you want to visit Europe and the UK? Had you always planned it?'

'No, we have come over with the intention to travel to as many nudist camps or resorts as we can fit in the two months that we are away. We have been to quite a few already as it is a bit more relaxed in Europe, especially Holland and Germany, but we have yet to find one that we do not like – that right, Borg?'

'Oh yes, I have loved it – especially some of the men. It is so good when you do not have to imagine what is hidden in those tight jeans and shorts, and see all the beautiful, lithe bodies; that is the bonus of being a nudist.'

'Give over, Borg; Leif will think you are perverted. You will always have me to fall back on.'

Borg rolled her eyes and nodded.

They planned to be away for three months but had open tickets in first class, and could book at the drop of a hat if need be.

The sun was just going down as we pulled into Yarmouth within an hour or so; having got dressed, we moored up.

'Hello, there, how are you today, sir?' said Einar to the harbour master. 'Any chance of you phoning us a cab? We would like to find a pub, or possibly two; can you recommend one, please?'

'Good evening – yes, no problem. Might I suggest the King's Head or the Wheatsheaf? Also the Bugle is quite good as well. I assume you will be looking for an evening meal? Then the Bugle has the best menu – in my opinion, of course.'

We went into the town, called in to a couple of the pubs for a pint, and then went on to the Bugle, where we had decided to eat. The grub was spot on; basic, but very nice.

'Well, I enjoyed that. I will pay,' I said as Ein was getting his wallet out. 'Put your money away, Einar; it's my shout. I insist on paying. I want to pay my way and not just take you for granted.' I was determined to pay, even if they wore more gold and jewellery than I had money in the bank.

We were out most of the evening and called a cab around 10.30pm to take us back to the harbour. Ein had had one too many, for English beer is a lot stronger than that American piss, and he had matched me pint for pint. Borg had a glow on as she had been drinking white wine; she had tried a French chardonnay-semillon that she loved and insisted on buying six bottles to take away.

Having got back to the boat, I was about ready for bed, but nope – we had to have a nightcap. Now, Einar was a bourbon man and insisted we had three fingers of Michter's No 1. I had never been an American whiskey fan; I'd tried Jack Daniel's and Jim Beam and wasn't that keen – give me a good single malt any time – but this was something else. It had a kind of caramel and vanilla taste, fruity with a touch of smoky finish. Yes, it was exceptional – I'd never tasted anything so lovely.

I looked at my watch; it was 12.30am. I had nodded off along with the other two, all of us in the lounge. I tried to wake the pair of them, but no chance – they were pissed out of their heads. I just left them and went to my cabin. I had pulled the bunks together to give me more room, as I preferred a double bed; maybe it was my size, but I had always had one.

I crashed out, and that was it until I woke up. It was 9.30am when I looked at my watch; my head was throbbing. Fuck, I felt crap, and felt even worse when I saw who was lying next to me – Ein. He was naked and must have been thinking about Borg. Well, I hope he was, for he was erect. She was right – there was not a lot to show, but still, he was in bed with me.

I moved a bit to one side and he groaned, mumbled, then opened his eyes. The look of shock on his face was not only a relief for me but an embarrassment for him.

'Morning, Einar, how are you?'

'Holy fuck! What the fuck am I doing here? What the hell happened?' he said.

'Don't ask me, mate; I have no idea. I have just woken up. I left you asleep with Borg in the lounge; you must have climbed into the wrong bed. Do not worry, it's no problem.'

'I can't remember coming to bed – as you say, I must have got into the wrong bed. I'm so sorry, Leif, please accept my apologies.'

We both got dressed and went into the lounge. Borg was still there lying out on the bench seat, still dressed in the same clothes as she was in the previous night, which made it a bit easier when we woke her up. She did not know me and Einar had spent the night together, and she was not going to find out, either.

Leaving Yarmouth, we set off down the coast heading for our next stop, Totland Bay; as we arrived, a small jetty was available to tie up to. There was a pub, the Waterfront Bar, so we headed up there for a walk and a few beers. We stayed the night, and the weather was still pleasant. I was enjoying this life, and wondered what the poor people were doing back home.

The next day we set off early for Alum Bay, not far from the Needles, a well-known visitor attraction if you can call it that sort of thing. It did not take long to get there, and we just dropped anchor in the bay and enjoyed the view. We decided not to stay there the night and headed off to Steephill Cove as it was getting late. We dropped the anchor and took the tender, or, for those not so up on nautical terms, the little dinghy we towed on the back.

We visited the little restaurant called the Boathouse, had a great meal which was an end to a lovely day. When we got back to the boat, we laid into the wine Borg had purchased and finished the lot.

The following day I knew I had had too many. We laid off the drink the day, all of us suffering from the previous evening; we were sitting around on the upper deck just taking in the evening air. Borg had gone down to get out of the sun for a while to have a few minutes by herself to read a book before the evening meal.

Einar turned to me and said, 'Leif, would you like to make love to Borg? Do you fancy her? As you Brits say – and does she turn you on?'

I did not know what to say. Was this a wind-up, or was he just testing me out?

'What made you think that? She is a very, very attractive woman, but we hardly know each other. I do not want to spoil our friendship as you have been very kind to me by inviting me to enjoy your vacation.'

'That does not answer my question, Leif. Would you like to make love to her? Yes or no? Please, just answer.'

Wow, he had me there. Of course I would, but why now? Why ask me now? Was him climbing into bed with me a tester to see if I was homosexual or bisexual? If it was, he was a good actor. I just said, 'Any red-blooded male would love to bed Borg. You are a fortunate man, Einar; you should be thankful she is yours.'

He looked at me and did not answer at first, but smiled.

'I will take that as a yes.'

He got up and went down to the lounge.

*

Nothing more was mentioned that night; we ate, had a couple glasses of Borg's favourite wine, and retired to our cabins alone.

The following day we set off. Within half an hour, we were all naked again, taking in the sun. I had learned from Ein how to steer the boat and use all the controls – even how to use the radar scanner; he was now confident enough to let me take charge and guide us to our next location, Ventnor Bay.

I was up on the flybridge steering the boat. I was loving it – the sun on my body, and master of my very own motor yacht… keep dreaming, son, I told myself. I was getting an all-over tan now, and my white bits had gone a light shade of brown; now, I was not vain in any way, but I loved seeing my naked body all one colour, instead of the white marks you usually had when out in the sun either abroad or even back in the UK. It always made your skin look so puffy and pale, like some sort of white bread dough.

It was not that far to our next stop, and as we arrived at the bay there was a small harbour where we could tie up. Ventnor was a thriving little town with lots of pubs and eateries, and it was decided we should stay a bit longer here and move on after two nights.

Once again, we hit the town, visited one or two of the local watering holes, and finished up at the Taj Indian restaurant. I had not really been a lover of Indian cuisine, and much preferred Chinese if I was asked to choose. I always believed that Indian food used too many different spices. I was not always sure what to order, but the look of the meals and the aroma coming out from the kitchen was nothing short of fantastic, and I still didn't know what to have.

We took a table, and the waitress came over.

'Good evening, welcome to the Taj; my name is Jayashree. Would you like anything to drink before your meal?'

'Yes, please, I will have a beer – and you,' I said, looking at Ein and Borg, 'what do you fancy?'

'I will have the same as you, Leif,' said Ein.

'White wine for me, please – dry white large one,' answered Borg.

'This looks a nice place – not like most Indian restaurants. They've not decorated it like some Taj Mahal lookalike,' said Borg.

'No, it's more like their living room,' I said, 'not that I have ever seen an Indian home. Love the mats on the walls – gives it a nice feel to the place.'

The waitress, who happened to be the owner's daughter, returned for the meal order. We had been going through the menu, and we did not recognise a lot of the dishes.

'Can you suggest any of the meals, please? As we do not know what to order; we are not sure?'

'That's OK. We are often asked the same question by other customers as we have included on the menu some meals made from an old recipe book my great-grandmother brought with her from India many years ago. She lived in Gulmarg in a remote part of the country, in the northwest Pir Panjal ranges.'

'Is that a lot different from what we might call everyday Indian cuisine, if that is the right word?' asked Borg.

'Yes, a bit. If you prefer, we can do you a banquet with tastes that will surprise you, and if you are not happy, you do not have to pay; how does that sound? I must ask, is there any preference? Do you like hot, as in curry hot, and does anyone have any allergies?'

We were all OK with that, she came back with a kind of carousel that she put in the middle of an extra-large table, but then I found out why.

She brought out starters of different pickles and other little morsels; some small golden discs of potatoes, crab and prawn cakes, something that had beetroot in it, chicken pops I think were wings fried in spices, and a few other items including poppadoms.

The main meals followed: six different dishes to share between us and three rice types. I'd never had such a variation, all washed down with nice cold beer.

Jayashree came back after we had finished.

'Was that to your satisfaction? I hope you enjoyed it?'

'It was wonderful – best Indian meal we have ever had; well, I've had, anyway,' I said.

'Can I ask you, does your name have an English meaning to it or translation? It is beautiful,' said Borg.

'Yes, it means goddess of victory – it is of Indian origin.' She blushed as she said it. 'Is there anything more you would like, or shall I bring the bill? Was there anything you did not like? For, as I said before, you do not have to pay for any dish you did not like.'

'No, everything was first-class; please bring the cheque,' said Ein.

We paid it in full and left a massive tip, as Americans tend to do, but it was well worth the visit. As we left, the whole family came out from the kitchens to say farewell, which seemed a nice gesture.

We had been in there about two hours and came out stuffed.

We got back to the Blue Moon, ready for bed. Einar said he was off, he was knackered; well, he didn't say that, being a Yank, but that's what he meant. Borg suggested a glass of wine – not her new one, that had all gone, but a beautiful red a merlot. 'OK by me,' I said.

She came back with two large, and I mean large, glasses, and sat down beside me. We clinked glasses and took a sip, then she put her glass on the table and touched my hand as she took the glass from me.

'Ein told me you were discussing me the other day, and he asked you if you would like to make love to me – is that right, Leif?'

I was a bit shocked to hear her being so open.

'Er... well, yes, he did, and I told him any red-blooded male would relish the chance of it.'

'But you did not say yes or no, Leif? Why not? Don't you want me? Am I not attractive to you? Is there something you do not like about me? After all, you have seen every nook and cranny of my body. Even my pussy the day you caught me sunning my vagina, and you pretended that you had not; I'm not stupid, Leif.'

She then went on to tell me that Ein could not keep it up any more. 'Oh, yes, he can get an erection, but it only lasts a couple of minutes, then goes limp again. You can see he is not that well endowed, anyway. It is so frustrating for both of us, as I just love sex – I need it, always have, ever since I was a young girl in high school. It seems the older I get, the more I need.'

'Borg, how long have you been with Einar, a long time?'

'Yes, we have been married thirty years, and for the past five, we have had separate lives. I can fuck whoever I like as long as the guy is known to Ein – that he has met him and verified that he thinks he is a decent, clean guy. That is why you were one of the "chosen ones" and why we have asked you to come on the trip. Einar isn't a perv; he doesn't want to watch me perform, although he does like listening from another room, as long as when I orgasm, I shout his name. He loves to shoot without an erection when he hears our lovemaking going on and me being satisfied.'

I was now hard, and she knew it by the bulge in my shorts.

'Shall we go up on deck, Leif, it's a nice night; it has gone midnight. There will be no one around this time of night.' She took my hand, and I followed like a puppy.

We stood just looking at each other holding our wine glasses, and then we kissed. Oh my god, she kissed so well – soft, full lips... her tongue opened my mouth and entered it, then she sucked my tongue. I was gone; she had me.

We stripped off – the breeze was so nice on that hot night. We lay on the lounger, and I was on my back looking up at the sky. There was not a cloud in sight. She bent down and took me. She was good – my word, she was good; she had done oral before, that was for sure, her lips only gripping on the upward stroke.

I wanted to get to Wigan – oh, how I wanted Central Park. She knew I was getting close, and smiled as she got astride me. I could feel the heat of her vagina as she lowered her self on to me. I felt her muscles gripping me as she rode me up and down. I was way past Halifax Thrum Hall and on my way to Oldham; wow, it was good. For her age she was an expert in her field. Then she stopped riding me and asked, 'Leif, will you take me from behind? I want you as we stand next to the handrail. I want to be bent over, looking at the sea. Please, baby – just for me, please?'

How could I refuse such a request? She got up from me and stood next to the side of the boat; she spread her legs as I entered her from behind. 'Oh, fuck,' she cried. 'Oh, yes, push, baby!' I was like a piston in and out. She was sucking me in with every thrust, pushing back against my groin as I went back up her. Warrington was close; oh my, it was close. I was on my way to Wigan, going down Greenough Street to the ground. Was Workington in sight? 'Oh, fuck, yes… Mmm… oh no!' I was there, and could feel her gripping me, then she shouted, 'Oh, Ein, baby! Ein, I love you!' Then we uncoupled.

I went limp, and it flopped out; the sweat was dripping off me. I just sat on the lounger and picked up my glass. Borg joined me, still licking her fingers, before washing them down with this beautiful merlot. It felt so right, just being naked in the warm evening alone with a lover on the back of a beautiful boat.

The following day I got up; there was no one on deck, so I made myself a coffee in the galley. I went and sat in the lounge and then Ein came up. 'Morning, Leif – enjoy yourself last night, I believe? Borg told me all about it. Having said that, I already knew when I heard her crying out my name last night. Thank you, son, for being so understanding. I enjoyed it – I came as well; I'd not brought so much up for many a long year. Thanks again, son – here's to the next time.'

We did not fuck again, not the next night anyway. I said 'fuck' and not 'made love' for I felt that Borg did not want love, just fucking, just the sexual act. She loved Einar, no doubt about that, and in a way, she was doing it for him as much as her satisfaction.

We left Ventnor and headed up to Bembridge, which would be the last stop before Ryde. Five days had passed, five beautiful days. I did not want it to end. I was like a kid on holiday with his parents; the only difference I was fucking my mother.

I had found out she was fifty-two, and Ein was sixty; I had never considered making love to a woman nearly twenty years older than myself. Still, I had, and, believe me, it was good. It had opened another world. I hoped it would not be the last time I got the chance to please an older woman, and would always look at them in a completely different light from now on.

We were all in our sailing uniforms for the next trip – naked. It was a bit cooler today, but we still did not put any clothes on. I was told just because you feel the cold wind on your body there's no need to cover it up; it's good for the skin. How true that is, I don't know, but I went along with it.

We entered the harbour; now, this was a big one, and we had to moor up at the Brading Haven Yacht Club at the far end. This was the biggest harbour we had been in, and it had everything. Good job it did, as we were getting a little low on fuel.

It was decided we were to stay here two nights to take a look around; there was a small airport near Bembridge. We asked about taxi availability and was told it was easier to take the local bus service as it ran every half hour into town and dropped you off in the centre. Taxis were much easier to get back if you stayed out late, but town was more accessible and cheaper on the bus.

Ein was struggling a bit with his back; he had done well up to now but had problems walking long distances. He told us to leave him in on the front at a small pub, the Pilot Boat Inn, while we went for a look around the place. We hadn't got far, and Borg wanted a coffee, so we nipped in a cafe down Love Lane. The Love Lane Coffee house – very apt. We picked a booth near the windows and sat with our backs to the others in the place; it was kind of horseshoe-shaped with a bench seat making up the booth, and we could look out of the window watching passers-by in the street. It also meant Borg could play with my manhood, without anyone seeing.

The waitress brought the large coffees we had ordered, and we started some serious talking. Borg wanted me again now if she could; her hand was down my shorts. I was hoping that the waitress didn't come back to ask if everything was to our satisfaction, for it very nearly was. I had been feeling horny all morning, and this was just what I needed – a nice, slow masturbation session, not on my own but by a woman.

'Shall I go down on you, babe? Right now? Are you close? No one will see – come on.' I was just about at Wigan.

'OK, do it quickly.'

She pulled the front of my shorts down. That was it, straight away – oh fuck, it streamed out; she was gagging, and that was it – all done. She came up, and no one had seen a thing. I pulled my shorts back straight, and she took a large mouthful of a large white – so that was two large whites in a matter of seconds that she had swallowed. She licked the foam off her upper lip and kissed me.

'Thanks, babe; you need more of the same tonight, OK?'

We got back to Einar about an hour and a half later. He was sitting chatting with a guy who looked like he had been sandblasted, for his face was like leather.

'Oh, hi guys, I want you to meet a friend of mine – just met him, been chatting about old times. He was in the Navy during the Second World War, on submarines; meet Noah.' We said our hellos and shook hands. Apart from being in the oil industry, Einar had joined the US Navy during the war and he had served on aircraft carriers on the USS Yorktown, aged nineteen, when she was first commissioned in 1943, until 1947, at the age of twenty-three, when she was decommissioned.

He had seen action in many theatres of war. Still, he did not go into any great detail apart from when they were in Tokyo Bay sending supplies to prisoners of war who were still living in the camps, staying there until the Yorktown left to go to Okinawa, where they loaded passengers and got under way for the United States and her decommissioning.

Einar and Noah had so much in common it was not funny. Noah had an old fishing boat and invited us out the next day on a fishing trip. Borg quickly declined but said to Ein,

'You go, baby – it will be fun for you. Do you fancy it, Leif?'

Borg shook her head, and looked at me as if to say 'no', so I said to Ein that I wasn't much of a fisherman and added, 'Go on, mate, you will have a good day.'

Ein booked a taxi for 5am the following day to meet Noah at the harbour office on the far side of the harbour, for that was where his boat, the Ark, was birthed.

We had a quiet night; we were all in bed by 10pm. I heard the alarm go off at 4am, and heard Ein getting his breakfast and calling out to Borg that he was going. Fifteen minutes passed and the cabin door opened. Surprise, surprise, Borg stood there stark-naked with the biggest grin on her face.

'Now, that's what I call good planning, babe; what about you?' she said as she climbed in beside me. She cuddled up and stroked me down below. 'You ready now, baby? I am.' I was soon ready, as she put it. I needed a piss; I got up to go to the toilet. Now, it's hard to piss with an erection. I don't know if anyone has ever noticed this, but it took me a while to empty my bladder.

I returned to the cabin; she was lying back, eyes closed, masturbating. Her back was arched; she was on another planet. I lay beside her, just watching her, engrossed in what she was doing. Borg did not know nor care who was there; all she wanted was another orgasm.

I had never been with a woman like her; three times she climaxed before I touched her. She stopped, opened her eyes, and whispered, 'Oh, baby, I do love sex.'

She leaned over and took hold of me. 'Oh, Leif, look, he is so soft, let me bring him back to life.'

'Mmm,' that was the bugle sounded, and old Dick was stood to attention. She climbed on board – phew, that was good – lowered herself down, rode rhythmically, and closed her eyes, biting her bottom lip. 'Oh, fuck, Leif, baby!' Her head went back. I was lifting my arse off the bed so I could get better penetration. 'Oh… My… God!' she whispered. 'Yes, darling, yes… oh, fuck… Yes…' Her hands moved behind her head, then she ran her fingers through her hair. Her body trembled once again as she climaxed. I reached only Swinton this time, but what a journey.

We made love all day. God knows how many times we did it. I was drained; even with rests in between, she was insatiable; I could not give her enough. My penis was red and sore with rubbing; the bed was soaked in our sweat.

I got up; I could not do any more. I put on a robe, and went up into the lounge, just waiting for her to come and join me.

I must have fallen asleep, for the next thing I heard was a car pulling up on the quayside – it was Ein back from his fishing trip.

'Had a good day with Noah, mate? How did you get on? Catch many?'

'Wonderful, thank you, Leif. It was one of the most relaxing days I have experienced for a long time. We caught quite a few cod, haddock, some flatfish, I think they were called lemon sole. I had had a couple for lunch; Noah cooked them on a little paraffin heater, just pan-fried, lovely sweet meat.'

It was then I felt hungry; I hadn't eaten all day. All I'd had was cream pie, and it wasn't very filling.

'Where's Borg, Leif?' he asked.

'She is having a nap. We have had a busy day – walked miles around the harbour and back; we went to a small restaurant on the side of the harbour about five miles down the road from here and then walked back.'

I felt terrible telling him lies. I suppose it would not have mattered if I had told him the truth. He knew I was fucking his wife, but only when he could hear us, and he was condoning it – not behind his back.

CHAPTER 21

LEIF

The Oil Man

We were sitting relaxing, just talking about this and that, and I brought up Einar's past life.

'Einar, during the war, were you only on one ship, then, or did you ever transfer to any other?'

'I did some special training – was loaned out to a new unit they were trying to get off the ground, and I was with them on and off. We were sometimes called up to do special services. I was with a behind-enemy-lines unit, mostly on dockyards, ports surveillance, top-secret stuff. We went away, then came back to our home ship, and no one knew what was going on. Don't suppose I should even be telling you about it even now!'

'Wow, like our SAS, that sort of thing?' I was hooked. God, he was a war hero?

'Enough of that – after the war, I went back to Texas to my job as an oilman. I had worked my way up from being a roustabout to management, and I am still working as a consultant in the construction industry relating to refineries and LNG plants. I have done quite a bit of work in South America, Brazil, Venezuela, Peru over the years, but am now semi-retired. Now and again, I get a call to assist in designing a new plant and assessing contracts, bids, that sort of thing. I have my fingers in a few pies.'

'That is a coincidence, for I am in the same line of business, been in it for several years, and I will be looking for a new position when I get home from this holiday.'

I gave him a brief rundown on my past life, wishing I had a copy of my CV with me. I told him I was interested in the South American thing, as I had no idea it was as big as he was saying.

'Have you any contacts in the USA or Latin America?'

'No; I have never even been there, never mind making contacts.'

'OK, I will give you my details before we part. We must keep in touch as I might be able to help you in some way.'

'Truly? You serious? I would appreciate that, Ein, very much.'

'No problem – just keep Borg happy while you are with us, and I will do as much as I can to help you, Leif; I mean that.' He put his hand on my shoulder and touched my face with his other hand as a father would do to his son.

I felt touched. I know it sounds daft, but I did; it was the nearest thing I had had to a father-son relationship. Was I the son that Leif and Borg had never had? The only difference I was having sex with my mother, and my father condoned it… now, how weird was that?

We left Bembridge and set a course for Ryde. It was a bit overcast as we cruised up the east coast. It was the hottest day of the year so far; we were all taking it in turns to lie out and toast our bodies. The fun bit was putting on the sunscreen; I really enjoyed that.

I had now got a great all-over tan, along with Ein and Borg, who were already brown all over even before we had begun our journey.

Borg was lying back once again, legs apart, pussy glistening in the sun; she was shaved, as was Ein. It was not a thing I had considered – it just wasn't the English stiff upper lip thing to do, shaving your body, especially the cock and balls regions. Then Ein said to me, 'Leif, why do you not shave down below as we do? It's much cleaner; you don't sweat as much. I much prefer being waxed rather than shaven; you must try it. Borg will do it for you if you ask her – she has all the equipment with her. She waxes regularly; sometimes I do it for her.' With that, Borg appeared. 'I was just asking Leif why he does not shave his pubes – I told him you would wax him if he wanted, wouldn't you, babe?'

'Of course,' she said with a glint in her eye. 'I'd love to do it – well, Leif, you game?'

I declined the offer, although I must admit I was very tempted. I fancied Borg fondling my limp dick as she put on the cream and shaved me.

'Come on, don't be shy; it's nice. The waxing after can be a bit of a shock to the region, but after the initial strip, you get used to it, especially as there are a lot of long hairs to pull out after shaving.'

'OK,' I said. 'When can you do it?'

'Now, if you want. Ein, you watch the bridge while we go down and see to Leif.' He gave the thumbs up, and we went below.

'OK, lie on the lounge. I will get the gear.' She disappeared into their cabin, coming back with a bag. She emptied it on the table, taking what looked like a small deep-fat fryer that contained the wax. She plugged the wax machine in; we had to wait for it to warm up, as it was only a 12v system on the boat, so it took its time.

'Now, lie back, and open your legs. Let's see him… mmm, he looks so sweet lying there.' She lifted my penis, and it twitched. 'Do not try not to get erect, babe, or we will never get this done.' That laugh again. I was at Barrow on my way to Batley, working my way through the league still.

She lathered me up, took the safety razor and started to shave me; it felt nice. She cupped my balls as she worked around them and into the crack of my arse, although it was not that hairy there – or so she told me; not that I had ever seen it myself.

'How far do you want to go up the arse?' she asked. 'Considering it will need doing every few weeks.'

'Oh, just what you can see, please.' I sounded like I was at the barber's. 'How much do you want off, sir?'

'OK, that's the shaving done – now for the waxing.'

'She took the fryer and put it next to us, taking what looked like a small spatula. She took some wax on it and layered it on my skin.

'Wow, that's hot,' I said.

'Don't be a baby; now, this may sting a bit.' She put some tape on top of the wax. Pain was not the operative word, as she ripped it off.

'Fuck me!' I screamed, and she laughed.

'That's only the first one; now just lie back and enjoy the pain.'

Enjoy? What the fuck was she talking about? Enjoy the pain? It did get more comfortable, though, and by the time she had completed the task, I was enjoying it.

'There you go, babe, just as smooth as the day you were born; how does that feel?' Then came the nice bit – she started to rub baby oil over me. Oh fuck, we were at Oldham.

She finished me off – a happy ending for us both – then kissed me fully on the lips.

I turned my face away. 'Nah, Borg, don't do that – I told you, that's not my cup of tea, that sort of thing; now, I will try most things, but not that.' She just pouted and kissed me again.

I went up on deck with a beer for Ein, showing off my new look to him as if I was showing a new pair of shorts or something; he agreed she had done an excellent job.

'She does mine once a month; you must keep on top of it when you get home,' he said.

I was now wondering which barber on Hessle Road would be willing to have me sit in a chair while he shaved my bollocks.

Borg came up. 'What you think, Ein? OK? Did a good job, you reckon? I mentioned about getting it done regularly.'

Shaving wasn't the problem; you could do that with a shaving mirror on a chair. It was the waxing, that's why she did it herself. She said to just keep on doing it whenever you took a standard shave, and whip it over your balls, easy as that.

We arrived at Ryde, pulling into the harbour at midday. We tied up and set off for a look around; there was a cafe just across the esplanade so we went in there for lunch. Once again, the food was lovely. Then we went for a wander. Ryde was quite a big place – the largest town we had visited on our journey.

Ein and Borg were discussing where we should go next – either back to Cowes before going up through the Solent towards Southampton, or they could fuel up here and go straight there. They asked me what would like to do, but I didn't give a toss, and just shrugged my shoulders. 'Up to you, I am not bothered.'

It was decided we would go direct – up towards Southampton, and to Hythe Marina. It was agreed that Southampton was too much of a commercial port with cruise lines running from there along with all other merchant shipping, Hythe seemed the right place to berth up.

We had been fortunate with the weather, but this time as we set off from Ryde, it became very dark, and a breeze was starting to get up. Ein checked with the coastguard about the forecast and logged in our destination to them; it was the first time he had done this, but considering we were crossing major shipping lines, it was the best thing to do. It gave them an idea of who was about in the area.

The coastguard told us there were no significant storms brewing, although they did say it could be a bit choppy; it was nothing that we could not handle considering the Blue Moon's size. Choppy was right. There were times I felt pretty queasy – no, fucking ill.

We had got midway across and it was blowing a southerly about force six or seven, a stiff breeze to near gale. The waves were relatively high and the old Blue Moon was rising and dipping quite a lot, the most I had encountered. We were all fully dressed now and wearing life jackets. When Einar had mentioned putting them on, I must have gone the colour of bad shit, but he told me, 'Only precautionary, we always do it – not to worry.'

We got through OK without sinking and got into the mouth of the Southampton Water. Once there, the seas decreased, and the wind dropped. We stripped off the buoyancy aids along with our clothes, but it was not long before there was an abundance of shipping around us; it was decided to put at least a T-shirt on – knickers or shorts were optional.

It was a pleasant trip up to Hythe, and what a marina this was. We had to go through lock gates, so we had to hang about a bit for the tide to change before entering. Once in, we found our berth; it was good job Ein had rung and booked, as it was jam-packed. We found ours just off Shamrock Way; I hadn't realised it was a village with lots of expensive houses, each with their private berth – very impressive.

It had been a second choice coming here, but Ein and Borg had some old friends who lived in the village and they hoped they would be home, as they were 'quite well off'. Now that, coming from these two, meant they must be minted.

'They quite often went on trips around the world,' Borg informed us.

CHAPTER 22

LEIF
Salvage

G eoff and Karen Oswald were the couple. He had been in the salvage industry for years. Geoff started as a deckhand working his way up, to mate, then skipper. He had gained the reputation of being quite brave – some said foolish – but he would go into situations no other salvage tug would go.

We went into the harbourmaster's office to pay for the berth, get some tourist information, and ask if Geoff and Karen still lived in the village, for Borg had lost contact with them over the past few years.

'Oh, yes, they still live here,' we were told. 'They have moved into the newer and more expensive area – here, this is their address, but we must let them know you are here.

Mr Oswald is a very private person, you understand?'

Ein explained the situation and promised the girl behind the counter that it would be OK; he was an ancient friend of Mr Oswald. 'We would like to surprise him,' he said. The girl accepted the story and agreed not to let the Oswalds know there was someone to see them; the fact that there were three people and two of those were men sealed the story.

I was reading a brochure – apparently, Hythe was the first marina village to be built in the UK, and it was very expensive.

We had hired a car for a couple of days on site and drove round to find the house; after half an hour of driving, we eventually found it – and wow, what a place. It was massive. The boat in the mooring must have cost a couple of million even then. It had a two-car garage, although none on the drive; very nice.

Ein knocked on the door and rang the bell. There was no answer. He tried again; no response.

'OK, they must be out,' I said.

We were just about to go, and the door opened; it was Geoff.

'Well, I will be fucked! Einar, you old bastard; how are you, mate? Come in, come in… welcome! Why didn't you ring to say you were coming? Come in… Jesus, it's so good to see you, and the lovely Borg as well.'

We entered what one only could say was a palace. I had never seen anything like this, just in magazines or TV programmes; this was something else.

'Wanna beer or something? We are up by the pool upstairs; come on, I will show you,' said Geoff, handing us a beer each out of the most oversized refrigerator I had ever seen – two doors, each three feet wide, and seven feet tall. You could have lived in it. We took our drinks and followed Geoff up the staircase – three floors until we got to the roof. It was kind of hidden from view; it was like a valley with a room on all four sides, all with patio doors. God knows what this place cost; I was just stunned by it all.

Karen was lying out in a bikini, and she looked a million dollars. They introduced me to them; they were all very friendly, and we sat down and chatted, and another beer appeared after a time. I saw Geoff whisper to Einar and then look over at me, nodding and smiling. He then suggested that we all strip off, as, like Ein and Borg, they were sun-worshippers as well.

'Leif's OK with it; we have converted him into being a nudist guy,' Borg said.

Once again, I was naked in front of strangers, but it felt natural, with no inhibitions.

I was talking to Geoff about his accent. 'Are you a Geordie, Geoff?'

'Nah, fuck off, ya cheeky bastard. I'm a Mackem.'

Whoops – I'd hit a nerve there. I'd forgotten that they hate one another, and to ask a lad from Sunderland if he was a Geordie was the biggest insult you could give.

'What do you for a living?'

'I am on deep-sea tugs – have been all my life. I'm working for a company in Singapore now. I had worked out of Holland for quite a few years but retired after making a few quid and settled down here in the south. I love the weather; much better than up north.'

He went on to tell me more about his job history as he was very proud of what he did, and how they got paid so much money for salvage; it was fascinating, but I was thinking, how could you get the sort of money to support this lifestyle? You needed a fortune.

'I used to take risks, to be honest,' he said. 'I would take my tug to places others would not go. I will give you an example: we went to a call for help from an oil tanker that had lost all power in a storm off the Philippines. Luckily we were in the vicinity at the right time, the seas were running, and we had a job trying to get a line on board to allow us to attach a tow rope on, to make it possible for us to pull them away from the shoreline and into a harbour for repairs.'

I was intrigued by his story he went on.

'The seas were that rough the waves were about fifteen feet high. We had managed to get alongside the tanker on the leeward side, which more or less protected us from the wind. We were going up and down like a lift, one minute up alongside, then the next fifteen feet below, as the troughs on the sea were that deep. The crew was a bit wary; now, most of the time, they would carry out my orders or be out of work, but this time they had more or less said, fuck you, mate, I am not going out in that weather. I had gone out on the deck and said, OK, I will do it myself. I told the mate to take the helm, and said if anything goes wrong, you are in charge.

'I stood on top of the side of the gun wall, holding on to a cable, riding the waves as it went up and down, a bit like a surfer rides a board, but this board was only ten inches wide. I was holding on to a cable as the two ships passed; I stepped off the tug on to the tanker, just like stepping off the pavement on to the road. I had a rope fastened around my waist, which now meant we had a cable on board. This was then attached to a thicker line, and so on. Until we had the actual tow rope on board.'

I was in awe of the man; he was a fucking idiot, by the sound of it, but he was telling me things that would make a great movie. How anyone could be so brave in the face of such jeopardy was beyond me. I could not believe I was talking to an actual hero.

'This now meant that we had salvage rights for that tanker,' Geoff continued, 'which allowed the company to claim a percentage of the cost of the ship and its cargo – in this case, a lot of money as it was oil.'

'Did it make a lot of difference what cargo these ships were loaded with?'

'Oh, yes, sure – one of the critical dangers was environmental and the threat of oil getting into a slick and making land.'

Geoff gave me a lecture on salvage rights. It appeared that traditionally, the salvage reward had been subject to the salvor or salvage ship/ company successfully saving the ship or cargo. If neither was saved, the salvor got nothing. However, much time and money had been spent on projects. This harsh principle was called 'No cure – no pay.'

In the 1960s and 1970s, several ageing single-skinned tankers were coming to grief and letting massive slicks of crude oil escape. While passing ships were obliged to offer reasonable assistance to save a life, they were reluctant to provide salvage services on a seemingly reckless adventure to keep a low-value hulk where third-party liability risks might be enormous. Instead, salvors preferred to work where there were richer pickings and fewer dangers.

'I have been on a few jobs where the saving the cargo and equipment aboard a vessel was of a higher priority than saving the vessel itself,' said Geoff. 'The cargo may have posed an environmental hazard or sometimes may include expensive materials such as machinery or precious metals. In this form of salvage, the main focus was on the rapid removal of the goods and included deliberate dissection, disassembly or destruction of the hull.'

I was intrigued by what Geoff was telling me; this is why he put his neck on the line. Maybe it was not the right thing to do, and there were times when the company did not know or find out what risks he had taken, but what they did not know did not hurt them.

He finished off his lecture by saying, 'I am a wolf if in a storm when there are two ships both in danger. I would look at my options and always go for the one with the most expensive cargo, and I would be asking the ship's master questions to help him make the decision. The ship's crew and loss of life did not come into it, as far as I was concerned.'

It sounded a bit mercenary and acting like God, but it was a business at the end of the day; if he was going to be away for three months at a time at sea looking for ships in trouble, he wanted as much out of it as he could get.

'I will give you an example of how good I am at my job. A few years ago, a company had built a brand-new super-tug, the most powerful in the world, built in Germany. They asked me if I would be the skipper of it. I was even asked if I would prefer bunks or a double bed in the skipper's cabin – now, that's being at the top of your game. I have now moved on from being a skipper and gone into kind of semi-retirement; I am now a called a salvage master, and the company now sends me to the "bigger jobs" where the skipper of the tug, or sometimes tugs, can't handle the job themselves. There are situations where more than one tug is required. Maybe more than one company is involved. I will fly out to the destination, be airlifted out by helicopter to the scene, and take over the salvage.'

'Can I ask, Geoff, and forgive me for being nosy, but how much better off are you than being the hunter, so to speak, or as a skipper?'

'I am now on a yearly salary; it's a kind of standby pay, but the rewards from the salvage money are megabucks. I would prefer not to discuss my earnings, but you can tell by looking at my lifestyle that they have been good.'

We went back to the others, and Karen said, 'Has he been boring you with tug talks, Leif? He can't wait to meet people he has never met to bend their ears on his triumphs at sea.'

'Shut up, Karen – it keeps you in the finery you always want. Don't forget when I first met you, and your life then, babe – you wore the same knickers for a week, and your tits weren't as big as they are now. Mind, I am not complaining about them, best three grand I ever spent.'

I had to agree with him there – she had a great pair of tits; in fact, an impressive body.

We had a few more drinks, and Karen said, 'You will stay for tea, won't you? You can stop and make a night of it if you want – be nice if you do, save you driving; mind, that doesn't matter they are all private roads. As long as you don't hit another car, it doesn't matter, and you can't get breathalysed on here either.'

It was decided we spend the night with Geoff and Karen. I didn't need a change of clothes, that was for sure; I was getting to like this nudist thing a lot.

I was sitting with Ein; the women were yapping away together and Geoff was at the barbecue. We dangled our legs in the pool; what a pleasant way to spend an evening.

'Leif, what do you think? This is the game, isn't it? He has done OK, the old boy – all this and a nympho for a wife. What more could a man ask?'

I just looked at him; there was no need to ask any more questions.

Ein carried on. 'Oh, yes, she is a right filthy bitch – we met them years ago, when I could perform. I fucked her along with five other guys at a party; that is how Geoff met her. She was a hooker in those days, living in St John's in Newfoundland, working in a brothel. He was in port refuelling his tug before he went back out on the hunt. All the crew was at this pub/brothel when we went to the party. Karen was the star attraction. If she gets enough to drink down her tonight, she may well perform some of her tricks. She does wonders with a Coke bottle, and ping-pong balls are like bullets with her usage.'

I could not believe my ears; she looked quite elegant and well to do, not like some old slapper from a brothel. It just went to show that first impressions could be deceiving.

'Geoff had fallen in love with her,' Ein continued, 'and on his three months off he left his wife and family in Sunderland and went back to

St John's to "save Karen". He proposed to her on the second night he was there, and she accepted – and that was it. They've been together ever since. They never talk of the past, mind you; you wouldn't advertise the fact that your old lady was an ex-prostitute and she not only got paid for fucking, but she also loved it. Looking over there, it wouldn't surprise me if Borg was discussing your cock and shafting techniques as we talk.'

As I looked over, Karen gave a little wave, and Borg laughed that laugh; it seemed I was the centre of the conversation.

'Please don't mention it, will you,' said Ein, 'but I thought you should know before the end of the night in case she hits on you. He would not be a happy bunny – he is not like me; he doesn't like anyone else fucking her now.'

I took heed of the warning. I was still sore anyway, but she sure was a good-looking woman, ex-hooker or not; prostitution is just a job regardless. It's a way of earning money like any other job, only you can have fun doing it as long as you are safe and the person you are with you 'like', or would make love to if you met socially.

We were sitting by the pool; it was just getting darker but still warm enough not to need clothes, which I was getting to like. I had always wanted to be naked alone in my room even as a kid; I loved having nothing next to my skin, but in Hull, in midwinter, it wasn't the best thing to do in a house with no other heating than a coal fire downstairs.

We were getting merry now as Geoff had brought out a single malt whisky, one I had never heard of, Aberlour. It was a highland malt, he said. 'Anyone want to try this? Just got it last week; it's supposed to be good as it's fifteen years old.'

Ein was spouting about the bourbons he liked and mentioned Michter's No 1, again. Geoff dismissed US whiskey as piss, saying bourbon was not a real whiskey. I wasn't going to argue – I will drink anything – but I had to side with Geoff; I do like a good single malt.

They begged to differ, and Geoff opened the amber nectar. I must say it was good; I have loved it ever since. Even Ein commented, 'What a good drop.'

The night drew on, and we were all getting tipsy. The ladies were on their third bottle of white wine. Borg was getting louder, something she did when drinking as well as making love.

Karen was just Karen; she seemed very deep, taking everything in without actually saying much. She kept looking at me and smiling. Was it me, but was it a sexy smile, a come to bed smile, maybe, or was I getting a bit carried away? One thing was for sure – if I were to make a play for her and Geoff found out, there would be hell to pay.

I had gone to the toilets on the roof; they were both through the same door from the pool area, but when you got inside, there were two more doors for separate sexes. I came out of my side, and as I was washing my hands Karen came in. Fuck, she was hot. We were partly dressed now as there was a bit of a chill in the air. I had on shorts and a vest, one I had picked up on our travels as a souvenir; it had 'Isle of Wight – Cowes Week' printed on it.

Karen had put her bikini bottoms on and wrapped her sarong around her top. It was kind of surreal; we just stood there looking at each other, not saying a word, but fucking each other with our eyes.

We just fell into each other's arms, kissing so sensually, and then she broke away, saying, 'No, we can't – please, no.'

I pulled back. 'I am sorry – that should not have happened,' I said, and opened the door and walked back to the others.

Geoff looked at me and smiled. 'Another dram, Leif?' he said, holding up a new bottle. 'I bought two, just in case I liked it. I will order a case tomorrow.' He poured a good three-fingers measure into my glass.

'Leif, you ever had a rusty nail, mate? They are unreal – think this drop will go just right; I'll be back in a sec.' Then off he went downstairs.

A few minutes later, he arrived with a bottle of Glayva liqueur. 'Now, I haven't had one of these for many a year; an old Jock I sailed with on the eastern seaboard of the States, he swore by this. We had just got a line on an old coaster off Charleston in North Carolina; we had been on the job down near the Bahamas and were on our way to pick up a ship that had been blown up in an accident and was going back to the UK for a complete refit.'

He was off again, reminiscing. 'Oh, yes, rusty nails.' He poured a shot of Glayva and then a shot of whisky in a tumbler with a couple of bits of ice. 'Pity to use ice with these two, but the guy said it was needed to bring out the flavour. Now, if you want a real refreshing long drink, add some lemonade, but I prefer this version.'

Well, I could not believe how good that was, and still is. I do remember having three of them, and that is the last thing I can recollect. I woke up the next morning still dressed in what I had on, and it was 11am. I haven't a clue what time we finished.

I got up, and oh, my fucking head, it was pounding; I ached all over. I felt as if I had done ten rounds with Joe Frazier. God, I felt rough.

I went in the shower, water cascading down my head and shoulders. It felt so good. When I turned it on cold, my balls disappeared into my body. Fuck, it was cold, but it did the trick – it brought me round. I finished off and went up on to the roof to see who was around.

Only Karen had surfaced; she was lying on a sun lounger, naked as usual. I would miss the nudity thing when I went back to the land of the clothed.

She opened her eyes and spotted me perving on her. 'You like what you see, Leif?'

'Mmm, yes, of course, very much.'

'While you are here, come put some sun cream on my back, please, Leif – there are spots I can't reach.' She rolled over on her belly. Her boobs never moved; they were as firm as two pumpkins – same with the cheeks of her arse. I applied the cream on her back, slowly rubbing it in. She opened her legs as I rubbed it on her buttocks; my fingers went between her legs, just that little bit too high, but she didn't complain – she just gave out a small sigh and soft moan.

'Mmm, that's lovely, Leif; you have a nice touch.'

God, I was hard but dared not go any further. 'That's it, babe, OK – nowhere else?' I stood up. She could see I was aroused. 'We better not do anything – we will be sorry if Geoff were to find out; it would ruin both of our lives,' I said.

She pushed her bottom lip out and looked down to the floor like a child does when you say they can't have any sweets. I smiled, but this stick of rock was not getting licked, not today anyway.

Everyone was up now, and I was sitting by the pool reading a book I had started. I had gone down below, if you know what I mean. I got a shout to go back to the pool; the others were planning a trip or something.

We were just chilling out, and suddenly Ein said, 'Borg and I have been discussing what we fancy doing and have decided we would like to go into Southampton. There is a regular ferry from Hythe that takes you straight into the centre of the city; we would love a look around.'

Geoff chipped in that he would show them around. 'Do you want to come?' he said, looking at me.

'No, thanks. Just wanna lay about if that's OK?' I still felt a bit rough after last night's session. 'Rather just chill out and read my book for a while, though I might have a walk around the marina and maybe call at the pub for a cold hair of the dog on the way.'

'What about you, Karen, or you not bothered?' asked Geoff.

She shook her head and said she was not that interested. It looked like being a beautiful day, and she would rather stay home and top up her tan, not that it needed much topping up, that is.

'OK, that's it settled then,' said Borg, 'Better get dressed. They won't like us walking around the town dressed like this.'

It was about 10.30am when they all left to catch the ferry.

'Just me and you then, Leif – no one to pester us now, eh?' said Karen. 'Can I just ask you something, please, and give me an honest answer?' she added. 'What do you think of Geoff? Be honest, now.'

I wasn't sure what she was getting at. What was she planning? It seemed such an odd question – was there a catch in it?

She went on. 'The reason I ask is I don't see many people; we don't have much of a real social life. What with him being away now and again for some time, up to two months, depends on how big the jobs are, when he is home he does not want to do anything – he has gone off sex, and I need cock. Sorry to be so blunt, but I don't know if you know the story of how we met; I don't know if Borg has told you?'

'Yes, she did mention it. I'm not telling tales, as just we were talking, and it kind of came out in conversation. She told me you used to be a "professional girl" in the USA and Canada, that you had moved over there as a young girl and served your passage on a ship from Liverpool. That you had stowed away but were found halfway across the Atlantic, and it was a foreign crew. The skipper wanted to throw you overboard, to save any hassle with the USA's authorities. Still, the crew talked him out of it, as they had been taking it in turns to sleep with you.'

'Wow, that is just about everything; I did not know Borg knew the full story.'

She admitted she had already lost her virginity by the time she was seventeen – she had been having a hard time with her stepfather, and her mother would not hear a bad word about him. He made her give him a blow job once, and more or less raped her. She had told her mum, but she did not believe her; her mum had said she was lying, trying to cause friction between them. It was then that Karen had run away to Liverpool from her original home in Bradford.

She went on with the tale; I could not believe what she had been through.

'The place they took me to was more or less slavery. I had been sold to a guy who ran bordellos in North America. I had been used for about four years, moved from brothel to brothel, finishing up in St John's, Newfoundland. The only good thing to come out of my upbringing was the brothel owner knew he had to keep us girls looking tasty and healthy. We were checked out regularly by a doctor and always had a beautician and hairdresser in the brothels; they were more like gentlemen's clubs and hotels than actual dens of iniquity. We had learned to like sex; I had become addicted to it, and it was a way of keeping my sanity. I met Geoff one night, and he fell in love with me. I used to do a "special show" in the bar – none of the other girls would have anything to do with it, but I loved it. I would take all the men, one after another, in any orifice. My only stipulation was they must use condoms; my record was more than fifteen men. I must admit, even after that, I was insatiable – I still wanted more. I was crazy, out of my head; it was the only way I could live with myself. Then Geoff arrived, and he paid for me for twenty-four hours a day when he was in port. He did this to ensure no one else could have me.'

I was sitting there, fascinated with her story. How could she have lived through all of this and still be able to talk about it so openly?

'Then he went away and on his return he asked me to marry him.'

She jumped at the chance of freedom; she never found out how much Geoff had paid for her, as he never mentioned it again.

'I could fuck whoever I wanted when he was at home from sea, as long as he could watch. He always said it took him back to the brothel when he had watched other guys with me, but whenever he was away, I was not allowed to entertain anyone. I am surprised he has not suggested a bit of an orgy, but he wasn't sure how Einar and Borg would respond.'

I was thinking there would not be much point as Ein wouldn't be much good; mind, I wouldn't say no to a threesome with her and Borg if it could happen.

'If Ein had rung up to ask if you could visit, he would have put you all off, made some excuse not to see you,' Karen said. 'When Geoff has been away, if ever he found out that I had fucked anyone, he would kill me. That is why we live here; I never go off the complex. Leif, I am terrified of him. He has spies everywhere. I have slept with other men, guys who have come in to work on boats in the harbour. One young boy I have seduced a couple of times, but they are gone after the work is finished, no real trace. The only way in is by boat or with a pass to get past the barrier. If you have not informed the gate who you are visiting, you cannot bring a car in. All visitors are logged in – who you are meeting, what time you come in, and when you leave. Geoff got a printout when he came home of who had visited while he was away. Even if anyone asks for our address, it is logged. I am a prisoner here, Leif, a fucking prisoner. I hate the bastard.'

I could not believe what I was being told; they had moved into this house after he had it built in 1982; it was an upgrade to a newer, more expensive part of the marina. Why had he left her here with me then?

Was it a test to see if she would fuck me? And how would he find out if we did?

She told me he had taunted her ever since we had arrived. When he saw me naked, Geoff knew she would want me. He had said, 'Your golden God has arrived, but you can't have him.'

Now, this was a red rag to a bull when she said that. 'When did you last have sex, then?' I asked her.

'With someone when he was away? Apart from the young boy and a couple of others I just mentioned, a year ago Geoff was gone for three weeks on a job off the coast of India. We had a blocked drain, and I had to get a plumber in. We had a regular that Geoff had organised; he was about sixty-five, a guy who Geoff just knew would never have attempted anything. He'd been told the consequences if he did. But he was ill and could not come, so another guy came, only young and very horny. I could not resist the opportunity; the drain was not the only thing he opened up that day. Geoff went berserk when he found out about it; he accused me of organising it, and had me by the throat saying I had fucked the guy, then realised what he was doing and let go. I was lucky he believed me after days of arguing.'

I looked at her and said, 'OK, fuck him – come on, I want you.' I grabbed her hand, but she pulled away.

'No, don't – we can't. Please, Leif, don't – it's not worth it. He will know. I don't know how, but he will.'

I stood up and started stroking my manhood, getting it hard. 'Come on, you want me to, don't you?'

I put her hand on me; she stroked it, looking at it, and then she started to work me with long slow strokes. I could tell by the look in her eyes she was dying to take me.

'Karen, you know you want it as much as me.'

I was throbbing; it wasn't going to be in Castleford the way I felt.

Oh god, she was good; you could tell she had been a real pro. I had never been deep-throated; I had only ever seen Linda Lovelace do it on film. Still, Karen knew how to open her throat to take a penis; she'd learned the trick to help take the entire length into the back of the throat, and knew how to try breathing out while taking it in to help stop the gagging reflex.

I had never had a blow-job like it; I needed to fuck her now, but no, it was over. She said, 'No, I daren't do it.' She got up and went to her room. I tried to follow, but she locked me out.

I took a quick shower, left the house, and went for a walk. I said I would.

CHAPTER 23

LEIF

First Time for Everything

I had not realised what a fantastic place the village was with shops, bars and restaurants all within the complex. I had a few cold ones in a couple of the pubs and met some fascinating people. I was sitting outside one bar enjoying the scenery, so to speak, when a guy at the next table said, 'Hello, how are you today?'

I smiled and said, 'OK, thanks.' He got up from his table and came over, and asked if he could join me. He didn't give me much option as he was already sitting down; I couldn't very well say, 'No, fuck off.'

We chatted a while; he was one of those guys who, within half an hour, you feel you have known all your life. 'My name is Eric, by the way. Have you got a boat, then?'

'I am Leif – and it's Norwegian, before you ask,' I said. 'No, I am with friends. We have been touring the Isle of Wight; we came up here to see some old friends of theirs. Geoff and Karen Oswald – do you know them?'

'No, sorry, I don't believe so; where are you from? I don't seem to be able to recognise the accent.'

'I'm from Hull, East Yorkshire; ever been up there?'

'No, I haven't, but I have heard of the place – a big fishing port, isn't it? Had a few tragedies. I seem to believe I do remember reading something over the years. Wasn't there a famous triple trawler accident one Christmas time, I believe, then another? Er, the Gaul, wasn't it? Wasn't that supposed to be a spy ship around the mid-1970s? Let me think…

189

1974, if my memory serves me right?'

'Yes, you are right, Eric. How come you know about the tragedies? There have been quite a few apart from those – back in the 1950s the Lorella and Roderigo went down with all hands.'

'Yes, I recall reading about most of them. Wasn't there a lady called… oh, hang on, I will get it in a minute… Lilly Locker, was that her? No, not Locker… ha, yes – Big Lil Bilocca, that was her name? Big Lil – did she go to parliament or something?'

'Yes, she did; why do you know so much about Hull?'

'I have always taken an interest in the sea and love its history, that's all.'

'Do you have a boat in the marina?'

'Yes, I live in the village, on the other side in an apartment, but it came with a mooring as most of them did. I am a widower; my wife died a few years back. We sold up our house in Surrey and made a fortune on the sale, so we came down to Hythe and bought this place, and a boat, and retired. Can't take the fucker with you! The money, I mean, with no kids to hand it down to. Shame, I suppose, but that's life.'

I felt sorry for Eric; he seemed so lonely. He just needed company, I suppose. He told me he came here every day for a couple of hours to help pass the time.

'Fancy coming over to my place?' he said. 'Take a look at my boat, have a beer over there? It's not far to walk.'

Why not, I thought. I wasn't doing anything else; might as well do my good deed for the day.

'OK, fair enough,' I said, and we finished our drinks and set off to walk to his place; it was a lovely afternoon looking at all the different types of boat – yachts, motor cruisers, some old, some new.

Eric knew them all – who owned what, more or less what they cost to buy and run – the man was an encyclopaedia on boats and the village. We walked past one huge ship with three sails. 'Looks like a square-rigger, is that right, Eric? God, she is a beauty.'

'She is a barquentine, but the Americans would call her a barkentine, and yes, you are correct – some have four masts, square-rigged to the foremast and sometimes to the aft also.'

That 'short walk' had taken over an hour, what with the stopping now and again to say hello to people who knew Eric. He wasn't as lonely as it seemed, but nevertheless he was a widower living alone.

We arrived at his apartment building; his mooring was at the end of the jetty opposite his block. We walked down to his boat, Jenny Wren. I assumed Jenny was his wife's name, and I was right; he told me the boat was named after her, and Wren was his surname. We went on board; everything was spotless – it looked as it had never been used. And it hadn't. He told me it had never been through the lock gates. When I asked him why, he said he didn't have a skipper's ticket to go to sea and had no interest in sailing; he only wanted it to remind him of his wife. The man was a fucking idiot; what the hell was he on about? He was devoted to his late wife, but this was taking it a bit too far.

'You think I'm a fool, don't you Leif? Keeping this boat when I don't use it, just sitting outside my apartment. I suppose I am, but this was our dream, something we both wanted to do when we retired. The time had come for all this to happen, we made good money on our old place, the price was right here, we both were going to learn how to sail and get the correct documentation to allow us to sail her across to Europe, but she died before we managed it.'

There was a tear in his eye as we sat there in the lounge on his Jenny Wren. He went through her illness, and how sudden it was – from being diagnosed to passing away was just twelve weeks.

'She had liver disease; they didn't know what had caused it. She had cirrhosis of the liver, and it was too late to get a transplant, for your liver is the only organ that can regenerate itself with the help of a piece transplanted on to it. But we needed a donor. There was just not enough time; she was too far gone, no real warning.'

'You must have been devastated, Eric?'

'Yes, it was such a shock. First of all, they said it was the drink that had caused it, but she was teetotal, had never drunk.'

I just sat and listened and realised how lucky I was, and decided there and then that this would not happen to me. I would not grow old, alone in some apartment, with no one else but a dog.

We went into his apartment, which was immaculate, not a thing out of place. I don't know if he had OCD, but it was spotless.

'Fancy a beer, Leif, or something stronger?'

'I am a whisky man myself – what about you? What's your favourite?'

'I love Lagavulin – really like that one. I've tried a few over the years, but it is number one for me. I started on Glenfiddich years ago; it was one of the most popular, but then got into some of the classic malts, and the old "Laga" became my preferred whisky.'

'Here, try that – tell me what you think of it.' He handed me a glass with a good three-finger measure.

'Mmm, that's nice,' I said, as I put a hand over the glass and smelt the aroma. 'It's smooth – what is it? I think it's Irish.' I took a sip. 'I had some once before… wait a minute.' I took another sip and then another. 'Jameson 1780?'

'Fuck me, you are good,' he said. 'How did you know that, clever bastard?'

'I had some once and loved it; there are some good Irish whiskies produced, like Blackbush, which is a well-blended one. Tullamore Dew eighteen-year-old is very nice as well; bit expensive, but still – if you can afford it… Bushmills is another decent blended. Hyde No 6 is another I quite like. It's made with a blend of Irish single malt and Irish single grain whiskey. This whiskey has been coupled and allowed a finishing period in sherry casks before being bottled; it has a punchy, fruity sweetness with plenty of vanilla to back it up.'

I sounded like a whiskey salesman. I had read it in a magazine once and had remembered it.

'You know your whiskies, mate; I will give you that.' He was shaking his head. 'I thought I was good, but you beat me, mate; well done.'

I told him a story about when I once worked on a job and I met a whisky salesman in a hotel bar one night. We'd got chatting and were discussing whisky what I liked best. I asked him what was the most expensive bottle he had ever sold, and he told me £6,000. I could not remember the name of it, but he promised me it sold for £250 a shot, and people bought it; most of the pubs he sold it to kept it behind the bar in a locked cabinet.

I said to Eric, 'Mind if I ask you how old you are?'

'I am fifty-two. I was married to my wife for thirty-four years; we got wed when we were both eighteen. I've never had another woman, never wanted another woman.'

He started to cry, and I mean crying – he was sobbing. I went and sat next to him; he looked so, so sad. I put my arm around his shoulders and cuddled him to me; I felt so fucking sorry for him. Now, I had never held a man close to me like this before; it felt so strange to be cuddling a man. It wasn't my thing but it felt right for Eric.

He finally stopped crying and was sniffing like a little kid does when they have a crying session. He did not move away from me; he was relaxed. Then he got up and went into the next room, which I imagined was the bathroom. He was gone a good few minutes. I was getting worried about him. After a bit more time passed, I called out, 'Eric, you OK, mate? You OK in there?'

No reply. Then the door opened, and he came back.

'Whoa, now just a minute, Eric – you got me wrong, mate.'

He was now wearing a woman's dress, blonde wig, high heels – the works.

'No, it's Erica now.' He walked over to me and took my hand in his.

I pulled away and stood up.

He was standing with his hand on his hip. 'But I thought you liked me, the way you listened to me, the way you held me close so tenderly... I hoped you wanted me. I want you to make love to me like Jenny used to.'

Now my mind was whizzing. 'Like Jenny used to? What do you mean, like Jenny did... you mean...'

'Yes, we had a strap-on she used on me. Oh, I miss her so much.'

'You had a what? A strap-on, like a dildo?'

'Yes, it was so good – it was her idea; she said she wanted me to feel the enjoyment she had in our sex lives. Please, Leif, make love to me as Jenny did.'

Now, this was uncharted waters for me – no way. 'Sorry, mate, not my scene. I am off – bye.'

I got out of there as quickly as I could. The last thing I heard was him crying again and calling my name. I ran out of the apartment block and down the road; why, I don't know. It was probably in the hope he wasn't going to chase me through the marina dressed like a woman. I stopped and looked back; he was not following me. I came to a bar and had to have a drink. Well, that was a new one; it did absolutely nothing for me, and there was no way could I be homosexual.

I got back to the house, and after my near-miss with Erica, or whatever he wanted to call himself, and after my conversation with Karen, I just had to have her; I wanted to feel her body against mine. I had made love to lots of women; none had ever used their lips on me like she had done this morning. I wanted her, even if it meant Geoff would be watching us.

I was now thinking about how I could plan a session with the two women. How would I approach Geoff? Or maybe that was why he had suggested he take the others away. I hoped I was right.

The others arrived back around 8.30pm. They had been on the piss; all of them were more than merry. Was this the opportune time to bring up the subject of a session?

'Hello, Leif, had a good day? We have; you should have come with us,' said Borg. I told them I had been OK, had a walk around the marina, a few beers here and there, nothing too hectic.

'See any fanny you fancied on your travels, mate?' asked Geoff. I told him I'd seen a couple of beauties lying on the sundeck of a boat over near the pub, and that I would have loved a sandwich with those two.

'You ever had a threesome, mate? I have; it's awesome, right, Karen?' said Geoff, winking at his wife. She just smiled and nodded.

I told him I had never had that pleasure. Ein and Borg were not saying much; they just sat listening. I kept looking at Borg to see if there was any reaction, but not a lot was coming from her face. Ein also was not giving much away, which surprised me a little.

It was getting late, and Ein was nodding off in his chair; Borg kept telling him to go to bed. Every time she did, he woke up, shook his head, rubbed his eyes, and said, 'OK, OK, I'm not tired.'

The same thing happened at least on six separate occasions. In the end, she got up, grabbed him by the hand, and took him to their room, saying, 'Good night all – see you in the morning.'

We all said our goodnights; it was still a warm, beautiful night – shorts weather again. Karen was looking fabulous in a bikini bottom, with a silk sarong wrapped around her ample arse. Oh, how I wanted her.

'Fancy another drink, Leif, just a nightcap?' asked Geoff.

'OK, might as well as wish I had.'

He brought me over another whisky; I was getting very fond of this amber nectar.

With that, Borg returned.

'He is hard on now; who wants to be?' she smiled as she dropped her robe, walking towards us, bending down, and then kissing Karen full on the lips.

Oh my fucking god… Karen put her arms around her neck, returning the kiss. It was a full-on snog, tongues the lot; I was solid instantly.

Geoff stood up. 'Well, that looks good enough to eat,' he said, staring at Borg's arse stuck up in the air, and he dropped his shorts, standing there stroking himself. He, too, was soon erect. My, he was a big boy when horny, that was for sure. I wondered what he was going to do with it, but he never moved, just stood there stroking, his eyes closed.

The girls had moved on to one of the double blow-up beds they used in the pool. They were now quickly into the sixty-nine positions, not wasting any time at all.

Karen was on top; she looked up and licked her lips, and mouthed, 'Come on, now we are yours.'

I was over like a rocket. Karen sat up and knelt over Borg's face for the second time that day; oh fuck, it was good.

I looked over at Geoff; he was now lying on a deck, no longer watching us, with the biggest smile on his face.

I was already at Bradford, but the train was at the station. Borg was stroking in between my legs, touching my arse; wow, I do love that. I don't know why, I just do. My shaft was throbbing; I needed Karen. I said to myself, sorry, Borg, you have had me, but Karen is a virgin to my shaft, so it was going to be her to feel me first.

I pulled myself out of Karen's mouth and told her to lie next to Borg, who was now rubbing herself and moaning. Karen laid back; I went over her, missionary position, on my knees. I entered her slowly at first; she was tight considering she used to take fifteen cocks a night at her best. But I could feel her gripping me as I pushed him home. Oh my god, it was so good. I felt her nails digging into the cheeks of my arse; I was well on my way to Wigan, now at Salford at least, but willing myself not to climax.

I heard Borg orgasm, shouting out Einar's name as she climaxed time after time; she came over, kissing Karen, and rubbing her fingers on her lips.

What an experience this was. I was still pumping Karen as she came up and kissed me; I was close to Workington. I was almost there.

'No, don't – we want to share your juice, baby,' whispered Borg.

With that, I pulled out. I didn't want to, but I did it. I was solid, and it was glistening in the moonlight. I stood up – both of them were on their knees taking turns on me. That was it – I reached Derwent Park and they were both kneeling, their mouths wide open, like two eagle chicks in a nest waiting for the mother to feed them.

I shot my load, and what an amount – I had never seen so much semen come out of me. They then kissed, licking the drops off each other's faces. Wow, I wished I had a movie camera to record the scene. Still, I needn't have bothered. I had forgotten all about Geoff when I realised he had been recording it all on a mini camcorder he had. He was still stroking, and as I watched, he unloaded all over the decking.

I had never seen one of those cameras before; he shook his shaft, squeezed the last drop out, and came over. 'Great film, guys – here, look.' He re-ran the tape and then showed us on the tiny screen on the side that pulled out. It was unreal watching us fucking, really horny – I loved it. I was a porn star.

The girls were hugging each other as we watched the orgy being played out on the screen, then they kissed again, both giggling like teenagers.

I asked Geoff where he had got the camera from and he told me that it he'd bought it from a guy in Holland who told him it was not on sale yet, but it had been stolen from a factory innovations laboratory and was one of just two available anywhere in the world; it had cost him a fortune,

'But what's money? It uses standard 8mm cassettes; it's the only one yet developed with a screen on the side.'

It just showed what you could buy if you had the money. I wanted to be in that league one day; I didn't know how, but I was confident I would do it.

We all relaxed after our session. Geoff reminded me, very forcefully, I might add, that when we were alone, I could not make love to his wife unless he was there. Otherwise, there would be consequences, 'You understand, Leif, don't you? I don't give a fuck how big you are, but you will die. I have the ways and means, OK?'

It sounded like some sinister baddie from a James Bond movie. I understood, but, fuck Geoff, I thought – I would have her again before we left, and alone. I was going to leave Leif's seed inside her.

We had been there nearly a week enjoying their hospitality, loving every second of our stay, when Borg came out with the bombshell that we would be leaving tomorrow to travel back across to the Isle of Wight to complete our little holiday. I was really pissed off.

CHAPTER 24

LEIF

It Just Had to Happen

I had not made love to Karen yet; I'd not had a chance to get her on her own. Little did I know that today was going to be the day. She had overheard Geoff and Ein planning a fishing trip with a friend of Geoff's; they were going to ask me to go with them, and she told me this when we were left alone just before breakfast that morning.

'You don't want to go, do you, babe? Please stay with me today. You can fuck me properly this time.'

I smiled. 'What about Borg?'

'She wanted to go shopping in Southampton with me, but I told her that I had started my period this morning. I haven't, but Borg doesn't know this, and she accepted the excuse. She said she would go alone as she needed some "me time" – so it's just me and you.'

We were having breakfast. I complained of a stinking migraine coming on; I didn't have a migraine, but they did not know that either.

'Oh, sorry to hear that, mate; that fucks the idea of a fishing trip I had planned for today with you and Ein here,' said Geoff.

'Don't let me stop you. I am going back to bed – can't stand this sunlight,' I said, even though I was wearing sunglasses – what an actor.

Geoff chipped in, 'You sure, mate? We don't want to leave you if you are feeling bad.'

'No, honestly, I will be OK; they take about six hours to pass. I will be OK by the time you get back. I just don't want to be around other people. I am sorry if I have spoiled your plans. Please excuse me; I am off back to my room.'

An hour must have passed. I had fallen asleep when I heard my door open; I pretended to be still asleep. I heard Karen whisper, 'Leif, baby, you awake?'

I was lying face-down on the bed, naked with a sheet over me; I felt her hand on my shoulder, her soft touch.

'Baby,' she whispered as she stroked my back, her fingers going down my spine. I opened my eyes, turned to face her, and smiled.

'Hi, babe, I knew you would come. They all gone, then, I assume? Just you and me, eh?'

She got in under the sheet; she was naked, and I felt her firm breasts against my back. We embraced, our lips touched, and her tongue entered my mouth; fucking hell, it was even better than the orgy session. I rolled on to my back, and she climbed on board, already wet; she opened up as she slid down on to me.

We were at Wigan within minutes. 'Wow, baby, you were horny – hope that's not it? That all I get?'

She got off and slid down my body like a snake, and I felt her caress my limp dick, kissing it and licking it.

'I love cocks when they are like this,' she said. 'So natural in this state.'

She continued the foreplay; it tickled like hell. As any man will tell you once you have ejaculated, it is hard to have anyone touch you, even yourself; it's all in the mind, supposedly. Still, I kind of wanted her to stop, but something was telling me to carry on, to be a soldier – where is your will to win? Fight on, son.

She was not having a lot of luck; she came up, we kissed gently, and cuddled up for a rest. All of a sudden, she got up quickly and went out of the room, returning within a couple of minutes with Geoff's camcorder. 'Here, let's watch our threesome; that will get you horny, babe.'

We lay there, her head on my chest as I held the machine. It was amazing watching the film while the girl I was fucking was lying next to me, stroking my penis and rubbing her thumb around the head, using my juice as a lubricant.

It didn't take long. It was hard again; we made love, again and again, all afternoon. When we got to the fourth time, I was spent, blowing hot air.

What a wonderful, sexy, beautiful woman. An expert in the field of intercourse and all the added extras. Once again, I think it was the fact that we were doing something wrong – a bit like drinking under-age; it's more fun when you know you shouldn't be doing it.

I had fulfilled my promise to myself – I was going to have her. In the end, it was she who had me, but who was arguing… she was yet another one who will be in my mind when they put the screws in the coffin.

When everyone arrived back, we decided to go out to one of the marina restaurants. We had a great night – fantastic company, excellent food and expensive wine. Oh, how I wanted this life one day, but I knew I would not get it working for someone else. I needed another way to earn some money, but how, that was the question.

Back at the house, everyone was fucked – two of us more than the others. It was Ein and Borg who said they were going to bed first; it was going to be a big day tomorrow, as they'd be up early to get the boat ready for the trip across to Cowes. I said I would not be long before I joined them, not in their bed, but going to retire.

Geoff got up and asked Karen if she was ready. 'In a few minutes, babe,' she replied.

'I'm off,' said Geoff, 'I'm knackered – that fishing took it out of me. See ya in the morning.' He gave Karen a peck on the cheek.

'Fuck you,' Karen whispered as he went out.

I looked at her, raising my eyebrows. 'What's wrong? What's he done?'

She told me Geoff had given her the third degree when he had got home from his fishing trip, accusing her of coming on to me all the time. He had said, 'Bet you wish you could have fucked Leif yesterday, when you were alone – it's a wonder you didn't try today.' But he knew she wouldn't dare, or he would kill her.

'I have had enough. I am going to leave him. I have even dreamt about killing him. I have been trying to think of a way of getting rid of him, but I just have no idea how to do it.'

I was waiting for the question… would I help her? Had she been setting me up for this last night? The sex we had – was that the carrot to get me on her side? She was a great fuck, but not that good, not good enough to turn me into a murderer – no way. I had too much living to do.

She went on about it, but I wanted out; no way was I getting involved with a murder.

'Karen, it's not worth that. You have a good life – not great, but a good life. You fucked guys for a living once. I'm not insulting you, but he brought you out of that life, and you were grateful – you said it yourself, you grabbed the chance with both hands. Just accept it. You have all this – what more could you want?'

'Leif, are you blind? Do I need to spell it out? It's you I want. It's you. I love you, baby; these last few days have shown me what I want is a normal relationship, and I want it with you.'

Oh my god, how the hell would I get out of this? I knew one day that my philandering would get me into bother, that my messing with the opposite sex would come and bite me in the arse – and this was some hell of a bite.

What a trip this had been; how many things could happen to a guy in two weeks? I had met the odd couple, become a nudist, been tapped up by a guy in a dress, and had a threesome. Now an ex-prostitute wanted me to run away with her or murder her husband, who was a pirate and a psychopath; you couldn't write a film script like it.

I did not know what to say. I was in above my head. She had not moved; she just sat there looking at me, waiting for a response. Help me, I was thinking. Allow me to give me an excuse to say something.

'OK,' said Karen. 'I understand what I have just told you may have shaken you. You don't have to say anything; I'm sorry. I get it – you don't love me, not enough to kill my husband. I will have to do it myself.'

With that, she got up, came over, took my head in her hands, and kissed me. 'Good night, babe, it was good meeting you.' With that, she was gone.

I sat there for a while; my head was spinning. I had got out of it – no, she had let me out of the situation. Thank fuck, I said to myself.

The following day we were all up around six having breakfast; everything was normal. I could not believe that, after what Karen had told me last night, she could act like nothing had happened.

We had one more coffee, and Ein said, 'Sorry, but we have to get going.' He stood up and kissed Karen; Geoff hugged him, then came to me and did the same. Borg joined in the hugging session, and within a few minutes, we had said our goodbyes and were on our way back to the Blue Moon and our trip.

We had left the marina and were heading into the Channel when Borg said, 'Well, that was different, wasn't it? A change of scenery. I really like those guys; they're two of my favourite people. I enjoyed myself being on dry land for a few days. What about you Leif, what do you think?'

'Yes, I enjoyed their company. He was a bit of an oddball, but everyone to their own, I suppose. He was different; a hell of a life he has lived. Karen – well, what can I say? She is one beautiful woman.'

'And a great shag, eh? I loved our session, Leif,' Borg added.

Ein wasn't saying much; there was a bit of a swell on and he was concentrating on steering the boat, as there was quite a lot of traffic around.

We arrived in Cowes late afternoon and pulled into the berth we had left; my car was still there. Ein asked me if I wanted to stay for one more night in the Blue Moon, but I decided it was best I got going. I thanked him so much for my last few weeks' holiday. It's one I will never forget; we had such fun. Also, them teaching me about being a nudist. I enjoyed the freedom, even allowing me to make love to his wife, and the introduction to Geoff and Karen.

We said our goodbyes; Ein gave me his business card and told me to keep in touch, as he was often in Holland, still acting as a consultant to some companies and even countries.

My two-week break had turned into nearly a month; I wasn't complaining, but it was time I headed home. Borg was in tears as I walked down the gangplank to my car, and as I drove away, I waved farewell, and I was gone. Another chapter in my life over – a few more boxes ticked, along with a few more boxes I did not know I was looking for.

CHAPTER 25

LEIF
Heading for Home

I drove back to Ryde and managed to get on the last ferry back to Portsmouth; my aim was to go as far as possible until I was too tired to drive any further. It was not the best plan or the safest, but I wanted to get back to Hull as soon as possible. I had missed the old place, as well as the decent beer – that southern stuff was piss.

I had been advised to follow the Fossway, an old Roman road that ran from Leicester to Chippenham, then the A36 to Portsmouth. I took their advice and hit the Fossway. In a couple of hours I decided another two hours would be enough, and I would look for a bed for the night. I was hardly keeping my eyes open when I reached Stow-on-the-Wold and decided to stop there. I booked in the Kings Arms, an old-world-type pub/hotel, and after a couple of pints and a great meal I hit the sack.

I slept like the proverbial baby, woke at seven, had a shower and then went down for a full English – which was tremendous. I then set off on my way again. I had thought it would take me about four hours to get home. I was wrong – it took me nearly five. I went straight home to my place in Hessle as I hadn't spent much time there. I got my washing done, not that I had that much, having been nude most of the time. I had enjoyed it more than I ever imagined I would when Borg had told me it was compulsory on the boat. I know I had had a little dabble all those years ago with Jenny in Devon, but that was only one day – in fact, not even a day, just the walk on a beach undressed. I hadn't been spending days on end wearing anything but a smile.

205

Yes, I liked it and would look into doing more of it, not even just for the sex, but the feeling of freedom, feeling the wind and sun on my body, felt so natural. Maybe that was why they called themselves naturists and not nudists, but it had me hooked.

I went round to Mum's the next day; it was all the usual stuff, happy to see me, all that shit. I was beginning to think I was an oddball, being the only one – well, that is not correct; I wasn't – but the only one that was in the frame, so to speak. Anyway, I liked my own space; I was not into families, and always being at parents' houses every week. Like when I left Mum, I did not say, 'Bye, Mum, love you' or any of that waffle – I loved being on my own. I did not envy kids with brothers and sisters; it did not bother me one bit.

The following day, the naturist thing was still on my mind, so I made enquiries at the local library. I found that there was one of the oldest naturist societies in the UK just outside Hull. On the way to Hornsea, delighted with my find, I decided to look into this. First of all, I gave them a call; no time like the present, strike while the iron's hot, and all that. The number rang for a while, and I was just about to put the phone down when a woman answered. 'Hello, Natsun here, can I help you?'

I explained that I was interested in visiting the club if possible, and she asked me if I was a member of any other society. I told her I wasn't, and she asked if I had any experience of being in a naturist environment, and why I wanted to visit.

I explained that many years ago as a teenager I had been to Devon, and I told her about the visit to the beach that day, then went on to tell her about my last two weeks in the Isle of Wight and the boat journey. I said I had enjoyed the feeling of freedom and was looking to get involved, and that I thought it was a great way to spend my leisure time.

'OK, you sound genuine,' she said. 'When would you like to visit?'

She explained that I would need two towels with me – one to use after swimming, the other to place on any seats I sat on as they had a 'no bare bums on seats' rule, which sounded fair enough. She also told me they had an 'even numbers' rule at the club, where they tried to keep up equal numbers of single members. Families came as families, so that did not matter, but they wanted similar numbers of single men and women, and at the moment, they had a vacancy for a single man.

I asked when it would be convenient to visit, and she told me any time I liked. 'But to be honest, the sooner, the better.'

It was Friday; I asked, 'Is tomorrow OK?'

'Perfect – there are always more people here over the weekend. Most of them bring tents and camp out in the grounds. We have plenty of room; over twenty-five acres of woodland is available. Even if they are local, it saves them going home; if you don't have a tent, we always have the odd one available to borrow – all you need is a sleeping bag, for let's be honest, Yorkshire weather is not that hot all the time, especially at night.'

'OK, I will visit you tomorrow.'

Once I had taken a look, I would look into buying a tent and camping equipment. The lady had said most of the members used the camp kitchen and the cafe to eat as it was run on a no-profit system, keeping costs down. They bought in bulk, so you could not eat as cheaply if you bought it and cooked it yourself. Sounded great. I could not wait for tomorrow to come.

I set off the next morning and arrived around 10am. The place, at the end of a country lane, took some finding, but it had taken me less than an hour to get there from Hessle Road.

I went into the reception and was taken aback; the lady on the front desk was naked. She must have been in her early fifties, and was rather well endowed in the top half of her body. She was not fat but cuddly, someone you would love to snuggle up in bed with on a cold night, and with a lovely smile.

'Hello, how can I help you?' she said. I recognised the voice; it was the lady I had spoken to yesterday.

'Hi, my name is Leif – Leif Askenes. I spoke to you yesterday.'

She stopped for just a second, then remembered the conversation, 'Oh, yes, pleased to meet you, Leif, thanks for coming; my name is Molly. Did you bring your passport with you? I need this form completed for identification. All the club records are entirely confidential and kept locked away in the club's safe, for we respect the members' privacy at all times. The membership fees can be paid yearly in advance or monthly, but it is cheaper up front. I told you, didn't I, about the opportunity that we have for a single male member and that they don't come round that often. If for any reason you decide you don't like it, you can leave at any time. We will refund the remaining fees quarterly, which means if you went in the first three months, you will get nine months back, and so forth.'

'That seems OK to me, Molly.'

'Now, as a day visitor, it is £3.50 a day or £20 a week, or membership is £100 a year. Well, what do you think? I will take £3.50 for today and, should you like it and decide you would like to join, I will knock the £3.50 off the yearly membership; how about that?'

I could not argue; she seemed such a lovely lady. I hoped they were all like her.

'Oh, by the way, you can have a look round whenever you want to, but you must undress in either of the attached changing rooms to the indoor pool and gymnasium; there are lockers in there, a lot like the ones at swimming baths, where the key is on a rubber wristband. Don't forget to take your towels with you and remember the NBBOS rule.'

I went straight for it – into the changing rooms, and stripped off. Believe it or not, I was feeling a bit apprehensive about the situation. I mean, these were total strangers to me, and to be wandering around naked was going to be a bit of an ordeal, but nevertheless, on I went.

I walked out of the rooms, towels in hand; the first people I bumped in to were a family of four, a couple about my age with two kids, a boy about twelve and a daughter about fifteen. We exchanged pleasantries; they didn't have a Hull accent, but sounded like they were from West Yorkshire. They asked if I was new as they had not seen me before.

'It's my first day,' I said.

They told me it was great and that I would love it. Mike, the father, said, 'If you fancy a beer, we are just in the first clearing round the "squirrel run". We have a tent there, you can't miss it – blue with side bedroom – call round!' And off they went.

Off I continued with my tour of the site. Molly had given me a map showing all the different areas and it included details about what was available in each one. The woodlands contained a wide variety of wildlife, including deer, rabbits, stoats, pheasants and owls. There were cabins around the grounds, built mainly by the owners themselves, and they were hidden from view, very secluded. There were also areas for touring caravans, pitches that could be rented by the year for those who preferred that to camping.

I was getting hooked on this sort of 'leisure' activity; the further I went on my trek, the more people I met. Most of them were families; I had not yet met any single people, either male or female.

CHAPTER 26

LEIF

Natsun

The sun was shining; it was a lovely day. I found a clearing just off the track not far past the owl sanctuary. I put my bath towel down with the smaller one rolled up for a pillow, lay back, and closed my eyes.

The sun felt great on my skin; it wasn't too hot and wasn't burning me – it just felt beautiful. I must have nodded off, for when I looked at my watch, it was 3.30pm. I heard female voices coming down the track. I closed my eyes and pretended to be asleep. As they got closer, I heard one girl say softly, 'Hey, Sue, look over there – he's new. I've not seen him before. Look at that body.'

'Oh my god, he is gorgeous,' replied the other girl. 'I fancy lying next to him. Wow, just look at him.'

'Do you think he is married, then?' Sue muttered.

'No, there are no family vacancies that I know of – only for a single guy. This must be him, or he would not be out here on his own. I would not let him out of my sight if he were my bloke.'

I was trying not to get erect. Batley, Bradford, Bramley… it was working again, but it was difficult, believe me. I didn't want to be thrown out on my first day. I was also still shaved, although the stubble was showing a bit now. I slowly opened my eyes and rubbed them, pretending I had just awoken. I sat up; the two girls were about thirty feet away, maybe a bit more, but still staring at me. When they saw me wake up, they looked away.

'Hello, how are you two? Lovely day, isn't it?' They were both in their

211

early twenties, I guessed, but beautiful girls; one a redhead with the whitest skin you ever did see, the other a blonde, and a genuine blonde at that. Both had great bodies; things were picking up, for sure.

They both said hello in unison, then started giggling when they realised what they had just done. 'Hello, I am Lynn; I have not seen you before. Where are you from? And this is Sue, my friend.'

'Yes, I am new, and from Hull, here on my own,' I said, just to put them right on their initial comments. They both looked at each other and smiled. 'I am Leif – want to sit down for a chat, or are you standing there all day? I won't bite, not at first, anyway.' They both giggled again and came over.

It seemed unreal to sit chatting with two gorgeous young women, all of us naked, with no form of sexual scenarios entering my head. They told me they were single members who had been coming here for years, first of all with their parents but now, as they had gone past the age of eighteen, they were full members. Their parents had caravans on the site and came most weekends, but this week and next, they were in Sweden on a naturist holiday; it seemed they went there every year.

They both worked in Hull, Sue at Marks & Spencer and Lynn at Smith & Nephew. 'In the office,' Lynn added quickly. They asked me where I lived, again, what I did for a living, how often I came to the club, why I had joined… a list of questions. We were getting along great, and funnily enough, I'd not had a dirty thought when we chatted. Once or twice I noticed the girls looking at my groin area but they looked away when I made individual eye contact. I asked if they had boyfriends, and they both said they were not seeing anyone 'right now' and were not looking.

'We enjoy our own space,' was one comment from Sue.

'Boys are such a nuisance; I prefer older men anyway myself,' said Lynn, blushing when she realised what she had said.

I just laughed and said, 'Good choice.' I looked at my watch, realising the time. 'I am hungry. Is the food OK here?' They both said it was plain and basic, but good.

'The burgers are great – homemade. The lady who runs the bar and cafe makes it all, and it's cheap,' said Lynn.

'Well, who fancies a burger and chips? I am sure I do. Will you ladies join me?'

I stood up and offered my hand for them to stand up. They both took each hand, and I lifted them; it was the first time we had made physical contact, and it was nice.

We walked back to the cafe area, all so natural – me with my bath sheet over my shoulder and carrying the smaller one, the girls taking their small towels, and no handbags. This was great; I loved it.

We sat outside at some picnic tables; they were right. The food was terrific; the chips tasted like they were cooked in lard, just like Hessle Road fish shop chips. The burgers were thick and juicy, cooked to perfection; you won't starve here, son, I thought.

I had seen enough to know I wanted to spend more time here when I was home. I decided to go and buy a tent. I hadn't a clue what I needed or where I could get one from in Hull, but I was going to get into this naturist life without a doubt.

We finished our food, and the girls said they were going back to the van; if I fancied a walk, we could have a coffee back there. Was this a plan to get their way with me, or was that just wishful thinking? I agreed – maybe I would get a chance?

As we were walking along, Sue said to me, 'By the way, Leif, this is not an invitation for your leg over, understand? Neither of us fuck on our first date. OK, maybe second.' She burst out laughing. Lynn was holding back, then she started grinning as well.

'OK, OK, I get it, no worries – you are both safe with me.'

We walked a bit further, then the track turned to the right. On the left were the vans, two of them more or less side by side and a small tent in between. I asked what the tent was for, and they told me it was storage; they had four bikes in there.

'Good idea.'

'Yes, the woodland is massive, and you can get away from people if you have a bike and know where to go; there are some very secluded spots.' They had that look in their eyes. An ulterior motive was on my mind.

I played the gentleman; I didn't want to spoil a great day. I had a coffee, once again I was sitting with two young naked beauties on a gorgeous English summer's day. Paradise, one could say.

It was time for me to go. I had outstayed my welcome and decided I would leave the girls in peace. 'OK, I'm off,' I said. 'Thanks for a great afternoon. I will see you both again, no doubt?'

They both stood up and hugged me; then each one, in turn, kissed me – not on the cheeks, but on the mouth, a full snog-type kiss. I must have jerked down below, but they said nothing. Now, that was a pleasant surprise. I bid both of them farewell, and I was gone before I tried my hand.

I got back to the changing rooms and into my civvies, and met up with Molly in the office.

'Hi, Leif, enjoy our little oasis? Had a good day, I hope?'

'I have enjoyed it, Molly, so much I want to join. I would like to take up the single membership you have vacant right now, OK?'

I told her I could pay cash if she wanted it and he nodded as she was making the registration form out.

'There you go, Leif – just put in your address, etc.; all the rest is completed. You only need to pay a deposit today, as it has to be verified by the committee; they meet on Tuesday next week. You can still come back; we will not charge you, as you are now a member, but if for some reason they decide you are not suitable… which they won't, as I am chairwoman.' She giggled, 'It's a formality, so that will be £25 today, is that OK?'

I paid my deposit and thanked Molly for her help; just as I was leaving, I asked her if she knew the best place to get a tent from in the area. She looked up for a minute or so, biting the inside of her mouth as if some voice from above was going to give her the answer. 'Right, yes… Hull does not have that many camping shops. The best place with the biggest choice is in York.' She looked under the counter and came up with a little card. 'It's outside York on the way to Scarborough; you can't miss it – they sell caravans and everything. Leif, I know it's early doors, but we do have a space for a caravan going next month. One of our older members passed away, and his family are taking the van away. They want to use it for touring, so if you are interested, just let me know. It has not been advertised yet. I do know none of the current members are keen, as they already have vans, so it could be a chance if you are interested. At £150 a year ground rent it's a good deal, and you can also leave it over the winter if you have nowhere to store it, at no extra charge. There is an extra charge of five pounds a week for electric; we sell bottled gas at £15 a bottle, which would last a small van about six months.'

What a saleswoman she was. Once again, she had me hooked. 'OK, Molly, I will think that one over – next month you say?' She nodded and gave me the thumbs up.

The next day, I went to the caravan dealers to buy a tent; they had all types on display indoors. It was quite pleasant walking around. There were no nagging salespeople. One guy came up, asked what I was looking for, and just said, 'If you need any help I will be over in the office, OK?'

As I wandered, there were a couple of tents I fancied – both the modern frame type with inner rooms. One had two separate bedrooms and a living area in the middle, with an awning-type thing that came out the front. The other had three different rooms – it was huge, but expensive for what it was. I took my time, and then the sales guy came back. I told him what I was looking for and he suggested a small second-hand caravan, of which they had quite a few that they were trying to sell off to bring in more stock. I was thinking that they might be a bit too much money for what I wanted to spend, and even the tents were a bit more than I had expected. Still, I decided to take a look. As the guy had said, there were quite a few on display but they were not really what I was looking for. To be quite frank, I did not know what I was looking for – really just a bed and somewhere to get out of the rain, which we get quite a lot of, I am sorry to say.

The cheapest one they had with a fixed bed was £3,000, which seemed a lot of money; they had another one that was a bit more reasonable, but it was only a two-berth, which would not have left anywhere to sit when the bed was made up. That was just a grand. It was old, but as I would not be towing it around, I supposed it would do. It was not much more expensive than the tents I was looking at, but I still wasn't sure.

'We will deliver it to the Hull area free of charge as we are always in that part of the country,' he said.

'Thank you, I will think about it,' I said, and left.

I came away a bit disappointed, but still wanted to get something to put on the Natsun camp.

I was in the King Edward pub that night talking to a couple of old schoolmates I had not seen for quite a while. We were discussing this and that when Billy asked me what I had been up to today. I told him about buying a tent or a caravan to put on a pitch near Hornsea. I didn't mention it was a naturist site; I kept that secret to myself, for now anyway.

I told him about the vans I had seen in the York place when one of the other lads, Ken, who was standing near us at the bar, said, 'You got a minute, Leif? I might be able to help you on your van thing.'

He moved away from the bar and gestured to me to go over to him, which I did. I always was a sucker for the mystery thing.

'Look, I overheard your conversation – I'm not being nosy, but I work at a caravan company in Hull and know of a guy who kind of borrows brand-new vans. He is a delivery contractor, and he has, well, what you might say is an arrangement with someone at our place. They take three vans at a time, that is a full load, mainly two to three-berth; he can get larger ones to order. They are, as to be expected, more expensive, but still a hell of a lot cheaper than the actual cost if it is a bigger van. He tows that one out with the other three but only now and again as the larger trailers are made to order and are a much greater risk to take than the others they turn out by the hundreds, and there is no security control. They go through the manufacturing system out into the compound, where they are checked over, and if they find any snags, they then go into a different workshop to be put right. This shop is off-site and no control of what is where ever takes place.'

I was all ears.

'The only way of identifying a van is a plate attached to the chassis,' continued Ken. 'He takes it off and replaces it with another with a number that means fuck all. Virtually untraceable. What do you think?'

He was looking around to make sure no one was listening, then added, 'I do know that they have two customers for the end of the month and are looking for another. Would you be interested?'

'Ken, how much do they ask? Do you know the going rate?'

'£1,000 cash in hand, no questions asked, delivered to your house or wherever.'

Now I was interested. I told him I had to make a phone call – it was 7pm, but I knew Molly would be still on reception at Natsun, and I needed to contact her ASAP.

I went to the public phone in the bar and rang the number. As before, it rang for ages and I was just about to put the phone down when she answered.

'Hello, Natsun Holiday Park. Can I help you?'

'Molly, it's me, Leif; how are you? Can you spare me a minute, please?'

'Of course, what can I do for you?'

'Is that caravan pitch still free?'

'Yes, it is. Do you want it?'

'Yes, but not for a week. Would that be OK?'

'That was a quick decision. Have you got yourself a van? You don't mess about, do you?'

'Yes, I have ordered a brand-new van, but it won't be delivered until the next Saturday morning, is that OK? The last Saturday in the month.'

What I didn't tell her was they did some sort of stock check on a Sunday morning.

'No problem,' she said, 'as long as you come in tomorrow and pay the rent for the year, the pitch is yours.'

It gave me a chance to go in and see where the pitch was and make arrangements.

'You are a star, Molly – thanks for your help. Take the site off availability as it is now mine, OK?'

'No problem, I will do that, and I look forward to seeing you tomorrow.'

I went back to Ken and told him I wanted a van – a three-bed if possible. 'OK, I need to make a call now,' he said, and disappeared.

A few minutes later he came back and told me it was on, and gave me the address where I could meet the caravan dealer – I say 'dealer' loosely – and a phone number to contact him on. He had told him he had known me for years and could verify I was OK, and that I could keep my mouth shut. He told me to ring him right away, tell him who I was, and to arrange a meeting.

I went back to the phone and rang the number; a voice answered – they didn't give a name.

'Oh, hi, Ken just told me to ring you; it is about the van you discussed with him.'

'OK, right. Now, I have an old warehouse near the docks where I take the vans straight from the factory. Here I remove the plate and replace it. We then take them using three separate cars with phony number plates on with a set already attached to the van, then take them to whatever address. Where do you want it delivering to?'

'Natsun Holiday Park on the way to Hornsea, is that OK?'

'Never heard of it, but no worries, I will find it. I guarantee to be on-site before 3pm that next week. I will deliver yours personally; all I want from you is a £25 deposit, the rest to be paid on delivery. I must add, no one must know where you got the van from, or there will be consequences, do you understand?'

'No worries.'

I had to go round to his address and pay him the deposit to fix the deal. The following day, I did, and then went straight out to Natsun to pay for the site. Molly was once again on reception; did she ever have time off?

We went through the paperwork; she told me she was surprised I had gone to the lengths of buying a caravan, and a brand new one at that, as I had only just joined the club.

I told her I was taken by the setup there and loved it. I had been travelling with work most of my life and was hoping to settle down; it meant I had somewhere to go and relax – even more important should I go back to working away. The opportunity may not arise again. I told her I had looked at tents, etc., but the caravan seemed more of a holiday home. We shook hands on the deal, and that was that. I hadn't even seen where it was on the site. I went into the changing room and stripped off, ready to go out on to the camp.

We walked about 100 yards past the other vans and into a secluded area surrounded by trees, and there it was – a pitch with an electric hook-up point. The communal shower block was between my pitch and the others; they also had a waste point and black water point at the same location. Molly told me the pitch I had was put in as an extra to a switchboard that was ready to take more pitches when they expanded the site, but there were no plans at the moment for that; therefore, I should be on my own for a year or two, which sounded great to me.

'The member who had passed away had only been on this pitch for about a year,' said Molly. 'That was when they had decided to do a bit of an expansion but didn't go any further.'

'Molly, I am not sure what you are talking about regarding waste and black water. I have no idea what is on a modern caravan.'

'The black water is from your toilet; they come in a cassette form nowadays. You pour in some blue chemical into the flushing tank and red fluid into the toilet waste tank to break down the solids. The waste-water is what it sounds like – the water from your sink and shower if you have one. Did they not explain all this at the dealers when you bought the van?'

I did not pass any comment for the sake of not getting any more questions.

On my way home, I called in the local newsagents and bought a couple of caravan magazines, one of which had a picture of the actual van I had bought, or thought I had, as they were doing a feature on it as a comparison with two other makes. My dealer did happen to name the model but not the manufacturer, so I had some idea what I was getting; it was either a two or three-bed. He did not guarantee it would be three but would do his utmost in getting one.

Having read the magazine, I was pretty chuffed as to what I was getting; central heating, cooker, fridge with freezer compartment, shower, hot water system. If it was a three-bed, it was a fixed French bed which meant it was on the side with the shower cubicle next to it at the back of the van. The other single bed was made up where the table and two double settees were located within the van's front kitchen area. The pictures looked great; the third bed was the same as a two-berth in the lounge area at the front. I was hoping it would not be a two, as you had to make the bed up, but for a grand who could complain.

The following week I went to a local caravan dealer and bought all the extras I would need as the van was in a pristine state, with no gas bottles, water carrier or wastewater 'hog', as they called them, no 240v extension lead – nothing. As Molly had told me, I needed blue sanitary fluid and the red, which dissolved the paper and broke the solids down. I needed cutlery, plates and a low-voltage kettle, otherwise, it would keep tripping the 10amp fuse. I was about to leave the shop when I remembered I needed a toaster and a frying pan. I could not believe how much stuff I needed. I totalled up my cost. I had spent enough – that would do for now.

The big day came. I had been into the bank and drawn out £1,500 – the extra just if he did come up trumps – and was on-site at lunchtime. I did not go far from the office and entrance to make sure I was there when my dealer arrived.

CHAPTER 27

LEIF
Pleased with What I Got

Bang on 2.30pm he drove up in a new Land Rover Discovery. When I looked at the van, it was not what I expected. It was what I was hoping for, a three-berth, but he had done well – it was a bit bigger than I ever dreamed of. He just smiled and said, 'You owe me one, son. This was parked where the three for the carrier were, so I hitched it up on the back; you have won one mate, she is spot on. Come on, let's get it out of the way. I took this one as I knew you would not be touring with it, so it would not be seen anywhere but here, not for a while anyway.'

I went back in to get stripped; Molly said it was OK for the dealer to come in without stripping off as he was not stopping; she opened the gate to let him through. He looked surprised when he realised everyone was naked; I had not told him it was a naturist site. When I got in the car, he smiled and said, 'Jesus, Leif, you weren't sat on the back row when they gave dicks out, mate. No wonder you have come here; I didn't know it existed.'

I showed him the way to my pitch and he reversed the van on it, he then helped me set it up to level it off. He even supplied an extension lead and gas bottles as part of the deal; luckily they were from the same supplier as the site used, so it would be easy to refill them. He showed me how everything worked; I was chuffed as hell as it was just like the one in the magazine. He had even supplied small bottles of the sanitary stuff and one toilet roll. I could not have wished for a better service. He had included a caravan battery as well, something I had forgotten. He told me as I was not going to be towing it, I did not need it, but it was always handy if the power went down.

'How much more do I owe you for the different size of van?' I said.

'Make it £250, is that OK?'

That was a bargain; good job I had some spare cash in the house. I handed him his reward, and off he went with a wave and a smile – another satisfied customer. The last thing he did was tell me his name. 'If you need anything else, don't forget to give Nick a call.'

I went back with him to the car park to bring my car in with all the extras I had bought, took them back to the van, and returned the vehicle to the car park; lucky no one was around as I nipped in and out without getting dressed.

That was it. I was now settled in my little holiday home. I had forgotten to get a picnic table and chairs for outside eating and needed a couple of sun loungers, but the grass was good enough for now. I had got a few necessary provisions to get me going; I was intending to eat in the café, but now I had this I needed to make a shopping list and do some real shopping. It was nearer to Hornsea than Hull, so I went there to do my big shop, as mothers used to say. It was a far cry from the old railway carriage on Nettleton's field in Withernsea and the transformed double-decker bus, where I lost my virginity to the lovely Dorothy from Pontefract. I often wondered what happened to her. She would have made some guy a great wife, I am sure.

A week later, the girls came over to see my new holiday home. 'Oh my god,' was the first reaction. 'It's beautiful,' was another.

'Look, Sue, a proper fixed double bed; you don't need to make it up every night. This must have cost you a fortune, Leif.'

'Glad you like it, girls. I looked at a second-hand one, and this came up as a special deal from a company down south trying to break into the caravan market in the North of England.' What a liar – but it sounded good.

'Why did you not buy a tent, Leif? Or have you decided you like being a nudist and are looking for something more permanent?' asked Lynn.

'I had also looked at tents, but they were expensive for what I wanted. I intend to buy an awning to extend the living space as I don't plan on touring with the van, not yet anyway.'

Just in case it was found to be missing at the manufacturer's factory. At least out of sight, out of mind, or in my case, on-site, out of mind. But I never said what I was thinking.

The next day I bought three sun loungers; why three I don't know, but I got a discount if I spent more money. I also bought a table and four chairs, a table lamp for mood lighting, and a small portable TV, which turned out a waste of money as I could not get a signal because of the trees. My fridge was full of beer and wine and enough food to last a week.

Molly came around to look at her newest van to be put on the club's site. She was also very impressed. 'Wow, you don't mess around, Leif – this is some van, you certainly do things big,' she said, as she looked down at my groin, smiling. 'What are your intentions? Do you intend to live in it most of the time or what? I could rent it out for you when you are away if you want me to. I offer this option to all the members who have semi-permanent holiday homes here. You would have no trouble getting people to hire this; it is terrific. Especially during the off season when it's a bit colder, a lovely warm caravan would go down a treat.'

I had not considered renting it out, but it was an option, I suppose. For now, I had no intentions of getting a job. I would enjoy my time in my little paradise.

I had not even told Mum and Billy about it; the least they knew, the better. Anyway, they would not be interested in coming to a nudist camp. I certainly didn't want any of the lads from King Edward to find out – that rabble would only take the piss and tell every man and his dog about it.

I told Mum I was going away on holiday touring the UK and would ring her now and again just to keep in touch. With no regular girlfriend in tow I could please myself, and apart from that I was going to work on the two girls, Sue and Lynn, and try and get into their knickers –

well, not so much their knickers as I had never seen them wear any – another bonus of this naturist thing. Molly was also in the frame; although a bit older, she was undoubtedly a sexy woman. Even at her age, I would not kick her out of bed.

There were often visitors to the site who came from all over the world; I had not realised what a big thing the naturist life was. I knew Einar and Borg were really into it, as they were the first ones I had met, apart from Jenny's day in Devon all those years ago.

I did not do a lot for a couple of weeks; just hung around the site, read a few books was getting a little bored. One weekend a Dutch couple came on site; they were from Vlissingen in the south of Holland. Now, I heard of this place – there was a nautical school there, where a few guys had been and done a survival course for the offshore industry; they all said they'd had a great time while staying there.

They were in a tent and had pitched not far from my van, so we naturally met up and started chatting. Both were in their mid-forties or thereabouts. I was sitting outside my van, and the guy called over, 'Hello, good morning! Beautiful day.'

'Yes, not bad for England, but don't rely on it stopping like this.'

He walked over, holding his hand out. 'Hello, I am Henne, and that lady over there is my wife, Juul.'

She was looking over and waved as he pointed to her. I gestured to her to come over for a drink. We got chatting and they pointed out that both names were unisex and could be used for either boy or girl. They had been nudists or naturists for many years, having met as teenagers, going to various beaches with their parents, who were also keen on getting stripped off.

'Do you travel abroad, visiting sites, or stay more in Holland?'

'No, this is our first time in the UK; our favourite beach we go to on holiday in Holland is at Callantsoog, which is not far from Amsterdam.'

'Is naturism big in Holland, then? You must forgive me; I'm new to this.'

'Yes, it is one of the oldest beaches; it was made an official nudist beach in 1973 following a court case related to nudism in public. It has a great sandy beach that stretches for over a mile, so there is plenty of room for visitors to enjoy themselves, and lots of privacy, although we are careful not to exit the nudist section, which is marked between two poles.'

'Forgive me for seeming ignorant, but what do you mean when you say the beaches were marked with poles? I have worked in Holland and been to the beach but never noticed the pole things.'

'Oh, that it is a way of identifying certain areas for safe swimming, that sort of thing. It's quite easy to learn once you've visited a few of them. A bit like the flag system in Australia.'

'Are there lots of beaches for nudists? As I said earlier, I have been but not that often.'

'Oh yes, there are numerous beaches all along the coast from Vlissingen in the south – all you have to look for are signs saying "naakstrand" or "naturistenstrand" – up as far as Den Helder in the north of the country. We love it, but we wanted a change and decided to visit England.'

The more they told me, the more I wanted to visit one day. They advised me that some of the beaches were kind of segregated from areas where nudists were not allowed, and the rules must be adhered to at all times. It sounded good to me; I just hoped I would get the chance to visit one day.

I was lying out on one of my loungers one afternoon. Juul was walking back from the pool and stopped to say hello; her old man was having forty winks, and she had been for a dip. I offered her a drink and she accepted, and asked if I had any white wine. I did have, as I don't mind a drop myself. I handed her a decent glassful as I gave it to her; her fingers lingered a little longer on mine than usual, which was always a good come-on sign, a bit like the old 'Freemasons' handshake' as she used two hands to take the glass from me.

We sat and chatted a while, and I was impressed with her excellent English. She told me it was their second language and was taught in all schools; most children spoke it quite fluently. She was asking about the van, and as it was getting a bit overcast, I offered to show her the inside and all my home comforts. She told me she had been trying to talk Henne into buying one, but he was a bit of a tight bastard and wasn't having a lot of success.

I picked up both our drinks and went into the van, closing the door behind me; you never know your luck, I thought. She was about 5ft 10in – pretty tall, as a lot of Dutch people are, with blondish hair. I didn't know if it was dyed, as she was waxed down below – another nudist sign, or so I was led to believe.

She was very impressed with the inside of the van; she loved the cooker and how well it was laid out as I gave her the full tour, not that it took long. I showed her the shower/toilet on one side at the back with the bed on the other side, and she sat on the bed and said, 'My, this is comfortable. Can I lie on it?' I told her to help herself, so she lay back and pulled herself up towards the head of the bed, opening her legs in the process. She then tapped the bed and said, 'Come on up here.'

Well, I was like a rat up a drainpipe and went straight up to lie beside her.

'You locked the door, Leif, didn't you?' I nodded without saying a word. She fell into my arms, our lips met – and bingo, I had scored again. I was about to break in my virgin bed.

Her body was very defined – not skinny, not fat, either; more muscular, her legs especially. She told me later she did a lot of cycling back home as it was her main form of transport.

I lay back, and she got on top and rode me like a horse, never mind a bike. God, she was good; it didn't take long, and I was at Wigan without a stop.

We lay there just enjoying the moment; that's one good thing about being nudists. You don't have to worry about getting dressed. Just give it a quick wash and go, and away you go. She told me Henne was another guy who could not get an erection, and he did not mind her fulfilling her needs as and when required, as long as he didn't find out about it.

I was starting to feel sorry for those unfortunate individuals who could not get a hard-on. I was thinking about how terrible and frustrating it must be not to be able to enjoy one of nature's pleasures for a man, to feel the joy of standing erect. The enjoyment of you having sex with it, plus, of course, the happy ending.

Juul said she had better go as he would be awake now. As she was leaving, I was invited to their tent for a drink and a few nibbles, which I was unsure about. I gladly accepted and said I would be there around six. 'Fine,' she said, and away she went, disappearing into the trees.

As she was going out of the door, Lynn was coming out of the shower block. She saw Juul and looked at me as I was standing at the door, waving goodbye. I got a really dirty look from Lynn, as I looked back at her and waved. Lynn disappeared into her parents' caravan without waving back; I think there was a hint of jealousy in her eyes as she went away. Good, I thought – that just might get me into her panties if she thinks I am game for some fun.

I lay on my bed for a while, reading a book, and nodded off. I woke up at 5.30pm, had a quick shower, and put on a pair of shorts and a T-shirt to go round to Henne and Juul's tent. Henne shook my hand, and Juul gave me a peck on the cheek as I arrived; they offered me an Amstel beer. We sat down at a table and chairs set up with napkins and candles; very civilised.

The tent was a frame one with two separate rooms on either side of a central kitchen-type area; in total, it was about eighteen feet at its most extended and seven feet deep with a veranda at the front, where the table and chairs were. They carried it all in a small trailer, behind a VW Beetle.

'Have you tried much Dutch food, Leif? Here, try these.' Juul handed me small balls of mincemeat covered in egg with breadcrumbs and deep-fried, served with Young Gouda cheese, a smooth, fantastic taste.

'Hey, these are great; what are they?'

'You never had bitterballen before? Wow, we always have them for starters.'

I had a drink of my wine, and she brought out what looked like sausages without skins on a stick. 'Try these; this is another European delicacy made up of meat, chicken, beef and sometimes horsemeat deep-fried and covered with mayonnaise and fried onions.' She then brought out some tiny chips, not like the fat ones we get in our fish shops.

'What's the sausage called, Juul?'

'Frikandel – they are very nice… you like?'

'Yes, love them. All the time I worked in Holland, I never ate anything like these; mind, if you told me there was horsemeat in them, I might have declined the offer, but they are lovely.'

We finished off with appelbeignets, or Dutch apple doughnuts. It was a great meal, all fried, of course, but lovely all the same.

'Juul was telling me about your van and how I should go and have a look,' said Henne. 'Save us having to set up every time we go away. I prefer free camping, where you just set up camp anywhere. You did not need electricity; I have my own generator; all you need was water, and that is it.'

'What about toilets? How do you go on with that?'

'It depends on where you are. I just dig a hole and bury it, as we have a separate small tent with a chemical toilet we carry with us. We've never had any complaints from anyone; I don't think it's actually against any laws or anything, we just did it.'

Juul was going on about the caravan; Henne agreed to take a look the next day, just to keep her happy. He had intimated that he might look at a pop-up trailer tent setup, which had become popular in Holland, as storage was the main problem. Quite a lot of people lived in apartment blocks, and it was hard to find availability for storing caravans.

It was getting a bit chilly after the sun had gone down, so I decided to say good night, thanked them for the lovely meal, and told them to come round in the morning, not too early, and he could look at the van.

As I was walking back, I met Lynn; she was taking her parents' dog for a walk. She did not want to make eye contact, but I said, 'Hello, how are you?' She kind of acknowledged me in a sort of grunt, but no real words.

'Excuse me, Lynn – have I done something to upset you? What have I done wrong?'

She just shook her head and said, 'No, not really.'

'I noticed you gave me a black look when you saw Juul coming out of my van earlier; why did you do it? What is eating you?'

'No, I didn't.'

'Oh yes, you did; if looks could kill, I would be dead. Now come on, tell me what's wrong. Lynn, please, I am not here to fall out with you; I like you too much.' Why had I said that? I don't know; it just came out. She looked at me and smiled.

'Oh, that's better – a smile.'

'Do you like me, truly?'

'Of course I like you. Why wouldn't I, a beautiful young girl? I would be mad not to; I just wish I was younger, that's all.'

'I love older men. I hate boys my age; they are useless – give me the more mature man any time.'

Now, if that wasn't an invite, I had never heard one. I just smiled at her, kissed her on the cheek, and said, 'Goodnight, Lynn, we must talk again.'

As I walked away, I heard her say, 'Yes, we definitely must, Leif, for sure; see you tomorrow.'

I got back to my van, had a leak in my special portable potty thing, and got into bed; I went out like a light.

It was past 9.30am when I woke up and could hear someone outside talking; it was Henne and Juul talking in Dutch, rabbiting on about something. I think they were discussing whether to knock or not, as no one was about, and the blinds were down inside the van. I did not move or get up; I was pretty happy to lie there a bit longer and wake up properly before meeting the outside world. I heard them walking away, still talking in their mother tongue, not a word of it I understood.

I left it an hour, and then got up, thinking I would have a shower later. I got some breakfast and went to sit outside, and not long after my new friends from the Netherlands called round.

'Goedemorgen, Leif – how are you?'

'Good morning – very well, thank you.'

After showing Henne around the van and explaining how everything worked, he then asked me, 'How much?'

Now I was in the shit. I hadn't a clue, and I had not looked at a three-bed van, never mind a brand-new one and this year's model at that. I told him I did not know the price in Dutch guilders.

'Pounds would be fine.'

How the fuck do I get out of this, I thought. 'Hang on a second. I will find the paperwork.'

I nipped back in the van and opened a few cupboards, slamming them shut when I could not find the relevant documents – because there weren't any. I came back out. 'I forgot I had taken them home, but I had a special deal from a dealer down south,' I said. Now I was guessing. 'I don't know the full price – I think it was about £5,000, including all taxes and extras.'

It was far too expensive for Henne; he went white when he worked it out in guilders, so that was out of the question, but Juul was still nagging him.

To change the subject, I asked Henne what line of business he was in. 'Oil and gas,' he said.

'Well, what a coincidence; so am I – well, sort of.'

I told him a bit of my history – where I worked over the past few years, including my spell in Australia, which was somewhere he had always wanted to visit; we were both on the same wavelength. I told him about being offshore and the Musk tragedy and nearly drowning, how I had worked at Immingham refinery on turnarounds – all my past came running out.

He looked interested; he told me his company was always looking for young, experienced engineering staff. Henne asked me if I had a CV handy, as he was HR manager at a large Dutch offshore contractor and could help me find employment in Holland. His company worked all over the world from the North Sea to the Gulf of Mexico and was breaking into South America – Venezuela, Brazil, Peru, to name but three countries; I was all ears.

I did not have an up-to-date CV, but I told him I could get one.

'When are you planning to leave the area on your travels?'

'In about three days,' said Henne. 'We are going south but will be returning here for a few more days to get the ferry back, so there is no rush – just try to get one up to date for when we return, OK? I won't be doing anything until the end of the month anyway.'

I did not get another chance to bed Juul. Still, I would not give Henne excuses not to help me gain employment with his company. They left early the following Thursday. I waved them off and looked forward to their return, for Juul had promised to make love before they left the UK.

I went home that day and updated my CV, ready for Henne's return.

CHAPTER 28

LEIF

Sad News

It was August 1986. I had visited Mum and Billy; things were all OK at home. Mum was fifty-seven now, and Billy getting towards retirement age but was still working locally with the outfit that I had called, hoping they would give him a start. He loved it and even talked about working past retirement age, as he was still fit as a fiddle, so why not?

Mum told me my uncle, Hans Snr, had passed away, and Auntie Angela was taking it badly. We were not a close family; never had been. Still, Mum wanted to go round and see her; she had only found out about Hans dying from a woman at the bingo club that she went to. She had missed the funeral and was feeling guilty.

We arrived at their house in Hessle just after lunch, knocked on the door, and Hans Jnr opened it; well, I assumed it was him. I did not recognise him and couldn't remember when we had last met. He did not know me either. Mum was standing behind me; he had not spotted her.

'Hello, what can I do for you?' he asked.

Mum popped her head around me and said, 'Hello, Hans, is Angela in, please? Just thought we would come and see her. We've just found out about your dad – so sorry to hear about your loss.'

'Fucking sorry? You haven't been near us for years, and now you come round to say you are fucking sorry? Well, I am sorry – sorry you bothered. Now fuck off back to where you came from. Mum doesn't want to see anyone.' He slammed the door.

'Well, that was a success, Mum, I must say. What now? Come on, let's go.'

Mum burst out into tears. 'But he was my brother. I know we did not see much of each other, but he was my flesh and blood.'

She started knocking on the door again. 'Hans, please open the door,' she shouted. 'Hans, please, please open the door! I need to speak to your mum.'

With that the door opened again, and it was Hans. 'Auntie Chris, please just go away – Mum does not want to see you; you haven't been round in years. You didn't come round when Dad was first taken ill. You never set foot in the door when he found he had the big C and now, because you feel guilty, you want to try and make up for it. Now, I will tell you once more – fuck right off.'

'Hey, cut the language out, Hans,' I said. 'There is no need to talk to her like that.'

'And who the fuck are you? Yet another fancy man boyfriend?'

I felt like ripping his head off but kept my cool.

'No, I am Leif, your cousin, her son. Now shut your stupid mouth and tell Auntie Angela we are here to pay our condolences on the loss of your father, or I will fucking rip you apart, you twat.'

Hans went white and closed the door and went inside, returning a couple of minutes later. We were still standing there. 'Sorry, come in – please come in.'

'It's OK to cry, Hans – let it all out, mate.' He had calmed down and started crying. Mum hugged him, and so did I. He rested his head on my chest, sobbing.

Angela was sitting on the settee in her dressing gown, smoking like a trooper. Her stained fingers showed she had burned a hell of a lot of cigarettes over her years. I would not have known her; mind, I would not have known most of my relations as we had lost touch. They say Hessle Road families are close; well, we broke the rules. Why, I don't know. We just had. Angela looked ancient compared with Mum; haggard. I know she must have had a hard time but to say she'd let herself go was an understatement. On top of the cigs, she was drinking whisky; there was a half-empty bottle of Bell's on the coffee table and empty beer cans on the floor. Mum went over to her. They hugged and started crying, both rocking together; it was awful to see.

I went into the kitchen – a pig would have been embarrassed by the state of it. I filled the kettle and looked for some clean cups or mugs and found four in a cupboard along with tea and a pot. The fridge had nothing in it but cans of beer and a bottle of milk that had gone off. There was no food of any description, nothing – god knows when she had last eaten, and what about Hans? Where did he live? I could not work out how old he was; it had been that long.

I remembered we had passed some shops in the square. Before I bought my place in Hessle I used to spend quite a lot of time up there in my younger days. It brought back some happy times. I went to my car and bought some essentials – milk, bread, butter, cooked meat, biscuits, and a bottle of Bell's. I knew it was the wrong thing to do, but if it was the only thing that kept Auntie Angela going, so be it; who was I to judge?

When I got back to the house, I made the tea and a few sandwiches and took them into the living room, where they were all sitting and talking quite reasonably now about past years, and discussing Uncle Hans, as you do when someone passes away.

I nodded to Hans to go into the kitchen. As I got up, he followed me.

'How long she been like this, living like this in this shithole?'

'About twelve months – ever since Dad started to go downhill,' he said. 'He was given six months to live but was dead within six weeks.'

'Fucking hell,' was my comment. 'Hans.' He looked at me.

'What?'

'Where do you live?'

'Anywhere.'

'What you mean, anywhere?'

'I don't have anywhere; Dad threw me out about eighteen months ago. His head was in shreds; it must have been the illness that got to him. He started knocking Mum about, and I tried to stop him, but he gave me a good hiding and told me to fuck off, get out, and don't come back.'

Hans Jnr had been moving around a few different mates' houses, but most of them were married, and he was getting in the way, so he had run out of places to go. He was also out of work and only had dole money, which didn't last long. I was gutted for him; I needed to help him – after all, he was my cousin,

'What did you do for a living, Hans? Have you ever worked?'

'Of course I have, but since Mum was going through such a bad time, I was sneaking back in the house to see she was OK and had lost my job because of lost time. They didn't understand the problem, but, having said that, I did not tell them everything.'

'Where had you been working before all this started?'

'Cager Engineering – I was a welder.'

It was a local fabrication company, and I knew the owner, Peter Cager. I'd been at college with him when serving my time. Peter owed me a favour. It was about time I went around to see him; it'd be a chance to see if I could get Hans his job back.

'Come on, let's get this place cleaned up a bit,' I said to Hans. Mum was still chatting to Angela while we tidied the kitchen. It was soon spick and span and we had filled the dustbin with loads of rubbish. Mum had managed to talk Angela into having a bath, which was well overdue. By the way, I'm not being disrespectful when I say that.

When she had got back down, we had tidied up the living room a bit; she looked a hell of a lot better than when we had first arrived. Mum asked Angela if she had heard anything from her other brother-in-law, Arkvid, Mum's brother, but she said no; they had moved away from Hull a long while ago. Mum admitted she had not heard from them either as she did not get on with Mary, his wife. 'She's a right toffee-nosed bastard,' she said. 'I don't know who the fucking hell she thinks she is, just because she comes from fucking Kirk Ella. I haven't seen them since God knows when; we just drifted apart. It's sad, really, when your very own brother disowns you. Mind, that is the Askenes clan to a tee; we were never a lovey-dovey family. Must have been the way we were brought up, I suppose.'

'You haven't missed fuck all, Christine; you have been better off out of it from what I have been told – a right pair of big-headed bastards, fuck 'em!'

After a while, Mum said, 'We had better be going now. We must keep in touch, Angela, let's not drift apart.' She left her telephone number. 'Now, ring me whenever you need anything – and I don't mean a bottle of Bell's, either.'

While we were cleaning up, Hans told me he had moved back home now his father had gone and had tried to find a job again. I told him to go back to Cager and ask them.

'I wouldn't hold much hope on that, Leif – the foreman is an arse-hole. None of the men liked him; as soon as he turned his back, they would toss it off until he came round the shop again. He is one of those guys who comes up to you, calling fuck out of one of the other guys, then goes up to the guy he has been bad-mouthing and does the same about you – a right trouble-causer.'

He told me that the 'gaffer' was shagging one of the secretaries.

I will ask Peter when I call him, I thought, and find out if the rumour is correct; I must ring him when we get home to get the ball rolling.

*

'Hello, Cager Engineering, can I help you?' The woman on the phone sounded sexy; I wondered if she was the girl Peter was giving one.

'Hello, my name is Leif Askenes. I am an old friend of Peter – is he in, please? I was hoping to have a quick word; it's a personal matter.'

She asked me to hang on and see if he was available.

'Now then, you bastard, what the fuck do you want? Hope it's not money? We've been struggling lately.'

'Hi, Peter, how're things? Don't give me that shit about being skint. I have a favour to call in – remember how I took the flak for you when we got caught at college giving them two girls one in the toilet block?'

He started laughing. 'Oh, yes, that saved me a bit of embarrassment. I was engaged at the time; you saved my balls then, mate. Listen – when you coming in for a coffee?'

'I can come now if you are not going out.'

'OK, I will look forward to seeing you.'

Ten minutes later, I was in his office. I told him what Hans had told me. He did not even know he had left or been sacked. That was all left to the supervision and personnel to sort out. He was sympathetic when I told him about his father passing away and the problems with his mum and all that; in fact, the whole story. Peter knew of him and was under the impression he was a good employee – a hard worker and a good welder. I now played my joker. 'By the way, is that girl on reception the one you are shagging on the side?'

He went blood-red. 'What? Er… no – who told you that?'

I told him his foreman was spreading rumours on the shop floor about his affairs.

'Oh, is he now? Hmm, I'll soon sort that twat out. Thanks for telling me. It's not Gwen, anyway,' he chuckled. 'I had her a while back. Still, I have another younger one started six weeks ago – she's stunning, works in personnel. Hang on, I will get her to come to my office and bring Hans's file to me; you can see for yourself.'

There was a knock on the door; Peter said, 'Come in,' and the most beautiful thing you had ever seen walked in.

'Here is the file for Hans Askenes you asked for, Mr Cager; would there be anything else you wanted?' she said with a cheeky grin.

'No, that will be all for now. Oh, by the way, this is Leif – Hans's cousin. We were just chatting about him. Leif, this is Francesca.' She held out her hand and I stood, like the gentleman I am, and kissed her cheek. As we shook hands, she smelt divine; I didn't know what fragrance she was wearing, but it made my balls jump,

'Pleased to meet you, Francesca; it must be a pleasure coming to work each morning,' I said, looking at Peter. She blushed, and her eyes fluttered.

'OK, that's enough, you two – off you go now, Francesca.'

'Of course, Mr Cager. Bye, Leif – lovely meeting you.' And with that, the door closed.

'You lucky bastard. You mean you are giving her one? How old is she?'

'She just turned twenty-one; she came to work for me in personnel straight from university, got a degree in human resources and administration and management – brains as well as beauty, and to top it all a fucking nymphomaniac; I can't give her enough.'

'If you ever want a hand, just give me a call, mate. I would love to help you out, without any shadow of a doubt.'

'OK, might be fun to threes-up with her – anyway, enough of that. About young Hans?' He read through Hans's file and said, 'OK, no worries – tell him to come and see me on Monday morning. I will give him his job back, but don't tell him that; leave that to me.'

I called at Angela's house and went around the back to the kitchen door. Angela was sober and was cooking tea. 'Hi, Angela, is Hans home? I need to speak to him.'

'He is up in his room; sit down. I will call him.' She disappeared, and Hans came into the kitchen. 'Hi, Leif, what's up?'

I told him what had happened. I didn't mention the bit about Peter getting his leg over, but said I hoped he didn't mind me putting my nose in, and Peter wanted to see him on Monday morning about his dismissal.

The look on his face was priceless. 'Wow – you mean I will get my job back?'

'I don't know what he has in mind, but he told me to tell you to go and see him; that's all I can say, but it's a start. Even if it's only to give you a reference as you didn't get one when they dismissed you, did you?' He shook his head. 'Give me a ring after you have seen Peter; let me know how you got on. I have to go now, but good luck, mate.' I left Hans with such a grin on his face. I love it when you can put injustice right.

*

I had gone back to my van when Henne and Juul arrived back on site a little earlier than expected and called round to see me. I was sitting talking with Lynn, still trying to bed her but not having a lot of success. Nevertheless, we were becoming good friends even without being lovers – something I hadn't done for a long, long while, maybe for the first time in my life.

Seeing as Lynn had not met Henne and Juul formally, I introduced them, and there was lots of kissing and shaking hands. Lynn and Juul were getting along great, considering what I had seen in Lynn's eyes when she had spotted Juul leaving my van only a few weeks ago. Nevertheless we all sat down, I got a bottle out of the fridge, and everything was going along nicely.

'Did you enjoy down south then? Where did you get to, and what were the sites like down there compared with here?'

'One of them was outstanding – that was Slapton Sands, near Pilchards Cove in Devon. This is one of the oldest in the UK, and has been a nudist beach since the 1930s. We found it hard to find places as easily available as they are in Europe, and we spent more time dressed than undressed. The only one anything like our paradise here, was near Looe in Cornwall. We stayed there a full week, touring the area. We went to Plymouth for a couple of days but had to go around wearing clothes. We also went along the south coast, working our way back up north. However, I must admit that most of the campsites we visited were brilliant, even if you had to stay clothed.'

Lynn said she had to go as she had to be up early. Juul also left us, as she was nodding off due to the travelling. She had driven most of the way up, which left Henne and me. The subject of work came up; he asked me if I had revised my CV. I told him yes and went in the van to get him a copy. As he perused the contents, he commented and nodded, talking to himself.

'Leif, very good – one or two things I would change, do you mind? Have you a pen? I will edit it for you; there are certain things they like to see in Europe.' He wrote in a few comments, and made six amendments, but nothing drastic; it was more moving paragraphs about than actual changes.

'There you go, that's it; nothing more. I think if you make these alterations, I can ensure you that you would be guaranteed a job in the Netherlands.'

I read what he had done and was very impressed. He did point out not to put my age, as most people did in the UK. He said it was best to let them guess, which was not hard to do if you had set your entire history down. He also suggested that I put a brief synopsis of my apprenticeship and early positions with more detail to my last posts.

'Always say the last four jobs, for companies are more interested in what you did in your previous post and maybe the one before; you must have done the right thing to get where you were, otherwise you would not have been given that position.'

Two days later, we talked and had a few beers around at my van when Henne went back to his tent and returned with his business card.

Henne Van Erickson
HR Manager
Vanderries Marine & Construction Services Pty
25/35 Anders Strasse
Rotterdam
Nederlands

'Here you are – please get in touch with me when you need anything, and I mean it. Do not hesitate. We could use you in our organisation; the numbers are on the back. I have also written my home number on there. We are leaving a day early as I had a message from the office saying they need me back urgently. We are leaving on the ferry tomorrow night; I needed to give you this while I remember. I am off to bed now. I will see you two in the morning.' He kissed Juul and said, 'Don't keep this young man up too long, OK?'

She promised she wouldn't and smiled at me. About fifteen minutes later, she stood up and said, 'Come on, I need you right now. I have been aching for you all the time we have been away; I have not had sex since we were here last. I want you inside me.'

I followed her like a puppy dog without a lead and locked the door behind me.

Another bonus about this nudist thing was there no messing about trying to get undressed to make love. It was straight down to it. She pushed me back on to the bed and I was left with my legs hanging over the corner. She went straight down on me, and I was standing erect.

God, it was good – she certainly knew how to give a blow job. Why they say blow, I do not know, but I digress.

Before I got to Wigan, I was lying on the bed; she rode me like Lester Piggott coming down the final straight at Epsom Derby. I could feel the cheeks of her arse stiffening as she gripped me. Wigan Central Park came in to view. I was sitting in the directors' box as she scored.

The next day I was telling Molly about my discussions with the Dutch couple and how I had got friendly with them. 'I heard you got more than friendly with what's her name,' she said.

'Juul,' I said.

'Yes, the wife – I heard you were very friendly; a little bird told me all about it. I am right, aren't I?'

'Molly, you getting jealous or something? I got the impression you were happily married. It never entered my mind you would even think like that.'

Molly just blushed. 'You are never too old for making love, Leif, and a change, as the saying goes, is as good as a rest.'

I had gone in to ask if I could borrow the typewriter to revise my CV again, which would save me going home. Molly offered to do it for me. 'I often have free time and would love to do it.'

I thanked her and gave her my old CV with the revisions on it as suggested by Henne; she said she would drop it off at the van later. 'Maybe you should take a better look inside my new van then, Molly,' I said as I walked out of the door.

I was about to score once again; this was getting a bit too much for me. I'd never done so much shagging. I needed to get a job.

Later that day I was in my van, and there was a knock on the door. 'Come in, it's open,' I shouted. Molly entered with my revised CV in her hand; I was lying out on the bed. She closed the door and said, 'Stay where you are; you look nice lying there.' She walked towards the end of the bed; she was wearing a tracksuit top as there was a bit of a chill in the air.

She gave me the manuscript and told me to look over it. I started to work my way through it as she stood at the bed end.

'Great, very good,' I said as I read through it. 'Yes – spot-on.' When I looked up again, she was naked.

'Well, do I get paid for it then, my boy?' She knelt on the bed.

'You don't have to give me money; I will take it in kind.' With that, she took hold of my manhood and licked her lips. Oh fuck, she was right – it did not take long, and I had reached Keighley. She then got on board and worked the final chapter off, and within minutes I was at Wigan again.

'Now then, my boy, you do not say a word to anyone about what has gone on today. You have made an old lady very happy, and you can do it again, without doubt. Nine-and-a-half out of ten – next time I want a full house, OK?'

Then she was gone. I felt great – I had got what I wanted, and so had Molly.

The next day I went into Hornsea and bought a few newspapers, some envelopes and had some copies of my new CV done at the library.

I decided to see Mum again a couple of days later and use her phone. I had had mine cut off at my flat as I wasn't using it enough. Billy was sitting at home when I walked in. 'What you at home for? No work on, mate?'

He told me they were on a shutdown at one of Hull's chemical plants, and he was on the night shift. He didn't like it much, but he got his head down when the work the foreman had allocated them was finished. He was with the hydro test squad, and there was not a great deal for him to do, but it was twelve-hour shifts and time-and-a-half for nights; he loved that bit.

I asked where Mum was; he told me she had got the bus to see how Angela was.

'Can I use the phone? Please.'

'No worries, of course you can. Bloody hell, it's your house. I am going to get my head down.'

I had a list of contacts of agencies and companies that I had either worked for or knew the right men to contact for work. I had been there an hour or so. Mum would go berserk when the bill came in, but I would see her right when she fronted me for it later on.

I contacted a guy I knew who I worked offshore with, and he gave me a tip about a company in Holland, Heldren, which had a lot of work coming up all over, or so he had been informed. He told me that one of Hull's agencies was doing a lot for them and suggested I should take my CV into them. Don't post it – take it in, was his advice.

I had heard nothing from anyone, and two weeks had passed. I thought there wasn't much about, but something would come up. I just knew it.

CHAPTER 29

LEIF

New Love in My Life

It was almost October, and it was getting a bit too cold to be running around naked at the camp. I decided to wrap the van up for the winter but needed to bed Lynn before she got a regular boyfriend.

I was at the camp, and her mother walked past my van. I shouted over to her and asked where Lynn was. She told me she was busy with work and would not be back so often as she was travelling more for a new company. She told me she had left S&N and was having to go away on different courses. I asked her mother to send my regards to her and wish her the best of luck. She told me she did not see that much of her now, for Lynn had got a place of her own on Beverley Road, but she would pass on my regards when they were next in contact. I asked for her number but she did not have it at the camp. Still, she would ring the site and give it to Molly.

I had sent my CV to the Hull area agencies and a few I had found in the national newspapers, along with the one I had taken into Jobnet, the agency supposed to be handling Heldren's work. As I said earlier, I had previous knowledge of them as a few lads I knew had worked for them in the module yards.

I got a call from a guy in Holland asking me what my current circumstances were and was I looking for work. It seems my name had been put forward to them; they were what you might call head-hunters.

After one or two telephone conversations with them, along with the client, I joined Vanderries, a massive Norwegian oil and gas contractor, with Asta Jacobs's help; she had been right to her word and got me a start with the company she was working for.

The company also had offices in Holland; it specialised in oil installations, both onshore and offshore. It was in the throes of setting up a fabrication and construction facility for its operation in the Netherlands. They wanted me as a lead piping design engineer working out of Rotterdam. It seemed they had been trying to get a Norwegian national to fill the position but could not find anyone; Asta had put my name forward, and luckily I got the job.

It seemed to be more than just a coincidence that Asta Jacobs, whom I had worked with, and Henne Van Erickson, whom I had met at Natsun, both worked for the same company in different countries. What had happened was that Asta had put my name into the Norwegian office HR department. They had passed it on to the Rotterdam office HR and, lo and behold, my new Dutch friend was head of that department. Bingo – I did not need any more information on me; they contacted the agency, and I was in.

As for Henne, 'The Van' had told me they had been working in South America for quite a while developing turnkey projects and joint ventures with contractors who had worked in several countries on that continent.

I got the ferry over on a Sunday night to start work in the Rotterdam office; it was in a perfect spot, not far from the docks, yet you could be in the city centre within minutes on the local tram and train system.

I was getting home one long weekend a month to start with, which was easy as I finished on the Friday and was allowed to go back a bit later on the Monday – not that much later, but it was OK with them.

I managed to get my feet under the table; after a couple of months, I asked my immediate supervisor, Aalt Daan, if I could work a four-day week and put my forty hours in over the four days. I wasn't doing much else at the time, just working, so I figured I might as well put more hours in while I was in Holland and have more extended weekends. If I wanted my leg over, I just got the train to Amsterdam, or went down the red light area in Rotterdam for a bit; it was a lot more relaxed than getting involved with a local girl. There were plenty of them around, but I was pretty busy at work and didn't want to get too close with a girl.

A couple of weeks later, I got the nod to work four days. OK, I had to work a bit longer to get away for the Thursday night ferry, but it was spot on – Rotterdam three nights, two nights on the ferry, and all day Friday. I had Saturday and Sunday at home, and went back on the ferry Sunday night; I didn't do it every week, but nearly every two to three weeks.

One weekend I went home and went back to Natsun to check the van out, and Molly gave me a message from Lynn that she had been given a few weeks previously by Lynn's mother. However, she could not get hold of me as my phone was still not connected. Anyway, she gave me the message with Lynn's phone number on it. I must get in touch, I thought, or she will think I am ignoring her.

Lynn had not been to the site much herself, and her parents had only been a couple of times, so, as Molly could not get a message to her, she tried to ring her, but she could never get hold of her. I had tried to get in touch too, but there was never any answer to my telephone calls, so I went round to her flat just on spec. No one was in; she must have been away with her new job.

Molly told me she travelled a bit now. Apparently her mother had said, 'She's doing very well, our Lynn. She has a vital role now with a new company and I don't see much of her – and she's too busy for boys.'

I thought I would try to ring her while I was away at work; it might be easier to catch her during the week and I could use my works phone to save me money. I tried every day, and still there was no reply. Then one Thursday, just as I was getting ready to leave the office, thought I would try again. I rang her number, and it rang for five or six times. I was just about ready to put the phone down, and then she answered. 'Hello, Hull 232323, how can I help you?'

'Oh, hello, it's Leif; how are you? I got your message from Molly a couple of weeks ago. I'm working in Holland. I've been trying to call you but you never seem to be in. How're things?'

Lynn sounded surprised. 'Oh, hello, how are you? What a lovely surprise. I have been away for a few weeks in Germany setting up a new franchise for the company I am working for now.'

'Oh, right, what are you doing there? Why did you leave your last job? Weren't you settled there?'

'I got headhunted and offered the accounts manager's position with them, and I am travelling most of the time. I will be in Belgium next week for a couple of weeks trying to sort another deal out. Maybe we could get together on the middle weekend if you aren't going home?'

'Wow, yes, for sure – I'd love to. Do you want to catch the train to Rotterdam or shall I come to you?'

'I am in Antwerp; it is only just over an hour on the train, and I am easy either way. Can you ring me next week on Thursday afternoon to finalise it?'

I rang her as agreed, and we talked for quite a while. After much consultation, it was decided. 'I have a spare bedroom,' she said. 'I'm in the suite at the Hotel Julien in Korte Nieuwstraat, in between the railway station and the Grote Markt; it's only twenty-odd minutes' walk from the station, so why not come here?'

That was it; I would get the train to Antwerp, a city I had not visited, but I was more looking forward to seeing Lynn again.

It was a beautiful autumn morning when I arrived at the station in just over an hour. The European railway system was amazing – it was always on time; you could just about set your watch by it.

Lynn met me at the station. She looked more beautiful than I remembered. She looked more mature and confident. We hugged and kissed each other on the cheeks; nothing too sexual – just friends greeting each other.

'Fancy a coffee?' she said. 'I know a great little coffee shop on the way back to the hotel; it's halfway there – come on.'

As we walked along, she put her arm in mine, like two close friends. I must admit it felt good. Her perfume smelt expensive, and her clothes were not from Hessle Road or Hammonds – no disrespect to them, but it was classic European.

We found a table, and Lynn went and sat down. I had not changed my sterling yet into Belgian francs, but I had some guilders with me and asked if they would take either. The girl accepted sterling without any problem, but just before I paid, Lynn came over and handed some notes over and settled in francs.

'No question – they are on me,' she said.

We returned to the table and waited for the coffee to come. I did not know Lynn that well; we had only met in the world of naturism and not talked about ourselves, our history, where we were brought up, etc. I knew she worked at S&N in the office; she had already told me that. To break the ice, I asked her what she was doing now, how she had got the job, and a bit more of her background. I had always found that getting girls to talk about themselves was sometimes a bit of a challenging task, as most did not open up that easy, but Lynn was not one of these girls.

'Well, where do I start?' she said. 'I was brought up in a multicultural family; my father was born in Hull, but his father was German and came over here as a prisoner of war. He stayed, having met his wife, who was French – what a mixture. As a child, I spent lots of time with my grandparents and picked up the different languages, and like most kids, I could mimic them; I was almost perfect in every language. Then when I went to school, I decided I wanted to learn more, and can now speak fluent German, Danish and French, with a smattering of Dutch. I am trying to learn that, for my new job is with a company that sells franchises all over Europe in the beauty/cosmetics industry. I have a goal in life. I aim to become the boss of my own company. What field it is, I am not sure, but what I do know is that the contacts I am making now will come in handy and will enable me to branch out on my own once I have found the niche that is missing.'

To say I was impressed is an understatement – she was the first girl I had ever met with a real purpose in life, a goal; apart from looks, she certainly had brains.

After our coffee, we walked back to her hotel and went straight up to her room, which had a spare bedroom; it was more of an apartment than a hotel room. It was very nice. She told me the company did not pay expenses as such, but booked her in a hotel wherever she travelled to and paid all the bills on a company American Express credit card. 'No limit within reason,' as she put it.

'How much better off are you working for this new outfit than Smith and Nephew, then, Lynn?'

'The basic salary is low, but I can earn an excellent monthly bonus on sales and percentages coming back from the franchisee. It's good enough to pay for my apartment in Hull, which is on a mortgage that I am paying off in larger amounts than were stipulated; I am doing this to reduce the years.'

Here was me, forty years old and still renting; where had I gone wrong? I needed some guidance from this girl on managing my finances; I wasn't broke by any means but needed to channel my money into making more money.

'I have always been an ardent saver, Leif. Since the early 1980s, just after Margaret Thatcher put the bank rate up to seventeen per cent, I have been putting my savings into fixed-rate bonds, hoping that I will get a good return on my investments over some time. Up to now, I am way in front.'

I needed a financial adviser urgently.

We got changed and went out on the town. She liked a drink, as I found out on our kind of pub crawl around the bars in Antwerp, finishing up at a nightclub behind the city hall. It was just after 2am when we got back to the hotel, and Lynn was, for want of a better word, arseholed.

I had to undress her and put her to bed, which was a pleasant task, I must admit. Although I had seen her naked before, I'd never actually handled the goods, so to speak.

I was looking for some sort of nightie or pyjamas, but couldn't find anything; she must have slept naked. I stripped her totally and put her in bed. I retired to my room like the perfect gentleman I was. Deep down wished I'd climbed in with her, but for some reason I didn't. Did I have more respect for Lynn than I'd had for my previous girlfriends?

It was around 10am when I woke up the next morning. I'd had a great night's sleep. I could smell bacon cooking and fresh coffee brewing. I got up and went into the living/kitchen area. Lynn was still naked, apart from an apron, cooking breakfast.

'Morning, Leif – sleep OK, did you? This is the only time I cook – on Saturday mornings; it's the thing I have always done since I started travelling. It's my day; I love Saturdays most out of all the days in the week. Pour the coffee, will you, please? This is just about ready.'

I poured two mugs of the coffee and sat at the table. I had my briefs on.

'You don't have to wear them,' said Lynn. 'There are no rules about bums on seats here,' she laughed. 'Feel free to take them off if you want. I am always naked when I'm at home; it's just something I'm used to since being a child. I find clothes so restricting. My parents have always been ardent naturists, as you already know.'

She placed the plates on the table, then took the apron off and sat down to eat her breakfast. I almost choked as she put a sausage in her mouth and smiled with her eyes. She held it between her lips, then bit some off and put the rest on her plate. I felt my groin stir as she repeated the action; she was teasing me, and it was so sexy.

'Come on,' she said after we'd finished the meal, 'we can wash up after. Come and sit in the lounge. I like to play some of the old music; I've got some great cassettes I carry with me. I just love the Stones and the Beatles. My dad got me into them.' That made me feel old, as I remembered them well; they were my era.

'How old are you, Lynn? Can I ask?' She looked at me with that smile again. 'You told me once you preferred older men; well, is forty too old, or not old enough?'

'I'm twenty-eight – is that too old for you? Or do you prefer younger?'

What could I say? I thought she was younger, but thinking about the life she had lived, I realised she must be a bit older. I hesitated, just teasing her; she was staring at me, awaiting my answer.

'Of course not, Lynn, not at all; it's a perfect age – but not just your age is perfect, every part of you falls into the same category. I think you are a beautiful, wonderful woman, and I am pleased to call you a friend. I was hoping I could call you my girlfriend?'

She looked down at the floor and blushed; she then flung her arms around my neck and gave me the best kiss I had ever had. It felt so good to feel her in my arms.

'Leif, I have wanted this moment for so long; I fell in love with you the first time I saw you when you walked into my life. I always imagined you fancied Sue more than me; you always seemed to be looking more at her whenever we met and talked. The time you showed us around your new van, you seemed to be concentrating on Sue, not me, and the day I saw that Dutch woman leaving your van, I was so really hurt; I was convinced you were not interested, or you would have made a play for one of us. Then when I got your message through Molly, I was so pleased, I could not believe it, that you, Leif, were trying to find me. Oh, baby, I love you so much.'

To say I was surprised at her response would be a significant understatement. I felt humbled by it but had I used the wrong terminology in girlfriend, had I overstepped the mark, it just came out of my mouth, but it did sound right when I said it.

When I was younger, when the lads on Hessle Road met a girl that they liked, they used to say, 'Will you go out with me?' which meant will you go steady, or shall we date regularly – there are lots of different ways of saying the same thing, but I had asked Lynn to be my girlfriend; yet another way.

We spent the rest of Saturday just chilling out in the apartment, talking about things we had never discussed – our upbringing, our interests away from work, how we both had European ancestors. Lynn's came to Hull because of the Second World War; mine because they just liked the city and its people. I had never been so close to a girl before. Was she the one I was going to settle down with for the rest of my life?

To be honest, I was frightened. I had never felt like this; Donna in Australia was the nearest thing I had got to being genuinely in love, always thinking about her, twenty-four hours a day. Then there was Mel, but it was never going to work out; we had been very close, mainly because we worked together, first in Queensland then again in Sarawak. We were thrown together, but there was no doubt the sex was good. Still, I was beginning to realise there was more to being with women than just sex, even though I would hate the day when I did not get a buzz from it. For I got great pleasure from giving pleasure, to feel a woman tremble and hear her moan as she climaxed to my touch or kiss in a certain way, to feel her body next to mine, the softness of her skin, the smell of her. Certain perfumes turned me on. Chanel No 5 was horny and Opium drove me crazy, especially when having oral sex; trying to lick and sniff simultaneously is the hardest thing you can ever try to do. It's bit like playing a didgeridoo, breathing in and out at the same time. To feel with a woman as one, our bodies connected, me inside her being part of her was always beautiful; I always say if God made anything better, he kept it for himself.

All my past seemed to be coming back to me; all the women had I taken to bed. I could not criticise them for at the time they were the ones for me, but I had never felt like I did at this moment in time. I was hooked, line and sinker, but – there is always a but – why did I feel like this? I was in another place, somewhere I had never been, with no one to ask; it was to be my decision.

Lynn had told me her feelings towards me; she seemed genuine or else why would she say such things? She did not have to; she did not come running to me, throwing herself at me, for Lynn had always been the one in the background. She was right when she said I always seemed to be talking to Sue, but deep down, I was more interested in her.

We had been talking for hours, sitting naked on the sofa or sprawled on the floor with 1960s music playing in the background. We hadn't attempted to make love; neither of us had made a move on the other, or made sensual touches such as a brush of a hand on her breast, her stroking me on my leg or even penis – nothing. We just loved being together; there was that word love – was this the real thing? I knew I was a lot older than her, but there seemed no difference when we were together; it felt just great, like it was meant to be.

We met on quite a few occasions over the next few weekends; it was much easier just to jump on the train and go to Antwerp. I never went home for a month; Lynn came to Rotterdam about six weeks after our first boy/girl relationship. We had talked a lot on the phone most days. I could not get her out of my mind; I was definitely in love, for sure.

We had gone for a day out on the train for a change of scenery to The Hague. Lynn was coming to work in Holland in a week. It seemed that one of her clients was looking for a place to open a franchise in the area, and she was going to look at where they were thinking about – without them knowing, that is. We were sitting in a cafe on the Turfmarkt, one of the main streets not far from the central station, having looked at the property. Lynn wrote notes before filling in a form of some sort; she had brought a camera with her.

I picked up the camera. Now, I was no camera buff, but this looked expensive. I had never seen one like it. I asked Lynn what it was and she said it was a Sony Video8 Handycam. She showed me how it worked; I was amazed. It had a little screen you pulled out at the side so you could see what you were filming. She told me her bosses had supplied it to help the franchisee learn more about the company and how they expected things to work. It was very similar to the one Geoff Oswald had when I met him on my Isle of Wight jolly.

My mind was working overtime. Yes, you guessed it – I wanted to film Lynn making love with me for the first time, for I had made my mind up that this would be the weekend it was going to happen. I thought Lynn was ready.

We got back to Rotterdam about 6.30pm and we both wanted a shower. 'You go first. I will wait,' I said.

'No, you go first.'

'No, let's do it together.'

This was something we hadn't done; we got into the shower, and it was a bit cramped but more intimate. It was amazing as we soaped each other down. As Lynn was washing my penis in a stroking motion, I was soon erect; I'd almost got to Wigan by express and this time not far from Workington. She warmed up – she was ready now, without a doubt. I was savouring the moment; I did not want it to happen straight away.

We had supper; just sandwiches as we had eaten earlier. I didn't want a lot, for I didn't like making love on a full stomach. We were sitting on the settee watching some BBC programme you could get in Holland; I was messing with the new toy Lynn had brought with her. I got up off the couch and started walking around using the camcorder. Taking a video of Lynn, she began to pose and act as if she was making a movie. She opened her legs to show her vulva; she was stroking herself. I could see she was getting turned on, and I was instantly erect.

'You want to do it, Lynn, are you ready to make love?' I said, and she closed her eyes and nodded; she didn't say anything, just nodded. I filmed her masturbating; god, it was horny. I put the camera on the coffee table and pointed it at the rug, hoping that was where we would end up. It was no doubt the best sex I had ever had in my forty years on this earth.

We got part of it filmed, and she said she was pretty pleased with our efforts, which were quite surprising. She whispered in my ear. 'We must try again – and we need to buy a stand for the camera.'

CHAPTER 30

LEIF

Will You?

After nearly four months of being together, Lynn had left Holland and gone back home to work for a few weeks before returning to Europe. Christmas was getting near, and we had got very close. I was besotted with her; she was the love of my life.

We had gone to Amsterdam to do a little Christmas shopping and take presents home to our families and friends. Walking through one of the larger shopping areas, we came across a jeweller's. Lynn looked at some rings in the window; I was looking at the watches in another display. I had always fancied a Rolex but could never come to buy one. I could have afforded one, but just never took the plunge.

I wandered over to her. 'What have you seen, Lynn? What takes your fancy?' Then I looked at the display. It said, 'Verlovingsringen.' Now, I didn't speak a lot of Dutch. Still, I had a vague idea of what it meant, though I wasn't admitting it, for I had not considered getting engaged. We'd never talked about marriage, but it seems Lynn must have thought about it, but not said anything. I watched her out of the corner of my eye, and she was scrutinising intensely the choice of rings laid out in the shop window.

I had always been single, never really tied to any girl. Mel was the nearest I had been to wedded bliss, and that was only because we had been living together, and it suited us in Sarawak. It had crossed my mind, but the split when we got back to Australia had turned me off the idea; it was not so much being tied to a woman but the excess baggage that often came with it, such as in-laws.

There was one consolation; I knew Lynn's parents from the campsite and got on well with them – very well, to be quite honest. Her mother, Gry, which is equivalent to Dawn in English, was sound as a pound, very protective of her only child, as is natural; her father Lucas was a quiet sort of a guy who seemed a bit under the thumb with Gry but was OK with me. How they would react to someone wanting to take their baby away was yet to be seen.

I sidled over and asked, 'What are you looking at those for?'

'Oh, nothing… just looking. I love that one there. Look, Leif.' She pointed at a blue stone surrounded with small diamonds; I assumed it was a sapphire, but it was kind of silver-blue, almost aquamarine. It looked great; I must admit I liked it as well. It must have been expensive, as it had no price on the label.

'Hang on a second, Lynn, we have not discussed getting engaged… or am I missing something here?'

'OK – will you marry me?'

I was stunned. Wasn't I the one supposed to do the proposing? I knew girls were only meant to propose in leap years, and 1986, as far as I knew, it wasn't a leap year. You had to be able to divide it by four, so the next one was due in 1988. What was going on here?

'Well, will you marry me? I know it's not a leap year, if that is what you are trying to work out, but, in your language – fuck it, I am asking now. I love you, Leif Askenes. I want you to be my husband. Now, will you marry me?'

How could I refuse? 'OK, I would love to marry you,' I said, 'and thanks for asking me.'

We kissed a long, lingering kiss, then broke away and opened our eyes. A crowd had gathered around us, something we had not noticed during our conversation; they started clapping, applauding my decision. We then hugged again at the reality of it all. We were going to be married. When, we hadn't a clue; where, we weren't sure, but most likely in Hull. All of this was going to be a new adventure – one that neither of us had expected when we went out shopping that morning.

We went into the shop and a girl came over. Luckily, as most Dutch people do, she spoke perfect English. We asked to look at the ring we had chosen, giving her the tray number, and she went to get it out of the window. She returned with the tray and placed it on the table in front of us; we had been invited into a more private viewing area by this time, and we had also been joined by the manager. I feared the worst – this was going to cost the Earth; when the heavies come in, you know something is expensive.

'Good morning; how are you both today? I must say you have excellent taste in gemstones. That is what we call a blue emerald and it's part of the sapphire family; that one comes from Pakistan in the Himalayas, and it is thirty-five carats.'

He went on to tell us about the unusual one we had chosen.

'One factor that affects the price of aquamarine gemstones is the colour of the stone. The most common stones have a medium to light tone and don't have any secondary hue such as green or yellow. The most prized aquamarine gemstones are medium to high blue saturation, which sometimes looks like a sapphire. And also the colour is called Santa Maria blue or double blue.'

'OK, enough of the waffle; how much is it?' I sounded impatient, and I was; I did not want it to be out of my price range, as it was supposed to be a once in a lifetime purchase. I didn't want to appear a Scrooge when he told us the price and I could not afford it.

He took a pen out of his pocket and wrote on a piece of paper without saying the cost; this looked pricey. 'I will do a special deal for you and give you the price in sterling,' he said. 'We will also take a sterling cheque, not a problem.'

I looked at the paper. Fucking hell – £3,500 – although I had thought it was going to be more than that. 'This is half-price,' he added. 'We have a sale on and that is one of our older stock items, which is why I can give you such a good discount. It is a beautiful ring, but not everyone's choice; I'm glad you two liked it so much. I would like to make it easier for you, and you can have it for that price.'

I looked at Lynn; she was begging me with her eyes.

'OK, it's a deal.' Good job I had my chequebook with me. I was going to go into a bank and withdraw some money anyway.

Lynn squealed with excitement, threw her arms around my neck, and kissed me again. I had never seen anyone so happy. The ring was also a good fit when she tried it on; it just slipped on her finger. It did look fantastic, I must admit. Her long slim fingers showed it off perfectly.

We left the shop, Lynn still wearing her new engagement ring. We went along together like walking on a cloud. What had I done? Gone and got engaged. I hadn't asked her dad for her hand in marriage, nothing – we'd just gone and done it.

'Come in here; I need a drink,' I said to Lynn as we passed a bar. 'Wow, what have we done? How the hell are we going to break the news to our parents? What will they say about this?' Lynn just shook her head; she was still grinning, looking at the ring. Then suddenly she broke down in tears, and I mean real tears – they just flowed down her cheeks, and she was sobbing, crying, smiling all at the same time; people in the bar started staring at us.

'It's OK, she is just happy – we just got engaged to be married; don't worry,' I said, and the crowd then all started clapping. I wondered if it was a Dutch thing, but it was beautiful for strangers to join in our celebration.

Eventually, we got out of the bar three sheets to the wind. We'd had one or two jenevas more than we should have, but hey, it was our day – the best day of my life. I'd never dreamt I would ever say that, but undoubtedly it was.

We had decided to stay in Amsterdam for the night. We had no change of clothes, so we passed a supermarket and bought some toiletries, along with some underwear for both of us. We found a little hotel just off the Oude Hoogstraat for the night. As we were checking in, Lynn, who by this time was a bit worse for wear, was showing the girl behind the desk her ring while she was trying to check us in. It took a lot longer than required, as they were then both oohing and aahing, then along came another girl chattering away in Dutch about how much they loved the ring, how lucky Lynn was to have been given it, then smiling at me. I had not a clue what they were saying to Lynn, as she had picked up a bit of the language by now. One of the girls came over and hugged and kissed me, and said, 'You are one fortunate couple – congratulations.' I was thinking we were never going to get to bed at this rate; then the manager appeared, and he wanted to see the ring, too.

'Ah, very nice. Give them the bridal suite. It is empty, I believe. No extra charge – my engagement present to you two.'

We managed to get up to our room at the top of this small hotel. I didn't think it was big enough to have a bridal suite, but sure enough, it had. When we entered, it was unreal; it had everything. A king-size bed was in the middle of the room, and above it was a mirror the exact size as the bed. The bathroom had a double-sized bath, walk-in shower, and everything that a couple would need to do everything together.

I went back into the bedroom, and Lynn was out cold on the bed, snoring; I undressed her and put her on top of the duvet, then stripped off lying next to her; that was it.

I woke up at about 7.30am with a mouth like the bottom of a budgie cage. You know when you wake up after being drunk, and you are not sure where you are, you open your eyes trying to focus… all I could see was the mirror above us and I was not sure who I was looking at; my brain was not working. I knew the girl next to me; she was lying on her back, legs wide apart like a starfish. I was at one side of the bed, more or less clinging to the edge; how I hadn't fallen out during the night I did not know, but having said that, I could have done.

I needed a drink. There was a mini-bar in the room so I got myself a bottle of fruit juice and downed it in one; it never touched the sides. I smelt my armpits. God, a shower was in order. Lynn was still out cold; so much for the bridal suite – it hadn't been much use to us. Anyway, I was in the shower, and was beginning to come round. I was feeling quite pleased with myself about getting engaged. I was washing my hair, with my eyes closed, when I felt a hand on my penis, stroking me, and it felt pretty nice. Then this body rubbed up against me, and I felt a kiss on my cheek.

Lynn was up, and it wasn't the only thing that was up. I put my head under the shower to wash off the shampoo so I could open my eyes.

'Good morning, darling,' she whispered. 'Mmm, you are hard… baby, that feels good,' she said as she stroked me. Oh fuck, I had gone past Castleford already. We covered each other in body wash, massaging each other; I was standing behind Lynn, rubbing her neck and shoulders, my shaft between the cheeks of her gorgeous bubble bum. The ring on her finger looked great. Why I was looking at that, I do not know, but I just did.

We both got to Wigan together, then we dried off and lay on the bed. Now, if you have never had sex with a mirror above you, I'm afraid you have not lived, for it's one of the most erotic things I have ever done in my life. It's like watching a porn movie, but you are the two actors. We both loved it – I lay back watching my face as she was on top, then the other way round. Lynn said she had never had such an intense orgasm. 'It felt like a thousand butterflies flowing out of my vagina,' was how she described it. Who was I to argue?

I had never in my life made love three times in the morning before breakfast. We sent for room service; Continental breakfast, the full works, even two glasses of Buck's Fizz, a mixture of cold meats – and cheeses, of course, we were in Holland. The service was brilliant, and we never got off the bed.

I rang the reception and asked if we could stay another night, apologising if they felt I was being cheeky, or 'brutaal' in Dutch, as the girl told me, giggling. There was no problem as the room was not booked out; she would ask the manager if we could have it at the same rate.

What a day – we did not leave the room until mid-afternoon. My old feller was sore with making love. She was an animal; what had I got myself into? I did not give a fuck, to be honest, or should I say I did more than once.

We had a couple of hair of the dogs, and did a bit more Christmas shopping. As we were in Amsterdam we just had to visit the red light district, complete with its unique shops.

'Leif, come here, just look at these. Oh my god, look at that there.'

Lynn was looking in the window of a sex shop, pointing at the vibrators on offer, 'My god, look at the size of that one! It would split me in half.'

Was this the quiet, unassuming girl I knew before we got engaged? She was now a sex maniac.

'Come on, let's go inside; I want one.'

We went in. I was looking around outside to see if anyone was watching us go in, just in case we knew anyone; it was quite stupid, thinking about it, but that's how we English are. Still, when we got in, I couldn't believe my eyes; it was a sex supermarket. Whatever took your fancy, whatever your sexual orientation, there was something here to satisfy every need.

We were wandering around, mouths wide open, just absorbing what was on view, from vibrators to dildos of every size and colour. I could not believe that a woman's vagina could take some of them. Mind, having said that, when you think a baby could exit that passage, I suppose some of those on view were minute. I was looking at some condoms called Long Love; now, I was not really into french letters, as to me it was like having a shower with your raincoat on. But these had a coating inside that numbed your dick to make you last longer without having to think of every rugby league team and ground on your way to the end of the line.

I would have some of those; definitely. I put three packets in my basket; Lynn wanted a vibrator. 'Mmm, I like the look of that one,' she said, and she picked up a box with one that had what looked like rabbit ears on the side. It had a lead about six feet long with a remote control attached. As she was reading the label, a lady of, shall I say, more mature years stopped and said in Dutch, 'Ik heb een van die het, is geweldig,' and smiled and walked away. I asked Lynn what she'd said, and she shrugged her shoulders. Then another girl who was looking at the array of sex eggs said, 'Oh, the lady said, "I have one of those, it's wonderful." I do, too – my husband works away, and I use mine a lot; it's really good when you are alone at night and need relief.'

I could not believe we were talking to strangers about their sex lives; we were just not brought up that way, were we?

Lynn placed it in the basket as if she was purchasing a tin of beans. We completed the shop tour, and when we got to the checkout there was a queue of people, all standing in line with baskets full of sex aids; it was a hell of an education.

The mixture of customers was quite diverse. I would say the oldest was about seventy if she was a day; she had condoms – surely not for her? Or were they just for protection? She also had a dildo about a foot long, complete with veins and a bell end like an Easter egg with a circumference of at least two inches; she had not a care in the world who could see what she was buying. Another girl about twenty had a set of handcuffs, some crotchless knickers, and a vibrator; she was fit as well. It crossed my mind that I wouldn't mind giving her one, and I smiled back when she saw me looking at her basket. She put her thumb up and mouthed, 'I love it.'

Our turn came to pay for our goods, and the pretty young girl on the till did not say a word until we had paid the bill and, as we were putting our goods in the plastic bag – plain, no adverts on it – she said, 'Thank you for shopping with us; enjoy them and please call again – bye.'

We went back to the hotel, dashed upstairs, and hurriedly opened the bag. One of the products I had bought was some love gel lubricant; it was supposed to have some additives to stimulate the woman's vagina. It would go well with my new Long Love condoms. We were going through our purchases, opening up the packages and packets – quite an array of sex toys. Christmas morning was never like this. 'I never saw you put that in,' I said as I picked up a dildo, jet black and a lot larger than my real white one.

Lynn smiled and said, 'I have never had a black one, either real or imitation, and just wanted to try it.' She was coming out of her skin, that was for sure, from the quiet, shy person I first met on the site near Hornsea to what sat before me in this hotel room in Amsterdam and who was now my intended.

'Can I ask you something, babe?' I said. 'Have you been waiting to let yourself go, and now you are engaged to be married you want to experiment in bed?'

'Leif, all my life, I have always said I would not let loose until I have the man that I know is the one. I must admit I did have a wobble once when I was younger, but the day I saw you sunbathing at the site, watched you lying there in your glory – such a beautiful body, perfect in every way – I knew I wanted you. Don't ask me why, I don't know; I haven't a clue. I had never even spoken to you or heard your voice, but something inside clicked. I had never felt like that about anyone, though I love sex; I wanted to try it from being fourteen, I suppose. When we were on holidays with my cousins, one of them was older – sixteen – and he was a lot wiser than us kids. I wanked him off, and he touched me – 'sticky finger,' as us kids called it. I liked it; I tasted my first one a year later at school behind the proverbial bike sheds, and yes, I loved that also, but it was just kids' games; it meant nothing. I wasn't the school bike by any means; I selected the boys I wanted and, boys being boys, I had many choices. I decided I would not go all the way until I was sixteen and ready, and it was legal. I wasn't sure whether I wanted a boy or a man to take my virginity, but I wanted to be sure it was the right person, whoever it was.

'Then some friends of my mother's came over to visit from France; their son was with them. He was so different from the boys I was used to; you can imagine the average Hull boy, couldn't speak proper English, never mind being multilingual. He was more grown-up than his seventeen years; his dress sense was impeccable – smart wasn't the word. His manners were typical French; he kissed my hand when we first met, his accent was so sexy and he was so advanced for his years – he was a man of the world in a young man's body.

'My legs just opened up for him; he seduced me one night when Mum and the others had gone out for dinner. He was a nudist, too; even then we were always naked in the house, all of us. His father was a stunning-looking man, and that is where he got his looks from.

'He was staying in the spare room; I had been to the toilet when I heard him in his room. I could hear the bed creaking and him moaning. He was masturbating. The door was not closed properly, so I slowly opened it and peeked in; he was well on the way, lying back with his eyes closed, giving it hell.

'I went in and on tiptoes and stood next to the bed; he was just about there when I touched him. He jumped, and I thought he was going to levitate off the bed, but I carried on stroking him and did not stop me. Then he shot his semen all over my hand and arm; it pumped out of him.

'It went on my breast – oh my god, it felt so hot. I rubbed it in my nipple, then we kissed and after half an hour or so he was rock hard again; he seduced me and fucked me, took my cherry – there was a trickle of blood, but not a lot. It felt so good to be a real woman; it felt so powerful to know that now I could have any man I wanted – but not just any man. I knew that after the only time I had succumbed. I would know when the right man came along, and then you came into my life, darling. I love you so much.'

CHAPTER 31

LEIF

Trying Out Our New Stuff

We never left the hotel that night. We tried all the toys and things we had bought, did everything in every position, and every time, I reached Workington; now that was a journey.

We played using her new black boy on her. I would slide it in her and let go of it; she would use her vagina muscles to push it out, then slide it back in again. She orgasmed time and time again; I had never been with a woman who had so many wild orgasms. Her body arched and trembled, and her eyes rolled back in her head as she climaxed. I put on one of my new condoms; didn't like them. Still, these were not thick; you could more or less see right through them. I had been inside Lynn for a few minutes when I realised I could not feel anything; my penis was numb, but I was still having great sex.

I pulled out and removed the sheath, and Lynn went down on me. Oh yes, she was like a vacuum cleaner. I still hadn't reached Wakefield. She then stopped and tried to say something. But it was like she had had a stroke; the sound was garbled. She then looked a bit worried. 'I can't talk.' Only it didn't sound like that. 'My mouf is mum… why can I mot feel my mouff?' I realised then the stuff inside the condom must have been like the stuff they rub on your gums to numb them when you go to the dentist just before they put the needle in. But this must have been much stronger. I started to laugh. She jumped on me and pushed her tongue in my mouth, licking the inside of my mouth, our tongues rubbing hard. It went numb. I started to try and talk, but my

267

words came out the same. We both fell about on the bed, nearly pissing ourselves. I went limp and had still not ejaculated even though I had been at it for almost an hour. The lube that I had used on Lynn, she said, was unreal. It was kind of tingling; her pussy lips were so sensitive to the touch, and when I was sliding in and out, she said she had never felt anything like it.

The numbness wore off, and we both had a very, very happy ending. We sent for room service and once again had a great meal, finished off with a bottle of Dom Perignon champagne; the end of a perfect day.

We took the ferry from Rotterdam on the evening tide, arriving back in Hull at 7.15am on the Friday morning. I dropped Lynn at her place before setting off for my apartment just after 10am.

We had said we would not go round to our parents' until after tea that night, and we also had decided we would not move in together yet. We would hang on for a few months and wait until Lynn had sorted out her business interests, as she was getting close to breaking away from her current employer and setting up her own business. She would not let me into her ideas just yet, but I was told, 'I am getting close.'

I rang Mum to make sure she was going to be in. She was not going out, but Billy would be in Rayners, his local. I made no mention of our intended news to ensure it was as big a surprise to her as it was to me.

I picked Lynn up; as she got in the car, she said, 'I have an idea; why don't we pick your mum and Billy up and take them to my parents' house, give them a chance to meet.'

I told her that Billy might could well be in the pub, as it was Friday, his big day out, but we could take Mum, as I also thought it was a good idea. It was not too far, as Lynn's parents were in Anlaby and Mum's place was on Hessle High Road.

We arrived at Mum's; I was nervous, as I hadn't even told her I was seeing anyone, or 'courting', as they used to call it. We pulled up outside and went round to the back door; no one ever used the front door – it was just one of those things.

'Hello, Mum, I'm home; where are you?'

She was upstairs. 'Be down in a minute,' she said, so we sat in the living room and waited. The look on Mum's face when she came in and saw Lynn sitting there was priceless.

'Oh! Er, hello, how are you?'

'Mum, I want you to meet Lynn. She is my fiancée; we got engaged while we were in Holland a couple of weeks ago – we wanted to surprise you.'

It was the first time I had ever seen Mum speechless. She took Lynn's hand, looked at the ring, then looked back at me, then looked at the ring again, and still hadn't said anything.

'Fucking hell, Leif! Fucking hell… why didn't you say something? Fucking hell!'

I stood up and hugged her. 'I wanted it to be a surprise.'

'Fucking surprise!' Then she realised what she had said and was quite embarrassed by her language. Still, Hessle Roaders weren't used to pulling punches, and what she said was just the way people talked 'down road'. In fact, the expression 'fucking hell' had numerous uses.

She hadn't said hello or anything to Lynn, then just grabbed her and hugged her like a bear. Lynn was looking over Mum's shoulder at me, with a sort of 'what shall I do?' look on her face.

'OK, Mum, let her breathe; you are smothering her – let Lynn go.'

Mum sat on the settee with Lynn, still holding her hand like a lost child; she started asking questions, such as how we met.

I had told Lynn not to mention the Natsun camp; that would have blown her mind. I then had a horrible thought. If we surprised Lynn's parents, would they be naked in the house? We told Mum what the plan was, and she thought it was a fantastic idea. I pulled Lynn to one side to tell her of my concern about what her mum and dad might be wearing – or not wearing – when we got there.

'OK, I will ring them and tell them I am bringing someone who is not a nudist to ask their advice about some business venture I am looking at, so they need to be dressed.'

'Can I use your phone please, Mum? Lynn just wants to ring her parents to make sure they are in.'

She went into the hallway and rang them, coming back after a short conversation. 'No problem; they weren't going out anyway.'

It didn't take us long to get round to their house, pulling into the horse-shoe drive and parking up in front of the entrance. Gry and Lucas opened the door as we were getting out of the car; they both looked puzzled, to say the least, to see me and a woman in a headscarf getting out of the car.

'Mum, Dad, you know Leif – you met at the caravan site a while back. This is his mother, Christine.' They put out their hands to greet her, both half-smiling, still unaware of what was going on. Realising we were all standing on the drive in the middle of December, Lucas was the first to speak. 'Oh sorry, come in, come in – you must be freezing.' He took my mum's arm and led her into the hallway, followed by Gry and Lynn with me following at the rear of the procession.

We got into the living room, and Gry asked us all what drinks we would like – tea, coffee, or something more substantial. We all settled for tea. Gry disappeared into the kitchen, returning after a few minutes with a tray with the best china on it. This was obvious, but a thing mothers do when unexpected strangers turn up at their houses.

Lots of small talk passed between us all until Lynn came out with the punchline.

'Mum, Dad, we have something to tell you; it is rather a surprise.'

'You aren't… are you? You're not…?' said Gry.

'Mother, no, don't you dare ask if I am pregnant – no, I'm not.' You could see Gry relax, then Lynn followed through with, 'But we have got engaged; Leif and I are going to get married.'

You could hear the old pin drop; then Lucas broke the silence.

'About bloody time you found someone, my girl, I was beginning to wonder.'

He stood up, kissed his daughter, then came over to me, shook my hands, and hugged me. It was like being gripped in a vice. Jesus, he was strong. I apologised for not asking him if I could marry her; he just shrugged it off.

'It's old-fashioned, son, don't worry about it. I am pleased you two have got together, especially as you already knew each other from the nudist camp.'

With that, my mother's mouth opened as wide as the river Hull. 'Fucking nudist camp? What's he talking about, Leif?'

Talk about shit hitting the fan – it had come in bucketfuls. My Mum had no idea, as I had never told her. I'd never quite known how she would react, and what she didn't know didn't hurt her.

Both Gry and Lynn looked at me, giving me daggers, not knowing what to say to follow that bombshell. Neither did I, to be honest; I just looked bemused.

'Well, I'm waiting. Have you something to tell your mother? Why be so secretive about it? I don't give a monkeys what people do in private. I have often wondered about it when I have seen things in the papers or magazines. It's popular, but I never knew there was anything round Hull. Where is it?'

I was taken aback by her response; you could feel the tension release as Mum made her statement. I told her it was nearer to Hornsea than Hull, that I had been a member for a long while, and that was where I first met Lynn, and she used to go there from being a young girl with her mum and dad.

Then the thing I never dreamt I would hear came out of Mum's mouth.

'Oh! I would like to try it. Can I come? But only when it gets a bit warmer, not now in midwinter, no, thank you.'

'Of course you can come to visit us,' said Gry. 'We have a cabin on the site, and of course, Leif has his caravan.'

Mum's head nearly twisted off her neck.

Gry went on to tell Mum all about the camp, and that she felt that it was a great place, and how the freedom of being naked was so refreshing.

Lynn stood up. 'Can we stop talking about the camp now,' she said, 'and discuss why we are here – to discuss our marriage and when it will take place.'

Now my ears pricked up; we hadn't discussed when the big day would be, never mind our parents.

'It has to be a June wedding when the weather has a chance of being good,' Gry chipped in. Then the open forum began, and I could not get a word in. I just sat back and let the others decide when I was going to tie the knot. In the end, we all agreed to think about it and come back later on.

We left Gry and Lucas's house and dropped Mum off on the way back to my place; we hadn't spoken much on the journey before Lynn said, 'I am sorry – I didn't mean to bring up the wedding date thing, that just slipped out. I had been thinking about it, and as I started talking, I just said what I was thinking.'

'Don't worry; we can let them know when it's going to be when we have decided.'

That was the last time it was mentioned for a long time, as we both had to be back in Holland after the New Year to get back to work. We had a great Christmas Day; we had lunch at my Mum's – full Christmas dinner, roast turkey, the complete works.

I went in Rayners with Billy for a pint before dinner, which was a bit of a ritual, and met some old faces I had not seen for years. I was standing at the bar near one of the four beer pump stations. It was supposed to be one of the longest bars in Yorkshire. There was a door at the back of the serving area that led to a passage to the smoke room and the singing rooms at the back of the pub. There was a lad waiting to be served, whose face I knew but couldn't put a name to him. He spotted me.

'Hiya, Leif,' he said. 'How are you? Not seen you for a while. Where have you been?'

'Here and there, you know how it is,' I replied.

Then another guy said, 'Oh, you know, Kenny, do you? He is always in here, him and his old man; you know the coal merchants.'

Then it came to me – Kenny Smith. I had not seen him since 1960 when we were in the same class together at Boulevard.

'Unreal! Not seen you for a while.'

What an understatement; but I suppose when you look back, when the fishing industry was alive, you could go for years without seeing people. And with all the people moving away to east Hull and the council estates on Bransholme, the community had been torn apart.

On Boxing Day we went to Lynn's parents for another Christmas lunch – once again, turkey and all the trimmings were on offer. If I never saw another turkey leg again it would have been too soon, and sprouts – oh, how I hated fucking sprouts.

On New Year's Eve, Lynn came to mine and we stayed in. We had a nice bottle of wine and a meal – steak, which I cooked – and a night by the fire, naked of course. We still had some presents to open, unique gifts that we bought each other over in Holland. We saw the new year in, wrapped in each other's arms after making love once again. Oh, how I loved this girl, the future Mrs Leif Askenes. I could not wait to make her mine.

We had got back to Rotterdam and work. I had been there about three weeks when Lynn came round telling me she was going to be transferred to Oslo for a month the following week.

She was devastated, in tears, but we knew it would happen one day; it was all part of our jobs. I hugged her and tried to console her, telling her not to get upset, and we would be OK. I could come and visit her every two weeks, which meant I would only see her for three days during the next month. Even when I thought of it myself, it did not seem too great.

The situation was not going to work; I never imagined that I would put anything in front of my work, but being almost married was getting to me; something had to be done.

I was in my apartment one evening, a few months later. Lynn was still travelling with her job; the company had given her a promotion, one that was so good she had put her idea of going it alone on the backburner. But – yes, there is always a but – it meant she would be away more often, and it also meant travelling further afield, as they were going global, plus they had offered her the overall control of the programme. We had discussed the situation in depth; she offered to knock the job back, but I knew she would never forgive me if she did, so I encouraged her to take it, even though I hated the idea.

I decided to go out for a few beers, got the tram into the city, and frequented a couple of bars. In the Atlas Bar, I was having a cold beer when I heard a voice I recognised, over at the back of the room.

CHAPTER 32

LARS

The Time Had Come – A Year Later

J anuary 1987 – a great time of the year, summer, and things were getting better and better. We had tried to arrange some time off to get back to Europe, but we could just not fit it in; the building game in NSW was unreal. We had expanded yet again. We were now one of the leading crane hire companies in Sydney, Wollongong and Newcastle. We had opened branches in Coffs Harbour on the north coast and Tamworth in the state's north-west.

We were looking again at going to the UK, and then the Wall Street Crash happened on October 19, when the Dow Jones fell more than twenty per cent in one hit; in Hong Kong, it fell a massive forty-five per cent. The world of finance was in turmoil.

It did not hit us that hard, but many companies suffered and building slowed down as people were worried about taking out mortgages. It seemed good to me to start thinking about that holiday; flight fares were lower, people weren't travelling. We decided, fuck it – you can't take it with you, so we began to organise our trip. We did have second thoughts at one point, though, after two major transport disasters. A cross-channel ferry capsized, and then there was an underground fire at King's Cross in London, which made us a bit wary about going. Then England also suffered one of the worst storms in history when hurricane-force winds hit much of the south.

The holiday took some arranging, and 1988 came around. There was always something happening at work. We had gone to the Bank of New South Wales's travel department and asked them to draw up an itinerary for a trip to Europe that must include Paris, Rome, Madrid, Amsterdam, London and possibly Edinburgh, as well as Hull and Blackpool. We had gone off Venice, as we had decided to get married in London; why not? I was a Pom by birth. We told the bank it was to be between six weeks to two months' duration.

We wanted to fly first-class, or if that was too expensive, we had read that Qantas had started business class in 1979 and we thought we would like to travel on that – nothing like economy. Qantas Airlines' main route was the Kangaroo Route from London to Sydney, with lots of stops on the way. They came back to us saying the best flights would be to travel via the USA with Continental Airlines, for they were the best seats and what you might call frills.

There was not much difference in the seats, but it was less hassle when you checked in, as well as better meals, boarding privileges and more baggage allowances. There was one other alternative – to fly over to Perth and take the one-stop in Bombay, a twenty-hour flight to London; there was no business class, but it was less hassle changing flights in the USA, so we plumped for this. We had to cut down a bit on baggage, but we decided we could handle that.

We also decided it would be a great idea to drive around Europe. We would fly to London to visit France. We weren't sure about Spain but would make changes if required. Then we'd head back up to Italy via the south of France, into Belgium, then on to the Netherlands and Amsterdam. Leaving the mainland of Europe, we could then cross the North Sea from Rotterdam to Hull and then up to Edinburgh. We'd work our way back to London and fly back to Perth, catching the Indian Pacific. We felt this would round off a fantastic holiday. This final part of the trip was the bugbear it tended to be booked up years in advance. The only way we could get on it was to book the platinum service, all-inclusive. Yes, it was expensive, but we wanted it so badly.

The advert read, 'From the glittering blue of the Indian Ocean in Perth to Sydney's cosmopolitan metropolis on the Pacific Ocean.'

For this reason, we put our trip back until 1988; it worked out well and enabled us to have everything in place.

Having chosen the self-drive option, it meant a hell of a lot of driving, but there were two of us to share it, and we had plenty of time over two months.

We left for Perth on August 20, 1988, on the early morning flight from Kingsford Smith Airport; we were due to fly out on the British Airways flight that evening. It was a great trip; the Poms had got it right. We had got ourselves extra legroom as our seats were near the doors, which took a bit of bribery, but we had booked the trip well in advance, and the bank had priority as it booked so many flights.

The journey was broken down with one stop for refuelling; when we got off the plane in Bombay it was like walking into a furnace; the humidity was unreal. We were pleased to get back on after about an hour. I was lucky that I did sleep a little in the next part; they offered us food every three hours or so and kept coming round with drinks, and to be fair, the service was spot on, no complaints at all.

When we arrived – talk about tired; I had never been so fucked in my life when we landed at London Heathrow, and it was dark and pissing down. What a terrible greeting to England at 9am.

We were booked in a hotel near Heathrow; we checked in by 10.30am. We had quick shower, breakfast and went to bed. I could not sleep; I tossed and turned, so I got up. Maya was still crashed out. I put some clothes on and went down to the bar for a couple of beers. There were four choices; I picked something called Briscoe's IPA to try. Oh my god, it was warm, and it tasted like piss – not that I have ever tasted piss, but it was terrible. The barman asked if I was OK. I told him I was going to call the police and tell them that he had tried to poison me. He just laughed, took the beer away, poured it down the sink and offered me a lager; whatever that was, at least it was cold, and it wasn't too bad.

After four pints, I was bloated and knew I had been on the beer, so I went back up to bed. Maya was still snoring. I joined her and woke up with my head throbbing at 1am.

Maya was sitting watching some old movie on the TV. I was starving, and decided I did not like this jet-set thing; I wished that we had never left home, and it was only our first day. We both crashed out again watching *The African Queen*; some guy was walking in the water and pushing this old boat through a swamp, with some sheila sitting in it talking with a funny voice.

At 10am, the telephone rang. It was some sheila with an accent I had never heard before wishing me good morning and reminding us that we had to check out at noon sharp, or there would be extra charges.

We had transport arranged to take us to Dover to catch the ferry across to Calais, where we had booked in another hotel for the night, as we were going to pick a hire car the following morning that would take us around Europe. We had been given a brand-new 1988 Opel Ascona, 1.8i engine, which only had 500 miles on the clock and was classed as a large family car. They had upgraded us due to the length of hire we had taken. I was pleased, for the legroom in a smaller car would have been tight, mainly as we were now both driving a BMW 6 series at home.

We set off for Paris; it was fun driving on the wrong side of the road. Still, they had conveniently moved the steering wheel over to the other side of the car. We soon got used to it, but what we didn't realise that most French drivers thought they were in the Le Mans twenty-four hour race; they were crazy, and driving in Paris was a nightmare. We always said Sydney was terrible. Home was like a country town compared with this.

Thankfully, the bank's itinerary was spot on, with directions to each hotel; this was OK as long as we followed the routes laid out by them, but if we decided to take a detour anywhere, this did cause a few problems. There was no satnav in those days, just a load of fold-up maps you kept in the door pocket or glove box. The bank had issued us one for every country we were due to visit, and the idea was to unfold it like a giant newspaper the night before and mark it up with a black pen according to the documentation they had supplied – and it was a bloody good job they had.

When one was driving, the other was navigator and, to be honest, Maya was a better navigator than me, so it turned out I did most of the driving. We had asked that we did not drive more than four hours between stops and no fewer than two nights in any one place, apart from the major cities, when we had asked for four nights.

They had come up with exactly what we asked; for now, we did not know that Paris was divided into twenty arrondissements, or areas. Our first hotel was the Hotel Regina, which first opened in 1900. It was unreal when you realised that Australia was only founded 112 years before. It was near the Louvre and a lot more of the Paris tourist traps.

We had four great days in 'Gay Paris', and off we went to Belgium. We stopped halfway in Amiens, about three hours' drive from Paris, in a small hotel in the centre of the town. It was the nearest hotel to the old city and only a minute away from the cathedral and the home of the writer Jules Verne; he spent eighteen years living there and wrote most of his work there. All in all, we had two beautiful nights in the city.

So far, we were having a great time; we loved France and all its history. The next stop was Bruges in Belgium. One thing we noticed was that there were no borders. We were told that five countries had opened their borders after some agreement was signed in June 1985.

We loved the ambience in every country we had visited and couldn't get over how green everything was, how close each town was to each other, how narrow the streets were in the old town areas, along with the new towns that had sprung up after the Second World War.

The next stop was Amsterdam, the sex city of Europe. I was looking forward to visiting the red light district – just for a look, you understand. We were booked in the Park Plaza hotel right in the centre of everything, within walking distance of all the tourist attractions, including the red light district.

On our first day, we visited the Anne Frank Museum, and the Rijksmuseum – the principal national museum of the Netherlands. It illustrates the art and history of the country from the Middle Ages to the present day. The Van Gogh Museum was unreal, but we had had enough museums for the first day; too many to mention.

We were sitting in our hotel room after having a swim in the pool and a relaxing massage.

'What's on tonight, then? Suppose you want to hit the girls?' Maya was laughing when she said it.

'Might as well while we are here – just a look… unless you want to come in with me and learn a few things, Maya, my friend,' I said, smiling.

'There is nothing I don't know about sex, thank you very much. You don't complain very often.'

We decided to eat out and find an Italian, or maybe an Indonesian – I had read that was very popular in Holland; the rijsttafel was supposed to be very good. The Dutch word that translates to 'rice table' is an elaborate Indonesian meal adapted by the Dutch.

We found a small restaurant recommended by a guy in one of the bars we visited; it was supposedly one of the city's oldest bars. Established in 1624, Café Chris was where, we were told, the Westertoren Tower construction workers received their payments. The famous painter, Rembrandt van Rijn, also lived in the area. He even had a studio nearby; it is safe to suppose that he probably frequented the café as well. The interior was exquisite and full of character. The ceiling beams were beautifully engraved, and the dark wood was stunning.

We left the restaurant heading for the windows in the red light district – unbelievable; I'd never seen anything like it. Whatever your fancy, it was here. Walking around the streets and passages was a lesson in itself. We stopped off for a beer or two on our walk, and in one bar we got talking to a couple from Newcastle in NSW, not UK, and they asked if we had been to one of the sex clubs or shows. We told them we hadn't heard about them, never mind visiting one, and they said they were going. Did we fancy coming along for a look as they had two spare tickets? Some friends had chickened out after purchasing them.

We accepted the invitation and made our way to the bar/theatre, which was only a short walk from where we were. Taking our seats at a table, right next to the small stage, there was a mixed audience, mostly tourists of all ages and nationalities. There was a big sign on the doors as we entered – 'No Photography.' We were searched for cameras, and if you had one, you had to hand it in and were given a ticket to reclaim it after the show.

The show started with a couple of strippers, good-looking girls with very fit bodies, who finished up doing a bit of a lesbian act – not too explicit, but enough to stir the loins.

Another girl came in with a snake about five feet long; it looked like a python, but I'm no expert. It wasn't black or brown, that was for sure, and where that snake got to was unbelievable; it actually disappeared between her legs at one point.

Another girl came on after a round bed was placed on the stage. She started to undress seductively; a vibrator appeared from I don't know where and she began to enjoy herself with that. The music was soft, which was more than I was, as I sat watching. I realised then why the round bed revolved, so that all sides of the stage got a perfect view.

Later on, there was a big black guy who must have been 6ft 7in; I'm 6ft 4in, and he was bigger than me. He was naked apart from a loin-cloth. They started to perform, kissing, stroking – they did everything one could imagine. She pulled off the loincloth, and he had grown another arm. I had never seen a penis as significant, not only long but thick. I looked at Maya; she was licking her lips staring at this monster cock. Looking around the audience, I could see every woman was fixated on this man.

He mounted the woman; I didn't think she would take him, but it went in up to the hilt. She was moaning and screaming. Believe me, this was no act; she was well and truly rooted. He fucked for what seemed to be ages – longer than I could have gone; I had almost shot in my shorts. He finished off by withdrawing and shooting his semen all over her breasts; she rubbed it in and then licked her hands.

They both got off the bed; the crowd gave them a standing ovation. The men were all standing in more ways than one, myself included.

That was the end of the show, and we left all discussing the last act. The couple we had gone with, Terry and Leanne, said they were off back to the hotel to tell their friends about it. 'And then an early night,' we laughed as they left us.

We got back to our hotel, and the only thing I can say if you have any problems with your sex life, is get to one of these shows. It's better than a porn film, being there next to the action – and that night we had the best sex we'd had for years. We were both that turned on; it was fantastic.

On our last day in Amsterdam, we did a canal cruise, which was a must. We did consider going back to the sex show but decided not to; instead we had a romantic meal in a nearby Italian restaurant.

We changed our travel plans as we had decided to visit Scandinavia. We left Amsterdam and made our way up through Germany on to Norway via Denmark, where, on our way back, we would get the ferry from Esbjerg to Harwich in south-east England.

We landed in Oslo, having taken the ferry from Copenhagen, which was a beautiful city; we just wished we had stayed there a bit longer.

I did not know a great deal about my Norwegian heritage, so I wanted to find out as much as possible. I hadn't realised how the famine in the 1800s had devastated the country and just how many people had left to go to the new world in the USA. Thousands had fled and lots more had perished. I could go on, but don't want to bore you – to me, though, it was terrific finding out how my ancestors lived; people I did not know existed until I found out about being stolen from my birth mother.

We had had a great time up to now; we then travelled back to Denmark to catch the ferry to the UK.

CHAPTER 33

LEIF
Old Friend

There was a group of guys, a bit rowdy but just enjoying themselves, when I noticed that one of them was Geoff Oswald, the guy I'd met on my Isle of Wight trip. I went over to say hello; he had his back to me as I walked over.

'Hello, Geoff, how are you? Been a while,' I said.

He turned, and a big smile came across his face. 'Well, I'll be fucked! How's you, Leif? My, you are looking well – come on, let me buy you a drink.'

We took our drinks and went and sat away from the other guys. We exchanged the usual banter; had I heard from Einar and Borg? He went on to tell me where he had been and what he had been up to since we last met. His favourite subject was still his seafaring antics.

After a few months off, he had gone back to sea and was now working for a Singapore salvage company as a captain on one of the biggest ocean-going tugs in the world. He had been on the job off Malaysia in the Strait of Malacca, which connects the Pacific Ocean to the east with the Indian Ocean to the west, and at its narrowest point, is 1.7 miles wide. He told me the job involved a collision between the Hiroshima Moon, laden with 40,000 tons of crude oil, and the Pacific Promise, a container ship. After the initial collisions, some 12,000 tons of oil had escaped into the sea and caught fire; both vessels were engulfed in flames. The rescue ships were floating around on a sea of fire, trying to put out the inferno but not getting set alight at the same time. Geoff believed it must have been the nearest thing to hell he had ever seen. All but four of the Pacific Promise's crew perished, and only three on the Hiroshima Moon survived. Several tugs, which had dashed to the scene in the hope of a salvage job, eventually helped extinguish the fire and tranship the cargo, and the vessel was safely redelivered to her owners. It emerged that the collision had been a result of the Hiroshima Moon being taken by pirates who, after locking the crew in the accommodation, then abandoned ship, leaving the vessel still under way yet without any bridge officers in control, and it had rammed the Pacific Promise.

Geoff was clearly traumatised by the whole event. 'It was the hardest job I have ever been involved with and will never forget the scene,' he said. 'It's hit me so hard I have given my notice in to my company. I felt I was getting too old for this swashbuckling life, searching the seas for ships in distress, like some sea-going hyena looking for its prey. I finish for good in three months. I am now officially semi-retired, enjoying my life living in the marina with Karen.'

'How is she, Geoff; well, I hope?'

'Oh yes, same, same – she often mentions you and the great time we had when you all visited us.'

I did not think he was fishing or trying to trip me up into saying yes, Karen was a great fuck, or the like, but I had to be very careful in picking my answers.

'Yes, I enjoyed your company. I have settled down myself and am engaged to marry a girl called Lynn; she is from my hometown, Hull. You must come to visit us here – that's my business card, and my private number is on the back.'

We spent the rest of the night drinking and relaxing; he never mentioned Karen again until we got up to leave. 'Now, don't forget you are always welcome in my house. I know Karen would love to see you and your fiancée.'

We said our farewells, and we both left the bar. He went his way along with the rest of the crew to get back to his ship. I turned in the opposite direction to go back to my place. I arrived home a bit worse for wear, but it had been an enjoyable night nonetheless.

I was woken up early the next morning when the phone rang; I answered it, bleary-eyed and head pounding.

'Hi, babe, how are you?' It was Lynn. I did not say anything for a moment or two, still half-asleep. 'Hello, you there, Leif? Answer me, Leif.'

'Yes, babe, sorry, I'm still not fully awake – how're things, OK?'

She told me that everything was going along great; she was making progress in Spain and would be staying there another week. She would be going on to Portugal for two weeks, then should be home for a few days before heading to a conference in Athens for a week. She would not let me get a word in; she never asked how I was, or how my work was. It was all her and her fucking company. I knew she was enjoying the job and the thrill of the environment she was now in, being a high-flyer in the firm. The only problem was I was missing her; never before had I played second fiddle, and I did not like it, not one bit. We chatted for about half an hour; most of it was her talking. She had changed, and I wasn't impressed. I cut her off in full flight.

'Lynn, we have to talk. We need to discuss the situation we are in; it's not working being apart, especially now when you are so far away we can't meet for long weekends. I miss you so much.'

The line went quiet for a bit. 'OK, I understand, babe. I agree we must talk. I'm sorry you are feeling neglected and missing me, for I also feel the same. But it's my job – we must be able to sort it out. Wait until I get back… I've got to go babe, speak later. I love you.' And she was gone.

We had only seen each other on the odd occasion; it was killing me. I had been celibate all this time, despite being close on a couple of occasions, but no, I was being faithful to my fiancée. There was no doubt my right hand was my best friend, and I had gone back to my childhood in doing it for myself; it was OK but couldn't beat the real thing.

I enjoyed being with Vanderries and had settled in quite nicely. It was a fantastic company to work for, the money was great, four-day week – what more could one ask?

But I was still missing my fiancée. Not being with her was something awful, apart from not getting my leg over.

CHAPTER 34

LEIF

New Kid on the Block

I had been home for a weekend and returned a couple of weeks later, and there was a new kid on the block who had started that morning. She was from the Norwegian office, a typical Scandinavian tall blonde going by the name of Ingrid.

She was unreal; she looked like she had been chiselled out of marble. She must have been six feet tall, with legs that were, well, the best I had ever seen, and a perfect face, high cheekbones, a mouth that just begged for it to be kissed… wow, she was absolutely stunning.

'Leif, I want you to meet Ingrid Neilson,' said my supervisor. 'She has joined the company as a quality control engineer. She has been transferred from our Bergen office to gain experience in the module yards.'

'Hello, Leif; very nice to meet you. I hope I can learn a lot from you during my stay in Rotterdam. I'm so looking forward to picking your brains.'

'Hi, Ingrid, the feeling's mutual. Welcome to Rotterdam; I hope we can help you in gaining some knowledge of the fabrication facility and what it is all about.'

She would be working alongside me to pick up how things worked in the yard. Now, that was all I needed – I wasn't getting my end away, and I get put with a Britt Ekland lookalike. Along with that, she had a fantastic personality; you could not help but like her.

We got close over the next few weeks, going out for a few beers after work a couple of times. It was the height of summer, and the weather was beautiful. I had been going to the local nudist beach on the weekend, on my own; Lynn had been when she was back in Rotterdam but very infrequently, if not at all.

I was bending over some drawings at work one day, and Ingrid came up behind me. My shirt had ridden up my back, showing some bare skin. I had topped up my tan, as being naked in the sun was one of life's pleasures.

'Hi, Leif,' she said, 'I could not help but see – how come you are tanned all over, with no white bits?'

I laughed and told her about being a nudist and going to the beaches at weekends.

'Oh wow, I am a nudist, too! Can I come with you next weekend, please? I did not know anyone in the company was into naturism; I would love to come.'

Oh my god, now this was music to my ears – I couldn't wait for Friday to come.

We got the train to Amsterdam and then the tram down to the local beach; as soon as we got there, Ingrid stripped off. What a body – fuck me, I could not take my eyes off her, and nor could most of the men as we walked along the water's edge; she was stunning. I could see the guys thinking, you lucky bastard. It was a pity they did not know she did not belong to me.

We found a spot a bit away from the crowds and lay down our towels. Ingrid started to put sun cream on as the sun was scorching that day. I don't usually use it, but she offered me some and started to rub it on my body. Ingrid put some on my back for me; her touch almost made me stand to attention. An unwritten law among nudists is never getting an erection. She then lay on the towel, asking me to put some cream on her back.

What a sight lay before me – a blonde goddess, a body like a statue, not a spare ounce to be seen, and she wanted me to rub cream on her. How could I do this without getting hard? I do not know, but I tried. Her buttocks were firm, with no marks, nothing, and perfect, smooth skin; she must work out, I thought. I had never seen her in this light, as at work, we wore boiler suits most of the time, and when we met socially, she was always in jeans and a baggy T-shirt. As I was rubbing her back, she said, 'Have I got my ass covered, Leif? I don't want to get that sunburnt – can you rub some on to make sure it's all covered, please.'

Fucking please? I did not need asking. Oh, Jesus, it felt so good as I rubbed the cream all over. She giggled when my hand went between her legs and said, 'That's near enough, Leif. I might start to enjoy it.'

We had a great day, and we did not need to leave to go for lunch as we had taken a picnic with us. The sun was going down; we packed up to set off for home. As we walked along back to the promenade, Ingrid put her arm in mine and told me, 'Leif, thank you. I have truly enjoyed today; when can we come again? I like being with you. You have made me welcome; to be honest, I was getting a bit homesick, missing my friends.'

'Of course we can; I also am enjoying your company. We are both in the same boat, working away from home and our families; it's not only great working with you, but meeting socially away from the office has been fun.'

She gave me a hug and smile; I almost melted.

I was getting close to Ingrid, maybe too close, but hey, I was only human. Over the next few weeks, we saw quite a lot of each other, and one day I was daydreaming and staring at her on the other side of the office.

I was thinking of Lynn and how it was not working. Our engagement was just not right, being apart like this, for it had been nearly a year. We had hardly seen each other, just late-night phone calls when it was all about her and that fucking job. When we did start talking about different things, telling each other how we loved and missed each other, we both used to masturbate on the phone until we both climaxed. It was a relief, no doubt. Still, it was no substitute, no way.

I did not realise Ingrid could see me staring at her until I blinked and then saw her. I quickly looked away and went back to study the documents on my desk. A couple of minutes later, she came over behind me, put her arm on my shoulder, and looked down at the drawing; I could feel her breath on my neck. Mmm, it felt good. She whispered, 'Are you

OK, Leif? Nothing wrong, I hope? Let's have a drink after work, OK?'

We worked late that night as we needed to get a report done for a meeting the next day, so it was about 7.30pm when we got finished. We were alone in the office; everyone else had gone. Ingrid came over and asked if I was ready to go. There was something different about her; I wasn't sure what it was until we got in the lift. As the doors closed, she put her arms around my neck and kissed me full on the lips.

Stunned was not the word; surprised came to mind… bowled over was more like it; I had not expected that. The kiss lasted longer than just a kiss; it was a full-weight snog – what a kisser. Ingrid pulled away and smiled, saying, 'Leif, forgive me, but I have wanted to do that for such a long time. When I saw you staring at me today, the look in your eyes made my mind up for me. Yes, I wanted you – I have wanted to taste your lips for such a long time and now I have, I want more.' She then came back to me for another helping.

What made it worse, so did I. Lynn was not going to like this, but she wasn't going to find out; what she did not know could not hurt her.

We left the office and went to another bar we used pretty often, knowing full well that it was one that none of the other staff frequented. We did not want to be seen as having an office romance. We found a booth and sat down next to each other, not across from each other as we had done on previous occasions. Ingrid took a drink of her beer and put the glass down; she then put her hand on mine.

'Well, Leif, what are we going to do about this situation? I want you, and I know damn well you want me, right?'

I just nodded in agreement, then finally managed to say, 'Yes.'

'As you said before,' said Ingrid, 'we are both alone in a city far from home, both missing our loved ones, for I am also engaged to be married to a guy who goes to sea. He is away months at a time, but we have an open relationship. We can both have sex with others as long as neither of us finds out about it.'

I was just sitting there not saying a word, then the question was thrown at me.

'Leif, can I ask you a personal question?'

'Of course, you can; what is it?'

'Can I make love to you?'

Now, that was one of my lines. I had used this many times, but it had never happened to me the other way round. You can guess the answer – we finished our drinks and went back to my place.

I had never been seduced by such a wonderful, experienced woman in my entire life. What she did not do to me has not been invented; you name it, we did it. I could not believe it; it was like a porn movie but in real-time.

We lay back on the bed, sweat running off the pair of us; talk about insatiable – she could not get enough. Still, she wanted more, but I could not get him up for it; we decided to rest while I opened a bottle of wine, and we went and sat in the living room, both still naked. God, I loved this nudist thing.

We sat on the floor just talking and touching. She was magnificent; I could not take my eyes off her. She told me how she used to be a gymnast at a younger age and a basketball player; she certainly had the size for it. 'Do you still work out or go to a gym when you are home?' I said.

'No, not at all. I do sometimes go to a sauna now and again; it helps my body keep in trim. Do you know of any around here? We could go together if there is a mixed one.'

'I will make some enquiries tomorrow; some of the guys might know if there is one about – it'll be fun.' She then stood up and bent over, her face nearly touching the floor; her arse, so perfectly round, was there in front of me. She started doing some gymnastic moves, standing on one leg and lifting the other straight up – I could not believe how supple her body was. She told me she was a bit out of shape. Well, if she was, I did not know what she would be like fully fit; the mind boggled.

To finish off her routine, she lay on her back, lifted herself until she was almost upright, resting on her shoulders, and opened her legs wide apart; they were horizontal to the floor, not trembling – solid as a rock.

I could not resist it; temptation got the better of me. I just had to go and stroke her. It was laid out in front of me like the proverbial buffet, ready to be eaten. She did not flinch as I stroked her, just a slight moan as my fingers ran over her entrance. I bent over and blew on to it as if I was cooling some chips; that was it – my face covered her.

'Can I talk to it?' I said.

'Do whatever you want, babe.'

I then said, 'Hellooo,' and my tongue came out to its fullest length, licking it like a cat lapping up some milk.

'Mmmmm, baby,' she sighed, and her body trembled; as she climaxed, it felt as though she was going to suck me in. I pulled away and went down on the floor, waiting for her to join me. She then lowered herself down ever so slowly and came back to me; we just cuddled up, opened another bottle, then retired to bed to finish off a great day.

We had to be up early. Ingrid had to go back to her hotel as she needed a change of clothes for work to enable us to meet again for the usual start of 7.30am, making out that nothing had happened that night. Still, it was to be the first of many, as I did not realise what I had got myself in to.

I went home the following weekend without Lynn. I am sorry to say I don't know if I was getting paranoid, but I felt we were drifting apart. I needed to see her face to face to sort it out one way or another.

CHAPTER 35

LEIF

Never Thought it Would Happen

I went round to Mum's, and we were sitting having a cuppa, when she came out with a beauty.

'When you taking me to see Natsun, then?'

'Are you serious, Mum? You want to go to a nudist camp?'

'Yes, of course, why not? I do fancy it.'

'What about Billy, Mum? Do you want him to come with us?'

'No way, he would be wanking as he walked around; best if he didn't know anything about it.'

We arrived at the site that afternoon. I had told Mum the rules; I was a bit apprehensive as I had never seen her naked for a long time, and she had not seen me without clothes since I was a child, so it was going to be a surprise for both of us.

We went to the reception. Molly was on duty as usual. Did she ever have a day off? Mum filled out the form and had a chat with Molly about the rules, which she already knew. Still, Molly insisted – protocol. We went into the changing rooms and came out a few minutes later. Now, I know I should not say this about my mother, but what a great body – I hadn't realised how fit she was for fifty-seven. Anyway, I digress. Mum looked me up and down and said, 'OK, take the towel away – I have seen it before.' I moved the towel. 'Wow, it's grown a bit since the last time I saw it, son,' she laughed.

We walked through the park towards my van, which Mum knew nothing about; as we passed people who knew me and said hello, Mum asked, 'Who's that? They seem nice.'

I pulled the van keys out of the small bag I had with me and unlocked the door. 'Wow, this is posh,' said Mum. When I told her it was mine, she muttered something about 'More bloody secrets.'

Going inside, I got a couple of sunbeds out from under the bed. Mum was going through the place like a burglar in every cupboard, asking questions and chattering away.

'Come on outside. I will put the kettle on for a brew.'

She sat down and started going on about why hadn't I told her about this before. How long had I had it – all the usual stuff. I brought out the tea, set it on the table, and sat next to Mum. Then came the inquisition. Oh my god, it must have lasted half an hour. 'Who else knew about this paradise? Can I come and use it when you aren't here?'

I was a bit apprehensive about that; it was not Nettleton's Field, it was my private place. I did not want Billy and all his Rayners mates coming down and trying to get in. When I told Mum this she was a bit upset; she did not say as much, but I could tell by the expression on her face.

'Mum – Billy would not fit in here, now would he? Be honest now; it is just not Billy.'

'Yes, I suppose you are right, son, but I can come on my own. I will just tell him I am going away to see friends or something.'

'What friends do you know outside of Hull? You have never been off Hessle Road. Billy would start to think you had got someone else. Also, how are you going to get here, for a start? There is no public transport to the site; you need a car to get here.'

'But there is a bus stop at the end of the lane; I could get off there or get to Hornsea and get a taxi back.'

'Mum, it is a good mile and a half walk from the stop to the site. What if it is pissing down? What would you do then?'

There were too many reasons why it was not feasible.

'Look, I will bring you now and again when I am home; I don't mind doing that – but it is my hideaway from everyone, and I want it to stay that way, understand? Apart from the fact it was my sex pad to bring girls to, and I did not want my mother cramping my style.'

That should not have come out, not to my mother anyway.

She went quiet then and, after a few minutes, agreed and said no more on the subject.

Not long after, Lynn's parents arrived; now, this was going to be an eye-opener when they saw Mum lying out in all her glory; you should have seen Mum's expression when she saw them.

'Do not say a word, Mum; now you have seen them, and they have seen you – just leave it at that.'

'But I would never imagine she was so fit for her age and him… well, he is…'

I cut Mum off in mid-sentence; in the end, they came over for a drink and a chat, but there was an air of… I don't know? They did not stop long and left.

Mum had decided she wanted to stay the night; I had to make the single bed up as she wished to have the double. I was a bit too old to sleep with Mum. I had never made love to a fifty-seven-year-old woman in my life, and I had no intention of starting with my mother. Fit as she was. Thinking about it, Molly was the oldest, with Borg a close second. There was a lot to be said for the older woman, without a doubt.

I was up early the following day and went for a swim in the pool. Lucas, Lynn's father, was in there doing his regular thirty lengths. He had done this every morning for as long as I had known him. He kind of blanked me as we met on the side of the pool; as I was about to start my swimming, he stopped in front of me, for he had finished his routine.

'How are things, Lucas, OK?' He looked at me strangely as if he did not want to talk to me. 'Hey, what's going on? Why are you avoiding me? I'm engaged to your daughter, for fuck's sake.'

He looked at me and said, 'I am so sorry things haven't worked out for you and Lynn, what with her job and everything.'

Things had not worked out? He must know something I don't, I thought.

'What are you referring to? I haven't spoken to Lynn for a few weeks. What the fuck are you on about? Come on, Lucas, tell me – what has she told you?'

He got out of the water and headed to the showers. I was quickly in there with him; I grabbed his arm and would not let go.

'Lucas, you must know something I don't know. Now, what's going on, or do I have to beat it out of you?'

He slumped down on the bench. 'I know that you have split up because it isn't working out with Lynn travelling with her job. What with not seeing each other for weeks on end, she said it was best you split up – that it was your idea. When you rang her and told her you were finished, I must say I think you did the honourable thing when you told her to keep the ring as a sign of friendship, a memento of great times. That was very good of you, son; unfortunately, when she rang us to tell us the news, she was in a hell of a state because you had finished with her. She was almost suicidal.'

'When was this? When did she ring you? I have not spoken to her; she is lying.'

'This was about three weeks ago. I must go. I'm so sorry, Leif. I liked you as well, son.'

I was gutted, to say the least. I had to get in touch with her. I rang her that night, but there was no answer, not even her answer machine was on.

The next morning I collared Lucas and Gry. I went to their cabin around 7am. I knew full well they would be up; they always rose early. Gry confirmed what Lucas had told me.

'I am so sorry, Leif, that you have split up, but understand your reasons.'

'Listen, Lynn is telling you a load of lies. I have not split up with her at all; I want to sit down and plan the wedding for the coming summer.'

They both shook their heads. 'You don't have to lie to us,' said Lucas, 'for Lynn told us, and we believe her – she is our daughter. You have broken her heart; she was besotted with you. Now you have dropped her like a stone. Sorry, Leif, but please leave us – and please, please, do not bother us again.'

I went back to the van to get Mum. I needed to get back to Hull to try and sort out this mess; it had gone too far. I needed answers, and I needed them quickly.

I dropped Mum off at home, without telling her. I didn't want her to worry about what was going on. I went back to my flat and opened a bottle of Johnnie Walker. The first glass never touched the sides; it was an hour or so later when I looked at the bottle. It was empty – as empty as my heart; I was totally in shock. Why had Lynn told these lies? I just had to find her to settle this situation.

*

It was a bright morning as the ferry pulled into its berth in Rotterdam. I got the tram straight to my office. I was early; the crossing had not taken as long as usual.

I had been at my desk a couple of hours when Jan, the mail boy, came round with the morning's post. 'Ah, Leif, I have something for you.' It was a small package, posted in Antwerp. I opened it – and there was the ring, with a note saying 'Sorry.' Nothing else; no explanation.

So she was back in Antwerp, was she? I had to see her, just to speak to her to get to know the truth. Luckily, Ingrid was on a week's holiday and had gone back to Bergen to be with her fiancé as he was home from sea, so at least I did not have to put on a brave face for her.

I rang Lynn's Antwerp office and spoke to the receptionist. I was told she was out of the office and would not be back until the following week. The girl could not give me an exact location as Lynn was in various places. But would be back for a week on Thursday, as there was an important meeting planned. I thanked her, and she asked who had called. I told her it was someone interested in a franchise and would rather not say at this moment in time.

Ingrid was back by now and was all chatty about her boyfriend – what they had got up to on holiday, and all the sordid detail. I did not need this, though I know I was cheating on Lynn, and she was cheating on her guy. I told Ingrid what was going on, and she took it OK. 'Let's just ease off, eh Leif,' she said. 'I understand – you get it sorted; no worries.'

The two weeks dragged by, but Wednesday came around at last. I had asked my boss for an extra day off; I explained the situation, and he said no problem.

I got the evening train arriving in Antwerp at around 9.30pm. I had booked a small hotel not far from where Lynn used to stay, hoping she still used the same place.

The following day I set off for her offices. There was a coffee shop across the road. I arrived there around 8am and sat in the window, watching people coming and going into the building.

An hour passed, but there was still no sign of Lynn. Then a taxi pulled up, and she got out – but she was not alone. A guy got out with her; he paid the cab, and as the car drove off, they stood talking for a moment. She kissed him on the cheek, then walked to the entrance; he waited a few moments, then followed her in.

Hmm… she was having an office affair. And by their actions, they did not want anyone to know what was going on. I could not stay here in the coffee shop all day. I gave it half an hour and used the public phone to ring the offices opposite. I was told everyone was in a meeting and would not be available until later that afternoon; it was scheduled to end around 4pm. Could I ring back around then? I said I would, and before she could ask me my name, I put the phone down. I had a day to kill. I had never really seen the city as a tourist so decided to take a look around. There were numerous museums and places of interest, but I decided to go to the city zoo, not far from the central railway station.

I paid the entrance fee and was given a map with all the information I needed. It said the zoo had been founded in 1843 and was widely regarded as one of the most beautiful zoos in Europe. I must admit I never expected this in the middle of a city, and spent nearly the whole day wandering around.

I met a lovely young lady called Frances, one of the resident keepers. She helped look after the sea lions. She came over, and we got chatting. She was a marine biologist who specialised in sea lions. I could not believe that she had such a wealth of knowledge about only one species of animal, and, me being me, I spent more time at their enclosure than at any other. But I was running out of time – I needed to get back to Lynn's office, so I made my excuses. Just as I was leaving, I asked Frances if she fancied a drink one night or maybe a meal. She agreed and gave me her phone number. Leif, you never lose it, I thought to myself as we said goodbye. I promised to ring her during the week.

I got back to the cafe and took my seat in the window; I was still reading the zoo's brochures and stuff when Lynn walked out of the office alone and started heading towards the neighbourhood where she stayed previously. I drank my coffee and took off after her, trying to make sure she did not see me, as I walked on the opposite side of the road and pretty well back. If she stopped, I stopped – I must have tied my shoelace at least four times. She came to a road junction and the lights.

I knew where she was going; she must have had the same place as before. I knew I could take a short cut and come to her home from another direction. I was right; as she approached the apartment block, I was already standing in a doorway opposite. As she approached, I ran across the road in front of her. 'Well, hello! Fancy meeting you here, Lynn. I hope you are well?' The look on her face was priceless.

'Oh, Leif, what are you doing here? What do you want? How did you know I was here?'

'I think I deserved a bit more of a welcome from my fiancée than that. And another thing – why all the lies? You have told your parents – why not tell them that you had finished it, and not me? We can't discuss it here, in front of the public – let me come in and talk. I need some answers, Lynn. I think I deserve some, don't you?'

At first, she refused to let me go into her place. 'We are finished,' she said. 'Let us just leave it at that.'

'No, I want the truth. I want to hear from you. Why have you blown me out?'

I was gutted. This was the first time it had ever happened to me. It hurt, more than words could say. I truly loved this girl and did not want it to end.

We entered her apartment; she must have kept it on even when she had been travelling. I did not know this and wondered why. I was trying to put the pieces together, but not very well. We talked about her travelling and why it was not working out, but she did not convince me with her answers.

I then hit her with the big one. 'Who was the guy you got out of the car with this morning? The one who you kissed on the cheek – the one who waited while you went in first?'

She looked shocked, like a kid looks when you find them stealing out of the sweet jar.

'How did you see that? Were you spying on me? How dare you follow me!'

'Guilty as charged – you are having an affair with a much older, most likely married work colleague, and you have binned me for him. That's right, Lynn, isn't it? You have ditched me for a man old enough to be your father. I know I am older than you, but not twice your fucking age, and don't turn on the tears; it won't wash with me. How long you had been fucking that granddad Lynn? What is it? Is he loaded or something? What can you get from him that I can't give you?'

She did not answer, turned her back on me, and started looking out of the window; it seemed like an eternity before she spoke. 'OK,' she said at last, 'I admit I do love you, only I have realised that I do not want to settle down; my job is everything to me. Having been with you has made me see life through a different pair of eyes. You have brought things out of me, something I never knew I had, how much I love sex, and now I have seen and done things I would never have dreamed would happen. Oh, Leif, I want more, and I do not need a husband; I need to be free. I am so sorry it has worked out like this, and the guy you saw me with, and I am sleeping with, is the managing director, Leif. I am fucking my way to the top, and nothing will stand in my way. I am so sorry, just let me go.'

I never dreamt I would hear that language coming out of her mouth.

'Leif, I love being single – I love being able to do what I want to do when I want to do it. OK, I admit when I asked you to marry me, I meant every word I said, but things have changed, and yes, I have changed. You understand, Leif, don't you?'

Gutted wasn't the operative word, but yes, I understood. I could not argue with her, for I had been that free spirit all of my life. Who was I to criticise?

She told me she was sorry about lying to her parents but had decided that was the easiest way to break it to them, rather than tell them what she had just told me.

We sat holding hands for a while, realising it was all over, but me being me, I had to ask. 'I suppose a fuck's out of the question, then.'

She just laughed. 'I don't think that's a very good idea, Leif, as much as I would love to feel you inside me again – but let's just have our memories, eh?'

I stood up, held her for the last time, tasted those lips for the last time, and left her. I still could not believe I had lost the most beautiful girl in the world.

CHAPTER 36

LEIF

Met Connie for the First Time

A week passed and I started seeing Ingrid again; she was still working in Rotterdam and had been home yet again for a few days as her fiancé was back from the sea. He had changed ships or something. She told me about her time with him; I don't know if she was trying to make me jealous or what, but it was working.

After work, we went for a drink, and sat in the bar just chatting casually; she told me she was sick of not seeing her guy and was thinking of calling off the engagement. She did not know that Lynn and I had separated. As far as I knew, anyway; I had not advertised the news since I had got back, so I didn't know who could have told her if she did know.

'Why are you telling me, Ingrid?' I asked.

'Just wanted to tell you I am a free woman again.'

'It never stopped us before, Ingrid, but while you are on the subject, so am I – free, I mean. Lynn and I have called it quits. It was not working out being so far apart, but do you think it's a wise move us getting together, as you do not know how long you are going to be in Rotterdam? In fact, neither do I.'

'I suppose you are right. But we can still be good friends, can't we? Nothing is stopping us from making love, for I need sex more than I need food.'

How did I find them? Here was Ingrid, a nympho, and Lynn, who had turned into one and just wanted to use her fanny as a passport to the top in business. There must have been some simple no-strings girls out there?

Three trips had passed, and I only went home for the third one. I was single again, with no ties. I had taken the ring into a local jeweller in Hull, and got a reasonable price for it – not as much as I had paid, but not far off it, as I told him I had spent more than the actual top-line price without the discount; he was happy and so was I.

I went out to the campsite to make sure everything was put away for the winter. I saw Lynn's parents, but they ignored me, which hurt a bit as it was not my fault. They had different ideas, but hey, that's life – shit happens, as they say.

I went in town one Saturday night for a few beers and called in at my local drinking hole, the King Edward. There were the same old faces at the bar, and the same old banter about Hull and Rovers, as a mixture of both fans used the pub along with several Tigers supporters in the mix. What a boring fucking life this lot lived; most of them had never been out of Hull, apart from two weeks every summer at Withernsea and a Wembley weekend for the rugby league cup final. I was not that badly done to. I was sitting on my own in a booth near the window – the place was heaving – when two new faces I had never seen before asked if they could sit at the table with me. 'Sure, they are free –help yourself.'

'Not seen you before,' one of the girls said.

'I come here quite a lot when I'm home but spend a lot of time working away.'

One of the two, the prettier one – that is no disrespect to the other one, who was more bubbly and definitely up for it – asked, 'Where do you work?'

'Oh, I work in Rotterdam in the Netherlands, or Holland, as it's better known.'

Then Bubbles came out with the old Hessle Road catchphrase, 'Fucking hell, what do you do?'

I did not go into any accurate detail, and my eyes were more on the pretty one. While we were chatting, Bubbles spotted someone who had just come in and said, 'Be back in a jiffy.'

'Well, that leaves you and me. I'm Leif, and you are?'

'Connie, and before you say anything, yes, my mother loved Connie

Francis, the old pop singer from the 1960s.'

We got a good yarn on; I went and bought a couple of drinks; Bubbles – or Anne – had taken the hint and got off with some guy and was slowly sucking his face in the corner.

It was getting towards closing time. I was starving and suggested to Connie if she fancied a Chinese; she said she would love to but had to catch her bus up to Boothferry Estate. 'Don't worry about getting home,' I said. 'I have a car. I can drop you off – if you want, that is?'

'Are you sure it is not out of your way?'

'No – no bother. I live off Hessle Road anyway.'

'Oh – OK, then, if that's the case, I would love a Chinese.'

We finished our drinks and walked over to the takeaway above Centre Bar, my favourite Chinese in Hull at the time. I always ordered the same meal – a special, with chips, which had nearly everything in it – finished off with an egg in the middle. Connie asked for chicken with black bean sauce along with a couple of beers to share.

I liked this girl; she was lovely, looked about twenty-eight, not too rough around the edges like old Bubbles, but a bit more, what you might say, classy.

We had a great meal and we talked about who we were, and our history; it turned out she was older than I had thought, at thirty. She was divorced, with one child, a boy named Martin, aged nearly fourteen. He was at Hull Trinity House School, and wanted to join the merchant navy like his father. She lived alone, as things had not worked out with her old man; they'd had to get married but they were too young – she was seventeen, and he was eighteen. It just was not meant to be. She now worked in an office of a small electrical engineering company. She had been there a few years, and loved it; they had been good to her. It all came out on both sides, and it was nice talking to a woman who could listen as well as talk, without discussing work all the time.

It was time to go, and I drove up to her house. It was now once again that moment when I wasn't quite sure what to do next. Should I slip an arm around her back and touch her neck gently, always a nervous time? Or let her make the first move? I chose the latter. She turned in her seat, took my hand and gently kissed my fingers. She looked at me, and said, 'I'm thrilled I met you tonight, Leif; it's been a long time since I was in the company of a man.' She then leaned over. Our lips touched ever so gently. I had never had an electric current run through my body just through one kiss. 'I must go. Would you like to do it again, Leif? I would.' She pulled a little notepad out of her handbag, wrote a number on it, and put it in my hand. With one more kiss, she said, 'Night – and thanks again. Ring me, please.'

I sat there watching her walk up the path; she turned as she opened the door and waved as she disappeared inside.

I looked at the note she had given me, Connie Winterton, and her number, 'ext 21'. Well, Connie, you have won me, girl, I thought. I would most definitely be in touch.

She knew I worked away and only returned to Hull every other weekend, so she was not expecting to see me for a couple of weeks. I had already decided to go home the following weekend.

Work was going well; we had several contracts on the go, two in the southern North Sea gas platforms, and two up north off Aberdeen. We were also looking at a new refinery to be built in South America and two in Asia on the drawing board, so it was a bit hectic.

We had taken on more staff to meet the demand, and there had been talks about opening an office in the UK, but nothing had been settled just yet, not that it concerned me; I was pretty happy doing my four-day week in Rotterdam, thank you very much.

I walked into the office one Wednesday morning and not been there long when the phone went. It was my boss, Aalt, who asked me to go up to his office when I was free. That was what I liked about him – no orders; he always asked you, never told you. Man-management at its best. I told him I had just a couple of calls to make and should be OK in half an hour.

'Come in, Leif.' Who should be sitting there at the desk, but Henne. 'Hello Leif – nice to see you again. Been a while; how are you?'

I was still quite surprised to see him again and was kind of stuck for words at first.

'I'm OK, thanks; sorry… but I was shocked to see you – pleased, of course, but just a bit taken aback.'

'You must be wondering why I am here and not in Norway? Well, there have been some changes made in head office, and I have been promoted. Don't ask me why, but I am now director in charge of worldwide support. What does that mean, I can see you asking? Well, I am now leading the new group in the company that will offer support to countries around the globe in organising their assets – oil and gas exploration offshore and onshore, mining, petrochemicals, and other industries that we have vast experience in, hoping to bring them into the twentieth century. We had found that it could be a bit of a minefield when it came to negotiating contracts with worldwide companies who didn't have the expertise in carrying out that scope of work.'

How did little old Leif come into this scenario, I wondered?

'Leif, as you know, we have been working in that part of the world for quite a few years now. But we have noticed there is a gap in the marketplace for this type of expertise. It has come to light that there are quite a few, what you might call, not so honest companies, who are, for want of a better word, ripping these countries off; it's our intention to make that impossible and also make money ourselves – a lot of money. They struggle to negotiate the right deals. We would be an independent advisory group, training their staff in the correct procedures in negotiating contracts, etc.'

'Sounds some task, Henne – you must be excited about what lies in front of you; when does this start?'

'It already has. I have been to Venezuela, Brazil, Peru, Argentina, Cuba, Colombia, Bolivia and Chile already, just spreading the word on what we are offering. It is a completely new concept. What is in it for us, you may ask? We will gain by supplying and training the right staff, for a start, and we obviously will be negotiating for some of the contracts. But even us as big as we are, we can't take on every job on offer, but what we can do is offer the service to ensure that each country is getting good value for money in the hope that it gives a fair playing field for all contractors, including us. Although we are offering this assistance as a company, it is independent; we would, of course, be charging a fee for our services. We help each nation set up; it is down to the individual nation's office to choose the winning bids with no influence from our department. The whole idea is to ensure that there is a standard set of bid modules set up so that each project is costed the same way. I won't go into the exact details, but I am sure you get my drift.'

I was wondering why he was telling me all this, when he asked me if I would be interested in joining his group.

'It would mean resigning from Vanderries, but that is only a technicality; there would be no argument with them. Leif, you do not have to give me an answer right away, but I would love you on my team. I will send you the details of the position's salary and conditions as per usual. Just let me know at your pleasure. One last thing – this is all hush-hush, so please do not breathe a word to anyone about it. We are not advertising what we are doing; the group will be set up in the Bahamas and not registered in any other country. Our offices would be in Nassau, and you would work out of there, with first-class hotels and airfares, and tax-free earnings paid in any currency you wish to any bank in the world. It's all in the pack that I will send you. Thanks for listening to me and I look forward to hearing from you soon.'

I supposed that was my nod to leave. I stood up and told Henne I would look forward to receiving the information and give him my response as soon as possible.

I got back to my desk. I was in shock; what the fuck had he offered me? It sounded too good to be true. I needed time for all this to sink in; I was sitting reading a contract for a project we were looking at when Jan walked up with a package. 'Hi, Leif, this just arrived special delivery. I signed it for you. Will you sign this for me? It's just procedures, OK?'

I looked at the envelope; it was the usual A4 size, but about an inch thick – it felt like a hardback book. I ripped the envelope open. I was right – it was bound in faux leather, but with no titles or anything. That was quick. Henne must have taken for granted that I would be interested in the position. It was the package for the job he was offering me, and what a position it was.

Position: Proposals Consultant Manager

Salary: BSD$ 200,000 (£130,000 approx) per year paid monthly free of tax in any currency nominated.

Expenses: all expenses including hotels, air fares (first-class), car hire, per diem payment of BSD$ 75 per day per week, 48 weeks per annum, paid monthly in advance by cash.

Use of company Amex card for all expenses to be included with expense claims.

Six weeks' holiday per year, return flights from the Bahamas to UK 3 times per year.

All expenses to be claimed through company accounts, monthly in arrears.

All flights and hotels to be booked by the allocated travel company.

The primary scope of work was to act as consultants on developing a standardised form of negotiating contracts between government agencies and worldwide contractors, creating a model that would work in both parties' interests.

I won't go into all the job details, but I was more than interested. I did not contact Henne for a few days, just to let him think I was not making a rash decision, but I knew that I wanted the job as soon as I had been through the information.

Aalt called me to his office a week later and told me that Henne had been chasing him up for an answer, totally discreetly, of course. I told him I had come to a decision, and as much as I did not want to leave Vanderries, it was too good an opportunity to let go. He understood and wished me all the best; he asked if I would do a couple of weeks or one trip handover with the guy filling my post.

Of course, I agreed, and that was that. I contacted Henne later that day and told him my decision. He was pleased to hear my answer, but he did say he knew I could not resist the opportunity to take up the offer and would not regret it; he promised me that this was the chance that only came around once.

I had got back with Ingrid; I did like making love with her – who on earth wouldn't have – but I needed more. It was time to take stock of my life – to sit down in front of a mirror and have a good conversation with myself as to what my intentions were, what with the new position I was about to take up with Caporal Industries, which was the name they had come up with for the new venture.

We spent the night at my place; once again, she did not fail to come up with the goods. I excelled myself, getting as far as Workington; occasionally, Derwent Park came in to view. God, she was hot, but I could not see myself settling down with her. How could I trust her if I would be working out of Nassau and roaming around South America for the next few years? That's if it worked out. No – I had had a word with myself. I decided I would make the best of her being in my life for now. Then give her the news that I was leaving in a week or so.

I was having a coffee in the small canteen-type area at the office when Ingrid walked in. I was alone; she came up to put her arms around me and stuck the lips on me. Wow – how the fuck was I going to let her go?

'Morning, babe,' she said. 'Thanks for last night – that was wonderful. I'm so glad we are back together. Oh, by the way, you remember us talking about going for a sauna one night? Well, I have found one. It is a mixed one – do you mind? It is in Dordrecht, so not far to go. I was talking to one of the girls in the typing pool; she goes there regularly. Fancy a visit? You need to be invited as it is a bit exclusive – members only, but I think she fancies me so she will sign us in if you want to give it a go?'

'OK, I am game; when do you fancy going? Any time suits me – just remember, only Tuesday or Wednesday nights. On Mondays, I am usually knackered with travelling and Thursday I go home, but I could make an exception if it is worth it,' I said, laughing.

'Mmm, babe, it will be well worth it; you know it will. I just think a mixed one should be fun.'

Ingrid had seen Tess, the girl from the typing pool, and arranged for the following Tuesday to 'welkom in het paradijs' – you can guess what that means in English. We went straight from work; all three took the train and found the place just off the market square down a side street.

Tess knocked on the door – three taps, two taps, and a three. I could not believe it – all these little secret things that went on; it must go back to the resistance in the war, I thought. Anyway, we got in, and Tess introduced us and did the business for us to join. We had to fill out a form, nothing too detailed, but as we were foreign, we had to produce our passports; Tess had already informed us of the requirements.

Rightfully paid up members of Paradise, off we went to the changing area, which was not segregated as it was a mixed club. It seemed odd getting stripped off with people I had never met; I was used to the nudist scene, but at least they always had separate changing facilities, if only to build up courage for the new starters.

I was stripped and ready for action when Tess came around the corner; wow, what a body. She was a pretty girl to start with, but her figure was something else – beautiful.

'Ready, Leif? Ingrid has just gone to the toilet – she won't be long. She said she didn't want to piss in the whirlpool,' said Tess, laughing. 'Right – you have to go through shower as you enter, which is compulsory, then choose what you want to do. I usually go in the middle-heat sauna. There are three – low, medium and hot. It is best to build up to the hot one, so, the usual thing is a spell in sauna, then the plunge pool, back in the heat, then the pool. I usually do three spells. Stay in as long as you can stand it, then the pool. You will get used to it, OK?' Tess disappeared into the medium sauna.

Ingrid joined me. 'Come on, Leif, let's try the low heat; take Tess's advice.'

'OK, that will do me.'

We entered the pine log cabin, which was not that big inside. I supposed it would take about eighteen people on the three levels as there were only two others in it. Bloody hell, this was hot enough for me. I sat on the lower level. Ingrid went over to the other side and lay out on the middle level. I had been in about five minutes, and the sweat was running out of me already. I put my small towel over my head. I heard the door open and a cold draught came in around my legs, and someone went on the top level behind me.

311

I took my towel off, about to go for my first plunge; being nosey, I turned to see who had come in. The first thing I noticed was this waxed vagina, directly in front of my face. I could not stop staring; it mesmerised me. Then this voice said, 'Hallo, je wilt?' – in English, 'Hello, you want?' That broke my concentration.

'Oh, yes, er… sorry… yes – hi, how are you?'

'You are new here, I see. Hello, I am Danique. Pleased to meet you.' She put out her hand.

'I am Leif – Leif Askenes. Yes, I am a first-timer. Pleased to meet you, must cool off – catch you later.'

I went out into the plunge pool, followed by Ingrid. The water was freezing.

'Who is your new friend, Leif? Didn't take you long; what's her name? She is gorgeous.'

It was the second time Ingrid had commented about a girl. I wondered if she was a bit on the lesbian side; she had never mentioned it before, but there again, why should she?

'Danique is her name. Why, you fancy women now, Ingrid? Fed up of dick?'

'Always have done, ever since I was a little girl. As you English say, a change is as good as a rest, Leif. Don't knock it unless you have tried it.'

I just smiled and nodded, climbing out of the pool, heading back to the next session.

We stayed there about two hours, not all in the saunas. There was also a steam room, and a massage room where this Turkish guy tried to rip you apart limb from limb. Still, all in all, it was a very relaxing way to spend an evening. I met some new friends and was wishing I was not going away as I had found another hobby. As we left, Ingrid was passing her new friend a piece of paper. I guess it was her contact number.

'All good there, Ingrid?'

'Don't get jealous. I am working on a threesome, babe, and you will be the one in the middle, OK?'

*

No one at work knew I was leaving as the new venture was still under wraps. I continued as usual, though one or two questions were being asked as to why was I spending so much time with Michael Van der Leiden, and who was taking over my job? We just made out it was expanding the division, as there was so much more work coming in. This seemed to keep the heat off.

My time with Vanderries came to an end, along with my current friendship with Ingrid. She took it quite well when I explained I could not tell her about my leaving before, but I had been sworn to secrecy. 'No problem, Leif,' she said, 'it's been good, and, if at any time in the future we meet again, just remember I want to fuck you, OK?'

How could I refuse such an offer?

CHAPTER 37

LEIF

Another Beautiful Evening

I left Rotterdam on Wednesday, September 30, 1987 on the night ferry back to Hull. I would have a week at home before flying out to Nassau to meet my new work colleagues.

I rang Connie to see how she was doing; I hadn't called her while I was back in Rotterdam, and I hoped that she had not forgotten all about me. I rang the number she had given me and got straight through to her office.

'Hello, Connie Winterton here – how can I help you?'

'Hi, Connie, it's me, Leif; how are you? Sorry I haven't been in touch, but I have been away in Norway and not had the chance to call you.' Which was a white lie. 'How're things?'

'Oh, hi, Leif – nice to hear your voice. That's OK, no problem, just glad you remembered me. I am fine – how long are you home for?'

'Only a week or so, then I am off to the Bahamas – Nassau, to be precise, on another job. I was hoping we could have a drink and possibly a meal again. Is that OK with you?'

'Wow, the Bahamas! You sure get about, don't you? And I'm stuck here in little old Hull; it's all right for some.'

We talked for a while, and set a date for the following Friday night. I booked a table at the Lantern, which was a small, intimate place, but the food was excellent.

I picked her up at her place. Before we left, she invited me in to meet her son, Martin; he seemed a nice, level-headed young man. We shook

315

hands, and we had a quick chat about this and that, after which he picked up a small bag and shouted to Connie, 'OK, Mum – I am off to Steve's. See you on Sunday. Bye, Leif – great to meet you, at last. Mum has mentioned you a few times – I've never known her talk about a guy so much; she must fancy you.' And, with a wink, he was gone.

Hmm… she had got rid of her son for the night. Was I reading the signs wrongly or was it just wishful thinking?

Connie came back down and said, 'He is staying over at his friend Steve's for the weekend; it's been planned for a few weeks. His parents are away, so he is keeping him company. I think he has a girlfriend, but he has not mentioned it. I did find some condoms hidden under his bed when I was cleaning the other day, and they are not there now. I just looked; at least he is acting responsibly. They have to start sometime, don't they?'

I just nodded; she was blushing when she told me the tale, so I did not pass any comment.

We went to King Edward first and had a couple of beers in there, then walked down to Ye Olde White Hart for a couple. We headed back along Whitefriargate to the restaurant, and had a wonderful meal – once again, they never failed to serve up great food. I had been going in there for a lot of years; it must have been the late 1960s when I first used it.

We finished off the wine and left, walking back to my car. Connie put her arm in mine and snuggled her head against my shoulder. 'Thank you, Leif, for another beautiful evening; it's been great. I don't know how I can thank you, do you?'

Now, if that was not a promise, I didn't know what was. We got back to her house, and she didn't ask me in; she just took it for granted as I was following her up the path. We entered the house, and she shut the door and locked it, kicking off her shoes, taking off her coat and hanging it on the banister.

'Want a coffee, or something stronger? I have a decent scotch in the cupboard, if you like whisky; it's a single malt my father used to drink all the time. Isle of Jura was his favourite.'

'I will just have a small one, as I'm having to drive – not far, but I still have to drive.'

As she was walking away, she said softly, 'You don't if you don't want to, Leif; you can stay the night if you want. You can sleep in Martin's bed if need be; it's your choice.' She turned to look at me and smiled.

We went into the living room, and I sat on the sofa. Connie handed me my drink and sat next to me, although there were two other chairs she could have used.

'Shall I put some music on, Leif? What do you like? How about Matt Monroe? I love his voice – it's so sexy. Will he do?'

She put on the LP and came back and sat next to me; we both put our drinks down on the coffee table. I put my arm around her. She smelt divine; I didn't know the perfume she was wearing, but it hit home with me. I was starting to notice different fragrances; was this usual?

I picked up her hand, kissing her neatly manicured fingers gently; not a lot of nail polish, just nice. Her head was on my shoulder. I lifted her chin, and our faces met. We had not been so close since the goodnight kiss she gave me last time we had met.

Our lips touched; she tasted terrific – what a kisser. I nibbled her bottom lip, and she moved towards me; our kiss was more in-depth now.

She straddled my lap. I was rock solid; I could feel the heat of her on my groin. It felt so good. I started to undo her blouse button by button until it fell away; she shrugged it off. I held her naked waist in my hands, stroking her back, undoing her bra. It fell away; what a beautiful pair of breasts, not big but still substantial, and the darkness of her nipples was gorgeous, and they were erect. I kissed each one, sucking on them; she threw her head back, sighing. I listened to her moaning as I nuzzled them, each one in turn; she was ready.

She stood up, slipping her skirt down. She stood there in panties, suspenders and black stockings. Wigan almost arrived just a bit too early. I stood up and stripped off while she watched me, licking her lips all the time and cupping her breasts.

I was naked, and standing to attention; she took hold of me and pulled me towards her. 'No – not here,' she said. 'Come on, we need the bed.'

We went upstairs and made love not just once, but at least three times, maybe more, I do not know; it was unreal.

We both fell asleep, and I woke up first, with her in the crook of my arm. The sun was coming up. I don't think we had slept much between the sex, but it felt so right; waking up with her seemed so good.

Looking down on her body, watching her breathing, she was so peaceful. I kissed the back of her neck, nibbled the lobe of her ear, and she woke up and turned. We kissed without speaking, and it was just perfect. She smiled a beautiful smile. 'Morning; you sleep well?' I nodded, then kissed her again without talking.

She looked up at me, with those beautiful eyes. 'Leif, you are the first man I have had inside me for such a long time, baby. That was so good. I have not felt so wonderful for years. I had forgotten what it was like to climax; you certainly can make women feel satisfied.'

'You are a wonderful girl, Connie. I feel something has happened to me since we first met, something I can't name, but I have to say it; it may sound stupid coming from a grown man, and I have never said it for years, but here goes – it's that old Hessle Road saying, "Will you go out with me?" But before you answer, there is a problem. I am going to be away for a while; I have not told you about all the details about Nassau and my new job. Would you be willing to wait for me as I will be away in a few days and I'm not sure when I will be back in Hull.'

She looked at me and cuddled up to me. 'Of course – I have not had a man in my life for a few years; what will a few more months matter? Let's just enjoy the time we have. Now make love to me. I want to feel you inside me again.'

We spent all day in bed; Martin wasn't due home until the Sunday evening, so we had until then.

We went out on the Saturday night for a drive to Beverley, had a few beers and a meal, and then back to Connie's place.

On the Sunday morning, I woke up late. She had got up early and was cooking breakfast; the smell of bacon was coming up the stairs. I went to the bathroom, then went down to the kitchen. I was still naked. She turned with a look of surprise. 'What are you doing? Why aren't you dressed, Leif? Go and put some clothes on!'

'I never wear clothes around the house. I just forgot, sorry. I'll go and get dressed.'

'What you mean you are always naked? You mean you are a nudist? You didn't tell me that, Leif.'

'You never asked, Connie,' I said, laughing; she wasn't amused.

'I'm not sure if I like it or not. I do like looking at your body, I won't say I don't, but if Martin was to walk in, what we could tell him? I wouldn't know how he would react, especially if I was naked as well.'

'We don't have to if you are not sure; I'm not forcing naturism on to you. It's just something I prefer. I've been a nudist for a while now; it's up to you. I'll go put some clothes on.'

Seeing as it was a gorgeous day, we had breakfast and sat out in the garden for a few hours.

I nodded off, and when I woke and looked at my watch, it was gone three o'clock. I heard Martin's voice coming from the kitchen,

'What's he still doing here, Mum? He has been here since Friday. You've certainly got the hots for him; hope you know what you are doing?'

'Martin, I like him very much; you don't mind me seeing him, do you?'

'You going out with him, Mum? You hardly know him. I hope he slept in my bed… he did do, didn't he?'

Connie didn't answer.

'Mum, you didn't… did you, Mum? Oh my god, Mum! I don't believe it.'

'Martin, I'm not discussing with a teenager what I did or didn't do. It's none of your business, for a start, and you have no room to talk. I saw the condoms under your bed, so don't you lecture me about my sex life, even if I had one.'

'Mum! Oh, Mum, when did you find them? Why were you snooping in my room?'

'I am sorry, but I was cleaning up your room. If you had done more of it yourself, I would never have found your contraceptives. I don't mind

– it is OK. I am pleased you are taking precautions; I'm quite proud of you, to be honest.'

I just kept out of it; I pretended I was still asleep when they came outside.

'Leif, wake up – Martin's home. Come on, sleepyhead, you can't be that tired.'

I stood up and shook Martin's hand; he was a bit reserved, obviously, as he was thinking about this stranger fucking his mother, a trespasser on his turf. A new man in his life – this was going to take some getting used to. But he kind of relaxed after a while, and we started to get on.

He was a Hull FC supporter and played rugby at school during the winter; we discussed how good they were and finished up the day quite good mates.

We were sitting chatting when I looked over at the house and could see Connie watching us; she had a big grin on her face, a satisfied look in her eyes. I was wondering, was this going too quickly? We had only known each other for a few weeks and I was thinking about becoming a fucking stepfather. Hang on, slow down, Leif.

I had a moment of inspiration. I would try to get to know the boy a bit better, find out what made him tick – maybe be the father figure I knew he had not had the luxury of, a bit like myself. I asked him why he was using condoms. Had he got a girlfriend?

'No, I haven't got a girlfriend, but you have to be careful you don't get an infection, don't you?' I nodded, but didn't really know what he was talking about.

'I use them when I'm with my friend Steve; he said we should use them.'

'Martin, you use them when you are with Steve?' Now he had my attention.

'Yes, we always put them on; it saves making a mess and stops you getting the white stuff on your hands.'

I was intrigued – then it dawned on me. They put condoms on to masturbate; now, this was a new one. 'Martin, you mean you put a condom on to have a wank?'

'Don't tell Mum, will you, but yes, we do. You can't get any disease if you do that. Steve showed me how to do it; he is older than me – he is sixteen and a half, and he has been doing it a lot longer than me. Don't tell Mum, Leif, will you, please? You won't, will you?'

'Martin, I won't say anything to Connie, I promise; it's just between you and me, but you don't need to use a condom to wank with. You can't catch anything playing with yourself. It's OK – everybody goes through that stage, even I did when I was your age.' Unlike Steve, I thought, playing the confidant and older friend; he seemed to be as immature as Martin, getting his younger friend to use condoms – unless he had other motives.

'Don't waste your money buying French letters, just use a tissue to clean up after,' I said, but my mind was working overtime. What else did this Steve have in mind for Martin? 'I would like to meet this Steve sometime.'

'Oh, you will; he is coming round here a bit later – we are going to another lad's house.'

An hour later, we were still sitting in the garden, and I heard this voice. 'Hiya, Martin, you home?' It had to be Steve; he came in through the back gate. Now I knew why Martin was being encouraged to wear a condom; this boy was surely gay, not that we called it that then.

'Hi, Steve, come in; this is Leif, Mum's friend,' said Martin. Steve walked up to us, and I put out my hand to shake his; limp wasn't the word. His hands were as soft as a girl's; in reality, he looked more like a girl than some girls I had seen.

'Hello, Leif, so pleased to meet you; I have heard so much about you.'

'Hi Steve, how are you? OK, I hope.' We exchanged a bit of banter and then Connie came out; she gave Steve a peck on the cheek and a hug.

Now, I had not had any homosexual experiences in my life. But this guy was leaning towards that tendency, without a doubt. I must admit that back then I could not understand why Connie could not see it or turned a blind eye to her son's relationship with Steve.

The two boys went off to Matthew's, their other friend's house; I could not resist myself. 'Connie, that mate of Martin's, he is a shirtlifter if ever I saw one; he is bent.'

'Do you think so? What makes you say that? He seems like a nice boy – always polite, and he has been a good friend to Martin. He has had some dark days over the years what with never having a man around to look up to, and Steve has always been there to give him a hand and help him pull through.'

There was no answer to that. I explained the condom situation and what Martin had told me; I could hardly keep a straight face. Connie at first looked shocked, then she started to laugh. 'I suppose it's better than him getting a girl into trouble.'

'What, are you joking? I would rather him be shagging some young girl than having a boy lead him up another garden path.'

'Oh, I don't think Steve is like that; you are wrong there, Leif.'

I was left speechless. OK mate, you have said enough on the subject; leave them to it, I thought.

The two boys came back for tea; I could not take my eyes off them. They were like two young kids, very touchy-feely, playing around together. I did not make any more remarks for the rest of the day.

I left them after tea and said I would ring Connie on Tuesday to arrange to go out for a meal and maybe Martin could come with us. I suggested she asked him after I had gone, rather than put him on the spot while I was there, as long as he didn't ask Steve to come as well.

*

I got a phone call from Henne giving me the details of my travel arrangements; they had been put back a few more days, which I didn't mind. I was now scheduled to fly to Nassau on Monday, October 1, on an 11am flight from Manchester.

I was booked into the British Colonial Hilton Hotel for the first two weeks of my stay until I found an apartment near Bay Street's offices.

It was getting close, and I was genuinely looking forward to it. I was to meet my new boss, Greg Preston, he was flying in the day after and was booked in the same hotel. An informal meeting had been scheduled for Tuesday evening, along with the local staff that had been taken on by Henne and the HR team. They had been up and running for a few months, under another name.

Connie and I met up a couple of more times over the next few days I was home. She stayed over at mine one night, which was nice. We never discussed Martin's situation; she did not bring it up, so I left it at bay.

My last night in Hull was on the Saturday. We went around town, met up with a few old mates in King Eddie, went for a Chinese again above Centre Bar, then headed back to Connie's place.

Martin was still up when we got back, and I was a bit nervous about sleeping with his Mum when he was at home, but he knew the score.

We were sitting having a coffee when he said, 'Oh, by the way, Leif, I have stopped using condoms now; it's so much better, you were right.' With that, he went up to bed. 'Night night, you two.'

Connie started laughing, with that 'told you so' look on her face; who am I to judge, whatever will be, and all that.

I was up early on the Sunday had booked a hotel in Manchester for that night, which would save rushing to the airport to catch the flight. Connie was very quiet that morning. We had said our goodbyes while making love, but there was not a lot more to say. I decided to get away without too many sad farewells.

Martin was still in his room doing whatever he did in there. I shouted upstairs, 'I'll see you, mate. Take care now, OK.'

'OK, bye, Leif, have a safe journey; see you when you get back.'

I hugged Connie; she did not want to let go, but I had to leave. I gave her one last kiss, and left.

CHAPTER 38

LEIF

The Bahamas, Here I Come

After a great flight, I arrived at my hotel around three o'clock, five hours behind GMT. God, it was hot – well, it was compared with Hull. It was around 80F, and I had read on the plane that it didn't get much below 72. There was a slight breeze, which helped, and I knew I had better get used to it. I had a light meal and felt knackered. I was in bed by 8pm; it was too early and I should have stayed up, but I could hardly keep my eyes open.

I didn't sleep very well, so I went for an early morning stroll around the hotel gardens and down to the beach area; there were not many people about, but it certainly was a hell of a spot. I had struck lucky here.

I went back to my room, got my swimmers and shorts, and went back to the pool area. The weather was ideal; this would do me. I was alone at first, then a few more guests started coming down by lunchtime; the sun was at its highest, and quite a lot were under umbrellas or in the shade. I wandered over to the bar, ordered a glass of white wine, and got chatting to a British guy who was with his wife on holiday. In his early sixties, he was a well-spoken chap called Bryan from the Home Counties; I reckoned Middlesex, around that neck of the woods.

We had been chatting a while when his wife turned up, reasonably fit for her age and a lot younger than him – meal ticket came to mind, but it was not good to judge; one of my faults. Bryan introduced me to Melanie; we said our pleasantries and ordered another round of drinks. It seemed that Bryan was with one of the big international banking firms and on the board of directors, but had had to retire.

'Company policy, you know,' Melanie added to the conversation. They went on talking about themselves, what they had and how well Bryan had done. I was getting pissed off with the continuous blabbing about the British middle/upper class and how the working class needed to buck its ideas up; I had not a fucking clue what they were talking about.

I made a quick escape when another couple arrived on the scene; believe it or not, this joker had a cravat and long white trousers on, and a white Panama hat – the old colonial look. My god, no wonder we had a bad reputation abroad.

I bid them all good day and disappeared into my room; I needed a shower and a snooze before the meeting tonight.

I woke up, looking at my watch; it was 6.30pm. Fuck I'm going to be late, I thought, then realised I didn't know what time Greg was supposed to be meeting. I was in the shower when the phone rang. I got out, and just as I was lifting the handset it went dead. I was just getting back in and it rang again; it was a woman's voice, but American, which surprised me.

'Leif, hello, how are you? It's Shannon – Shannon De Vries, from Caporal; welcome to Nassau. How are you finding the weather? Not too hot, I hope?'

'No, it's fine, and how are you?'

'I am excellent, thanks – just calling you to let you know that everything is set for tonight's meeting in the bar at 7.30pm, followed by a meal. There will be six of us – Greg Preston, the new boss; Michel Andrews, the office manager; myself as PA to Greg; Deide Bakker, the accountant; Frederick Meyer, the engineering manager; and you. There's no need to dress for dinner; it is not the done thing in the Bahamas.'

'Look forward to meeting you all; see you in an hour, OK.'

'Great – bye, Leif.'

I finished my shower, had a shave, and was ready to meet the gang. I arrived in the bar for 7.30pm prompt, but hadn't a clue who I was looking for. I just stood at the bar looking for five other people who were in a group.

There were just two women, and one guy. Could they be the ones? I went over.

'Excuse me, but are you three from Caporal Industries, by any chance?'

'Oh, hello, Leif, I am Shannon. This is Michelle, and this is Frederick; so pleased to meet you. We are just waiting for Greg and Deide; they will be down soon. What are you drinking?'

'Just a beer, thanks, Shannon – anything will do.' She went to the bar and left me with the other two when Greg and Deide arrived, introducing themselves; Shannon came back and got their drinks order when she returned, and we went over and sat in a booth.

Everything seemed great; they seemed friendly, sound people. Greg was visibly the boss – he had that presence, that stature some guys high up in the chain of command have. Having said that, he seemed OK. Deide could not be anything but an accountant, with half-rim glasses on the end of his nose. Frederick was the typical Dutchman, tall with a big handlebar moustache. Michelle was a local girl from Nassau, and very attractive; she had been to the London School of Economics and come out with a masters in economics, which was all above my head. That left Shannon De Vries; she was tall, with long, blonde hair, and athletic-looking; my kind of woman. Hang on, Leif, steady up, son, you have only just met, I told myself. She was also from Nassau, of American parents who had retired very early from the States after making a fortune in the Texas oil industry. She also had been to university in England – Oxford – with a master's degree in corporate law. And then there was me, a raggy-arsed kid off Hessle Road. How about that?

We talked all night about work. Greg went through the ideas of setting up the company, his intentions, and what would be required from the group. He did not go into detail. He seemed happy with the group put together for him by Henne in Norway; that was about it.

We left the restaurant and retired to the bar once more, with a couple of whiskies to finish off, then we split up. Greg and I retired to our rooms, and the others left the hotel to go home, wherever that was.

The following morning we all went to the offices just off Bay Street, which was a short taxi ride from the hotel. We all more or less arrived at the same time, just before 7am; it was an early start, but also it was to be an early finish as office hours were 7am to 3.30pm Monday to Friday. The hours could be flexible, though; as long as the core hours of forty were put in, Greg was not bothered.

After being shown our offices and issued with all the consumables, we were called into Greg's office to receive the lowdown on what Caporal was all about. Greg went around the table, telling us in detail what was expected of us as individuals and what was required from us as a whole. We were given a questionnaire that needed completing. Greg also informed us he was going to interview each of us for our position to ensure we would all fit in the team and that he was happy with what Henne had provided. 'Just to satisfy myself,' were his words.

You could feel an air of uneasiness among the group after he had finished talking, but he was the gaffer – it was on his head if anything did not work out. None of us knew what he was looking for, but we were soon to find out.

We all went back to our offices to read the notes he had given us and re-read our CVs to make sure we were singing from the same song sheet when we were called back in to see him. Within an hour, my phone rang; it was Shannon. 'Hi, Leif, would you come to Greg's office? He wants to chat.' She then whispered, 'You are the first one.'

'OK, on my way.' The questionnaire was a simple tick-box form, and the schedule meant nothing; it was merely a list of requirements.

Greg was sitting at a big old oak desk. He got up and walked towards me, offering his hand once again, which seemed odd, but maybe it was just his way.

'Come in, Leif, take a seat; want a coffee?' he said, pointing to the percolator on the side table. 'Just brewed a fresh pot.'

'Yes, please – white, one sugar; thanks.'

After some small talk, Greg got down to the nitty-gritty. He asked about my background since I left school. I was right; he wanted to go through my CV to make sure there were no lies in it. I had it off pat – where I had been, my success story, everything, warts and all. After a few questions to try to catch me out, he was nodding with every statement I made.

As the proposal manager, I would be accountable for the bid cost structure definition, he told me – analysing the tender documents and studying the scope of work, project schedule, potential primary resources and construction equipment to be used. It would be down to me to develop the bid cost estimate of project activities and services, including staff, workforce, construction equipment/consumables, assets, plant materials and subcontracts. I would need to identify the critical materials to be estimated on a vendor quotations basis. He went through the complete list of what my position entailed.

'OK, Leif, now one last question. Do you think we can pull this venture off? For if we can, we will all finish up very rich, both company and our staff.'

Now, what did he want me to say? 'No, I think it's a load of shit,' or, 'Of course, Greg, we can do anything that we are prepared to put our backs into.' I took the latter option.

'Yes, of course, we can. I think you have got an excellent crew together, and with your leadership, the world is our oyster.' What a grovelling bastard I was turning out to be.

Greg went on. 'This,' he said, showing me a set of documents, 'is what we are going to strive to set up for each South American government energy department. It will be issued to all contractors from every country in the oil and gas exporting business; it's going to be a hell of a challenge and is going to take some time.'

'Greg, as far as I am aware, this has never been done before; if we can do it, everyone must be singing from the same song sheet. It will boil down to whoever gives the right price and who wants it more than the other, but there will be no hidden agendas – everything will be in the open.'

'Leif, there is one thing – we will have the foot in the door. We will be "the consultant" to each government. It will be down to us to advise the best quotes as an independent group, not officially part of any significant players. They have no idea who our parent company is, for the groundwork has been going on for more than twelve months. I have been in touch with all the government bodies in all the South American countries involved; they are just waiting for the model to be handed over to them. Now, open that and tell me what you think.'

I opened the file. It was chapter and verse, and was precisely what I imagined would be needed to obtain the goals required. I did not understand why they wanted me to be involved.

'How come you want my input? At first sight, it's just what I assumed would be required. I would need to go through it in more detail, but it looks OK to me. My main worry would be what they haven't included in the relevant bids, but this is covered on the schedule in the last section.'

'There is only one thing we can't make allowances for,' he replied, 'which is that all of the countries use one man as their liaison. How this guy got so much power we don't know. He is an American from Texas; no one knows his name. He set himself up years ago to act on behalf of each country. I have had private investigators trying to find out who he is but no joy so far. He more or less decides who gets the contracts; we believe it's to ensure there are no under-the-table payments or bribes handed out by individual companies to any high-ranking ministers or the like. This guy is squeaky clean as far as we can find out.'

'Does he know about our plans? Is he aware of what we are trying to implement?'

'No, he has no idea, as far as we can tell, as to what we are proposing to try and instil into these government organisations, for we have gone over the top of the energy ministers, and in some cases, we have been selling this to the presidents themselves. The response has been first class; no one as yet has declined our offer. It's up to you – yes, you – to finish off the pitch. What do you think?'

Wow – what a position to be put in. Down to me? Fucking hell, what could I say?

'Well, it's some task, but I'm up for it, Greg. I'm sure we can pull it off. Let me go through your model to see if I can pick any holes in it, but looking at it, it seems it's all covered. What's the time schedule for it to be handed out? I assume each country will all get it at the same time?'

'Yes, we are looking at four months from now. It seems you will be doing some travelling in the next year – is that OK with you? Once we have issued our plan and model, and once it's accepted and put into their constitutions, they will be going out to all contractors for them to issue all new bids for all the new works both offshore and onshore. It's not so much the individual oil companies in South America that designate who gets what job, it's the governments; they work in partnership almost like turnkey projects, and share the profits from the oil.'

I didn't say a word, just listened. Greg was thoroughly engrossed in this idea and was convinced it would work, but I still had my doubts; I'm not sure why – just a gut feeling.

'The government foots the bill for the production platforms and the assets; this is then taken out of the profits to make sure the oil companies don't make any profit out of the initial outlay for the plant, etc. It helps the oil companies so they don't have to lay out millions of dollars at the front end. We hope that doing it this way, the cost of the drilling, etc., should be more or less the same. Most of the exploration has been done for the next ten years or so anyway. Onshore might be a different story, but when you read the models fully, we have covered them slightly differently.'

I went back to my office with the model and a lot of hard reading to be done.

I spent a week perusing the information. It was OK but had a few holes in it. I knew this could not work with Brazil, for its leading oil company was partly owned by the government; it had a 63 per cent holding in Petrobras. No way in the world would we get in there and try telling them what to do. They had been operating in the oil game since the 1950s; that was one out of the equation.

I then spent another week looking at all the other nations that were going to be targeted. The big players – Argentina, Venezuela, Bolivia, Brazil, Peru and Colombia – had all been established for years. I was having doubts about what Caporal was trying to break into. My main problem was I did not want to go in and piss on their parade; they had put a lot of work in setting up the system, and the idea was right in principle. With these organisations being in the game for so long, it would be like telling them to change everything they had created over the years.

Was I mistaken? How could the hierarchy in Vanderries get it so wrong? In my mind, that is. Had I made a mistake in taking the job? I did not feel comfortable with the situation.

But I was in it now and needed to give it more time. Was being I too pessimistic? Time would tell.

CHAPTER 39

LEIF

Houston, Texas

A month must have gone past when Greg called me into his office to inform me he had set up a meeting with 'The Man' who was acting for most of the organisations involved; he said they did not know his name, or he did not want to tell it to me.

I was to fly to Houston and meet 'The Man' at a hotel; he was fully aware of what we were trying to bring to the party. All he could give me was the hotel name – that was it.

I arrived in Houston and booked in at the Marriott down town. I had a deluxe room with a city view, which must have cost a few quid, but hey, I was promised the best by the company.

The meeting was organised for the following day; therefore, I had a night to kill, so I had a shower and went down to the bar. It was a hell of a place – all chandeliers and old furniture; very posh, as Mum would say. As it was a bit early for getting on the drink, I changed my mind and went out of the front entrance for a breath of fresh air. I was standing looking about, when the concierge came up behind me.

'Can I help you, sir? You seem a bit lost, if you don't mind me saying.'

'Oh, hi – no, I'm OK. Just thinking about going for a stroll, but don't have much idea where to go.'

Henry, the concierge, asked me to come back to his desk; he gave me a map of the area and pointed out some places of interest. It was getting a bit late in the afternoon to travel far, but with the hotel being on Main Street, there were a few bars and restaurants to visit if I just fancied a bit of a pub crawl. It was a pretty safe area to walk about as long as you weren't out too late, which I didn't intend to do anyway.

I went out with my little map, with the recommended drinking holes marked up. I decided it was still a bit early for the drink, so just went for a walk. There was Market Square just around the corner, a green park-type area, with a water feature. I called at a newsstand and bought a paper to read about what was going on in the world.

I sat there for a while, watching people hurrying about as they do in most big cities in the world, when this old grey-haired black gentleman stopped to say hello. He reminded me of the country singer Tom T Hall, who used to sing 'Watermelon Wine'.

'Mind if I sit here, sir, take the weight off my old legs? Not like they used to be.'

'No, please join me. How are you today?'

'Oh, a limey, eh? What are you doing in Texas? You're a long way from home, sir. I haven't met many Englishmen lately – you are English? I can tell by your accent; you're definitely not Irish. I have a friend, Paddy, who is from Dublin – you don't sound like him – and those Welsh folks kind of sing when they talk, don't they?'

I hadn't got a word in, but he seemed OK, so we chatted a bit. He told me that he was eighty-six, and had come to Houston when he was eighteen and looking for work. He was from Alabama initially and born in 1900; he missed the First World War and was too old to serve in the second. He had been through some tough times, being black and all. Still, he had no hard feelings; he had married, and brought up three kids. His wife passed away thirty-five years ago, and his kids had moved away.

I felt sorry for the man. I supposed that, finding me, a stranger who would listen, was a godsend to him. I listened to his story, and he wanted to know what the UK was really like.

'Is that right you limeys don't have racial prejudice problems like we do here?'

'I could not honestly answer that; I suppose we don't have any problems, not in Hull, anyway. We don't see many black people, the odd

Asian or Chinese, but nothing like the USA.'

One thing that had got to me why we were always called limeys. I asked the old man why – he had been around a long while, did he know?

'You mean you don't know why we call you that, sir? As far as I can recall, the term originated in the 1850s as lime-juicer, later shortened to "limey", and was used as a derogatory word for sailors in the British Royal Navy.'

'How come you know so bloody much?'

'I don't know, must have been at school, I suppose, or I must have read it somewhere. I believe since the beginning of the nineteenth century, it had been the practice of the Royal Navy to add lemon juice to the sailors' daily ration of grog, which I believe was a watered-down rum. They believed the vitamin C in citrus fruits prevented scurvy and helped to make these sailors some of the healthiest of the time. Am I boring you, sir?'

'No, far from it.'

'I studied modern history at college before I left. English was my favourite subject of them all. I seem to remember the term may have been used earlier in the US Navy as slang for a British sailor or a British warship. I believe the usage of "limey" in American English was used to mean any British person, and the term was so commonly known that it was featured in American newspaper headlines. That's all I can tell you – hope it helped, sir?'

I looked at my watch; an hour had gone by, just like that.

'Don't want to keep you, sir, if you have to be going.'

'No, there is no rush. I have plenty of time; I love history myself, and I appreciate your knowledge.'

We carried on chatting; I really found it enjoyable, hearing about his past life, but I had to go in the end.

'Been lovely meeting you.'

'Marlon, sir, the name's Marlon – and thank you for your time, sir, it's been a pleasure meeting an English gentleman like yourself.'

'Well, thank you, Marlon, and the feeling's mutual. Goodbye and take care.'

With that, I left him. I had left my paper on the bench. As I turned to go back for it, he had picked it up and was walking away with it. No problem, Marlon, you keep it mate.

I was getting a bit hungry so thought I'd call in somewhere for a sandwich. I didn't want much as I had a table booked in the hotel restaurant. I looked at my map; Pat's Irish Bar was the nearest with a ring around it. I called in there. There were not a lot in, but it was still early; the office workers wouldn't finish for an hour, or so I supposed.

The barman just had to be Pat, the owner. He had a face like a battered boxer, just like that guy Jimmy Cagney I used to see in the old black and white movies. He was watching a rerun of *I Love Lucy* on the TV.

'Well, hello, how the hell are you today?' he said in his Irish brogue.

'I am OK, thanks.'

'Oh, bejaysus, an Englishman – what will you be having?'

'Do you sell the Guinness on draught in here?'

'Of course we do, sir; what will it be, a pint or just a half?'

'I will have a pint, thanks, and do you sell food as well? I just fancy a sandwich or something.'

'I'll bring you a menu; the hot roast beef is very nice, even if I say so myself.'

Pat returned with the menu. 'The beer will be just a moment – you know you can't rush the black stuff.'

He then returned with the beer. If it was as good as it looked, it was not going to touch the sides.

'There you go – enjoy, sir. Have you chosen your food yet, or you want a bit longer?'

I told him I would take his advice. I would have the hot roast beef sandwich with fries and salad.

'Good choice, sir, be back in a jiff.'

The beer was unreal, just like it was in Dublin the last time I was there – a fantastic pint.

As soon as the glass was empty, he returned with another. He was a good barman, this bloke; even if you didn't want one, you could not refuse it when he brought it over.

'I see you enjoyed it; I thought you would like another with your food, which will be here now. I'll go and get it.'

I'd never seen a sandwich like it – it must have been five inches high and eight inches square, filled with succulent roast beef with the juices running out of it and covered in fried onions. The plate was eighteen inches square and loaded with salad and fries – not skinny American fries but thick-cut chips.

'Oh my God, what's that? How many is that for?'

'Just a regular serving – I didn't think you would want to go big, sir, when you said you just wanted a sandwich.'

It took me nearly half an hour to finish it, and I did not eat all the salad and only half the chips; it was beautiful. Mind, the extra pint of the black stuff I had to wash it down didn't help; I was packed like the proverbial boot. I had to undo my belt a bit, I was that full.

Pat came back over. 'Enjoy that, did you? I see you left a bit; most people do. I don't know why they give you so much, but we always have. We don't want to get the reputation of being stingy. Once a place gets that, it's a downward trail. Our food brings back the regulars, and also people come in when visiting because they know we give great value for money.'

'Yes, the concierge at the Marriott told me to come here.'

'Oh, Henry – yes, he's my cousin on the wife's side, nice fella; tell him I was asking after him. Not seen Henry for a while.'

I returned to my hotel. What with the Guinness and the monster sandwich, it had knocked me back, and I was feeling quite tired. I couldn't wait to strip off and lie on the bed. I turned on the TV; an old Western starring Gary Cooper was on. I started to watch that.

I nodded off, and when I woke it was 8pm. After a quick shower, I headed down to the restaurant. I was shown to my table; I had a lot on my mind. The waiter brought me the menu, but I did not hear him at first. 'Yes, a couple of minutes, please.'

I could not get this guy I was going to meet out of my mind. It was getting to me. I hated being kept in the dark. I couldn't wait to see him, find out who he was and how the hell he got into such a dominant position. He must be as old as Methuselah, I thought, to have gained the trust of so many top men and organisations worldwide. Still, I would be finding out pretty soon.

I ordered a bottle of white and a Mexican chicken dinner. When it arrived, I realised why the Yanks were all obese; the portions they consumed were unbelievable. Mind, the food was good. After the food and wine, I was feeling tired again all of a sudden. It was time I went to bed. It would be a big day tomorrow, and I needed to be at my best.

*

The meeting was to be held in one of the conference rooms in the hotel; why, god only knew. As far as I was aware, there was just going to be the two of us at the table – me and Mr X, whoever he was.

I had a phone call about 11am and was asked if I could meet earlier as Mr X had to catch a flight later in the day. I agreed, and was all set to go to the meeting at 1pm prompt.

I looked through all my paperwork to make sure it was all in order and headed off to the conference room, one of five that were in the place.

I knocked on the door; no answer. I tried again – still no response. The door was open, so I had a look in the room, but there was no one else there. I wondered if I had got the right place. I went back outside to check; yes, it was the right one – number four. I went back in and sat down at the table. This was stupid; it was big enough for twenty people. I went over to the window to look at the view and street below. Then the door opened behind me. I turned around. Well, fuck me. I could not believe it. Einar Hegdahl, my old Isle of Wight buddy, was standing there.

'Hello, Leif, nice to see you again! How are you? My, you are looking well, my friend. I hear you are making quite a name for yourself. Been getting good reports about you, my boy.'

I was stunned. Of all the guys to meet again. No way in this world did I ever expect the mystery man would be him –why would I? – but it was great to see it was someone I knew, never the less.

'Hello, Einar; great to meet you again. How is Borg? Well, I hope? Is she with you on this trip?' I was hoping.

'No, she is back home in Florida. She never travels with me on business trips; she gets bored easily, if you know what I mean.'

He came over, and we shook hands. We sat down at the table; he placed his briefcase on it, and opened it up.

'Well, now, I have been informed that you will be my contact on this little venture that your company is hoping will change the way the oil business is run in the Americas – is that correct?'

'Yes, you are correct. Do you know much about what we are trying to put forward?'

'About setting up a sort of standardisation of all working contracts between the client, namely the country and contractors, bypassing the oil companies altogether. Yes, I have heard a little, and it interests me, for there has always been that bit in between where the clients finish up paying double for the installation hookups, maintenance, etc. It drew my attention when I heard a whisper of what you had come up with.'

'I have brought with me a copy of what we are proposing the model will look like.' I said, handing Einar the document.

'I would like you to go through it with me chapter and verse,' said Einar, 'for if I am right, this could be a winner for all concerned. The oil companies won't like it, one little bit, as they have always creamed off the top, shall we say, an extra profit, when all they should be making money on is what is coming out of the ground.'

I opened my copy of the documentation and laid it on the table in front of me.

'Where do you want me to start? Right at the beginning?'

'Yes, please,' said Einar. 'I will make notes as we go through it, so if I ask you to stop in between, please forgive me, OK?'

We went through the document page by page, which took us hours to complete. We even broke off for something to drink and then went back into it again. In the end, Einar gave me a look. 'I am not sure,' he said, 'but I am willing to go through it and make some suggestions. There are some points that I know the ministers will not like. I am quite influential with most of them, although I just can't get into others, for one reason or another. I must add I am working on that small detail.'

'Einar, it seems my company is under the impression that you are the in-between man for all of the South American countries, that you are more or less the guy who makes the last call when it comes to which contractor gets the relevant contract in question.'

'Who on earth told them that? I did not know that was common knowledge.'

I told him what the company knew about this unnamed individual who could help set up the company's ideas, and that it was intended to protect all contractors and give them all a fair playing field on negotiations.

'I don't know how they set up this meeting as they did not give me your name,' I said. 'I don't know if they know your name.'

'They don't know my name, but I found out you were involved and, because I know you and like you, I decided we should meet. You see, no one knows who I am but you, and that is the way it must stay if we go forward – for I believe we could all do well out of this situation, especially me and you, my son.' As he said the last sentence, he put his hand on my shoulder.

He told me he would keep the paperwork for a couple of days while away on a trip, and we would then meet up again. I could take what we had come up with as a deal that would work, in his opinion, for all parties including the oil companies. We would need to get on board; it was no good us thinking that they could be left out, as it was impossible, but he had friends in high places whom he believed might well go along with the recommendations once he had tweaked it. I agreed; I could not do much else as he held all the cards.

The following day I went to the pool area to relax and take in the sun. I had got up and was dangling my legs in the water when this little black girl came up to me.

'Hello! Can't you swim? Want to borrow my armbands? You can if you like; I have some over there with my Daddy.'

'Oh, hello! No, thank you. I am fine, just keeping cool.'

'Don't you talk funny! I never heard anyone talk like you; where are you from?'

The little girl's father came up. 'Oh, there you are. I hope she is not pestering you, sir. Now, come on, Rhaelyn, stop annoying the gentleman.'

'It's OK. Rhaelyn is not bothering me; she is fine.'

'I was worried – she can't swim yet and needs her armbands on. I am trying to encourage her in learning, but she is not keen on water.'

He turned to talk to his daughter; I just loved that southern drawl.

'Now, come on, honey, I think it will be a good idea if you put your armbands on now if you want to go for a swim.'

'Where did you get that idea from, Daddy?' she said, putting her hands on her hips; she rolled her eyes and looked at me.

I was pissing myself listening to the conversation; no way was she going in the water.

'OK, come on back over to the shade; Mammy will be down in a few minutes. She wants to go for a swim, OK? Nice meeting you, sir; you have a nice day now, you hear.'

With that, he took his daughter's hand and left, still trying to convince her to go swimming with her mum. She turned and waved at me. 'Byee, sir, nice meeting you! He sure does talk funny, Daddy.'

*

I called Greg back in Nassau and told him the script, chapter and verse; he sounded a bit worried when I told him Ein's comments, remembering not to mention that I knew Mr X. I told him I would call him as soon as I had met 'The Man' again.

Einar returned from his trip. He did not tell me where he had been, nor did I ask, as it was not my business. He told me he had looked through our model and proposition and had one or two misgivings. He said the preferred bidder option was missing from the plans. The bidder is selected by the vendor, usually to some predetermined criteria, as the party to whom it intends to award a contract, subject to the completion of negotiations and legal arrangements. Also, he noticed that there was no reference to the situation where each contractor must show they have a culture and track record of an integrated management system – which is proof that they are committed, thus enhancing performance while remaining cost-effective, increasing employee and customer satisfaction, and facilitating continuous improvement.

He also pointed out that the suppliers would register at their own cost. This guy knew what he was talking about. He would earn his coin, no doubt about that. I did not realise how clued up he was; he was undoubtedly a good ally. Having said that, he was having doubts that the oil operators would buy into the scheme. He was saying that too much would be taken away from them by the governments seeking too much power over who did what, and no way would they accept that scenario. For it was the operators who had done the initial exploration and drilling.

We had another couple of days of meetings, and Einar told me he would write a report and send it to me in a few days once he was convinced what he was going to suggest was going to be his ultimate decision.

As he rose from the desk, he looked down, and his last words to me were, 'Leif – as a friend, I would look for another job, for I don't think this will work.'

I flew back to Nassau the following morning with his words at the back of my mind.

CHAPTER 40

LEIF
Back to the Cold

I got back to the office that afternoon, and Greg was straight in to see me. 'How did you get on, then? What did the man say about our proposition?'

He was not happy when I told him Einar's findings, without mentioning his name.

'What do you mean he doesn't think it will work because of the oil companies? That's what it is all about – them ripping the governments off and the contractors not all singing from the same song sheet. That is what we are trying to do – to make sure it is the same on every contract. It's the model that every project should be priced to. Does he not understand that?'

I told him a couple of things that we had missed out; essential elements that needed to be included in any contract drawn up.

'Ah well,' he said, 'we might have made a couple of mistakes, but you can't say it won't work because of something like that.'

I could see the look of terror in Greg's eyes; panic was setting in.

I was beginning to think Einar might be right. 'Look for another job.'

Another two weeks passed and we received Einar's report, which was quite damning; it meant more re-reading and making amendments. We were sending letters to the Norway head office without getting any help back. In the end, Greg could not take any more; he more or less said, 'Fuck it.'

A week later, he called me in and told me he had been on to head of-

343

fice, and they were wrapping it up. Although we were not supposed to be part of them, the board of directors had decided that they would not pursue the situation any longer and had pulled the plug. He told me they would pay me four months' pay in place of notice. They did not have to, but considering that they had asked me to leave my previous position, they would do the right thing by me as they did not have a similar situation to offer at the time. I was OK with this; it would give me six months of being on their payroll as I had started at the beginning of October.

On Tuesday, December 8, I arrived home, out of work, but glad I had come out of it OK. I had a few quid in my bank account that would tide me over for a few months as it was usually hard to find work over the Christmas period.

I spent the holiday period at home and had Mum and Billy round for Christmas dinner. It was the first time for a long while that I had spent a Christmas with Mum; she loved it, and so did I if the truth were to be known.

We opened our presents; Billy got the usual socks and underpants – they were more like football shorts. Martin opened his, which were mostly clothes. I gave him twenty quid, and the same for Billy. I opened mine – a bottle of Isle of Jura whisky, and socks. I had bought Mum an LP, *Behind Closed Doors*. I knew she liked Charlie Rich. I had seen that it had on the playlist, 'The Most Beautiful Girl in the World.' She loved that song. It was straight on the record player.

New Year's Eve I spent with Connie, as we had got back together. After I had got home, I contacted her. I was starting to like her; I trusted her. What happened with Lynn had made me wary of women who did not want to get involved too deeply. But I enjoyed Connie; she was not too demanding, and seemed quite happy with her lot – plus, she was pretty good in bed, which was always a bonus.

We had been out a few times over the past few weeks; I was getting a bit sick of the bloody UK weather. I was looking to get away for a few weeks until a job came up, for I did not think I had a chance until after Easter, which was April 17 that year. I asked Connie if she could get some time off, but the boy was the problem with his schooling and everything. I suggested he could come with us. Why I said that, fuck knows. Still, it just slipped out one night when we were in bed. It wasn't the only thing that moved out, as you can imagine.

I had forgotten all about what I had said when Connie came back to me a few weeks later. 'Leif, you know when you suggested Martin could go with us on holiday for a week? Well, I have been thinking about it. He asked at school, and they said they did not mind as long as it was only a week, as he is now fifteen and is doing well. They said he would not miss a week. We had told them that you worked away a lot, and this was the only time we could get away as a family. I did bend the truth a bit, I must be honest, so if it's OK with you, we can go?'

Fuck. I did not think for the life of me he would get away, but what I was snookered; no way was I going to be able to get out of it now.

'OK, great. I will book somewhere not too far but sunny. How much notice do you have to give work?'

'None – they said I had some lieu days owed for the extra time I have worked, and things have been a bit quiet since Christmas, so I can go when I like.'

That made it easier. I went to Thomas Cook the next day and booked a holiday in Tenerife. I was surprised they both had passports, but Martin had one as he had been abroad with school and Connie had travelled a bit with work.

We were all set. I managed to get a week beginning Thursday, February 9 in Playa de Las Americas at the Hotel Rebecca. It was a bit away from the beach area but still a four-star hotel. We got a two-bed apartment, which meant the boy would have his own room.

We landed at the Reina Sofia airport just after 11am. It was not far on the coach to the hotel, and by mid-afternoon, we were all settled in. I was ready, with my swimmers on; it was a pity it wasn't a nudist holiday – that would put the cat among the pigeons if I could find a naturist beach we could visit. We went around the pool for an hour or so. There were not so many people about, and plenty of sunbeds available; the

Germans must have stopped at home.

Connie came down in a new bikini. She looked hot; it was the first time I had seen her in swimmers. I'd seen her naked plenty of times, but sometimes a girl looked better in swimwear. Indeed, she turned a couple of heads as she walked past, especially the old pervy pensioners – and there were lots of those around at that time of the year.

Just lying around doing nothing – I was great at that. This was the life; a bit of sun on my back, a pretty girl on tap, and plenty of beer and decent food, I hoped.

We were on B&B in the hotel, so we either stayed for a meal or went out looking for restaurants; I said I would ask one of the old codgers near the bar. They looked as if they had been there a while, their skin like tanned leather.

'Hi, fellas – how's things, OK?'

'Hello – you are staying here, mate?'

'Yes, we have just arrived.'

'You look as if you have; your tan just needs topping up, son.'

'Oh, thank you for the compliment, cheeky bastard.' I laughed as I said it so as not to cause offence.

'Only kidding, mate,' said the old man. 'Yes, we've been here a nearly a month. We came for Christmas as it was cheaper than staying at home, with the cost of gas and electric being what it is. We come here for four months every year, have done for what, four years isn't it, Mike?' He turned to the guy sitting next to him at the bar.

'Yes, this is our fourth year here, mate – love it. Fuck being back home freezing your bollocks off! Got a great deal, full-board, me and our lass – £1,800 including flights for both of us for 128 nights. I don't know how the fuck they do it. That's flying from Manchester.'

I was looking at this Mike, and he had a twitch; it appeared like he kept winking at me, then I realised what it was.

'So you recommend the restaurant, then, it's OK?'

'Yes,' they both said more or less in unison. 'It's brilliant – all buffet stuff,' said the first man, Eddie, 'so you help yourself. It's not à la carte, but it's always spot on.'

'We have to pay for the beer – that's not included,' added Mike, 'but it's cheap enough anyway. It's that San Miguel stuff, but it is not that bad; you get used to it after a month. To be fair, every time we get back home and back on the local brew, I quite miss the old Miguel.'

I went back to Connie. Martin was actually chatting to a young girl in the pool, so maybe he wasn't batting for the other side after all.

'The two old geezers at the bar were telling me the grub's OK in here – we can try it tonight if you like? Save us messing about looking for somewhere we don't know, OK?'

She was just lying back, bronzing, and never even looked up. 'Yes, OK with me.'

Another couple of hours passed, and I was getting peckish, 'Come on, shower – look at the time.' It was six o'clock. Shit, shower, shave; we were ready by seven. 'I will see you both down in the bar. Don't be too long, Martin – don't put your make-up on tonight.' He frowned when he looked at me but then smiled; he was warming to me, and I was to him. This holiday was going to be great.

They both came down, and I ordered a couple of more drinks. We went straight in and were given a table on the balcony overlooking the pool. It was a lovely spot; it looked like we had picked a decent place to stay.

We chose the buffet at a set price – all you could eat. The old guys were not wrong; everything was available. The usual stuff – pasta, pizza, chicken, more or less everything you would expect on a buffet, plus great French fries; that was Martin fixed up. All washed down with a glass of white wine, it was a super end to a perfect first day.

We had finished our meal and were about to leave as Eddie and Mike came in with their good ladies. Mike winked again; they were all were dressed as if they were going to the captain's dinner on the QE2 – they even had ties on.

'Evening all, you were right.' I said. 'The grub is spot on; thanks for the tip.'

'No problem. Pleased you liked it!'

As we were walking out, Martin said. 'What was that guy winking at;

was he OK?'

'Yes, just a nervous twitch.' It seemed he was trying to say something, you know when someone makes a statement and then winks to say told you so.

'What you on about, Leif?' said Connie.

'Oh, forget it.'

After dinner, a few more drinks and finishing off with a couple of single malts, that was me fucked. As soon as my head touched the pillow, I was gone. It was 8am when I woke up, and the sun was streaming through the blinds.

Connie was sitting up reading. 'Good morning, sleepyhead. Jesus, you died when you got in bed last night; never even said night-night.'

'Sorry, babe, I must have needed it. I was cream-crackered – I can't remember falling asleep. Where's Martin?'

'Oh, he went out early. He's down by the pool with that young girl he talked to yesterday; I think he is smitten. She is French. I believe he is parle-voux-francaising – all that work at school, he's probably practising it on her.'

'I hope that is all he is planning on practising.'

'Trust you to think of that. One day, you're saying he is bent, and now he is after a French *jeune fille*.'

'A what?'

'*Jeune fille* – that's French for a young girl. Don't you speak French? Come on, Leif, you must speak French. Everyone does!'

I just shook my head. I did not know what this world was coming to; here was a Hessle road lass who could speak French – unreal.

We got ready and went down to the pool. I was sitting reading, but this French thing was fascinating to me, and I needed to find out more. I turned to Connie and asked, 'How come is it you both speak French so well?'

'My father was in France during the Second World War – don't laugh, but he was a spy. He was sent there because he could speak the language; his mother was French, and growing up, that is the only language they spoke in the home as she could not speak English. Anyway, he met up with a French woman who was working for the resistance. He brought her back to the UK, and she also could not speak English too well, only the basics, so we all sort of picked up the lingo. Martin, as a boy, has always been a studier and took a real interest in it, I even bought him a course on French lessons, and that's how come he can speak it so fluently.'

'Wow, you live and learn.'

'There they are over there, look; she is gorgeous.'

It was too much – I decided I must meet her. I walked over to them; they were standing by the diving platform.

'Bonjour, OK.'

'Oh, oui, très bon, merci,' she answered.

Martin looked at me, clearly wondering how this bastard could speak French. Little did he know that was just about my vocabulary used up.

'Vous devez être Leif, Martin m'a parlé de vous,' she said – 'You must be Leif, Martin has told me about you.'

'Is it OK if we speak English? My French is not that good.'

She smiled and then said, 'No problem, Leif.'

'So who is this, Martin?' I said. 'Don't be ignorant; what is her name, do the honours?'

'Oh, er, this is Juliette.'

'Hello, Juliette, what a beautiful name – pleased to meet you. Yes, I'm Leif – what's he been telling you about me? Good, I hope?'

'Oh, yes, he speaks very highly of you; he tells me you are very kind to his mother Connie, she is such a nice person. He says she is fortunate to have found such a nice boyfriend, after all she has been through.'

I wondered what she meant by that; Connie had told me she had got married too young but had not gone into too much detail, and I had not asked.

I was getting out of my depth with this French-speaking lark. Martin spoke it like a local in Paris, so it was time for me to make a retreat.

'Nice meeting you, Juliette, catch you later?'

'Merci – au revoir, Leif. Venir, Martin, permet de trouver quelque part où nous pouvons être seuls.'

I wasn't sure what that last bit was about; I would ask Connie she spoke the dialect.

Connie had gone back to the room, as the sun was getting too hot for her; she was lying on the bed in just her bra and panties. She was starting to wear a little more sexy underwear lately, and I liked it; I hoped it was just for me.

'Hi, is Martin still with that French girl, Leif?'

'Yes, I left them down by the pool, but they disappeared as I was walking away; Juliette said something to Martin as I was leaving but did not know what she said.' I told her roughly what she came out with.

'Oh, did she now? You know what she said? "Come on, Martin, let's find somewhere where we can be alone."'

'Sound good to me, love; at least he was not disappearing with a man or a boy.'

'Oh, give over, Leif, you have an obsession with Martin. He is not bent, as you say. God, how I hate that expression; he is just a young man coming out of himself. He is just experimenting, call it what you like. Surely you went through that phase when you were younger? Now, do not tell me you never did.'

My mind went back to my first holiday in Withernsea when Dougie and Dot taught me my first sex lessons. OK, she was right; I should not be critical of Martin – he wasn't doing anything wrong.

We met Juliette Blanchet – which in English means blonde, pure – Martin's new love, officially the following day. It turned out she was a little older than Martin, being seventeen; we had not seen much of him since he had become friendly with her.

We were sitting having a few cocktails before dinner one night when Juliette joined us.

'Come and sit down; what would you like to drink?'

'Could I have a Coke, please?'

'One Coke on its way.'

'There you go, Juliette; forgive me for being a bit forward, but I noticed you have a beautiful colour – so natural. Do you live in a sunny climate at home in France? Are you in the south?'

350

'No, Leif, my mother is from the West Indian island of Martinique. It's one of the Windward Islands. It was a French colony; my for fathers were Huguenots.'

'Never heard of them?'

She looked shocked, like everyone should know. 'They were French protestants who held to the reformed tradition of orotestantism. Its origins are from the sixteenth century.'

'Wow, have you been there to look for your roots?'

'No, all we know is they had fled to the West Indies to get away from persecution in France. One of them took a local for his wife, and as the majority of early descendants were of the African continent, my dark skin was handed down through the generations, and here I am to prove it.'

We had an excellent meal; Connie had a go at me for asking too many questions about Juliette. And at the end of the night, Martin disappeared with his *jeune fille*, and we retired to our boudoir.

The following morning, I sat by the pool waiting for Connie to come down when Juliette turned up.

'Good morning, Leif; how are you this beautiful morning?'

'Oh, fine, Juliette. How are you, OK? What you up to today?'

'Just waiting for Martin to come down – we are going on a bus trip today. My mother has bought us the tickets. You have not met Mum yet, have you? I will make sure you meet her tonight. You will just love her; she is so sweet.'

'We will look forward to it, thank you, Juliette. Is your father here as well?'

'No, my father passed away when I was very young. I do not remember him. He died at sea; his ship was lost in a storm off Martinique, one of many shipwrecks that occurred off the eastern coast.'

'Oh, I'm sorry to hear that.' I shook my head. I could not believe how she came out with every detail when answering questions; it was as if she was programmed.

Martin turned up. 'What time did you get up, Leif? I never heard you. Mum's getting ready – you know what she is like; she takes forever and a day.' He put his arm around Juliette's waist and kissed her – not a peck, a full-blown kiss.

'OK, what time is the bus leaving?'

'Er, it's picking us up at 8.30am from the front of the hotel. We will be gone all day – is that OK, Leif? You won't mind?'

'Why should we mind? Don't be so stupid – you kids get off and enjoy yourselves. Just don't do anything I would not do, OK?'

Juliette smiled. 'We will try not to, Leif, but won't promise. Come on, babe, let's go, or we will miss the bus.'

She took Martin's hand in hers and led him away, like a lamb to the slaughter.

No wonder he was smitten; she was overpowering. Why had she picked on him, I wondered. He was nothing but a wimp.

Connie arrived. 'Right, what are we doing today? Fancy a day on the beach, or we could hire a car or a scooter. Now, that would be fun – we could get a scooter each. I haven't ridden one of those for years; one of my old boyfriends had a Vespa 125. Wow, that brings back memories of before I got married; I must have only been sixteen or so. What do you think?'

'Oh, yes, a scooter – sounds good to me. I noticed the garage just down the road had some outside the other day. They must be for hire; we can nip down there and take a look.'

We walked up to the garage. The guy outside was the typical second-hand car salesman, but the Spanish version – slim, dark skin with a thin moustache. I didn't like the look of him one bit.

'Are you sure these are safe?' I asked the guy in the garage. 'They look a bit battered to me. Do you provide helmets with them?'

He said that they never got asked about helmets, but if we wanted them we could for no extra charge; he did not think we needed them as the scooters only had 50cc engines and the roads weren't built for speed.

Connie was sitting on one of the machines, 'Look, Leif, no gears – just twist this thing towards you, and they go, easy.' She turned the grip, and off she went, nearly into a passing car.

'We will have two helmets, mate, and a suit of armour for her.' He did not crack his face. He had no sense of humour, not Hull humour anyway.

We were off down the road towards the beach. The scooter man had given us a couple of maps of the area, showing all the beaches and coves to visit. He mentioned Playa Montana, which had a nudist beach if we were interested, and it was only a mile or so away. Also there was no need to travel on the main roads.

Now, Connie knew I had a liking for being naked, but not in public, and I did not know how she would react to arriving somewhere where no one was wearing clothes – but I was about to find out.

I looked at the map and the route, assuming it was well signposted. 'Follow me, love, and take care, OK?' I said.

Twenty-five minutes later we arrived OK; the road was a bit twisty and downhill but we did not see many cars. We never saw anything until we arrived at the beach. There was a small car park where we left the scooters and a signpost saying 'To The Beach'. Underneath, in small letters, it also said 'naturist' – but Connie did not read it. I took her hand, and off we went. We had bought some sandwiches and a couple of bottles of water from a cafe on the side of the road; we were set for the day. Plenty of sun cream to lather on our white bits, and off we went.

It had a winding path leading to a staircase that guided you down to a beautiful beach of rocks and coves. It was very well hidden, and what made it so special was its crystal water, the breakers just rolling in with hardly a wave – it was paradise, and not many people were there when we arrived. There were a few more along the shore, but you could not see they were naked; not without binoculars, anyway. We walked along the water's edge. The sea was beautiful and warm; it felt so good as it ran between your toes as you walked. That sensation has always made me feel so alive.

As we got closer to the other people, Connie said, 'Fuck me, Leif, they are naked! Look, there – he has no trunks on!'

'I know – it's a nudist beach.'

'What, you mean you knew? Why we have come here? We are not

nudists.' She shot me a quizzical look.

'Connie, it came up once before in conversation a while back, but we didn't discuss it. There's something I haven't told you before – I am a naturist. I belong to a nudist camp near Hull.'

'Near Hull? What do you mean, near Hull – where?'

'Not far from Hornsea. I have a caravan there. Mum has been to visit, and even she loved it.'

'Your Mum, Christine, naked? You've got to be joking. I don't believe you – you are taking the piss.'

'No, honestly, come on. You will love it. There is no better feeling than swimming nude; the water running around your body feels so natural.'

'No fucking way I am stripping off in public. Now, come on – we are going. I am disappointed in you, Leif.' She turned to walk back.

'OK, you go,' I said. 'I am staying. It is up to you; it is easy to find your way back.' I hoped she would see sense and stay.

'You mean you would let me drive back on my own, you bastard?' The Hessle Road lass was coming out in her now. 'You fucking no-good bastard.'

'Calm down, Connie, it's only clothes. Look at those people over there; they have no inhibitions. Look, no one is perving on them. No one is bothered if they are naked or not; no one is walking around with their hands covering their wobbly bits or tits. It just so natural; it's only in people's minds that they think it is wrong. Just try it, please, for me, babe. It is like swearing; you are brought up to be taught that swearing is wrong. If you had been told that a fish finger was a swear word you would have called me a fucking fish finger instead of a no-good bastard. By the way, "bastard" is not swearing. It comes from the Old French "bastart", perhaps from "bast" in the phrase, *fils de bast* – son of the packsaddle, that is – of an unlawful union and not the marriage bed, or a child born out of wedlock.'

'I don't want a fucking history lesson, Leif.'

'There you go again, swearing, just because –'

'Shut up, silly bastard.' She was beginning to soften her tone; she was surveying the surroundings. 'Hmm, OK,' she said, 'but if I see anyone giving me dirty looks, we are off. I am not showing my fanny to just any randy old man, OK?'

I dropped my swimmers, threw off my T-shirt and was stark-naked in a flash.

'Hang on, give me a second – pass me a towel,' said Connie.

'You have got to be kidding. You don't need a towel to strip off; you aren't putting anything back on to cover yourself, are you?'

Connie looked a bit sheepish, and began to undress. She was down to her bra and panties. 'Come on, all off,' I said. She was looking round to see if anyone was watching her exposing her white parts. 'Go on, it's easy – just drop them.'

She stood there naked as the day she was born, and did not move a muscle, like a statue.

'Come on, let's go in the water.' I took her hand as we walked towards the surf. No one stared at her; one or two ladies of, shall we say, mature years, nodded and said, 'Hello.'

One elderly gentleman, who must have been in his late sixties and who was not on the back seats when they gave dicks out, stopped to say hello. He was clearly a long-term naturist; his skin was dark brown all over, and I mean all over.

'Beautiful day, isn't it? You been here before?'

'No, it's our first time here,' was our reply.

'Looks like it. Never mind, get some sun and make sure you get plenty of cream on that virgin skin, my boy – don't want to get any burns on there. It bloody hurts. I did it years ago, never again. Have a nice day now – bye.'

'He was nice, wasn't he, the old man? Did you see the size of his todger, Leif? Bet he has pleased a few damsels in his time.'

'It's OK for you to perv, but not for anyone else? Look at you, behave yourself; it's not the done thing.'

'Yes, you're right; sorry, babe. I must admit, it's great in the water – I love it now I'm in. It also covers you up,' she laughed as she took hold of my manhood.

'Don't do that! That's another unwritten law – no fondling the goods. I don't want to get a hard-on, or I will never get out of the water.'

We stayed all day. Connie loved it once she got used to being naked; she even stood talking to a few people, including men, without folding her arms to cover her breasts – she was just so at ease with her body. Still, everyone was the same who went to such retreats – I'd got another one hooked, and I was very happy for her.

We went to the same beach three days on the trot, and Connie made some great friends; she even invited them to 'our caravan near Hull,' as she put it, 'at our club site.'

I thought it would be a few months before we hit Natsun, but I hoped we would still be seeing each other then. Was I falling in love again? Well, I thought I was; she was such a wonderful girl.

Our week passed too quickly; Martin had met the love of his life in Juliette and Connie was now a confessed naturist. She said she could not wait to do it again.

We went home with all-over tans – no white bits; she was going to enjoy telling those at work about it and even had photographs on her camera to show her mates at home. I wondered how they would go down at the local chemist 'on road' when she took the negatives in to be printed.

Billy and I went in Gipsyville Tavern for a couple of pints before Sunday dinner at Mum's. Afterwards we were sitting having a few cans of Long Life beer and watching a film on the TV when Mum, who by this time had had quite a few snowballs, said, 'Well, we are all here, my little family – well, most of them. I just wish my other son was here; he will be one day, you see – he will come back from Australia to his real mum.'

'What's she on about?' I mouthed to Billy. 'It has been ages since I came back from Aussie.'

'Come on, Christine,' said Billy. 'Time for bed; come on.'

'No, Billy, I want my boy back. He will come home one day; you just wait and see.'

Billy looked at me and smiled, but it was not a genuine smile. He picked Mum up, and carried her up to bed. 'See you in the morning,

Leif; Christine's had enough – she always talks shite when she is pissed.'

I thought that was strange; he'd never reacted like that before. Did he know something I didn't? Why Australia?

THE END

THE ASKENES TRILOGY: BOOK THREE
THERE WILL BE NO MORE LETTERS

CHAPTER 1

LEIF

Another Job

After putting Mum to bed, Billy came back down. He still had a funny look on his face, a kind of embarrassed look, and it was bothering me what Mum had said about her son coming home from Australia.

'Is she all right, mate? She hasn't thrown up or anything? Those snowballs always send her over the edge – why she drinks them I will never know.'

'Yes, she is fast asleep now. You are right; when she drinks them, she gets fucking delusional. I think that's the right word – she starts talking rubbish.'

'So this stuff about her son from Australia is a load of shite? What do you reckon she means by it?'

'I don't know, son. Your guess is as good as mine; I know she went through a bad time when you went. You might not like what I am going to say, son, but you broke her heart, you leaving her like that; I know – I was there. She could be thinking about those days, I don't honestly know, but I wouldn't worry about it. She won't even know she has said it in the morning, so don't you go reminding her, dragging up bad times, OK?'

'Yes, sorry, Billy, you are right; must have been those memories flooding back. OK, I won't say another word on the subject. Thanks for telling me – I never knew; she never let on.'

'Well, she wouldn't, would she? Her fucking blue-eyed boy could do no wrong, but I got it in the fucking neck. That's why I'm telling you now. Let's leave it at that, OK?'

To be continued…